Black Market

By

Ross Page

Acknowledgements

I would like to thank those kind and supportive people who have helped me get this far.

Foremost, of course, is my adorable wife Celeste, who believed when I didn't; there is no possibility that I would have written a single word without her enthusiasm and love.

Thanks to my editorial team; Alice, Duncan, Celeste, Kevin and Rob. Your ideas and critique were invaluable.

A special thanks to Father and Son, Ken and Kevin who gave expert advice on the Cricket match.

To Rhisiart, Anwen, and Jen, thank you for your guidance on the Welsh language and for helping me to discover Trefynydd.

Plus, a thank you to Aaron. Also, Greg, how could I have catalogued my research without your example.

Last but not least, Lolly and Dexy, who took me on the long walks, during which the ideas came, and we met with the characters.

Dedication

In my story, I clumsily tell a tale of a Canadian crew of RAF aviators who perish whilst training in the Brecon Beacons. Although my account is fictional, there are a number of real crash sites dotted around South Wales from this era. These young men were brave, so far from home, and came to fight for freedom; We must remember them always.

1

He's not yours – A Village Butchers in South Wales - 1941

Ceridwen backed away. "No, you promised, you promised never again. You put your hand on the bible, your father's bible, you swore it."

His rage was beyond reason, and her appeals were in vain. She steeled herself to the pain, the pain she had come to know so well. She held her hands together in front of her chest, almost like she was praying. Her fingers interlocked so that they would stay together during the beating. The thick, heavy leather strap, used to sharpen the butchers' knives, would rain down in blow after blow. They were never aimed at her head; the marks would reveal the truth of their loveless marriage to the world. He favoured the bottom of her back, her buttocks, the backs of her legs, all excruciating targets. His favourite was when she dropped her guard, and he lashed the heavy belt across her breasts; he knew that she found the agony to be unbearable. Ceridwen was reeling from the pain. She wretched dryly and thought that at any moment, she would pass out. She had turned round, facing away from her abuser, and for a moment, she had hoped that he would be content to hit her across the back. But then he grabbed her left arm and spun her, pushing her hard. The base of her back hit the corner of a wooden bench, adding to her agony. A set of knives, carefully lined up, cleaned, and sharpened, ready for the next day's work, spilt to the floor. Ceridwen grabbed onto the worktable behind her to stop herself from falling. With her arms out of the way, her psychopathic spouse aimed a colossal blow at her chest. Ceridwen fell to her knees, trembling amongst the sawdust and knives, waiting for more blows. She was screaming, but over her screams, she heard the cries of another. Through the fog of pain and humiliation, she looked up and saw her boy, her own boy, the one good thing in her persecuted life.

Owain had heard the noise, and he had run into the workroom. He tried to hold back his father, pleading with him to stop.

"This is none of your business, boy. Leave me alone."

But the young man had no intention of leaving him alone. He punched the older man in his back. He was no fighter, though, and the ineffectual blow only antagonised the bully even further. However, it diverted the older man's attention from his mother as the next blow came crashing down around Owain's ear.

"You do not beat him; He is not yours to beat." Ceridwen barely recognised her own voice as she shouted the words firmly and evenly at her abuser. "He's not yours to beat," she repeated, quieter this time, as she rose to her feet.

As David Morgan turned towards the unrecognisable voice, Ceridwen held the knife behind her back. It was a filleting knife with a long-pointed blade sharpened to perfection.

David Morgan stood motionless, bemused, appalled by the words of his wife.

"You were never man enough to father such a son. He's not yours to beat, I tell you." Her bitter words were firm, unbowed, and most of all, for the first time, unafraid.

Morgan lifted his hand high, the loathsome strap was poised to swoop down once more, but the blow never came, as the honed tip of Sheffield steel pierced his cowardly heart.

2

Not just any old Joe – London - 1940

The war saved Joe Turner from a life of wrongdoing, which would have seen him prosper or be killed trying. Humble beginnings had forced him to choose between a harsh and tedious, for a man of his intellect, existence working at the dockyards or the excitement and reward of villainy, with no chance of an education and no possibility that his talents would be channelled into worthwhile and wholesome advancement. Joe's choice, and there really was no choice, had been crime.

Somehow avoiding Borstal in his early clumsy escapades, Joe had become a clever and careful crook. He had always been prepared and capable of looking after himself whilst avoiding violence just for the sake of it. He moved on the edge of a world that wrestled for control through brutality. Skilfully, he had remained on good terms with the mobsters despite his despising of their cruelty and ruthlessness. Just as adroitly, he had avoided the attentions of the custodians of the law. Of course, they knew of him and suspected his involvement in many felonies, but their attentions always seemed focused on frying bigger fish or, frequently, too busy counting the proceeds of expediently looking in totally the wrong direction.

Joe picked his jobs carefully. They had to be profitable but not big enough to attract too much attention. Either from the law or from his rivals. He worked alone mostly; he trusted few people, especially when his livelihood and liberty were at stake. Neither was he greedy, working when he needed to. He saved carefully. In this way, he could lie low when the spotlight might be expected to shine in his direction inconveniently.

Victims were equally prudently selected. Joe intensely disliked the idea of profiting from those in society who could ill afford any loss. Drugs, prostitution, and extortion were never a part of his activities for the very reason that they were parasitic. They sucked the life and soul out of the communities he loved.

3

Crucially, those were the preserves of the gangs and organisations that Joe wished to have nothing to do with.

When the war came, it was lucrative for Joe. Things changed overnight; the waters were muddied very quickly. Crime rates soared as the criminal fraternity cashed in on the confusion and new opportunities. As the competent and honest coppers signed up and went off to war, detection rates plummeted. Hordes of people turned to petty crime in desperation, as many lost their homes and all they possessed to the Luftwaffe; the Government was slow to compensate or even rehouse. Whilst others struggled as families were torn apart, the breadwinners set off to wreak their own revenge on the Nazis, perhaps a little negligent or forgetful in sending money back home.

Joe's own forte was housebreaking. Even though his targets were usually in the more prosperous areas, away from the East end, the target of so much attention from Reich Marshall Himmler. To him, the blackout was the gift that kept giving. He could easily move around undetected in the dark streets. The furore of the bombers, the Ack Ack guns, and each heart-stopping explosion covered any noise he made during his uninvited visits. His well-chosen, carefully selected quarry conveniently trembling in their Anderson shelters, leaving him free range of their homes and possessions. Even the obliging Air Raid Wardens would sound the 'All clear', advising him it was time to take his leave.

Joe was smart, streetwise smart. Hard as nails and gutsy, but in a gentle exterior. Stocky, muscular, and imposing despite his 5' 8" height. Joe's angular features, square set jaw and high cheekbones insinuated an Adonis-like beauty. Especially when combined with blond wavy hair and piercing blue eyes, which any aspiring Hollywood actor would kill for. His eyes, his defining feature, were mesmerising. People could not look away from them. They were warm, honest, perpetually smiling, impossibly blue, yet they had a steely indomitability that told of his purpose and determination.

While Joe profited from the war, he felt uneasy that he should be doing his bit. Joe loved his Country despite the little it had done for him. He had hope that things would change after the war. He was no revolutionary, but society would have to move

4

on. There would be opportunities for him in the time that would come. First, the war had to be won, and he knew he had to help.

Milkmen and Butcher's delivery boys had always been a reliable source of information for Joe. Who better to know the comings and goings of a family? "No deliveries this week, please" meant one thing: the house would be empty for a while. A discrete chat, just everyday gossip, with a more than eager kitchen maid would supply enough details. Joe cultivated numerous such informative individuals. Paying handsomely even if the information was not used. Indeed, he got far more intelligence than he could possibly act upon. From this he was able to identify the choice opportunities carefully.

If a house were to be left empty for any length of time, then the valuable contents would be secured elsewhere or taken with the family. A short absence, a weekend visit to the country house or a trip to stay with friends was what was required. It is too short a time to warrant moving the silverware to safer places, and it is not worth emptying the safe. Yes, staff would be left behind, but they would often be given nights off or even leave to visit family. Naturally, there was always risk involved. Plans changed at the last minute. As much as the war had helped him, its unpredictability was a potential enemy.

3

Intervention – A village Butchers in South Wales - 1941

Myfanwy Thomas was worried; she had not expected David Morgan's refusal to continue participating in their scheme. They had started off the business in a small way. Myfanwy supplied the odd extra beast to the abattoir, and Morgan slaughtered the animal and divided up the meat. Ceridwen, David's wife, distributed it through the butchers' shop, alongside the rationed food, to their friends and neighbours in the village. Morgan had started to object when Myfanwy had upped the ante. She had said that they could make even more money, and the risk was small. For David Morgan, though, it wasn't about the money. They had been helping their friends and their community. Now Myfanwy was getting greedy, and they were selling the illegal meat to people they didn't even know. He'd had enough. He knew he should report it but didn't want to get into trouble. In particular, he didn't want his boy, Owain, who was learning his trade, to get in trouble. Ceridwen was too influenced by that woman, Myfanwy Thomas, he reasoned. She deferred to her every wish. He hated her and her interference. She had been looking at him judgementally of late. Had Ceridwen complained to her of her treatment at his hands? She had no right to come between a man and his wife; it was not her business.

Morgan had written anonymous letters to the Ministry of Food, suggesting to them that someone in the area was breaking the rationing rules; he had told no one about them, not even Ceridwen. He hoped that the authorities would send more inspectors to the area and Myfanwy would be forced to scale down her plans. But they hadn't, and now that woman was expanding even more. It was time to put a stop to her, whatever the consequences. Morgan had told Myfanwy he would go to the police if she didn't stop. To Myfanwy, he was a fool, a coward, and he would ruin everything. Myfanwy would have to find a way to convince him, but for now she was worried for her friend. It was no secret that Morgan beat his wife. It had been going on for years, but recently, Myfanwy had seen it taking its toll on her best friend.

She had decided to follow the couple back to town, where they lived above the butcher's shop. When she arrived, she could hear raised voices, her friend pleading with her husband, and the unmistakable 'thwack' of blows being delivered by a belt. Unsure how to proceed, she was about to cross the road and knock at the door when she saw Owain Morgan ahead of her—the young man running into the building. There was more shouting and then silence.

Myfanwy entered the room as the lifeless body of the butcher slid to the floor. His wife was standing before him, straighter, taller than her usual stance. Her hand, still holding the knife. Blood on her arms and best dress. No trace about her face of her usual twitching, faltering, compliant mannerisms. For the first time in a long time, Myfanwy was witnessing her friend smile.

4

On the farm – South Wales - 1941

Rosie wielded the pitchfork like a stoker on a steamship might shovel coal. Each time she stabbed at the straw; it was as if her whole being depended on striking to the heart of the pile. She lifted the tool, piled high with the yellow stubble, and threw it across the floor of the cow shed. She worked like a titan; few men could have matched her pace.

She loved this job. Although she had grown up in the industrial murk of Northern England, she had spent her school holidays at her grandfather's farm in North Wales, and they were the happiest of times. Being a Land Girl, one of the Women's Land Army, who were helping to feed the Nation, was a dream job for her:

"Back to the Land, we must all lend a hand,
To the farms and the fields, we must go,
There's a job to be done,
Though we can't fire a gun,
We can still do our bit with the hoe."

The patriotic song played over in her head as she worked up a sweat and a thirst. A thirst she would no doubt quench at The Dragon's Tail Hotel later that day. If only she could just do this job for the rest of the war. Do her bit by helping to keep this farm running. But fate had tougher and far more dangerous roles for Rosie to fulfil. Her skills and intelligence would be needed elsewhere before the Nazis could be defeated.

Rosie was her undercover name; she was born Amy Kathryn Percival in Salford, Lancashire. The daughter of William James Percival, a motor mechanic and part-time singer/entertainer. Bill 'Percy' Percival had met Amy's mother towards the end of the Great War. Percy had been injured at the Somme and discharged from the Army. He had returned home to Salford and resumed his job as a Motor Mechanic at a small garage in Ordsall. Percy could hold a note and loved to sing, so he gave much of his spare time to entertaining the recuperating soldiers at a nearby sanatorium. It was here that he met Kathryn Knighton, who was nursing the broken bones and minds of the invalided servicemen. To him, a man who, like so many of his peers, had seen so much ugliness, her beauty was breathtaking. To her, he stood for everything she hoped for, brave, strong, and kind. Their love was almost instantaneous and, as it turned out, lifelong.

Kathryn was from a wealthy family who owned extensive lands around Chester and North Wales. She feared that her family would not approve of her marrying a lowly mechanic, so they eloped and married as soon as she turned twenty-one. Kathryn adored the tiny two-up-and-down council house where they set up their home. Despite her mother's relentless efforts to spoil her happiness, she revelled in the love she had for Percy and for the life that grew inside her. She knew that her Percy would prosper, and in the heady excitement and optimism of the end of the war, she looked forward to her future with hope and joy.

The epitome of her bliss was the birth of Amy.

Most people at that time thought that death would have had its fill, having feasted on millions of young men taken before their time. Surely, the peace would see the grim reaper return to the shadows, sated by the senseless slaughter of the War. But without mercy for the bereaved, caring nothing for the grieving multitudes, Death was not yet finished with this cursed generation and embraced his old accomplice, disease.

The "Spanish Flu" killed more people than the war had managed. Some estimates say 50 million people worldwide. From Percy, it took his Kathryn and broke his heart.

It was a crushing blow, but Percy had Amy to think of, and despite the entreaties of his mother-in-law, he was determined he would not part from her. How could he when each time he heard her cry, or chuckle or coo, he heard the voice of his Kathryn? Each time he looked at Amy, he saw her face, smile, and beauty.

In his heart, he knew that he was being selfish. Her grandparents would give her so much more than he could afford. But he understood that they would send her away to a boarding school when the time came, and he knew that Kathryn would have hated that. So, he persevered and did the best he could. He worked hard at the garage. For a time, things were good; they had all they needed, and he even managed to save a little money for his dream of owning his own garage one day. Then, for no reason that he, or anyone else for that matter, could explain, things got hard. Money was tight, companies went bankrupt, and work dried up. Someone tried to explain to Percy that it had to do with the stock market in New York, but that didn't make any sense.

Amy was just about to move up to secondary school. She was a bright student, and her grandmother was more insistent than ever that she be sent to boarding school to fulfil her potential as a young lady. Percy resisted as ever, especially as the child was not the slightest bit interested in being a young lady. She delighted in helping him in the garage after school. She understood the workings of the engines he worked on and could always be relied upon to pass him exactly the right spanner when asked. At school, she excelled at maths, French, and Latin. She had scant regard or interest in cooking or sewing. The two of them struggled, but the garage was short of customers, and his working hours had been cut. Percy had taken an evening job singing and entertaining at the Palais Night Club and dance hall to make ends meet. It was a rough place and not really the sort of establishment Percy would have been seen dead in. But needs must. Fate intervened, and Percy was forced to accept the inevitable and agreed to let Rosie attend a boarding school in Chester. He moved to a Garage in Sandbach to be nearer to her and eventually was able to buy the business with the help of his father-in-law. Amy spent the holidays at her grandfather's farm, and her life was incredibly happy. She loved the farm, especially when her father would visit. She had a keen interest in mechanical engineering and would help with both the farm machinery and the garage. She loved to assist with the horses and became a competent rider. She was also very fond of her grandparents' housekeeper, Morfydd Thomas. Mrs Thomas was a rotund lady of a perpetually cheerful disposition. Being a fiercely proud Welsh lady, she was loath to speak anything but her native tongue. Amy helped with the household running. Immersed in the constant chatter, stories of the mythology of the principality and proud singing of the redoubtable lady, Amy could not help but learn and love the sing-song language. Much to the irritation of her grandfather, whose knowledge of Welsh was scant, and who struggled to keep up with the babble of the ladies.

One afternoon, whilst exploring the farm, she discovered an old motorcycle, abandoned and rotting away in a barn. Eric had acquired it as a part payment on a business debt and had forgotten about its existence. Amy begged her grandfather to let her have and work on it. Eric's business associates would have been astonished to see how this hard-nosed, intractable, and wily businessman was putty in the hands of this sweet young girl.

Within 3 months, working mostly alone and with minimal assistance from her father, she had the machine running like new. She fell off the first time she rode it on the farm roads. She pulled on the front brake as she attempted to bank the machine right. The wheel locked and slid away from her. The bike ended in a hedge; she was blooded and muddy, and her leg, hands and backside were grazed. Tears welled up in her eyes, but she fought their bitter sting as she jumped to her feet, righted the bike, started the engine and rode on. Lesson learned: Do not brake while turning. It was the beginning of her lifelong love affair with two wheels.

At school, she excelled; although she railed against the constraints of the dated syllabus, Amy was desperate to follow her own interests. Those interests, whilst at odds with those that a young lady was expected to pursue by the school, were at least encouraged by her family and a new teacher who came into Amy's life at that most formative of ages.

Miss Boushear was a once-in-a-generation teacher who recognised that talent came in many different forms and didn't always fit neatly into the constrained stereotypes of British society at that time. She herself had been a square peg forced into the round hole of conformity to gender roles. Recognising a kindred spirit in Amy, she did everything she could to guide her along a path that would fulfil her potential. Doing this with stealth to avoid conflict with the school.

Mathematics would become even more of a pleasure to Amy as the ambitious teacher guided her towards applied mathematics, pushing her on until she was accepted to study her master's in mechanical engineering at the Victoria University of

Manchester before moving on to Oxford and applied mathematics.

As a student, she raced motorcycles sponsored by her Grandfather and her father's garage. She became one of only three women awarded a British Motorcycle Racing Club Gold Star for lapping the Brookland's circuit at an average of over 100 miles per hour on her Norton M30.

At Oxford, her talents had been recognised, and the Government had drafted her as the war approached. She was a perfect recruit. Brave, clever and resourceful. Her mechanical knowledge and her gift for linguistics were a huge advantage and she excelled at everything thrown at her during her Special Operations Executive (SOE) training. She had been selected for a mission to France, where she was to liaise with emerging local resistance movements. Her object was to set up the proper organisation of networks, readying them for the important work they would do to disrupt the Nazi war effort. There was one problem. Although an excellent French and German speaker with impeccable grammar, her French accent was just not quite right. Whilst a German soldier may not notice, it would be clear to any French person that she was not French. The danger of a French collaborator questioning her authenticity was too much of a risk. Try as she might, Rosie could not get it right. To everybody's disappointment, she was pulled from the mission. She feared her espionage career would never get off the ground. But she need not have worried as her talents would be needed on the home front and not just baling hay.

5

A bench and a meeting – London 1941

Simon Bach realised that he had reached the place of his meeting, checking his watch; he was just a little early. He took a seat on the park bench as instructed, dressed in civvies, smart business attire, the appearance of a young professional taking advantage of the pleasant London spring weather. He took a paper packet from his briefcase, unwrapped a sandwich, and started to eat exactly on time.

"Sorry about all the cloak and dagger stuff, Bach." the voice came from a small, neat man who had just taken his position at the other end of the bench. "My name is Robinson, Ministry of Food."

"Pleased to meet you Sir, Simon Bach, Lieutenant British Army currently without attachment."

"I say, Bach, is that a German name?" Robinson's tone was somewhat haughty.

Simon was used to the jibe "Actually, it is Welsh, Sir, means little, I believe."

"I hear very good things about you from Major Calderdale. Rotten luck about your injury. It doesn't seem to bother you much, though. Hardly any limp."

Simon had been sitting a few minutes when Robinson arrived. Yet he had observed him walking; had he been following him? Simon realised that he had been careless. He wasn't on a case, yet he had been warned to always be on his guard. And there he had been, strolling across London, daydreaming like a schoolboy in a least enjoyed class.

"Yes, Sir, it hardly gives me any trouble at all, thank you." Simon replied nonchalantly.

"But you aren't passed for jumping?" Robinson probed.

"The Doctors seem to think that a heavy landing might shatter the ankle completely, Sir. I can run for miles, still manage to bowl

13

a decent off-break, and my tennis is better than ever. It's just the impact of the landing, you see, Sir."

"Damned shame. The Major told me that you were one of their Stars at the SOE. Had big plans for you I understand."

Simon shifted on the bench nervously. He had no intention of discussing the SOE with this man. But it was always awkward when you were talking to a Senior Officer if that is what Robinson was. "I am sure I don't know what you mean, Sir."

"Quite right to old chap. You don't really know who I am. Let me assure you that I have full access to your file; my position allows me those privileges. Major Calderdale recommended you to me for a little job I have on. I can tell you he was none too pleased to lose you. Especially as I am also taking a couple more of the cream from his crop. He called me all sorts when he found out, the language of the man."

Simon nodded "Yes he has quite a turn of phrase when he is displeased." Both men smiled at the understatement of the Major's character. "May I ask who you are, Sir? I don't wish to be rude, but one likes to know who one is working for." Simon ventured tentatively.

"Quite understandable, young man; I like that you ask me that. Unfortunately, I cannot tell you too much. Officially, I am with the Ministry of Food. But I can tell you that I report to the very highest level." Robinson paused and looked straight into Simon's eyes. "The very highest level you understand." He stressed.

Robinson edged very slightly closer, and his voice dropped into a conspiratorial tone. "The job we have been given is vital to the war effort. Our success may be pivotal in our winning this war." There could be no doubting that Robinson was serious. He wasn't a man to gild a Lilly; Simon was sure about that. "Let's walk while we talk; one gets so little exercise these days."

"You should try a few days at the Majors health spa." Simon quipped, referring to the universal nickname for the training camp that had made or broken countless promising young men and women of the SOE.

"Bit too old for that caper now." Robinson smiled; somehow, Simon sensed that in his day, this diminutive man had done his share. Now, as they walked side by side, the Military bearing of his new boss was obvious.

They walked in silence for a few minutes. Simon sensed that he should be patient. As they walked, Simon saw that Robinson was carefully surveying the area. His own training alerted him to the subtle glances of his companion. Simon, too, had been spurred into using his craft and was sure that they were being followed.

"Tell me what you see." Robinson gently commanded.

"50 yards behind on the other side of the street. Tall man. Trilby. Carrying a heavy overcoat on a day with no prospect of rain. He is alert to his surroundings. Probably looking for a tail. He appears to be making signals to a comrade. He is frequently adjusting his hat and changing the arm on which he is carrying his coat. I am afraid that I cannot spot his comrade. Whoever it is, they must be very good. I simply cannot pick them out." Simon was frustrated at his apparent failure.

"Very well done, young man. And thank you for the compliment. Yes, he is signalling. And his comrade is me. That gentleman is DI Covington. He is my personal protection officer. There are still some old friends who would like to settle the odd score with me." Robinson seemed unconcerned by the serious threats he faced. "Covington is dull as ditch water, but I would rather have him on my side in any sort of altercation than any man I have ever met." Robinson paused and looked intently across at Simon as if he was making his mind up about something. "Tell me what you know about the Black Market."

6

An easy entrance – London - 1940

Joe carefully walked up the street and watched the house. No lights were visible, but then there was a blackout. All the heavy curtains were carefully drawn against the watchful eye of the Luftwaffe. Joe was confident the house was empty. His informant was first-class.

'Jeff the Chef' was an amazing cook. He plied his trade to those social climbing households who could not afford a full-time chef but wished to convince the world that they could. He had many regular clients, and his art was highly valued. Especially as he used his contacts to obtain ingredients that were not easily available legally. The trust afforded to him by his devoted patrons and the necessity for them to book his services well in advance gave him unbridled access to the running of their homes. Most importantly, to their diary.

Jeff had two weaknesses: fast women and slow horses. Unfortunately for Jeff, he had no perspicacity about either. Despite life continually issuing him warnings, Jeff repeatedly put his faith and his money behind his ill judgment. Thus, he was in a continuous state of financial penury. Joe, as Jeff's friend and confidant, was perpetually on hand to support him in his many hours of need. Always ready to help alleviate his monetary woes and relieve him of his valuable information.

Jeff had informed Joe that the family were visiting friends at a country estate in the North. They would travel on Friday and return on Tuesday. They had two permanent staff. An elderly housekeeper and a versatile Maid who was required to perform many household functions. The Maid was considered invaluable to the lady of the household and would accompany her on the trip. The Housekeeper was to be given time off to visit her sister. The house would be empty all weekend. Perfect.

Joe walked the street one more time, happy that the persistent drizzle was keeping most people tucked up at home. All the houses were quiet, and the traffic was non-existent. The Luftwaffe were late tonight; perhaps the weather didn't suit their purposes as much as it did Joe. He slipped across the road as he drew level with the house. He was inside in just under 3 minutes. Carefully avoiding standing on the flower beds, he had climbed up to the roof via a sturdy drainpipe at the rear. As he expected, the dormer window opened easily; people were much less careful about locking windows so high up. Joe found that such an entrance had another advantage. Any damage caused when opening the window would be much harder for any passer-by to spot. Additionally, as soon as he was a few feet from the ground, he was out of the eye-line of most people. Rarely did people look up from under their hat or umbrella when it was raining.

Inside the attic room, which was usually occupied by the maid, Joe checked the fireplace. It had been made ready for lighting but was cold. A good sign that the house was indeed empty. His next task was to secure his exit. Cautiously, he made his way down the stairs. He stepped at the edges of each stair tread, where the wood would be held firmer in place and less likely to creak. Advancing by feeling his way along, using his excellent night vision, not yet prepared to risk any lighting. On reaching the ground floor, he used the first door to his right into the Morning room. Careful not to trip over furniture, he edged to the French windows. Heavy curtains were drawn across the expansive windows. He drew them back silently, allowing enough light for him to work with. The doors were bolted, top, bottom and across, but not locked. A good security measure to prevent entry from the outside whilst allowing a quick and convenient exit point in the event of a fire or other such emergency.

Satisfied with his chosen escape point, Joe made his way across the hallway to the front door. A set of keys hung conveniently on a hook next to the hat stand. People were so often generous in their predictability. Joe warily drew back the heavy black-out curtains that hung inside the door. Carefully unlocking, drawing the top and bottom bolts he cracked the door just barely open. There was activity on the street; a dark figure walked slowly away from him along the far pavement. He couldn't make out the man's features or even his clothing. The rain was still falling, but he carried no umbrella. A Special Policeman, perhaps, or an ARP (Air Raid Precautions Warden)?

Delicately, he closed the door and slid the top bolt partway. Thus, any copper who might check the house was locked up securely would be satisfied. For his own part, a hasty exit would be a simple matter. Now, he would find the kitchen and take similar precautions. But his favoured exit, especially if it was a Special Constable out front, would be through the French doors from the morning room to the patio. He had already identified his route over the garden wall should the need arrive.

But he paused for a moment. Something was wrong. What was it that just didn't feel right? Then it struck him. The blackout curtains; why had they been drawn by the front door? There would be no light in the house during the weekend. He could understand the windows being covered, perhaps ready for a late return on Tuesday. But drawing the curtains behind them would be awkward as they left the house. Maybe they had made their final exit through the kitchen. That was possible; he would check to see if that door was covered. Hold on, they must have left by another way; this door had been bolted on the inside.

He was crouched down behind the front door, not wishing to throw any kind of shadow on the glass on the upper portion of the door or the windows at the side. He deliberately slowed his breathing and willed his senses to a heightened state. His eyes scanned the silent hallway. Was that a glimmer of light under the first door over to his right? It was very faint but discernible in the darkness. Joe lay down on the floor and squinted towards the danger. A red glow, not the white glare of a table lamp; it was the flickering light of a dying fire. Now, all his senses were shouting out to him, vying to be heard and understood. Joe realised that the house was warm. It was far too warm for an empty house of almost 2 days. There was a faint smell of freshly smoked cigars. Joe liked a cigar himself, and he fancied that it smelled like a good one. More odours suggested themselves, and Joe closed his eyes to concentrate on them. The fire smell was there, coal undeniably, the sulphur of a lit match. Along with another sweeter and yet still smoky aroma, Whiskey. Closer by, the scent of damp clothing and recently dubbed leather.

Joe heard a soft drip of water next to him. The sound was minuscule, but in the darkness, and with his elevated senses, it sounded like an explosion. He realised it came from the direction of the Hat stand. He slid his hand across the floor and felt the cold chill of water on the tiles. Reaching up, his hand brushed against a coat. A man's coat, dark, heavy material and wet. Wet from today's rain. In fact, this evening's rain. Joe thought quickly, yesterday was Friday, and it had been dry all day. The rain hadn't started until this afternoon.

On the floor next to the stand, he found wet boots. These were not the footwear of a worker, nor were they dress boots; these were military boots.

Joe didn't like it. There was somebody here, and he had no desire to wait around and find out who it was. He was getting out of there and fast. Which way? Not the front door. It was the easiest and obviously closest, but there was the dark figure patrolling outside to think about. He had no yearning for a tussle with the law, even if he was an ageing part-timer.

The French doors. The Morning room was diagonal across the hall from the heated room and was, therefore, his best bet. Moving stealthily across the floor, Joe put his hand on the door handle, pausing to listen; his ear pressed against the wood panel, he gently opened the door. The room was dark and thankfully unoccupied. Joe had moved just one step towards his escape when he felt cold metal touch softly against the back of his neck.

7

A job description – London 1941

Simon was taken aback. It was not the sort of question he was expecting. "Well, Sir, the Black Market, not a lot, I guess. Everyone is aware of it. Although it is seldom discussed in polite society, most people would see it as disloyal. But I guess the same people might dabble if tempted by something they need." Simon thought his answer sounded wishy-washy; he realised that he knew nothing and that he had taken no interest in the subject before now. To cover his embarrassment, he quickly added. "To be honest, Sir, I have not thought much about the subject."

"You and most people, my boy, which is exactly as we, the Government, would like. The truth is that it is far more serious than people realise."

"Do you mean that there is more going on than we know?" Simon asked earnestly.

"There is much more going on than the public realises, which is good. I mean, it is good that the people are ignorant. The various Ministries have been working hard to keep a lid on it. The Black Market is both an inevitable evil and a thorn in our side. If it gets out of control or worse, if people become aware of its true extent, then it would be an absolute disaster for the war effort."

Simon was now even more confused, and it must have shown because Robinson continued.

"Sorry, old chap, I am not exactly explaining this very well. Let me start at the beginning. When the Government realised that war was inevitable, we knew we had serious problems. Firstly, as a nation, we only produce 30 per cent of our own food. Having a large empire with plenty of trading partners that was not a problem during peacetime. We have plenty of advanced industry and technology to trade and many willing customers. At first sight, not being able to feed yourself might appear to be a problem. But think about it as a Nation; if you were 100 per cent self-sufficient, all well and good, but what happens if there is a drought? A couple of years of bad crops or disease in your livestock. Then you have a big problem. Suddenly, you must source food from abroad but don't have a supply chain. Plus, you do not have as many manufactured goods to trade because your manpower is in agriculture."

Simon listened intently; he could see the logic but didn't know where it was going.

"You studied Law at Cambridge, I believe. So, if the War had not so rudely interrupted your studies, you would be practising by now?

Simon nodded; he hadn't thought about Law and his studies for some time. He was a soldier now and probably would be for a good while.

"Law is a good profession. Well paid. When you want to eat, you eat. If the restaurant doesn't have any food, you go to the next one. You can even decide what food you want to eat. But if you decide to grow your own food, you will rely on good fortune and weather. Also, the range of food you could grow is limited to the climate. Try growing a banana in the Yorkshire Dales. Do you see my point?"

"Yes, Sir, I think so. The Government were deliberately preventing the economy from being dependent on agriculture." Simon thoughtfully replied.

"Spot on. It has been a policy of the British Nation for a long, long time. The beauty of it is that as an Island, we are by necessity a sea-faring people. Over the centuries, we have built a large merchant navy that, through the Empire, trades all over the globe. If one region has low commodity supplies, then another will usually take up the slack."

"And we are paying for this with our manufacturing industry, right, Sir?"

"Spot on, top marks," Robinson remarked jovially, like a patient teacher with a favoured pupil in class.

Robinson nodded enthusiastically before continuing. "There is another major advantage with this policy: more men are available to the armed forces in times of war. If we grew more of our own food, we would need more men to stay in the fields." Robinson's enthusiasm so far had been like that of a car salesman extolling the virtues of the latest coupe. However, Robinson's

21

tone changed as he elaborated further: "All of this is well and good in peacetime but can get a little tricky when your enemy is particularly good at making submarines and can sink your merchant ships almost at will."

"That wasn't foreseen, Sir." Simon regretted saying it. It was almost treasonous to criticise the government in such a way. "I am sorry, Sir; I didn't mean to er…"

"No, you are quite right. The thing is, we expected that France would hold out. Stop the Germans with the Maginot line. We didn't expect that the Nazis would be able to build massive U-boat bunkers on the North Atlantic coast. Normally, the only coast available to them Is the Baltic, and that is relatively easy for the RN to patrol. Now, their blasted U-boats have less distance to travel to intercept our convoys. They can stay at sea longer. In addition, the French Navy no longer exists; it had the fourth-largest navy in the world. It would have been much easier if they were still fighting alongside us." Robinson looked worried as though explaining the problems brought home their magnitude to him.

"Are we losing more shipping than is being reported?" Simon had also picked up on the mood; he feared he already knew the answer to his question,

"Yes, we are, a lot more. Of course, we expected losses, but the weight of shipping being lost is staggering. Last month, forty-eight ships were sunk, over 600,000 tonnes, countless men. Each ship downed is a body blow. We lose experienced men, valuable ships, and vital cargo. Twenty-five per cent of the cargo that we shipped, we lost, and in return, we only managed to sink two U-boats." Robinson was more than worried; it seemed like it was personal.

"Surely we are growing more food?" Simon asked hopefully.

"Yes, we are. Production has risen markedly; however, we can only do so much. British farming has always been defined by what we can grow. Traditionally, we tend towards meat and dairy production because many of our farms are hill farms. We don't have as much low-lying, flat, arable land. Schemes like Dig for Victory are helpful. Especially as they give the participants a sense of purpose. What we worry about the most is the rationing system."

"But I thought that Rationing has been a great success." Simon was surprised.

"Well, it is certainly the impression we like the nation to have. In theory, rationing works fine. Every British person gets the same crack of the whip. The available food is shared equally. That is how it works on the surface. However, although the boffins assure us that the rations are enough. Only the most frugal and skilful cooks can make palatable and nutritious meals from the meagre allowance. Of course, one can always go out to eat, as you know eating at a restaurant doesn't count towards your allowance. One can eat every meal out without needing to use your vouchers. A happy circumstance for those that can afford it. But of course, our workers are not in that position. And they are the very people we need to be well-fed. We also need them to be happy and motivated. To try to even things out, we set up the British Restaurants. Fair value meals are available off ration and priced to be within the reach of more humble budgets. A remarkable success for as long as we have supplies. The same goes for Works canteens and free school meals. We worry that the U-boats are winning, we cannot increase domestic production enough, and we are approaching a time when there will be real shortages."

Robinson paused to let the information sink in. Simon was concentrating hard; none of this had occurred to him before. He was starting to see the enormity of the problem.

"Now consider this." Robinson continued, "If you have enough, you don't mind too much if someone else has more. Naturally, there are richer and poorer people. But if you do not have enough, you can't feed your children adequately, then you might be somewhat aggrieved if you feel someone else was getting more than their fair share."

"You mean through the Black Market, Sir?" Simon interrupted.

"Yes, exactly. So far, the Black Market hasn't worried us too much. Of course, we have run campaigns against it. We have toughened up laws and introduced harsher sentences for people caught. But in a way, we have ignored it."

"Why would we do that?" Simon's innate sense of fair play riled against such a policy.

"Mainly because we do not have the resources to do much about it. The Police forces are stretched; it is not widely reported, but serious crime is dramatically up on pre-war levels. Secondly, we thought much of it was chicken feed, small deals and often in commodities that are not rationed, like tobacco and alcohol. We don't too much mind if people get a few extra fags or a bottle or two from time to time. Probably good for morale."

"But it is food you are most worried about?"

"That and Petrol." Robinson continued, "Petrol because we need it to wage a war. Food because we need a well-fed workforce, and, importantly, we need a happy workforce. Or, to put it another way, a workforce that is not discontented. The truth is that we don't really know the extent of the Black Market. By its very nature, most of it goes unreported. Many people think that a few extra sausages here and there is a victimless crime. However, we are beginning to suspect that it is far more extensive than we first thought. There are indications that organised crime groups are getting in on the act. We even suspect that our enemies are fuelling the fire".

"If that is the case, Sir, surely that indicates that it is big business. Why would gangsters be bothered with a few sausages?" Simon spoke as if thinking aloud. He was beginning to see the problems.

Robinson was impressed; he understood why Major Calderdale thought so highly of this young man. "Certainly, that is how we see it."

"But why would Jerry get involved? Surely, they can't think that they can make much of a difference?" Simon was still a little bemused by the complexity of the issue.

"Well, Jerry stands to win in two ways. Firstly, diverting food away from the workforce and into the already ample bellies of the better-off in Britain cannot hurt his cause. Secondly, if the Black Market is as big as we think it might be, then a serious injustice is happening. People are not getting a fair crack of the whip. The problem then is, if it gets out about the extent that the middle and upper classes are, shall we say, suffering a lot less than Joe Bloggs, there could be serious civil unrest. Bear in mind that whilst most British people are solidly behind the war effort, there are still discontents in our society. The communists, or at least some of them, are still committed to revolution even though we are fighting the Nazis. We still have Union leaders taking their members out on strike."

Simon was aghast. "I didn't know that, Sir?"

"No, naturally, we have kept that from the National Press. Most of it has been quickly sorted out, and to be fair, some of the grievances were not without merit. What we fear now is that we could lose the goodwill of our people. Empty bellies are what usually start off revolutions."

"Do you really think it could come to that, Sir?" Like most British men of his class, he had never taken the idea seriously of Britain becoming a socialist state.

"Well, we do not intend to let it happen. You can see there is a lot at stake here, Bach."

Simon nodded gravely; he didn't like what he heard.

"There is one more thing that could make matters even worse." Robinson paused to collect his thoughts. He looked like a doctor who, having already given his patient bad news, was about to tell him the worst. "We have intelligence that a rogue unit of the IRA is involved in smuggling livestock to Ireland."

"The IRA? But why, Sir?" Simon could not believe it. "How would they benefit?"

"You may not realise that the relationship between Britain and the Republic is somewhat strained. Ireland is a new nation struggling to find its place in the world. Its government can see the horror that the Nazis are inflicting on Europe. However, politically, they must remain neutral. Britain is still hated by most of the Irish public. Add to that the injustice that they perceive as being caused by the division of Ireland. If that wasn't enough, when we declared War on Nazi Germany, we took the stance that neutral countries should be supporting us. If they were not helping us, then they were essentially against us. The decision was taken that Britain would embargo any exports to Eire. Including food and agricultural products. The Republic is somewhat behind the rest of Europe in Agriculture and Industry. They have been trying to catch up, but as I say, they are a new state. They heavily depend on importing grains, seeds, and agricultural equipment from the UK. So, the embargo is hitting them hard, and in addition to that, the fact that their shipping is being sunk by German U-boats at the same rate as everyone else's. In short, their rationing is more punitive than ours. Irish stomachs are rumbling, and to them, it's the Brits that are to blame. So, if a group of Irish Nationalists were to get hold of a significant load of goods from the British Black Market, they would make money, look like heroes for feeding their people, damage the British war effort and embarrass both the British and Irish governments."

8

Not alone after all – London 1940

Major James Wilber Rider Calderdale was no stranger to the house. He knew its sounds, smells, and draughts—the draughts that changed as the fitted doors opened and closed.

His visit had been unplanned and last minute. Disappointed that his parents were absent, he had no complaints, though, as he had not wired ahead. It was still surprising to him that he had managed to get the time off. He had not wanted to disappoint anyone by promising a rare visit only for the usual change of plans. He realised, guiltily, that he was glad his old home was empty. He loved his parents, but he knew he would soon tire of their constant questions, worried entreaties to look after himself better, interrogation about lady friends and overbearing pride in his achievements. The solitude would be a godsend, even if it would be just one evening. He was loathe to admit it, but the stresses and strains of his calling were taking their toll. He longed for the peace and quiet of his own company.

He had walked from the station, unable to find a cab; he consoled himself with the promise of a gentle stroll along much-loved streets. Then the rain started. Glad of his coat and hat, he quickened his pace, anticipating the warm fire that his childhood home promised. On letting himself in with his old key, he dutifully dealt with the blackout. Bolting the front door and drawing the luxuriant curtains. Only once was he sure there were no gaps for the light to escape from, and after checking the downstairs rooms, he flicked the switch for the electric lights. Nothing; his father was distrustful of electric power, and even if he had been away for just one night, he would have thrown the switch on the main circuit board. James smiled at his father's circumspection. The electricity panel was in the basement, and James had no wish to navigate the twisting, rickety stairs. No matter, there would be candles in the dresser drawer. He had matches on him. He knew where Father kept his best cigars.

There would be whiskey, and a fire could be made in no time at all. As no bed would be made up, he would sleep by the fire in his clothes and bathe in the morning. Thus, James encamped in the front living room. The fire had been made ready for the family's return and was blazing invitingly within minutes of his applying a match. The cigar and whisky soon soothed stretched nerves. The fire hypnotically warmed and entertained with its capricious shapes. The candlelight palliative; so much less offensive than the discordance of the electric bulb. James was jolted from his reverie by the flickering of the previously steady candle flame. He looked suspiciously at it as if he expected it to speak out and tell him what it was about. Again, the candle flickered, its flame bending towards the fire as if genuflecting to its superior cohort. Dark smoke rose from the flame as it writhed in the turmoil of the draught. James was instantly alert. His training and peerless instincts fired up like a finely tuned engine roaring into life. The draught had not been there before, of that he was certain. He knew the house and its eccentricities well. Something had disturbed the calm of the air; a window or a door had been opened somewhere in the building. That drew him to the obvious conclusion: someone was here.

James quickly and carefully extinguished the candle. The fire would be difficult to put out without making a noise. Fortunately, it had died down, and its remaining embers cast just a paltry glow. Knowing the room's layout, he avoided the furniture and reached the door. He listened intently for the slightest sound. Was that a creak of a stair? Surely it was. Ever so slight, he knew better than anybody that avoiding any noise on those stairs was impossible. In his youth, he tried many times, usually after a late night out, as he strove to avoid waking the household and the inevitable lecture from his parents. James heard the door to the morning room open, then silence. He was sure of his hearing and waited patiently until he could just make out the padding of soft shoes moving gingerly across the hall floor. The ruffle of curtains being drawn. Then, the sharper sound of a key turning a lock, culminating in a distinctive click. Bolts were pulled, and another pair of clicks were made as the door was gently opened and closed. Had the intruder left? James doubted it; no doubt he was just securing his exit in the event of an emergency.

James was unarmed, his service revolver in his case in the hall. His father kept a Walther P38 in his desk drawer. It was a present from James, who had acquired it in an altercation with its previous owner. Making his way via the library, where his father's desk loomed menacingly in the centre of the floor, James collected the weapon. Passing through the dining room, he skirted around the hallway, positioning himself behind the door in the Morning Room.

9

The Irish question – London 1941

Time was moving on and Robinson and Simon Bach had already walked some distance. Simon was not sure where they were exactly. Robinson had a suggestion. "I say my club is just around the corner; what say we pop in there and continue our chat?" He didn't wait for an answer as he marched off with Simon and, somewhere behind, DI Covington in tow.

Once settled into a quiet, dark recess of an opulent Gentleman's club, Robinson continued the briefing. "Now where were we Bach?"

"The Irish Sir."

"Ah yes, the Irish. We are not going to win this war alone, Bach. Thank God for the Russians. Germany attacking the Soviet Union will buy us time and take up a lot of the enemy's resources. But alone, we can never hope to liberate Western Europe. We just don't have the manpower or the industrial capacity to take on that sort of an operation."

"Do you think that the Americans will join in, Sir?" Simon guessed what Robison was getting at.

"Now that is the question young man, that is the question." Again, Robinson gathered his thoughts. "America has political problems. Many Americans see Hitler as a European issue, not their fight. Don't forget that a large portion of Americans are of German descent. Another very big and influential portion of the American public is Irish Americans. These guys see themselves as Irish first and American second. They are very much against fighting alongside the British, whoever the enemy is. You will remember the IRA bombing campaign on the British mainland from 1938 to 1940. Much of the funding for these outrages came from America. Not from the US government, obviously. Officially America denounces the actions of the IRA. However, many in America support them, and even the former ambassador to the UK, Joseph Kennedy, speaks warmly of Irish freedom fighters.

Then there are the American Southern States. Many people in these states identify with the Nazi's views on racial purity; they probably think Hitler is doing a good job. Add to that that most American housewives don't want to see their husbands and sons go off to die in a foreign war; the memories of the Great War are still very fresh. So, Roosevelt must walk a tightrope of public opinion. Eventually, the hope is that the majority of the Great American public will see the Nazis for what they are and do the right thing. In the meantime, Britain needs to be seen as being on the right side of the argument. Suppose for one moment that quantities of rationed commodities were finding their way from Britain to Ireland. If that became common knowledge in this country, then the British public would demand that the government act against the Irish. Most people don't see much difference between the IRA and the Irish Government. The pressure on our Government would be immense. Plus, there would likely be reprisals against Irish people living here; a great many Irish people are working here in key jobs such as construction, for example. If this were to play out in this way, if Irish people living in mainland UK were attacked by mobs of angry Brits, as happened to Italians living here when Italy declared war on us, then the Irish Americans would have a field day. They would claim that the British are a nasty colonial power, no better than the Germans. Our hope for the Americans to join us in the fight against the Nazis would be set back years."

Simon had been listening intently; it was all incredible to him. Like most Brits, he saw the world in very uncomplicated terms. The British were the good guys. Standing up for freedom and democracy. The Nazis were evil. They started the war by attacking Poland. They had overrun France, Holland and even plucky little Belgium. And if it hadn't been for the RAF, they would have no doubt tried the same thing in England. That America should even hesitate to join in and get rid of Hitler had seemed amazing to him. Robinson's explanations seemed to make sense, though. "So, if I understand what you are saying, Sir, the government is concerned about the Black Market because it could get out of control and cause massive dissension in the

British public. It could spark diplomatic tensions with Ireland, and that could stop the Americans from joining the war against Germany."

"Yes, that just about sums it all up quite neatly, Bach." Robinson smiled. "I say the sun must surely be over the yard arm. I don't know about you, but I could use a snifter." Robinson raised his hand, and almost immediately, the attentive steward nodded towards him and, without asking what he required, turned away and returned in no time with two very large whiskeys.

10

Time to leave – London 1940

Joe's skin crawled at the thought of the frigid steel touching his neck. He hated guns. They were the weapon of cowards. Any man or woman could kill with a gun. It was impersonal and, to him, immoral. Joe knew he had to move quickly. He had no intention of spending the next few years in prison. Equally unappealing was having his head blown apart by a trigger-happy homeowner. He would much rather take a risk.

Obligingly, at that moment, the air raid sirens started their evening chorus. Would he get another opportunity? He hoped the sudden noise would distract his foe.

His movement was swift and decisive. Spinning on his right foot, he snapped his head and shoulders around as his dance teacher had taught him. He liked dancing; good dancers got all the best-looking women, and that was reason enough to take lessons. As he had learned, the sharp movement of the head carried the momentum down through the body. In this situation, it had the added benefit of momentarily taking his head away from the muzzle of the gun. The would-be shooter was now aiming at fresh air. As he spun clockwise his right arm came upwards, his hand grabbing the forearm of his adversary, pulling it out straight. His left hand, arriving slightly later, punched into his shoulder, further straightening the arm.

Joe shot his left arm over the top of the gunman's shoulder. His chest now pushing against the extended arm. His weight fell, putting further strain on the shoulder and elbow joints. The man grimaced in pain but was temporarily quietened as Joe's elbow smashed backwards hard, glancing him just above his right eye. His assailant stunned long enough for Joe to snatch the gun from his hand, push him away and twist back around with the gun raised.

Joe saw that his attacker was an army Major, but he didn't recognise the badges of his unit. He was older than Joe around

40 maybe. Three or four inches taller and probably a couple of stones heavier. As the Major drew himself back up from the indignity of falling to the floor, Joe could see that this was no desk soldier. His uniform fitted him well and told of an active man. Joe's aching left fist was a testament to that; punching that shoulder had been like hitting a tank.

"Well done, young man, that was quite a move." The Major's voice was calm; he didn't seem the slightest concerned that a man had broken into his home and was now aiming a pistol at his chest. "It has been some time since any man has taken my gun away from me".

Joe said nothing as his mind raced. He didn't like this situation one little bit. He hated that he had been caught in the act. The situation was better now but ultimately far from perfect. None of the options that lay before him attracted him. There was just enough light in the room, and he felt sure that the man would be able to identify him.

An option was to silence him permanently. He had the means in his hands. The thuds of the German bombs landing were far away, but they might cover the sound of a gunshot. The prospect was distasteful to him. Shooting any man was not his idea of fair play, but killing a King's officer seemed unpatriotic. Like he was doing Hitler's job for him. The idea of dangling from a noose was equally unappetising.

"My name is Major James Calderdale; this is my parents' home. They are away for this evening, but I suppose you know more about that than I do." James studied the young thief carefully like a man might judge a horse he wished to buy or bet on. "You are unfortunate; I very rarely visit, I am little busy at the moment, small matter of a war on. The chances of me being here at the same time as your visit are a million to one against; sorry about that old chap."

"Forgive me if I don't share my name with you" Joe felt strangely at ease with this calm military man.

"So, what should I call you then?"

"Call me Joe if you like, but I don't intend to spend too much time chatting if it's all the same with you."

"Ah, your real name then, clever "

"How did you know?" Joe was aghast.

"Well, I wasn't sure until you just confirmed it." James smiled.

Joe felt foolish; he had been easily duped.

"Don't beat yourself up, young man. I figured a clever man with a reasonably common name would use it. You assumed I would think you had made it up; therefore, you might as well use it. Save you having to remember what you had said."

Joe felt like he was at school again, only this teacher was far better than any he had ever had.

"I just called your bluff; if it had been an alias, well, nothing ventured, nothing gained," James explained further. "Besides, what have I gained? There must be thousands of Joes in London. You are from London, no doubt, somewhere around Bethnal Green, I fancy".

Joe was astounded by the man's insight; he was spot on, but this time, he managed to contain his surprise and give nothing further away.

"Forgive me. I hope you don't think I am showing off, but regional accents are something of a hobby of mine." James carried on certain that his guess was correct. Joe was even more shocked; even when he was sure his reaction had been neutral, this man could see straight through him. Joe made a mental note never to play cards with this one.

"Nice work on the break-in, by the way." James continued the dialogue. "You came in via the roof, I suppose, one of the rear dormer windows?"

Joe nodded. "But how did you guess that?"

"Not a guess this time. I know this house well, and there is an extraordinary draught when one of those windows opens." James explained.

"You felt the draught?" Joe exclaimed in awe.

"Candle flickering. Electric is off, you see. Another bit of ill fortune for you old chap I might never have noticed if I had been sat with the electric lights on."

Joe nodded; this was a man to be reckoned with.

"I was impressed that you secured your exit first. The French doors and then the front door." James didn't wait for confirmation from Joe. He just continued with his appraisal. It was as if he was marking an exam paper.

"You were leaving before I so rudely stopped you? James asked. "Why?" He continued. "You knew I was here?"

"Yes." Joe felt compelled to answer. What was this man about? Joe had the upper hand; he had a gun aimed at him, for God's sake. And yet the Major was calling the shots, it seemed.

"Good effort. How?" James's voice was insistent; it seemed vital for him to know.

"Wet coat and boots, cigar and whiskey smell, room too warm. I could make out the fire glow under the door." Joe barked off the answers like a class swot, eager for top marks.

"Bravo, young man." James seemed genuinely pleased.

Joe's chest swelled with pride; what was this man doing to him?

"Why aren't you in the Army?" James blurted out.

Joe didn't answer.

"Dodged the draft, eh?" James accused.

"For now." Joe was defensive; he didn't like this line of questioning.

"Well, you're not a coward, is my bet. You're as cool as a cucumber; I doubt your pulse has exceeded 60 beats a minute since you broke in here. Not even when I had a gun to your head." James mused. "Perhaps you are a Commie or a conchie?"

"Never, I love my country as much as the next man" Joe voice sounded hurt and appalled. "I just want to serve on my terms." Joe countered.

"And you think you deserve that, do you?"

"I just don't want to end up as bloody cannon fodder. It's all right for people like you; you get to choose what you do. People like me are always the ones in the front line." Joe's passionate rant, fuelled by his guilt and shame, rang through the room.

"Maybe I could help you?" James deliberately lowered his voice to a soothing level.

"And why would you do that?" Joe asked with bitterness.

"Because we, I, need good young men like you. This war is being fought on so many fronts. It's a new age. Things are happening that you have no idea about. We need people with your skills, with your coolness and intelligence." James sparked an interest in Joe but dare he trust him?

"You're good at what you do, I can tell that, but I could teach you so much more."

"What, like how to keep hold of your gun?" Joe mocked as he waved the weapon in front of his would-be teacher.

James smiled and nodded slightly. "Touché, touché" his words chuckled out. "Well, I could teach you how to tell if a pistol is loaded or not just by the weight of it." James's voice was now serious and challenging.

"You're bluffing" Joe realised the implication. The gun was empty, and the Major had let Joe take it from him. "Nah, you're having me on."

"Only one way to find out." James teased.

The noise of the bombing had grown steadily louder in the last few minutes. Joe was sure that a gunshot would go unnoticed in the furore of the blitz. He raised the gun and aimed at the Majors nose; just before squeezing the trigger, he diverted his aim just to the right of the implacable soldier's head. Joe hated guns; he squinted as he anticipated the noise and recoil of the released bullet.

Click.

Silence.

No shot. No recoil. No smoke. No deafening noise. Just a click and then pain.

11

What to do? – London 1941

"So how do the Government propose to handle the problem, Sir." Simon sipped at the spirit; it was a little early in the day for him, but he had to admit he needed a drink.

"Well, old chap, that's where we come in. Firstly, we need to establish the extent of the problem. Exactly what is going on, and who is up to what? When we know that, we can act accordingly. Whatever happens, we must be discreet. Whatever action we take, we must keep it out of the press and away from the public. There can be no official involvement; we cannot use the police, for example."

"So, what do you have in mind?" Simon was beginning to think that there might be something that he could get his teeth into with this mission. Since his injury, he worried his espionage career might be over.

"We have been getting some information passed to us from an anonymous source. The Ministry of Food has been receiving letters from someone in South Wales who claims a Black Market racket is selling large quantities of livestock. You see, every farmer must declare how many animals they have. They are allowed to keep a small percentage for their own use, but other than that, they are obliged to sell their animals to the Ministry of Food at a fixed price. These are then distributed via the rationing system. Of course, we know there is a huge temptation for the farmers to underreport the numbers and keep more back. They can sell these for much more through the Black Market. We expect this to happen, but these letters were implying that there is an operation being organised on a much bigger scale."

"You say were implying Sir, does that mean that the letters have stopped?" Simon asked.

"Exactly, Bach," Robinson was beginning to like this young man more and more. "The letters stopped abruptly some months ago, just as they were getting interesting."

"Do we know where they were posted from, Sir?" Simon suggested.

"We can track them down to a post box in Brecon, South Wales. Brecon is a Market Town, and the date of each letter corresponds to a Market day. So, anyone visiting the market on those days could have posted them, and that means anyone in a 40-mile radius, we estimate. We have made some discreet enquiries in the area, and eventually, one thing did pop up." Robinson paused and sipped his whiskey.

"No doubt you looked at the Death register for the surrounding areas, Sir. Hospital admissions, that sort of thing." Simon blushed; he wished he hadn't questioned his new boss with such obvious suggestions.

"Quite right, quite right, Bach." To Simon's relief, Robinson didn't seem at all insulted by his questions; he was beginning to see that this was a man who was more interested in getting the job done than worrying about egos. "There was nothing at first. Then we came across a missing person report from a small town nearby. The local Bobby had investigated, but his wife had told him that her husband had joined up. The copper seemed to have accepted her word on that and closed the case."

"Who had made the missing person report, Sir?" Simon was intrigued.

"Apparently, the man's elderly aunt lives in a Retirement home on the South Coast. She normally gets a regular letter from him but hasn't heard from him for some time. However, she is a little vague, well into her nineties, fit as a fiddle but not fully compos mentis according to the Retirement Home manager."

"You sent someone to see her, Sir?" Simon enquired. "Did they get hold of one of his letters to her?"

"Yes, and yes, the handwriting did match our anonymous correspondent." Robinson was clearly pleased that Bach was measuring up nicely to the high expectations he had of him. He was already confident that they would work well together.

"Have you reopened the missing person case?"

"Would that be what you would have done?" Robinson was keen to know this bright young man's tactics.

"No sir, I don't believe I would. It could only muddy the water. It seems likely that this man's disappearance is suspicious.

39

I would tell the old lady that her nephew is fine, can't tell you where he is, top secret and all that, put her mind at rest so she doesn't make a fuss. It seems a little devious, but I can't see any merit in worrying her. I assume we can't find any record of this man joining any of the services. I would suggest that he knew something important and has been silenced. If that is right, then this is a serious matter. People are not generally hushed up for a few extra pork chops."

"Our thinking exactly, old chap." Robinson nodded and waited for Simon to continue.

"So, if there is a conspiracy, it must be somewhere in the region of this man's hometown. The conspirators must believe that there is no further suspicion about the disappearance. The policeman who investigated must be suspected, although it is equally likely that he is just incompetent. The conspirators may or may not know about the letters to the Ministry. They certainly won't know their exact contents. What exactly did the letters tell us, Sir?"

Robinson thought carefully as he took a good slug of the whiskey. "They suggest, without giving any real details, that a group of people are organising the production of extra livestock and concealing them from the ministry inspectors. You understand that many of these farms are remote, and there are too few inspectors, so hiding extra cows is much easier than we city dwellers might imagine. Again, there were no definitive numbers mentioned, but the implication is that they could be significant. As you so eloquently put it, it's much more than a few extra pork chops. Our earnest would-be informer seems to be opposed to this practice. If I had to make a guess, then our man has made his objections plain to these people and threatened to expose them. Our hope is that he hadn't told them that he had already informed us."

"If I may, Sir, what makes you think that?" Simon wondered.

"We had a couple of shrinks have a read through the letters. These are clever people, and they reckon that they can guess, although that is not a word that they use, from his letters his state of mind."

"That's incredible, Sir, surely."

40

"My thoughts exactly, old boy, but what they came up with seems to make sense. They think that he is only reluctantly involved with the, shall we call it enterprise? He feels it is wrong, but he is even more reluctant to inform on his colleagues. This makes perfect sense when you think about it. Why didn't he just write one letter and tell us everything?"

"Perhaps he is afraid that they would find out it was him that gave the game away?" Suggested Simon.

"That is certainly a consideration, but the shrinks seem to think that he has people or at least a person close to him who is heavily involved. He asked in his letters for immunity from prosecution. He hinted that others involved feel the same way he does. That would imply that some power is being exerted over them to comply with the operation."

"You mean that they are being forced?" Asked Simon.

"We think that they are being coerced. Perhaps this started off as a smaller deal, with a few sausages, as we said. But maybe it has grown into a larger concern. More risks, perhaps other parties involved?"

Simon realised he hadn't asked the obvious question. 'Sorry, Sir, what does this man do for a living? Why would he be involved?"

12

At his mercy – London 1940

To this day, Joe could not tell you what happened next. The Major could, but to Joe, the speed and violence of the attack were inexplicable. There was sudden and agonising pain in his right knee. The room blurred before his eyes as his body spun and fell. There was intense pressure at the bottom of his spine, and the hair on the back of his head was being pulled from his scalp.

Joe found himself face down on the floor. The Major above him with his knee in his back and a handful of his hair pulling on his head so that his throat was exposed and at the mercy of a large knife.

"Where the hell did that come from?" Joe screamed silently to himself as the realisation set in that he was helpless and about to die.

"Drop the gun" The Major's command was non-negotiable. Joe complied without hesitation. "Slide it away." The useless empty gun glided out of reach.

"Just for your information and education, the gun isn't empty. There was no round in the chamber. I thought I might relieve you of the opportunity of discovering that for yourself." The Major's calm voice was beginning to get on Joe's nerves. But he couldn't deny the man was a swell.

"By the way, thank you anyway for pointing it away from me before testing it. You were most gentlemanly."

"You're welcome, I am sure." Joe strained to remain calm.

"Well, at last, your heartbeat is up a bit", James joked.

"So, what is it going to be?' Joe enquired, "The Police?"

"Afraid not, old boy, man in my position can't afford that sort of publicity. Far too much inconvenience as well; I told you I am a busy man." The man's voice, which had been charming and jovial, now carried a menace; it was cold and calculating. Despite himself, Joe shivered.

It is not an easy thing to cut a man's throat. Even the sharpest blade needs strength and precision. Joe didn't doubt that the Major had the capabilities, neither did he question the sharpness of the blade. When it came, the incision was wickedly swift. The blade sped across in front of Joe; he felt its sting, and he fell flat against the carpet.

Instinctively, his hands clutched to his throat as he sought to stem the flow of life from his body. There was no blood.

"Get up. You are OK." James commanded.

Joe rolled on his side and looked up at his would-be murderer. "You bastard"

"Now, I thought you might be a little more courteous under the circumstances."

Joe touched his neck gingerly. There was the slightest of cuts, no more than a scratch really. A drop of blood smeared his fingers. He'd had worse shaving.

"Right, young man." Having regained the gun, the Major was in control now, as he had been all along. "Get yourself up; you're leaving. I meant what I said: I am too busy a man to be dealing with the police. What's more, I don't want my parents to know that their defences have been breached. That's the one thing you guys don't think about when you invade someone's inner sanctum. Yes, they may be insured, but what about their peace of mind."

"Easy for you to preach, easy to be smug when you have your choices and opportunities." Joe's pride was hurt.

"Now, don't get all commie on me. I understand, to me, the crime is that someone of your talents isn't utilised properly by society. I meant what I said: we could help each other out. Whitehall 3633, call that number in 3 days' time, ask for Major Calderdale, and give your name as Joe Crook, and they will tell you when and where to report." The Major was all business now. "Tell me, did you do any damage upstairs?"

"Of course not," Joe replied indignantly.

"I thought not; now away with you, please; I will lock up after you."

Joe didn't need too much encouragement; he turned towards the French doors.

"One last thing", The Major called after him; Joe paused without looking back. "The next time you enter a room, make sure that you check to see if there is anyone behind the door. Jerry won't be quite as hospitable as I am."

"Yes, Sir", Joe shouted with a sarcastic tone. It would not be the last time he used those words when addressing the Major, but he would be far more respectful every time thereafter.

Joe called the number as instructed, starting him on a path leading to the training Camp and his new life as a Special Operations Executive agent.

13

The Missing Man – London 1941

"He is the local butcher and runs an abattoir." Robinson let that bombshell hang in the air for a few moments. "So, he would be integral to an operation of this kind."

"He would, especially initially, in a smaller operation, a single farmer with an extra beast or two would need a friendly butcher to slaughter the animal and sell it on, under the counter, so to speak. It may be that for the operation to get bigger, they would need to distribute the meat further. We are thinking of the cities where there would be a higher demand. That may mean transporting the animals live and slaughtering them later. Thereby, they wouldn't need to keep the produce cool." Robison waited for Simon to draw his conclusions.

"If that were the case, then they wouldn't need a butcher at the source. Maybe our informant is being cut out of the deal. That's the reason he has become so public-spirited." Simon was guessing, and he knew it. The butcher's motivations were a mystery.

As if reading his mind, Robinson continued, "The fact is Bach that we don't know. We are somewhat in the dark, playing a guessing game. We need someone on the ground looking into what's going on."

"You mean me, Sir?" Simon didn't wait for an answer; Robinson hadn't told him all this as idle chatter. "Might be a bit tricky; these communities are usually very tight-knit Sir. I am not sure that a stranger poking about would go down too well."

"We agree, our thinking exactly. You would need a plausible reason for visiting the area. Your cover would need to be carefully worked out and watertight. Most importantly, you would need time to build trust. This must be done very discreetly. If you do find something serious going on, we would need to think very hard about what we do about it. As we said earlier, it would be an absolute disaster if news of this sort of thing became public knowledge. I want you to be very cautious and keep in touch as much as possible. This in itself will be tricky; country telephone exchange operators are notorious for brightening up their tedious shifts by listening in to calls."

"Radio Sir?" Simon suggested.

"Risky Bach. If someone discovered your radio set, they might think you were a German spy. Can't have you being lynched by some angry mob; you have cost too much to train."

"Your concern for my safety is most heartening, Sir." Simon smiled at his senior officer's levity.

"I want you to report to our people at this address." Robinson scribbled in a small notebook he took from his pocket before tearing out the sheet and passing it to Simon. "They will spend some time with you putting together a suitable identity and producing the right paperwork to cover you. We must get this right. It may be dangerous if you are found out. Be careful and the very best of luck, old chap." Robinson stood and stretched out his hand for Simon to shake. With that, Simon knew the interview was over.

14

The Silver Screen – London 1941

Joe was puzzled by his orders—not for the first time. He was learning that it was best to accept that there were things he would never know about and adopt the old mantra, "Ours is but to do or die."

As instructed, he sat in the cinema and watched the Pathe newsreel without interest, as it promised good news in North Africa. Joe was unsure how the siege of Tobruk was good news, but he was persuaded that Bob Danvers-Walker, the voice of Pathe news, knew what he was talking about.

The cinema was almost empty. This didn't surprise him as the advertised feature was old, and a daytime show would not be a crowd-puller. The few that had shunned the pleasant early summer's day were all most certainly with the security services. The courting couple who canoodled in the back row had a good view of the entire auditorium. Joe wondered how enthusiastically they were enacting their parts. He hoped they were not too engaged in their role.

A tall man with a trilby balanced on the back of the seat in front of him and a heavy overcoat laid across the arm of his chair stared intently at the show from his seat close to the exit. Joe knew that the man's job was guarding that door. Why, in an empty theatre, would a person with the choice of any seat choose to sit away from the centre and so close to the screen? Copper, he could smell 'em a mile off.

Feeling well protected, He slumped in his chair as his eyes drooped, and he pulled his hat down over his face. Get rest when you can, eat when you can and drink when you can, had been the Major's advice. Good counsel for any soldier, wars were said to be 90% boredom and 10% terror.

"At ease, soldier." the Major's voice rang out in the unoccupied cinema. If it had meant to surprise Joe, it appeared to have little effect. The slumbering Joe had not flinched.

47

"Good afternoon, sir. You're late." His languid voice was muffled by the material of his cap.

"Bloody insubordinate……." James Calderdale let the rest of his tirade fade from his lips as a smile came to his face. Joe had always been the officer's favourite ever since they first met at either end of the Major's pistol. No other operative would have dared to address him in such a manner. No amount of training had dampened his independence. He was an excellent agent, one of the few who really thought for themselves. Even if his sense of humour was a little unorthodox and his deference to authority practically non-existent. "Joe Turner, permit me to introduce Mr Robinson, who is here to assign you a mission. Is that convenient for you?"

Now Joe did sit up. "I am sorry, Sir." He addressed Robinson directly as he stood and shook his hand vigorously, "I didn't realise that someone important was coming."

"One day, Turner, one day" James smiled and shook his head resignedly.

"Turner, do you know who I am or what I do?" Robinson asked.

"Yes, Sir. I understand that you and your role in the Government are top secret, so naturally, I have heard everything about you."

It was Robinson's turn to smile at the defiant young man. "We want you to go undercover on a vital operation that will put you at grave risk of danger."

"Can't be more dangerous than the grub in the mess at the Health Spa, Sir," Joe mused, "I'm in."

"You might not be quite so enthusiastic when you hear the details, but we wouldn't ask you if this was not crucial. James, be so good as to explain to Mr Turner exactly what we would like him to do."

"Joe, you are to return to your old ways. It's back to petty pilfering for you, only this time you will get caught again." The Major was always one for the dramatic introduction. Joe didn't rise to the jibe; he waited patiently for the officer to continue.

"From here, you will be taken to a remote safe house; you will liaise with Susan Cartwright; I think you know her. She will help with your cover. Basically, we want you to return to your own persona. Joe Turner, expert thief living and working in the east end of London. Of course, you have been away for some time, and we will produce unbreakable alibis for that absence. You will resume your career in crime and settle back into your old ways. After several successful jobs, you will be arrested."

Joe was surprised and smiled at the Major. "Really, what for?"

"Murder."

"Murder?" Joe's smile disappeared from his face. "You have got to be joking."

"Deadly, serious old chap, if you will pardon the pun." James realised that Joe would rail against this idea, so he pushed on to explain the whole plan to put the would-be criminal's mind at rest. "You will be arrested for a crime you did not commit. Evidence will be planted; unfortunately for you, your alibi will be weak. You will be remanded in custody. To the criminal community, you will appear to be just an unfortunate victim of police incompetence and corruption. Hopefully, this will engender their sympathies."

"Just a minute, who is it that will arrest me with all this compelling evidence? What is going to happen to me? I very much want to serve; I think I have proved that already, but I am not sure I fancy a meeting with the hangman even for King and Country."

"You will not be hanged; in fact, you will get off Scot-free. The evidence will conveniently go missing thanks to DCI Wilkinson."

"Backhander Bill, that bent bastard?"

"Detective Chief Inspector William Wilkinson is perhaps the bravest man I have ever met and certainly the most honest." Robinson intervened in the conversation.

"You got to be kidding, right? Bill Wilkinson has seen more backhanders than Fred Perry. He is as bent as a nine-bob note."

Robinson smiled at Joe's colloquialisms "It would appear that our erstwhile DCI has been doing a very good job of establishing his reputation as a corrupt police officer."

"Wait a minute, you're saying that he is undercover, aren't you?"

Both Robinson and the Major nodded. Joe looked aghast. It took him a few moments to take this all in. He still wasn't completely convinced. "But I know for a fact that he has taken money, and what about Blind Bob? They say he beat him to death with his own ledger."

"Every penny that DCI Wilkinson has taken from the criminal community, and yes, that is a considerable amount, he has paid over to the authorities. There is a bean counter in Whitehall that can account for every ha'penny. He has ingratiated himself into the very core of the serious crime scene in London. In doing so, he has put himself at very serious risk. If his true colours were revealed, a mile-long queue of villains would want him dead." Robinson's tone had turned grave. "We must insist that none of what you are hearing goes any further; trust no one with this; a very courageous and diligent man's life is at stake. To be honest, we weren't too sure about telling you. Not that we don't trust you; it's just that the fewer people that know, the better. However, given the risks we are asking you to take, we thought it proper that you know the full picture."

The Major took up the narrative. "Blind Bob, Robert Justin, was, as you probably know, the accountant to the Baker Family. The Bakers, father and son, head up perhaps the most powerful crime syndicate in the East End. Ted Baker suspected that Bob had been skimming some of the cream off the top of his milk, so to speak. Ted asked his son Eddie to take care of him. Fortunately for Bob, DCI Wilkinson was at that meeting and offered to deal with the problem for them. He managed to convince the Bakers that they would be too close to Bob and consequently would be too much under suspicion. So, Bob was snatched by a masked gang from a pub in Stepney. Witnesses gave evidence at the inquest that Bob was thrown into the back of a van. At the very moment that Bob was snatched, the Bakers, father and son, together with all their known accomplices, were at a banquet hosted by the Mayor of London, ten miles away. Their alibi was further enhanced by the fact that they were being watched by several Scotland Yard undercover detectives." The Major paused to make sure that Joe was understanding all this. He needn't have worried.

"So Back Hander Bill, then spirits Bob away, after no doubt getting the low down on all the Baker's activities from him. But

50

if he wasn't killed, what about the inquest, the body?" Joe's quick brain was struggling to fill in all the pieces of the puzzle.

"A body was found a couple of weeks later by a bobby on the beat. An autopsy was performed by a home office pathologist, and a genuine inquest was held that concluded death by murder by a person or persons unknown. In reality, there was no corpse; the autopsy report was concocted. Photographs were not shown to the inquest jury because of the horrific injuries and the fact that the body had been ravaged by rats. The coroner accepted the pathologist's testimony because he had no earthly reason not to. The case file remains open, but the police have absolutely no leads to go on. Blind Bob is now enjoying his new life in one of the colonies, I believe."

"Well, bugger me, I always hated Back hander; I was sure he had it in for me. I thought he was as thick as two short planks, but I am guessing I was wrong about that as well." Joe shook his head in disbelief. "So, backhander is going to stitch me up for a murder; who?"

The Major continued. "There was a break-in at a large house in Kensington a couple of months ago. The robbers were surprised by the unfortunate elderly housekeeper, and they beat her to death. Nasty business. The police are under intense pressure to solve the case. The foreign office believes they know the culprits and given that they were foreign nationals on shore leave from a ship at dock, they are not too keen to try them in open court. The sensitivities are immense. The public outrage would threaten the diplomatic relationship between the King's government and a neutral nation. The matter will be dealt with in another way; justice will be done. Unfortunately, it will not be seen to be done in this case."

"So, Backhander pins it on old Joe Turner and probably gets a promotion for solving the case. The thing is, nobody who knows me will believe it. Just not my style. For one thing, I only ever break into houses I know to be empty, present company excepted."

"As you know, it is always a risk you take; things can and do go wrong."

"But if I were surprised by an old lady, I would just do a runner. You know that I was trying to do just that when you

51

stopped me. People know that, they won't believe that Joe Turner would murder an old lady, no way."

"Joe, you are missing the point here. DCI Wilkinson wants a result; he, in his persona as a bent copper, doesn't care if he has got the wrong man. In fact, he knows it wasn't you. But a result is a result. The fact that the rest of the criminal community will suspect that you are being fitted up just adds to your credos for what will happen next."

"Uh, Oh, this is about to get even worse, isn't it, Major?"

"As we said, you will be remanded in custody. While inside, you will play the part of the wronged innocent. Talking about the Bakers, I believe that you were once invited to join their exclusive little club."

"Oh, I do not like where this is going. Yes, I was, several times, in fact."

"But you managed to escape their clutches?"

"Yeah, just about. They are not the sort of people you want to work for or be in debt to."

"So, whilst you are inside…."

"Hold on, just one minute," Joe interrupted abruptly. "Let me guess. Backhander will offer to get me off for a consideration. Of course, I will not be able to afford his fees. So, Ted Baker will pay Wilkinson off for me. To pay him back, I will have to work for him. Correct?"

"That just about covers it. My only thought is that Ted Baker will approach you rather than vice versa. He likes to take credit for new ideas, so Wilkinson will plant the thought in Ted's head and let him come up with the solution. Ted needs a new lieutenant. His natural successor is his Son, Eddie. However, the boy is a psychopath, practically out of control. His Dad doesn't trust his judgement and wants someone with a good brain and someone less highly strung to keep Eddie in check. He likes you for the job and will jump at the chance of recruiting you."

"You do realise that I will have to earn my keep. They will want me to prove myself and do things that are highly illegal and very distasteful. I assume that I will be there to provide information about their activities. Is there something specific that you are looking at?"

"We learned from Blind Bob, by the way, why is he called blind Bob? I understand that he has perfect vision." Obviously, the conundrum had been playing on the Major's mind.

"Bob liked to play cards, blackjack, and poker most of the time. He has a very quick mind and can work out odds in a flash. But when he was playing, he would only look at some of the cards dealt to him. He would gamble based on the odds for the cards he had seen. Essentially, he would play Blind. The name stuck. He reckoned the policy was lucky for him. So lucky that he got into massive debt and had to steal from the most dangerous man in the UK."

"Mmm, anyway, Bob told us that Ted had been working on a new scheme. He only knew that the plan was in partnership with another firm. Most unusual for Ted. All Bob knew for certain, all that had gone through the books so far, was that Ted had bought a farm just outside Slough, had set one of his teams to locate and steal Lorries for animal transportation and had been meeting with Fergus McDowell."

"Sounds like Ted is going all Old MacDonald on us. Retiring to the country possibly? Who the hell is Fergus McDowell when he's at home?"

"All we know about McDowell is that he is the son of Irish Catholic immigrants. He is suspected of having Irish Nationalist sympathies. He was questioned by Special Branch over the 1938 to 40 IRA mainland bombing campaign, but nothing stuck. Since then, he has laid low, kept his nose clean, he even volunteers as a fireman."

"But if he was born here, why has he not been called up?"

"Works at the docks. Union shop steward. Protected occupation."

"So, crime lord and Irish Nationalist, not a good mix. But what does Ted want with a farm and lorries? Hang about, not black-market meat?"

"Yes, at least we think so. We have a hunch that Ted has cooked up a scheme that involves large numbers of livestock, probably petrol and other rationed goods as well."

"Surely not, there can't be enough bunce in it for the likes of Ted".

"Bunce? Do speak English Joe."

"Profit, money and I am speaking English. I just don't have a plum in my mouth."

"Why does everybody think the Black market is small fry?" It was Robinson's turn to speak his mind. "Have you any idea what some people will pay for a nice piece of steak or a gallon of petrol?"

"I hadn't thought about it like that; I suppose you are right. Ted Baker will get involved in anything that will turn a profit. I guess there is plenty of gravy in black-market meat." Joe chuckled at his own joke as the Major lifted his eyes to the heavens.

Robinson was too concerned to get his point across to even notice. "You guys must realise the importance of this. Trust me, we would not be asking you to do anything as risky as this if this operation wasn't vital. We need to keep a lid on this sort of thing. We are concerned that too much off rationed food is being sold, and do you think it is the average Joe who is getting the benefit? No. We are worried that this could cause disaffection amongst the population. Plus, it's a double-edged sword; if extra agricultural production is filtering into the black market, a reduced amount is going into the rationing system. Less and less for the people sticking to the rules and more and more for those that aren't. If it gets any more out of control, the people just won't stand for it."

"So, I am to get inside the Baker operation and find out what they are planning?"

"Yes, but more than that. We need to shut this thing down and we need to do it discreetly. We cannot allow the general public to become aware of the size of the problem."

"You said 'you guys,' Sir; I take it that there are others involved in this operation."

"Yes, Joe, there are. If Ted Baker is getting his hands on Black-market produce, it must be coming from somewhere. It would seem that large quantities of foodstuffs are being diverted away from the legitimate food chain. We must end the whole lot, production, distribution and the sales outlets. You will be working to find out how and where Baker is getting the stuff and how he is selling it. Plus, is he trading some of it onto the Irish Black market? We have other operatives investigating what we think might be the source of all this. With luck, we can move in and shut the lot down when the time comes."

The Major now continued. "We have an operative working undercover on a farm in Wales which we have strong reasons to believe is involved. Amy Percival is highly competent and is already producing good information. We also have a pal of yours, Simon Bach."

"Simon, what's that bugger up to".

"Simon is posing as an injured Naval Officer, recuperating in the Welsh Hills. He is walking in the Brecon Beacons, getting to know the locals, seeing what he can find out."

"The lucky bugger, Silver Spoon Simon, I bet he is staying in some lovely country hotel, top nosh, living the good life at the Ministry's expense, no doubt. An' here am I, dodging the bombs in the smoke, serving time in the clink, cosying up to psychopath gang leaders, putting my Alberts[1] right on the line."

"Yep, and who was it told you that life was fair? Isn't it time you got used to it?

---

[1] 'Alberts' is cockney rhyming slang – Albert Halls – Balls (testicles)

15

A ride in the country – South Wales - 1941

Simon Bach was enjoying himself. The sun shone, and his powerful motorcycle purred along the Welsh country road. The Vincent Rapide 1000cc V Twin had been a 21st Birthday present from his father and was his pride and joy. On hearing about the gift, his mother had at first refused to speak to either his father or Simon for several weeks. Not that she minded the expense, she doted on her only son, her own money often being lavished on anything Simon's heart desired. Her objection was the danger the machine represented. When she resumed communication with her son, much of the discourse was confined to the subject of the safety, or lack of it, of these 'infernal' machines. She had lectured him on the tragic loss of the British great war hero T. E. Lawrence, who had perished on his motorcycle just 2 years before. Simon's attempts to assuage her concerns were not enhanced when she learned that his new Vincent was even faster than the Brough Superior, which had caused the demise of her hero, Lawrence. The 'blasted thing' was advertised to top 110 miles per hour 'for goodness sake'. Her outburst had shaken Simon's resolve, as he had never heard her swear before; he hated that she would be so worried. The matter had been finally settled when he had pointed out to her that Lawrence had not been wearing any head protection, and it was this that had caused his death. Simon received an extra birthday gift, a newly designed motorcycle helmet, and goggles soon afterwards. He had been required to solemnly swear to wear them on all occasions.

It was not clear to him how long his father would be the object of the lady's wrath, but he was in awe of the man's bravery; he must have known the consequences of his purchase, and yet he had persisted, knowing how much Simon would appreciate the gift, despite the certainty of his own personal suffering. Greater love hath no father.......

It had been some time since Simon had ridden the complex machine. The cost and availability of petrol since the start of the war was the primary factor in its frequent idleness. However, this mission required Simon to have ready access to transportation. So, his suggestion to his superiors that his character would ride a motorbike had been readily accepted. Simon smiled to himself at his good luck. As he mused, the road opened before him. He rounded a long bend, and as the road gently fell away, it straightened. He could see for at least 2 miles into the distance. What was more, He was sharing this glorious highway with no other vehicle. The sun shone high in the sky above him; its warm rays had completely dried the tarmac. It was time to test The Vincent HRD Co Ltd.'s claim to be "The makers of the World's fastest motorcycles". He shifted his body forward until he was almost lying on the petrol tank. He firmly twisted the throttle. The engine roared its delight. With one eye on the road ahead, he watched the dial as his speed gathered.

It had been an intense fortnight for Simon since he had met with Robinson. He had spent a large part of it inventing and learning his new identity. The address that had been given to him was that of Baxter House, a small lodging house in one of those parts of London that was once prosperous and now teetered on the edge of run down. To all appearances, the occupants of Baxter House were just your usual collection of displaced people seeking inexpensive housing in the great City.

The Landlady was Mrs Craddock, who was the very embodiment of her trade. Impossible to accurately age, she was well past the flush of youth and yet as far from decrepit as it was possible to be. Her hair had probably not been seen by man nor beast for at least a decade, perpetually concealed in a hair net and headscarf. Her tiny frame was held steadfastly together by tightly stretched sinew and leathery skin. In fact, her husband had been the last to see her hair, in all its beauty and glory, whilst he was on leave from France in 1917. He had been a Sergeant Major in the Royal Fusiliers (City of London Regiment). He died fighting for the country he loved, attacking a German machine gun nest that had Captain Robinson and his men tied down at the Battle of Arras.

Robinson always looked after his men and felt a responsibility for them and their families. When he joined the British Intelligence service, after receiving a Blighty wound later in that same battle, he recruited Sergeant Major Craddock's wife to run Baxter House, a cover for the housing of agents and their instructors. Mrs C, as she was universally known, oversaw the running of a very tight ship. Meals were taken on time or not at all. Guests were required to be home by 11:00 pm or would be required to sleep in the Anderson shelter. Guests were not allowed in each other's rooms under any circumstances; after all, she was running a boarding house, not a 'house of ill repute'.

Despite the outward appearance of toughness, Mrs C loved every one of her charges, they represented the children that war had denied her. She now channelled the love that she should have been lavishing on her own children and her beloved husband into those brave young souls. Each time one left for one of their incredibly dangerous missions, her heart broke. She cried, secretly and alone, over each and every one of them.

Simon's instructor was a lady called Susan Cartwright. Simon liked her immensely. This would be the first of many operations on which they would work together. He would come to trust her without question. Theirs would be a lifelong friendship.

Sue was a little older than Simon. Slightly taller than average, with a somewhat muscular frame, she carried no discernible body fat, giving her the aura of an athlete. She was pleasant to look at, but she was not a natural beauty. Her face was a little too long, her chin slightly underdeveloped, and her small eyes sunken. Her mannerisms were quick and agile, and they gave her the air of one who was slightly nervous. In truth, she was nothing of the kind.

What set Susan apart was her mind. She had that rare mixture of high intellect and practicality that gave her an edge in her profession. Her ability to follow complex patterns of facts whilst seeing the simplicity of potential solutions was her inimitable talent. Her gender and humble origins had of course hampered her career in the old boy network of espionage. If she was disappointed by that, as she had every right to be, she wore it well. Carving out for herself a unique role and achieving a peerless status and level of respect from her colleagues, even from those inane enough to regard themselves as her superior.

Susan and Simon set to work immediately to develop a cover story that would place him in the town where the butcher had disappeared without raising any suspicion. It was a tall order. They could not doubt that a small town like the one in question would be a hotbed of gossip. A stranger arriving would almost certainly attract the interest of the locals. If there were a criminal conspiracy at large in the locality, then the participants would be somewhat cautious. Any enquiries Simon made would have to be very discreet indeed.

Trefynydd is a small town in the Brecon Beacons, South Wales. It is an area of outstanding beauty and was popular with Climbers, hikers, and cyclists before the war. This particular tourism trade was somewhat on the wane due to the war; nevertheless, those hardened enthusiasts who could afford the time and expense would still take short breaks at the Dragon's Tail Hotel, Trefynydd.

The Dragon, a 16th-century coaching inn on the historic London to Fishguard old road, is at the heart of the Trefynydd community. Before the war, it had an excellent reputation for its homely accommodation and traditional Welsh fare. The owners had struggled as the war had taken away their staff, now operating in a much smaller way, they kept open a few rooms for guests and the public bar for the local trade.

Simon would arrive as a Royal Navy officer who had unfortunately suffered injury when his ship had been torpedoed in the North Atlantic. Due to his injuries, he had been advised by Navy doctors to recuperate in the country where the air would be better for his lungs; mild exercise was also prescribed, and walking in the hills would be perfect.

Sue had advised that Simon's cover story should be as much based upon fact as possible. Simon loved hiking and had even done some serious climbing in India. He had some sailing experience and knew something about maritime navigation. He had a knowledge of the Royal Navy, which he had mainly picked up from friends in the service. Any shortcomings in his knowledge would easily be covered by the fact that officers or any enlisted men were forbidden from discussing their postings.

'Careless talk cost lives' was the motto on the posters. His background and family would be broadly his own. Even his Christian name would be kept as it was sufficiently popular to be difficult to check up on.

Simon had questioned Sue's caution regarding his surname. Surely, the people involved in this wouldn't have the resources to check up on his identity. Sue had explained that with the possibility of organised crime involved, they would take no chances. The authorities understood there were sufficient corrupt police officers to provide the criminal gangs with all the information they needed.

Simon Bach, a lieutenant in the British Army without attachment, had entered Baxter House, but it was Lieutenant Simon Lewis, a second officer in the Royal Fleet Auxiliary, who left. He was equipped with the relevant papers, ration vouchers, and family letters. Simon even carried the dogeared photograph of his former fiancé.

16

Time for a pint – London 1941

Joe had not been seen in the Dog and Duck for over 10 months. Not much had changed. The décor hadn't been updated since Mafeking; probably the last time the floor had been mopped was armistice day, and the cleaner used to clean for Miss Haversham. Still, Joe felt at home, the kind of feeling he experienced in very few places.

He strolled to the bar through the hustle and bustle, where piano music battled with the noise of the punters. Joe looked across at old Ivory Ivan as he struck the notes like his life depended upon it. For now, he was losing the battle against the exuberance of the clientele, but later, as the mood mellowed, he would be centre stage as people took turns to sing their favourite songs to his gentler melodies.

Upon reaching the bar, he was faced with a giant of a man who stared across the countertop at him. The man couldn't have weighed less than twenty stone and towered over Joe by at least 12 inches. To call him imposing was somewhat of an understatement, like calling the Atlantic a bit of water or the Eiffel Tower quite tall. Joe looked up at the steely eyes of the monster and held his gaze steadily. There was a long moment of silence as the two searched for weaknesses in each other. At length, the man mountain spoke, "What the bloody hell do you want?" His voice boomed as though it echoed from the depths of the very earth he stood on.

Joe's reply was prompt and steady: "I'd like a pint pot with a quarter of a pint of your best bitter, filled up to the top with tap water, please."

The mountain stared deep into Joe's eyes. "We don't sell that here." The booming voice was full of chagrin and menace.

"That's funny because that is exactly what I have been served every time I have been here in the past, and they say it's what you have been serving here for the last thirty years." Joe's voice was calm and challenging, his gaze unwavering.

The Titan straightened his back, and his fists clenched at the insult. His chest swelled as his large right hand swung savagely across the bar. It was met midway by Joe's hand. The impact was like a clap of thunder. Joe felt his hand being engulfed in the gauntlet of muscle, sinew and steel that was Charlie Crispin's handshake.

Joe was barely ready for what happened next. Charlie Crispin, The Cockney Calamity, Prize Boxer, Wrestler and Pub Landlord, pulled ferociously at Joe's hand, dragging the smaller man across the counter and into an embrace that threatened to squash the life from his body. Joe braced for the impact, but still, he felt his bones falter against the immense pressures of the 'loving' clinch.

"Joe Turner, you cocky little bugger, where have you been. Not seen you for ages. Here, Marge, Joe's here."

"Who?" The lady, who was busy stacking glasses on the shelves under the bar, looked languidly over her shoulder towards her husband. Her eyes caught sight of the crushed customer as he fought to regain his breath after his merciful release. "Joe, oh Joe, where have you been? I missed you so much. Have you been eating properly?" Marge Crispin had ducked under the counter with surprising dexterity for a woman of her stature. She now charged forward towards Joe, who just had time to fill his lungs with air before her embrace. Her hug was just as intense as her husband's, but her ample bosom somewhat softened the effect.

Marge released Joe momentarily, holding him by his shoulders at arm's length while she surveyed his physical well-being. "You've lost weight. I knew it." She pulled him back to her breast. Joe equated it to falling into a soft mattress, one that didn't let go. "Where have you been? I've been so worried. Thought the Jerry's had got you. Oh, we've missed you around here. Things are not the same anymore. Not like the old days."

Joe was happy to see the woman who was the closest thing he had ever had to a mother. She was a lady of unimaginable toughness but with a heart the size of London. Blond curls framed her moon-shaped face. Her alabaster skin stretched smooth over her plump cheeks. Round, owl-like eyes, light blue, smiled and shined like jewels.

Joe kissed her cheeks and hugged her back. "Marge, when you gonna dump this grumpy old ogre and run away with me." Joe teased.

"What would she want with a cocky young wimp like you when she already sleeps with a real man every night?" Charlie had come round the bar and joined in the banter.

"Well, that's just the problem, Calamity. All you ever do is sleep!" Marge burst into an infectious cackle of laughter, and in seconds, everyone in the room joined in.

Charlie swooped down behind his wife and wrapped a huge arm around her waist, sweeping her high into the air and out of the arms of his would-be love rival. Marge squealed in delight as he lifted her, spun her in mid-air, and caught her in both arms, planting a long and passionate kiss full on her still-smiling lips. It was an impressive feat of strength; Marge was a substantial woman.

Joe laughed with the others as he looked on at the spirit of the people in the packed bar. His people, the salt of the earth, decent people who would share their last piece of bread with you. People who would stand by you through thick or thin. People worth fighting for. Hitler had picked the wrong Nation to mess with, he thought to himself.

But the best embrace was yet to come. Joe looked around the room as he counted off the familiar faces.

Red Ron, shop steward down the docks, politically slightly to the left of Lenin. Always ready to bore a stranger to death with his views, those who knew him were wise to steer clear of him when he was espousing his militant ideas.

Jenny, Julie and Jess. The three beauties were deep in conversation with a group of sailors. An array of expensive-looking drinks were lined up on the table. The sailors looked pleased. They were obviously in for a good night. The girls were friendly and clearly not averse to their charms. The boys had already made a significant investment in the success of their evening; the exotic drinks, although costing them much of their pay, would surely lessen any resistance later. Their own beer drinks heightened the attraction of the ladies.

Joe smiled to himself. It was the oldest con in the book. Probably been happening in dockside hostelries since the first ships in history set sail and the earliest sailors alighted on foreign harbours. The drinks were bogus. Non-alcoholic coloured water. The fourth member of the team, the barmaid, would supply the drinks requested by the ladies and charge the boys the appropriate high price, which they were only too happy to pay. The girls would feign tipsiness, followed by ever more advanced drunken behaviour. The boys getting ever more excited by the teasing, flirty girls. Convinced that success was just a few more drinks away. When the evening drew to a close, the girls would suggestively talk of moving on to a place more intimate. First, they would just have to powder their noses. Leaving the boys to get ready for the night of their lives. The girls would retire to the lady's room, slipping out the back door instead. The profits from the sale of tinted water would be divided up later between the establishment, the barmaid and the temptresses. The disappointment of the sailors was the cost of a lesson hard learned.

Joe knew that Marge and Charlie were not enamoured by the practice on their premises. That said, they knew that the profession that the girls might be forced into as an alternative was much worse and far more dangerous. The sailors would initially be furious, but few cottoned on to the true state of play. They just assumed that the girls had got cold feet, and of course, the tales that they would tell their shipmates would have a far more satisfying ending.

Red Ron's colleagues from the docks were the majority of the crowd. With wives and girlfriends, they sought to wash away the thirsts hard gained by their labours at the heart of the empire. Harsh, gruelling and dangerous work, as vital as any bullet fired or ground conquered in this total war.

Joe's eyes settled upon a girl standing in the far corner of the room. She had flame-red hair that tumbled down from her head like larva from the mouth of a raging volcano. She stood straight and proud, tall and confident. Joe couldn't take his eyes from her vivid jade green eyes; it was as if they had searched into the depths of his soul, and they liked what they had found there. She had high cheekbones and flawless, pale skin. As their eyes remained locked, she swayed from side to side, her long skirt swished at the command of her gently twisting shoulders. Her head tilted in a coquettish manner, her eyes maintaining contact with Joe's. Teasing, provocative, daring and yet loving. Then, without warning, she flicked back her head, the ruby locks of her hair spread outwardly, like rings on the still water of a pond, disturbed by a heavy stone landing in its centre. She rose to her tiptoes, teetering as she fell forward into a sprint towards her Joe. She traversed the room single-mindedly. Oblivious to the spilt drinks and annoyed shouts of the people, she pushed aside in her reckless charge. Two paces from her target, her pathway was clear; she leapt trustingly and landed in the willing arms of her lover. They melted together, crying with joyfulness.

Joe had known Amber for as long as he could remember. They had been together at the orphanage, both largely ignorant of their pasts and desperate to be part of a family. Neither would ever achieve such normality. They were friends from the start and looked out for each other down the years.

It was a tough upbringing for them both. Most of the Nuns were gentle and kind souls who did the best for their young charges. Others were harsh and cruel, blaming some of the innocent children for their crimes of original sin, especially those brazen enough to be illegitimate. These embittered Sisters dished out punishment without hesitation and with little regard for justice or rehabilitation.

Education was framed along gender lines. The girls were mainly prepared for service. The boys, at the same age, would, naturally, enter trades more suited to the male sex. None, not even the brightest, would continue their education beyond their years with the Nuns. At 14 they would leave St. Mary's and take up their appointed position.

Amber was sent as a junior maid to a house in Lewisham. It was a position that did not suit her talents, and she hated her servitude. Joe persuaded Charlie and Marge to give her a position as barmaid at the Dog and Duck.

"Oy, Amber, where's those glasses?" Charlie shouted from behind the bar.

"Give 'em a break, Charlie; they haven't seen each other for ages." Marge entreated her husband. "Remember when we were young and in love? Amber, take the night off; we can manage, can't we, Charlie?"

"Bloody hell, I am trying to run a pub here." Charlie's grumpiness was soon placated by one of Marge's engulfing cuddles.

Amber had wasted no time fetching her coat, and the amorous couple headed out the door before Charlie changed his mind. Laughing together, they didn't see the policeman until they ran into him just inside the front door.

"What do you want?" Amber was immediately on the defensive, which was the natural reaction to her experience. "Ere get off me, take your 'ands off."

The officer grabbed Amber by the arms and roughly pushed her aside. Joe looked to his rear as he suspected more bobbies had entered the pub from the side door; his escape route was cut off. He turned back to the door. Having cleared Amber from his path, the constable advanced with handcuffs in his hand and took the opportunity to secure his prisoner.

Joe didn't offer any resistance; he was clearly outnumbered.

"DCI Wilkinson, fancy seeing you here." Joe tried to sound unconcerned as the crooked Detective advanced through the door and into the centre of the room. He looked around, making sure that every eye was on him. He waited for quiet before turning back to the prisoner.

Wilkinson cleared his throat and, like a Shakespearean actor, projected his voice so that all, even those in the cheap seats, could hear. "Joe Turner, I am arresting you for murder."

A pin dropping to the ground would have been easily heard as the pub's clientele took in the shocking news.

"Yes, folks, you heard it right, Joe Turner, good old Joe, he beat an old lady to death with his bare hands, and I am gonna make sure he swings for it." Wilkinson's voice was full of hate and gloating.

Joe was manhandled from the pub and straight into the back of a waiting Black Maria[2]. Amber was left standing by the door, aghast at what had happened.

---

[2] A Black Maria is the traditional English name for a police van that took away arrested criminals.

66

"No way, not Joe, he wouldn't, not Joe," Amber whispered to herself. Marge was behind her a moment later. "Get the girl a Brandy you great oaf." The landlady urged her husband.

"Brandy, Brandy, are you mad woman? We haven't seen Brandy since Dunkirk," the landlord complained.

"Charlie Crispin, I know for sure that you have a bottle tucked away behind the barrels in your cellar that you think I don't know about. Get it now; the poor little lamb is shaking like a leaf."

Amber sat at a chair offered to her. She rarely cried, but the shock caused her eyes to water. "No way, Joe wouldn't hurt a fly. He couldn't; he just couldn't have murdered an old lady."

Amber reached into her pocket for her handkerchief and found a small package there. Brown paper roughly tied together with coarse string. Typical Joe, quick thinking; he must have intended to give it to her later. Knowing it was the sort of thing that just might go missing down the nick, he must have slipped it into her pocket just before the copper had cuffed him.

Amber pulled at the twine, and the knot unravelled; the paper opened, revealing a necklace. Lifting the fragile item, Amber held it to the light. It was a delicate pierced link chain of silver supporting a pendant of a carved pastel green gemstone. Two beads of the same material nestled in the chain just above the main stone. The carving was exquisite; flowers curled around each other in endless swirls of light green. Realising what this was, she could hear Joe's voice, what he would have said to her had he had the chance to give it to her properly. "It's Jade, and it's the colour of your eyes."

Now, the tears came.

17

A raging thirst – South Wales - 1941

Amy, or Rosie, as she was now known as a land girl, heard the dinner gong sound from the farmhouse. The reverberation was soon chorused by the laughter of Dot and Betty as they came in from the fields. Saturday night dinner was always a rushed affair and was taken earlier than other nights of the week. A night out down the pub was an event to be looked forward to. Dresses had to be ironed, hair crimped or rolled, make-up put on, tea and eyeliner pencil applied to legs[3]. The table buzzed with the excitement of the hard-working girls. Myfanwy Thomas was less amused by the thought of the girls gallivanting around the town dressed like hussies. Rosie looked at her employer as she sternly passed out the food and mused that Mrs Thomas had the look of a woman chewing a wasp.

Myfanwy said little as the girls scoffed their meal. She hoped that the ample portions would absorb some of the alcohol about to be consumed and preserve the ability of the young ladies to maintain a level head and, therefore, their virtue. She knew that the meagre wages paid to her land girls would limit their buying amount. However, pretty young girls, and they were pretty, she had to admit, rarely had to pay for their own drinks. Especially when there were still some young men left around the town, including her own dunce of a son, who would invest their hard-earned wages in the chance of loosening some morals.

Instinctively, she looked at her son. He was a beast of a man. Tall, broad, muscular, not bad looking, she ventured to think. The girls seemed to like him, especially Dorothy. He was the product of generations of working Welsh farmers. Tough and relentless, unbowed by the hardships that the land they loved bestowed upon them. They were fuelled by the fruits of their labours and

---

[3] Due to war shortages and expense, young ladies would mimic the look of stockings by applying tea to their legs, then using and eyeliner pencil to imitate the stocking seam.

moulded by the sun and the rain, just as much as the livestock they tended. Looking at him was like looking at her husband in his youth, before the Great War, that he had needlessly and stupidly rushed to join. The war that had broken him, body and spirit, and had tossed him back to his family without even the decency to finish him off. Alwyn was just as his father had been back in the day, all muscle and vigour, without a brain cell to call his own. That hadn't mattered to Myfanwy in 1912, as they planned to marry. She had loved her Dai since they were toddlers together, and he had worshipped her. Her father's farm and Dai's parent's farm were adjacent. Theirs was to be a marriage of 2 families and 2 businesses, made in heaven.

Of course, she had known Dai's shortcomings. He was not the sharpest sickle at the harvest. However, what he lacked in brains, he more than made up for in vibrancy and endeavour. To Myfanwy, they were perfect together, as she had all the intelligence, ambition and schooling they would ever need. They were not long married when the war came along. In the remote Welsh mountains, she was sure that it would never touch them. Surely, if anything, it would be good for business. The nation would need feeding. They could expand their farm. Their future was bright. For once, they could benefit from the English and their war lust. Then Dai's head had been turned. The local Magistrate was a man called Sir Cecil Kege Le Burg. He owned the lands to the west of Trefynydd, all the way up the valley to the foothills of the mountains. He claimed a lineage back to the Norman conquests. But then He claimed many things of dubious merit.

At the onset of the war, he had been bestowed with the honorary command of the regiment of South Wales. With its proud history of valour and bravery in many colonial one-sided conquests. Shamed by the willingness of the "Pals[4]" battalions of the industrial north and midlands of England, who had responded

---

[4] Pals battalions were an idea used in the recruiting drive of the early part of the Great War. Many men were recruited to serve together in these battalions. The sad consequence was that many communities lost many of their young men as these volunteers fought in the same battles.

to the call to arms of Kitchener with his taunts of "Your Country Needs You". Those brave young men, happy to escape the bondage of factory purgatory, assured that the adventure of war would be a happy holiday from the misery of their futures. Proudly, they marched off to bloody the nose of the dreadful Hun. Le Burg had to do something. He had to match or better the commitment of those city dwellers. It didn't occur to him that his young men served better by putting the meat and veg on the tables of the factory workers. Who, in turn, fed the machinery of war. Trefynydd must match the fervour of the rest of the country to do its bit and send its youth off to its destruction.

Le Burg organised rallies on Market days in Trefynydd and the local towns. He spoke passionately of the evils that the terrible Hun had inflicted on brave little Belgium. How they had bayoneted babies and defiled the maidenhood of those innocent lands. He reminded the people of the proud tradition of Welsh regiments who, many times, had stood firm, outnumbered by marauding hordes of savages. Wasn't it Welsh archers that had carried the day at Agincourt? Dai Thomas was no match for such rhetoric. He could not stand by and watch others do their duty whilst he slept safe in his bed. He would fight to protect his young family and the land he loved. Besides, it would all be over by Christmas. True Dai, or what was left of him, was home soon enough. His mind was shattered by the noise, carnage, and violence of that senseless conflict. His body was wasted by the poisonous gas which would, to his last days, deny him the sustenance of the pure, sweet air of his homeland.

Myfanwy looked resentfully at her husband as he muttered to himself over his barely touched food. Aged well beyond his years, his body shrivelled and gaunt. He was a ghost of the man he had been. His only cares in life now were the mangy old farm dog who never left his side, how soon he could get down the pub and who would buy him a drink. His son, who sat beside him, seemed to mock his plight with all his strength and vitality. She hated Dai now much more than she had ever loved him. His foolhardiness had robbed them of their dreams and cheated her of her happiness.

Hate was an emotion that came easily to Myfanwy these days. She hated her husband, the English and their wars, Le Burg and the aristocracy, and the young land girls who now seemed to ridicule her with their youth, chatter, enthusiasm, and beauty. They were everything she had been, representing everything that had been torn away from her.

But now she had a plan. A way to restore her fortunes and put one over on the establishment.

"Alwyn, did you meet the truck as I told you?"

"Yes, Mother," Alwyn replied, as addressed in their native language. The only other Welsh speaker in the house was Dai, and he was away with the fairies as usual. So it was safe to discuss the business. Besides, the girls were so full of their relentless babble of dresses and make-up to take any notice of the conversation.

"You took the cattle to the field, I said?" Despite the knowledge that the conversation was unfathomable to the girls, Myfanwy was still cautious. She kept her voice low and neutral. She didn't use the field's name, just in case it was recognisable to the girls.

"Yes, mother. There was one lame, but I don't suppose we need to worry too much, do we?"

"I'll take a look when I go over when you go out. There'll be enough light for me to get there and back. Take your father with you to the pub".

Myfanwy scanned the table to see if there had been any interest in the conversation. Dot was holding up her hair to show how she would wear it tonight. Betty was nodding and saying it suited her. Rosie was helping herself to more potatoes and gravy. That girl could eat, and she always drowned her food in gravy. Must be a Northern thing. But fair play to her. She needed the energy, she could match Alwyn for hard work. She caught the girl's eye. "These potatoes are belting Mrs Thomas. Thank you." The thick accent left no doubt that the young lady hailed from the northern counties of England. Manchester, or was it Leeds? She couldn't remember. But she was a good worker, and that was for sure.

Myfanwy had been careful to take a friendly interest in the girls when they had arrived. They were a necessary evil, as many of the farm workers had foolishly joined up despite their protected occupation status, just like Dai had done. She had considered refusing the Ministry's offer of Land Girls, but she thought that it might have led to suspicion. As it worked out, they were a bonus. It meant that they could do the farm's day-to-day work, leaving more time for her to devote to the extra business, which proved to be very profitable. She made sure that their work was close to the farm buildings and well away from the extra land they had acquired for the business. Land that few people knew about.

"You're welcome. Thank you for your hard work this week; it is much appreciated."

Alwyn nearly dropped his fork; his mother never thanked him for his efforts. Nor had he ever heard her thank anyone for anything. He was about to say something when his mother's gaze turned to him, and he knew better than to challenge her.

"I have told you we have to keep these girls sweet. We need them, and we don't want them complaining to the ministry or making any sort of a fuss. But that doesn't mean you must be too nice to them, my boy. Keep your hands to yourself." Aware that she had changed to Welsh, she switched back to English, addressing herself to Rosie. "I was just telling Alwyn that he had to be buying you ladies a drink tonight and to make sure you get home safely".

"That's so nice of you, Mrs. Thomas. Thank you so much." Rosie's response was swift and sincere. Although the dialect of the South Wales Welsh speakers was somewhat different, the North she was used to was a much harsher tongue, whilst the South was much more sing-song, musical even. Rosie had no difficulty understanding the gist of her host's conversations. She had kept her knowledge of the Welsh language to herself, and that was proving to be very useful.

Rosie wondered about what Mrs Thomas and her son had said. In the nearly 2 months she had been at the farm she had heard the "business" referred to several times. Also mentioned were deliveries that had not been made to the main part of the farm. She was curious but knew to tread carefully. Myfanwy was a shrewd woman; Dai would surely know nothing; Alwyn was the weak link. But he was in awe of his mother and would certainly mention it to her if anyone asked him questions. The meal was over, and the diners started heading off to their rooms to prepare for the evening frivolities.

"May I help you with the dishes, Mrs Thomas?" Rosie offered.

"Bless you, child, thank you, but no. There's a concert on the wireless shortly. I will leave this lot to soak whilst I listen to it. Be nice to have a bit of peace and quiet around here for a change." Myfanwy looked towards the stairs as if she could see as well as hear the commotion of the youngsters getting ready. "You go and get ready with the others."

With this dismissal, Rosie caught up with the other girls and feigned interest in their fashion. It was a long and tedious procedure for Rosie. Her frustration was soon echoed by Alwyn's entreaties to "Hurry up; we are wasting good drinking time." and "They'll be calling last orders soon."

At last, the revellers set off down the lane towards Trefynydd. After only a hundred yards, just out of sight of the farmhouse, their progress was halted. Rosie had broken a heel on her new shoes. Dot and Betty were sympathetic, but Alwyn was furious at the potential delay. Dai had not missed a step. His gait was somewhat less hampered by his frailty when carrying him towards the pub. The dog trotted alongside dutifully.

"Don't worry, I can walk back and put my other shoes on. You lot carry on, and I will catch you up." Rosie was insistent and Alwyn was all for the plan.

"Are you sure you will be all right? I could come back with you." Dot's offer lacked any serious conviction. She knew Alwyn would be carrying on to the Dragon, and she didn't like letting him out of her sight. She was suspicious of Sara, the barmaid at the Inn. She had an idea that Alwyn fancied her, even though she was engaged to his best mate. Dot had other ideas for Alwyn's love life.

"No, you carry on. I will catch you up in no time." Rosie turned and limped away back to the farmhouse.

"Come on. You heard what she said." Alwyn grabbed Dot's hand and dragged her off. Dot was, at first, annoyed by the rough treatment at the hands of her would-be beau, but he was holding her hand at least. Progress, she thought.

73

Rosie approached the house cautiously. Her ruse with the shoe had worked perfectly. She wondered if the Ministry would reimburse her for the expensive item. She doubted it very much. Ah well, many much more valuable sacrifices were being laid at the altar of freedom. She stopped by the gate and waited just out of sight of the front door.

At that moment, she heard it open and close. Rosie expected that Myfanwy Thomas would come down the path and bump into her at the gate, but no. After she had counted off 60 seconds, she was sure that her employer must have gone a different way. Creeping forward, she could see the front of the building. No one was in sight. She moved up to the door and hobbled through it, ready with her plausible excuse for her sudden return.

The house was empty. Moving quickly to the kitchen window at the back of the house, she looked down towards the fields. No sign of Myfanwy. Returning to the front door, she skirted round the house to the side. The ground rose steeply from here, up towards the mountain. Rosie would have to hurry. She grabbed her replacement shoes from her room and slipped them into her bag. Then she slid into her work boots and set off uphill in pursuit of her quarry. Rosie was a fit girl, but the terrain was tortuous, and the early evening sun was still warm. After no time at all, she was sweating, and her skin glowed with her exertions. She pushed on and hoped that her appearance would not be noticed when she eventually made it to the pub. Myfanwy had only a few minutes start on the girl half her age, but she was born in these hills, and the climb was nothing to her. Rosie wondered why she was heading this way. The livestock were in fields away to the west of the farm. As far as she knew, Mynydd Farm's lands ended at the ridge just above the farmhouse. The land above was unused. Probably too inaccessible even to these hardy Welsh farmers.

After ten minutes of hard pursuit, Rosie caught sight of Myfanwy, who was off to the east, rounding the base of the mountain that gave the town its name. She paused as she thought about the maps of the area she had studied back at the ministry before setting off on her mission. She wondered as to the object of the lady's route. There was an old, abandoned quarry some 2 miles or so in that direction. Little else she could think of.

Rosie checked her watch. She had already taken too much time; her absence mustn't be thought suspicious. Turning towards the west and the lowering sun, she tracked around the mountain base away from Myfanwy. She fancied there was a way to drop down into the town directly from where she stood. Being a more direct route than returning to the farm, she would be at the pub not too long after the others. It was a difficult descent, made all the trickier by the unsuitability of her attire. Arriving at the road, just before it joined the main street leading into the town, she hoped she hadn't been seen. There was a watering trough at the junction, a throwback to earlier times when the stagecoaches would thunder by this way. It was still fed from a natural spring, and the water was sweet and clear. Having attended to her toilette and changing her boots for her dress shoes, leaving the boots to be collected later, Rosie marched into town looking as good as new.

The pub was a buzz of excitement. Dot was attached to Alwyn, who barely noticed her as he started in on his third pint of the evening. Undeterred, she talked incessantly and pushed herself close to him. Turning his gaze away from the bar and "that hussy" barmaid.

Dai had taken his customary seat by the fireplace; despite the warmth of the summer night, the kindly Landlady, Mrs Williams, had made up a small fire. She knew the old man's bones caused him discomfort, and he valued its soothing glow. Dai might be the butt of the jokes of many people in the town. His constant grumblings and his eccentric devotion to that old dog were often teased by her clientele. However, she remembered that fine young man who had done his duty and marched off to that terrible war. These youngsters had no idea what he had gone through; she feared that some of them might be about to find out what war can do; it chilled her bones to think of it.

Mrs Williams took the old man's drink to the table. Carelessly, she forgot to collect the money, the exact change he had put there. She bent over the dog and laid a dish of chicken in front of it.

"Diolch", muttered the old soldier as his trembling hands lifted the nectar to his lips.

Betty was in the company of Owain, the Butcher's lad, and three young men from the Army camp. The men were Indian,

75

from Punjab. They were part of a contingent of 500 based locally. Betty was enthralled by them. In their smart uniforms, they were courteous and polite, and to her, they represented the romance of the East. She equated them with the roles of her favourite film star, Errol Flynn.

Owain jumped up to meet Rosie and offered her a seat next to him. He had already bought her a glass of sherry, and hoping to please, he pushed it across the table to her. He watched and waited for her approval. Rosie tutted, lifting her eyes to the heavens before reaching past the proffered tipple and taking Owain's own freshly poured pint.

She lifted the dark brew in the air and surveyed it as an art expert might look at a masterpiece, "Eee, I have a thirst I wouldn't sell." She remarked before offering up a salutation of "lechyd da!" She then proceeded to down the beer, in its entirety, in one go; not a drop was spilt. The room echoed with cheers and applause as Rosie pushed the emptied glass back to Owain, "I'll take another of those, thank ye kindly." She requested in her broad Lancashire accent.

18

A Home from Home – The Dragon's Tail Hotel, Wales - 1941

Simon arrived in Trefynydd in the early summer evening. The sun was still warm, and he was glad that his machine would soon be allowed to cool after the long, demanding ride. He pulled in through an archway in the wake of many a weary traveller. Finding himself in a courtyard that housed disused stables, he spotted an open door and rode the bike straight into one of the stalls, as he had been instructed when he had telephoned ahead.

Like an overly enthusiastic clock, the bike's engine clicked loudly as it began to cool the instant Simon had cut the ignition. The shelter was warm and dry, better than some places he had stayed in himself. It boded well for his own accommodation, especially as he anticipated being here for some time.

Lifting the saddlebags from the bike, he headed off looking for the entrance to the hotel. Crossing the yard, the ground sloped upwards and plateaued out to a small garden. From here, steps led down to a lower terrace and an immaculate lawn. French doors promised a way in, which Simon took. Finding himself in an elaborately furnished lounge here, he dropped his bags and headed to the door marked Reception. Unmanned, Simon could hear voices coming up the stairs. He rang the bell and waited. The sound increased as the door at the bottom of the stairs opened, and light footsteps skipped up from below.

Simon almost gasped as the young lady arrived in the room. He had met his fair share of beautiful women. The elaborate receptions that His Mother would host in her role as wife to a British Consul exposed him to a seemingly never-ending array of daughters and wives of both local dignitaries and British officers. At Cambridge, there had been many young ladies hoping to catch the eye and heart of the privileged young men. Not to mention the nightlife in London that was awash with WAAFs and Wrens.

Never had Simon seen, to this level of perfection, the type of beauty which stood framed by the doorway, like a masterpiece painting of the most refined kind. The young lady seemed startled as if she had not expected to find anyone in the room. For a moment, neither could speak. The girl was perhaps not more than twenty-five. She stood frozen in the doorway. Her left hand lightly held the doorframe as if steadying herself. Her right held a tea towel, which she clinched to her chest like it was a prized possession. Plainly dressed, her beauty did not need the finery and jewels of Indian society or the rouge and lipstick of the London girls. Her hair was straight and held back in the simplest of styles; a single bow directed the shining blond into a tail that rose upwards, just a little, before cascading down her back. Her eyes were a delicate grey, soft and honest. Her skin was clear and smooth, finely shaded by the sun. Her mouth was perfectly proportioned. Lips classically bow shaped and unsullied by unnecessary pigmentations.

At that moment, the girl smiled, and the effect on Simon was complete. There was a humour to the smile, a soft chuckle of sincerity, an innocence to the gesture that was full of good will, seemingly ignorant of its power to captivate.

Simon broke the silence, stuttering he realised he couldn't remember his new surname. "Hello, I am Lieutenant Simon." Was all he could manage.

It was enough to free the girl from her bondage and she moved elegantly into the room. Lifting a flap in the countertop she ducked through and took her place as the receptionist. Simon marvelled at her movement. She had the grace and precision of a ballet dancer. It was if each step had been carefully choreographed and yet, was natural and instinctive. She moved through her environment barely touching it, as if gravity had chosen not to affect her and she had no weight at all, whilst her presence enlivened and enriched every atom of her surroundings.

"Welcome Lieutenant Simon." Her smile now seemed permanent, and her words were gently mocking to his discomfort.

Simon blushed before regaining his composure. "I telephoned yesterday, spoke to a Mrs Williams."

"We have been expecting you, Lieutenant Lewis. Did you manage to park your motorcycle?"

"Thank you; yes, the stable is perfect. I hope my room will be just as suitable." It was his turn to smile as he relaxed in the company of the young lady.

"Oh, I think we might manage something less draughty for you Lieutenant Lewis."

"Please call me Simon." Realising that it was perhaps a little too soon to dispense formalities, Simon blushed a little and continued, "After all, I may be here for some time."

"I hope so. I am Sara. I am the receptionist, maid, barmaid, cleaner, head cook and bottle washer." She joked. "You are Royal Navy?"

"Yes, currently without a ship. My last ship had a little altercation with a U-boat, and I am awaiting new orders."

Sara could sense an intense sadness about the young man. His comments were casual, but the levity was forced, and she could feel the tragedy that lurked behind his smile. Despite herself, she asked, "That's awful. Were many killed? Were you injured? What a beastly thing to happen?" Immediately she regretted her outburst, the last thing she had intended, was to pry. "Oh, I am so sorry, I didn't mean to…"

Simon sensing her discomfort quickly interjected "Yes it was ghastly, we lost many very good men. I injured my ankle quite badly and got my lungs full of fuel oil, from the water. I was very lucky compared to many. The Sawbones recommended that I get some fresh air and gentle exercise whilst I wait for my new ship. I have always wanted to walk in the Brecon Beacons, So here I am."

"Sawbones?"

"Navy slang for Doctor."

Sara laughed and the sadness was cleared from the air. The two young people were silent for a moment. Already they were relaxing in each other's company. The initial discomfort of their shared attraction receding. Sara wanted to ask more, she had to know everything about this man. It was more than idle curiosity, so much more. But now she didn't know what to say, where to begin. Before the silence became awkward a deep voice boomed up the stairs. "There are people dying of thirst down here, Sara. Shall I pour my own pint, is it?"

"You stay on your own side of the bar Alwyn Thomas and don't be touching those pumps, if you know what's good for you." Sara's voice, which had been soft and friendly, now echoed with the strength and fierceness of her race. And yet her words were almost sung, like an enthusiastic chorister belting out a favourite hymn. Simon smiled at the charm of this lovely girl.

"I am so sorry. My Aunt, Mrs Williams, had to go out earlier this evening, her friend is sick, and I am here on my own, on the busiest night of the week. The bar is packed. Your key," Sara handed the item across the counter. "Your room is at the top of the stairs," she pointed towards a corridor that led further into the old building and to a steep incline, "it's the last door on the left. The bathroom is the very end door, next to your room. Do you need help with your bags?"

Simon smiled and shook his head. "No, I am fine, I can manage." He desperately wanted to prolong their chat, but he realised that she was just too busy.

"Will it be all right if we do the registration later? I must get back to the bar or there will be a riot." Again, that captivating, chuckling, smiling voice.

"Of course." Simon looked around to where he had left his bags, momentarily disoriented. It seemed an age since he had walked through the hotel's door, as if so much had happened.

Sara skipped towards her duties at the bar, leaping down the steep steps two or three treads at a time. Her voice called out, "Oh, I am sorry, you must be famished; I didn't offer you anything. The kitchen is closed this evening, but I can make you a sandwich, cheese, ok? Come down whenever you're ready." Before he could answer, the girl was swallowed up by the cacophony of noise and cheers that greeted her long-awaited arrival at the pumps.

Simon stood motionless, still in shock and wonderment at the blast of energetic beauty that was Sara Lloyd, head cook and bottle washer of the Dragon's Tail Hotel, Trefynydd.

19

You know when you are beaten. – London 1941

Joe smiled to himself, happy that he had managed to slip Amber the package. He wondered when she would find it. He could picture her smile and her gleaming jade green eyes as she took the necklace of the same colour from the parcel. He felt guilty that she would be worrying so much. He wanted to tell her what would happen but was under express orders not to tell anyone. Everyone's safety, including hers, was tied up in the arrest being believed. The reactions had to be natural and realistic. The fewer people who were acting, the better. As far as he knew, it was just him and DCI Wilkinson, and fair play to him, the Chief Inspector's performance had been Oscar-winning.

The Black Maria police van plodded its way through the unlit street towards the station. "Damn!" Joe thought to himself. He had always prided himself on never having been a passenger in such a vehicle as this. Now, his duck had been broken, his first arrest. The van lurched to a halt, the doors swung open, and Joe was hauled out. As he struggled to find his footing, a leg came out and tripped him. His hands behind his back, held tightly by the 'darbies'[5], Joe fell heavily to the ground face first. Blood trickled into his eyes from a cut on his forehead. His shoulders strained as he was dragged upright by the arms. A practised move by the coppers, a way of inflicting pain without causing too much lasting damage.

Joe had expected this. After all, here he was, a murderer of an old lady; the constabulary was hardly going to treat him kindly. He'd expected a beating. The fall from the van, an accident, would be a good cover story for the injuries he would sustain this evening. It would be a long and probably painful night.

---

[5] Darbies were a common name for police hand cuffs.

20

"Careful she bites" – The Dragon's Tail Hotel – Wales – 1941

Simon changed and washed quickly. He was indeed famished and keen to resume his meeting with Sara. Leaving his unpacking for later, he made a brief inspection of the room. The furnishing was somewhat dated but didn't lack charm or comfort. The style spoke of an earlier time of elegance before bombs, war, and austerity had found their way to this forgotten outback. Simon felt that he had been given a larger room than expected. Mrs Williams had told him that he would be the only guest for this weekend at least. A large picture window faced west, and the sun was gently sliding down the sky, looking for its nightly home, nestled in the imposing mountains that rose high and far into the distance. The old road that had brought him this far into the country now cut its way between a few small shops, closed at this hour, terraces of cottages and then open fields before disappearing from sight. It was a beautiful vista, and Simon, still elated by the adrenaline of the ride and enthralled by the meeting with Sara, started to calm into the quiet nature of his new home. He would have to be cautious to remember that he was on a mission, not a holiday, and that dangers may await him even in so perfect a setting.

Simon followed the stairs down to the public bar. As he opened the door, the sound hit him. The laughter, shouted conversation, heated discussions and singing almost bowled him over. The sounds were amplified by the low-timbered ceilings and stone floors. He pushed into the room, his eyes watering at the dense fog of tobacco smoke that hung in a haze below the once-white ceiling lathe and plaster. Slowly, he navigated his way through the press of bodies. The sound abated slightly as, with each step, a new member of the clientele spotted his presence. Their conversation paused momentarily to greet the stranger in their midst. Nodding heads bobbed in his direction as he greeted one after another with a smile and a cheery "good evening". At some length, Simon managed to gain the relative peace of the room's far end. A table, set with delicate China, laced tablecloth, a small posy of flowers and a plate of neatly cut sandwiches, tucked invitingly in the corner offering its generous hospitality. It contrasted with the harshness of the other tables in the room, which were crammed with variously filled and emptied glasses of beer and overflowing ashtrays.

"I hope that cheese is okay with you. We have some Welsh cakes as well. What would you like to drink? We have tea, of course. Or would you prefer a glass of beer? Or lemonade?"

Simon turned to the speaker, quite forgetting to steel himself against the beauty of those keen grey eyes. Again, he was tongue-tied. The couple stood in silence for a moment as the revelry of the bar continued unabated around them.

"Could I please have a beer?" Simon answered at last. Thank you for the food; it's just what the doctor ordered."

"You're most welcome. I'll get your beer," Sara answered but didn't move immediately.

Simon could feel eyes around the room watching them. He suddenly realised that he had been staring at the young woman, so he deliberately turned and sat down to his food.

There were eyes watching. Alwyn Thomas watched through jealous eyes as the naval officer chatted to his best mate's girl. Dot watched Alwyn as he watched Sara. Rosie watched Dot, Alwyn, and the stranger. She had been expecting someone, and now he was here.

Simon settled down to his supper and tried to observe the room as inconspicuously as possible. He tried to play the part of a weary traveller, enjoying his food and drink. Sara brought his beer over to the table; he thanked her politely but consciously made no effort to make further conversation with her. He felt instinctively that they could become friends, but he was loathe to complicate matters. He would have to tread carefully if he was to build the trust of the community. The beer softened his nerves a little. He hadn't realised how hungry he was, and the food was much enjoyed. The room quietened as some of the clientele moved on to another pub in the next village, apparently nearer to

83

their homes. As the crowd thinned, the volume dropped, and the atmosphere mellowed.

An open doorway stood away to Simon's left as he sat with his back to the window. It led to a smaller room, more decoratively furnished, a lounge bar perhaps. Unlit, not used so much these days. Next to the opening was a small fireplace, which was lit despite the warmth of the evening. An old man huddled close to the flames. He was mumbling to himself. A timeworn dog, who sat at his feet, also availed itself of the heat of the fire. As Simon looked at the dog, it raised its head towards him. Their eyes met. The canine's eyes were clouded, perhaps from cataracts, but Simon fancied he could still see a fire in them. The dog stared at him for a long moment. Then she rose, arthritically and painfully, to her feet, pausing before slowly padding across the gap towards Simon.

The dog was a Welsh Collie. She was a rich chestnut colour, mixed with bluey grey and white, perhaps greyer than in former years. Her eyes were a deep and soulful hazel; despite the clouding of the cataracts, they told of her sharp intelligence. When she looked at him, her head tilted slightly, as though judging his character. Simon felt he could imagine the lithe power the dog had once possessed. Despite the toll her years and usage had exacted upon her, she was still a magnificent animal. Simon's hand hung languidly from the arm of his chair. He didn't move. The dog approached cautiously and sniffed at Simon's hand.

"Careful, mate. That dog will bite you as soon as look at you." The warning came from one of the young men sitting at a table halfway across the room.

Simon was unconcerned. There had been many dogs in India. Street dogs, wild and untamed, who roved in packs. The trick was not to show fear. Simon would leave food out for them, much to the annoyance of his parents. Some would growl at him, at which he would just walk slowly away. Never once was he attacked. The dogs would come and go. Some would play with him. They were the pets he was never allowed.

The elderly man stirred in his chair and looked across at the dog as it took in Simon's scent. "He's right; she does bite. Be careful, lad. She don't take kindly to people. Best working dog I ever saw, though. Run all day. Best dog I ever saw." The man's voice trailed off, and his eyes stared off into the distance as he was lost to his reminiscences. "Best working dog I ever saw, won prizes. Bred her too. Her puppies won prizes. Chap down in Cornwall had a couple of her pups. Bitches. Bred 'em. Won prizes. Best working dog ever, I saw."

The dog worked closer to Simon's hand. "Careful lad, careful. Best working dog....."

Simon didn't move. He looked towards the muttering man, ignoring the dog. He could feel a wet nose against his hand. It licked his skin. Simon looked down into its misty, fiery eyes. The dog licked him once again and then lowered her head. Simon gently stroked the animal before she circled and lay down at his feet. She looked into his eyes before resting her head on his foot and falling asleep.

"Bloody hell." Exclaimed the gentleman who had warned him.

"Well, I never. Never seen her take to anyone before. Usually bites anyone she comes near. Best working dog I ever saw though, won prizes, bred her too....." The old man's words died away into his mutterings. The ancient bitch snored at Simon's feet.

"What's her name?" Simon asked the old man.

"Cae, it's Welsh for the field. Best working dog I ever saw, won prizes...."

Cae lifted her head at the sound of her name. Realising she wasn't being called, she returned to her sleep.

Simon's table was next to a small window that looked out onto the high street. The road was narrow at this point, and a colourful, well-stocked hardware store stood just across the cobbles. It boasted of being family-owned and established in 1896. Signs offered all manner of necessities; browsers were 'most welcome'. A poster on the wall beside the window reminded all that 'walls have ears'.

Simon wondered about the blackout, as the curtains in the bar had remained open, even as the lights were gradually turned on, the summer evening sun had finally given way to the pending darkness. As if reading his thoughts, one of the young ladies, who had been sitting in a group with some men who he fancied were farmers and three soldiers who looked to be Indian, started to draw the curtains of each window in the room. The girl was tall and athletic-looking, and she carried herself with lissom strength. She was attractive without being as beautiful as the barmaid. When she arrived near Simon's window, he stood and offered her his help.

"Why thank you, kind Sir, a gentleman, a rarity around these parts, that's for sure." Her voice, with its thick northern accent, out of place amongst the lyrical Welsh twangs, was deliberately cast towards her male companions. Who grumbled and made unintelligible comments in her direction.

"Oooh Navy too, don't see many of your boys around here, more's the pity." She continued. "Staying here long, are you?"

"I hope to. Just recuperating. I'd like to do a bit of walking and get some fresh air."

"Oh, I would have thought a health spa might be better for recuperating, besides not much fresh air in here, this lot haven't washed since the Coronation. I am Rosie, Land Girl, for all my many sins." Rosie winked at the attractive sailor.

"Simon Lewis, pleased to meet you, Rosie."

"Careful mate, that one definitely bites" quipped one of the farmers loudly.

"And she hasn't been fed this evening", another joined in the fun.

"Aye, but I am the best-damned working bitch you gentlemen ever saw." She quickly responded, and with that, the room exploded into laughter.

Simon was grateful to Rosie. Her intervention broke the ice, and his status as a stranger softened as he was invited to join the conversations of the local crowd. He bought a round of beers for his new friends and was generously supplied with refreshments in return. Understanding that he must tread carefully, he limited his questions to general matters. Where could he get some hiking boots? What were the best walks in the area?

All the while, the dog slept at his feet.

Shortly before 10:30, Sara rang the bell for last orders. Simon had a fresh pint before him, and he started to drink. "I suppose we better drink up then."

"There's no rush." Came back from one of the farmers as he nodded towards the door. At that moment, a minute before closing time, the door swung open, and a Police Constable walked briskly into the room. Polite greetings were exchanged as he strolled to the bar. Sara had a glass waiting for him, probably whiskey, despite its scarcity. The officer downed the liquid without comment. No money or thanks were exchanged. Turning, he retraced his steps, offering good nights here and there. Fresh orders were placed at the bar as the door shut behind him. Sara ran off her feet once again.

The farmer smiled at Simon. 'We're good til ten to midnight. Better drink up then, though; Mrs Williams won't sell alcohol on the sabbath.'

Simon looked woefully at his beer; he'd already had too many, but he sensed it would be rude to go to bed just yet. He steeled himself and prepared to do his duty for King and country.

Finally, he got into bed just after midnight. Satisfied that the first day had gone well. He had made contact with some of the locals, putting out his cover story. In a community like this, the word would soon get around, which was good. He expected that any person involved in a criminal conspiracy might hear of his arrival and would soon want to check him out. If they hadn't already.

21

The sirens were late. – East End London – 1941

Jim Blakely drove carefully through the dark streets. The glare from the fires marred his vision, and he knew not to look directly at them. He'd been an ambulance driver for over 25 years, and instinctively, he felt that rushing was a fool's errand. Driving at speed through blacked-out London was suicide.

His trades apprenticeship had been a baptism of fire on the Western front. For 4 long, horror-filled years, at just 18 years old, he had carried wounded warriors from the battlefront. Across precarious duckboards. Mud threatened to suck him under, down to oblivion, if his foot strayed or slipped from its path.

4 years of dodging bullets to carry men away from the lines, most no more than frightened boys, often knowing that their mortality was precarious, many dying before the stretcher was placed down before an exhausted medic. Many more leaving this life despite the attentions of those helpless officers.

4 years of collecting body parts and handing them over to some poor sod, whose job it was to sort them, like a macabre jigsaw, a puzzle with no pretty picture on the box lid and always numerous pieces missing.

4 years of noise so intense it was beyond terrifying. The endless barrage from artillery miles away, the short ominous silence, the whistles, the shouting, the volleys from manifold spitting, venomous, malicious, cowardly and godless weapons, the cries, the screams.

The cruellest noise, the one that still haunted his dreams and probably always would, the cries of boys, desperate to hear that they may well live, begging that they might be saved, calling for their mothers, praying to a God that had been absent without leave since the very first shot had been fired.

Now, here he was again, pulling bodies from war-torn wreckage. Same enemy, same constant fight for lives. Only this time, it wasn't a foreign field; it wasn't only men and boys; it was Women, old ladies, old men, children, and babies. In this war, you didn't have to wear a uniform to die.

Jim turned right onto a long road stretching a mile or so down to the docks. There were fires all the way along the thoroughfare. The Jerry's must have lined up perfectly on their target of the wharves and warehouses that snuggled up to the river. Every fifth or sixth house seemed to have been hit. The bombs had dropped early. The bombers were a little too eager to discharge their destruction. Fire crews struggled to put out the fires, all too aware that their glow could be easily seen from the air and would be the perfect guide for the next wave of aircraft.

Jim saw an ARW (Air Raid Warden) chatting animatedly with a policeman; he pulled alongside, winding down his window. "Casualties?" He called. Not the time or the place for the niceties of a polite conversation.

The ARW nodded resignedly. "Everywhere, mate. The sirens didn't sound in time. Many of the houses were occupied. People hadn't gone to the shelters yet. They'll probably need you down at the pub. On the corner down there." The man pointed without looking, keeping his face turned towards the ambulance so that his voice wouldn't get lost in the noise. "Pub was full, jam-packed apparently."

Jim nodded and drove on without answering. Snaking his way down the street, past rubble that had been blown from each of the wrecked buildings. At 50 yards from the street corner, he stopped. The doors of the pub had been ripped from their frames; someone had used them as makeshift stretchers; they lay across the road, and on each, a blanket covered the bodies they bore.

The ground-floor walls of the building were largely undamaged, and any fire had been extinguished. The main hint of what had happened was a large crater that stretched from the far side wall most of the way across the road.

"I reckon the bomb went off in the cellar." Bert Evison's comment was something of a question. Bert had been riding with Jim for six months now. He was a volunteer, and fair play to him; he had stuck it out much longer than most on the job. His experiences rapidly trained him on what to look for.

"I would say you are right. It probably came in the roof, straight through the first and ground floors, then exploded when it hit the solid floor of the cellar. Better take a look, but I doubt anyone survived that. The pair walked slowly towards the building, looking up at the sign on which 'The Dog and Duck' still proudly displayed its name above the blown-out doors.

22

A Good First Day – The Dragon – Wales - 1941

Simon thought of the people he had met. Could any of them be involved? Certainly, any of the farmers might be. But the ones he had talked to were mainly young, and he wondered if they would have the organisational skills or authority to mount any serious breach of the rules.

It was too soon to speculate. There would be much more careful research needed before he could do that. One thing did strike a chord with him. It was what Rosie had said, the girl who was doing the blackout. What was it she had said exactly? Simon fought hard against the blurriness of his brain caused by the beer and exhaustion. What was it she had mentioned? A health spa. Why would she have said that? Was it a coincidence, or was she secretly referring to the nickname for the training camp, the Major's health spa? Was she testing him or letting him know who she was?

It had occurred to Simon that other operatives from the ministry might be working on the case. Robinson might want to back more than one horse. A land girl was a clever cover. In many ways, it was much better than his own.

Obviously, he had never met the girl before; she had not been at his training camp. But there were rumours that the Major had other "Spa's". It made sense; why have all your eggs in one basket? For occasions like this, it would be handy to have operators working separately, without prior knowledge of each other.

Had she been briefed that he was coming? Maybe she had seen through his story, in which case, so could others. Was she telling him of her presence or just looking for his reaction to test her suspicions?

If she were from the Ministry, she would be in a better place to discover any criminal conspiracies in the area than he was.

This, in turn, raised suspicion in his mind that maybe his true role here was to draw attention to himself and avoid other investigations that might be taking place. It was all conjecture. Simon had his orders and knew he needed to carry them out as instructed.

Nothing could be gained and everything could be lost by trying to communicate with Rosie. He would blow his own cover if she were just a Land Girl. If she is a ministry stooge, like himself, then he could expose her to suspicion. She had obviously gained the trust of the locals; if that was her mission, then she was doing a bloody good job.

As he drifted towards sleep, Simon thought that Rosie had intended to subtly let him know of her status. When it comes to the crunch, they may have to team up at some point in the future. For now, they both had a job to do.

23

Any survivors? – East End London - 1941

Jim and Bert jumped from the vehicle and carefully picked their way through the debris towards the front doors. A fireman called across to them, "Hello Jim. Nice of you to show up." The man's tone was mocking but good-natured.

Jim didn't mind. He had long since learned that many of those who were forced to witness these atrocities, night after night, only hung on to their sanity through their humour.

"Yeah, sorry we are late, Stan; we heard you were out, so we popped by to see your Mrs on the way." Jim teased. He had known the man for years; he had never seemed to change, but he had seen him age rapidly since the first German bombs had fallen. "But the queue was too long, so we thought we had better get round here and help you out."

"Ah, well, at least she won't be asking for any housekeeping money this week." Stan swotted away the mock insult. "Are you going in there?" He nodded towards the pub.

"Thought we would take a look, see if the Mild[6] is any good. Has it been checked?"

"We took a quick butcher's[7], doesn't look like there are any survivors. The walls and roof seem stable, but be careful."

"Always am, mate."

Jim reached the front door and peered in. Both floors were blown away. Looking up, Jim could see the roof. Most of the slates had been blown off, but the timbers remained. They looked to be solidly holding the external walls and the walls holding them, in the mutual self-reliance of which they were built. The internal wall that closed off the back of the first-floor living space was also intact.

The ground floor had been blown away. Just a small ledge remained around the right-hand edge and in front of the bar.

---

[6] Mild was a type of ale popular at the time, usually darker that Bitter.
[7] Butchers is rhyming slang for looking - Butchers Hook = Look

Below, the cellar had been opened up like a gaping abyss. Bits of fallen masonry and some wrecked tables and chairs littered the mud floor where they had fallen after they had been catapulted into the air. Hitting the roof timbers before falling back, past where they had sat for years and down into the chasm below.

Bert stood at Jim's shoulder and looked at the carnage. He looked askance at Jim, who was happy to oblige with his theory.

"Probably dropped straight through the roof just in front of that wall above the bar. Went through the first and ground floors before coming to a halt eventually when it had ploughed into the earth below the basement floor. It must have gone a fair way down, judging by the depth of the crater. The earth seems to have been quite soft. Probably wet from the proximity of the river. It would have exploded then. The blast seems to have been directed forward through the cellar, which extends out under the pavement outside, where they deliver the beer barrels. By the looks of how it has made a hole in the road, most of the energy went that way. The blast also went upwards, taking out what was left of the floors and the slates off the roof."

Jim was silent for a moment while taking in the rest of the scene. Bert and Stan, who had joined them at the door, waited for him to continue.

"Look at how the ceiling has fallen down over there; the rest of it has been blown upwards and totally destroyed, but that bit has fallen down and is intact." A section of the first floor had broken off just above the bar. It had hinged down and was resting at an angle on the solid countertop. A heavy cast iron bath sat firmly on the sloping floor.

"The bar is untouched." Jim mused, his whispered thoughts hard for the men to hear in the night's carnage. "I wonder if the old place was modernised. Probably when they put that bath in. They will have reinforced the floor to hold it; I bet it weighs a ton. They probably also strengthened the floor under the bar. Put a supporting wall under it. Maybe even filled in the cellar behind that wall for some reason."

"Maybe to control flooding, like you say there has to be water in the ground this close to the river." Stan jumped in with a suggestion.

"Might be the case. It would certainly explain why the force of the explosion went straight up and forward but not back that way; look, that wall is barely scratched." It was true the cellar wall seemed to have remained entirely intact. "It looks like the bar has hardly been touched," Jim repeated to himself thoughtfully. "I guess if the sirens had not gone off, they would still be serving. There would have been people behind the bar." Jim's voice was louder and more excited now. "I reckon that with the way the bar is still solid and the flooring from above covering it, someone behind the bar might just have a chance of surviving."

Jim looked expectingly at the two men. "Stan, see if you can get a bit of hush around here, can you. Bert, that floor won't hold both our weights, and I will need you to come and get me if it doesn't hold mine." He pointed to the fragile remains of the ground floor, which skirted the side wall and no more than 12 inches in front of the bar.

Stan moved away back to the street and shouted lustily. "belt up everyone, listening for survivors. You," pointing towards a shocked-looking fire volunteer, who was wandering aimlessly, unsure how he could help, "Grab a rope from the truck and take it to that man there." He pointed animatedly towards a lorry and then Jim.

Bert had run to the Ambulance, coming back with a roll of canvas, a spare for the stretcher and a crowbar. He handed them to Jim and nodded in support. Jim threw out the roll over the first section of the rickety floor. Tucking the crowbar through the back of his belt, He tied the rope around his waist and gingerly knelt on the fabric, lowering himself forward until he was prostrate. Laying his torch on the canvas under his chin, the light spread across the dusty floor in front of him. Using the canvas as a slide, he carefully pushed it with his feet. Inch by inch, he edged across the floor. Staying as close to the wall as possible, not wanting to put any more strain on the remaining timbers than was necessary, he prayed that by spreading his weight, the tortured wood would hold.

As he went, he used his arms to brush stray rubble from the floor out of his way, the debris falling into the chasm below. The dust stung his eyes and choked his throat, and its clouds, illuminated by the torch, blocked his vision. So that he had to wait for it to settle before he could carry on. Further slowing his progress. His ankles ached from the repeated pushes, which propelled him agonisingly slowly to his goal. The rope snaked out behind him as Bert let it out. Jim needed to secure the rope to something as he reached the corner of the room. If he carried on with the rope attached to his waist, then it would end up swinging out over the void. This was a further risk as he would need to continue without the lifeline.

The noise outside had abated, but each groan of the battered building teased his nerves, every sound the potential harbinger of his doom. He moved along to as close to the centre of the bar as he dared. Rolling carefully onto his back, he looked up at the solid-looking structure. Thick oak-framed panels, each 18 inches wide, maybe 24 inches high, were secured to the frames by quarter-round beading, the weak link, he hoped.

Jim tapped on the centre of one of the panels, five taps in quick succession, then a slight pause, and then two more. It was a very deliberate pattern that was unmistakable to anyone listening. Jim listened hard, with his ear as close to the panel as he could get it.

Nothing. He tapped again, using the same pattern but slightly harder. Listening intently. Nothing. Again and again, he tapped, each time harder. As he did so, he mulled over his options. This was a dangerous situation. The fall into the cellar was big, heightened by the huge crater the bomb had created. Plus, the landing would not be soft. All manner of splintered wood, twisted metal and jagged masonry could do all sorts of damage. Likely as not, he would fall headfirst, with little chance to protect himself.

He should make his way back to safety. After all, he had no idea if there was anybody behind the bar when the bomb hit. Even if he accepted that there had been, the likelihood of their survival was slight. Everyone else in the inn had been killed outright by the blast. His theory that the strength of the bar, the protection of the fallen ceiling and the apparent direction of the blast was just a theory after all.

Yet he felt strongly that he was right. There had to be someone behind these panels. Someone had to live from this abomination.

These people were just ordinary people enjoying a night out. A few drinks with their friends. Trying to forget the war for a while. Ready to run to the safety of the shelter when the sirens sounded. Let down by the warning system.

Tears of anger and frustration filled his eyes. He wanted to scream. Shout at those bastards. Senseless, senseless killings.

"Are you all right, Jim?" Bert called from the doorway, worrying that his mate had been still for a while.

Jim choked back his feelings and took a long, deep breath. "Fine, mate, never better. Can't hear anything. I am gonna just try and get one of these panels out, see if I can see anything." He couldn't leave without trying one last thing.

Taking a penknife from his pocket, he scraped at the varnish around the edge of the beading on the right side of the panel above him. Managing to get the blade into the gap between the thin bead and the panel, he worked away at it until he had made an indentation large enough to fit the end of the crowbar. Jamming the heavy metal bar into the gap, he pushed against it. The wood gave just a little. Moving the lever to each end of the gap in turn, the bead began to come away from the panel slowly until suddenly it snapped, the stick of wood shooting off and falling to the rest of the debris below.

Jim turned his attention to the top bead. This had already been weakened when the side bead had given way and was easy prey for the heavy lever. The left side followed with equal ease, as did the bottom. Being a keen amateur carpenter himself, Jim knew that the panel behind would be smaller than the frame to which it was fitted. This allowed the natural material to expand and contract without putting strain on the frame. Grabbing the crowbar with both hands, he swung it at the panel, hoping to shock the wood loose from its home of many generations. But he was a little too enthusiastic, and the momentum of his arms caused the canvas under him to slip on the dusty floor. Jim slid dangerously towards the edge. His body only stopped when the cloth snagged on a loose nail that protruded from the wood.

Jim's right arm and leg hung over the edge of the precipice. He froze, sure that any sudden movement would complete his demise. Fighting to control his breathing, sweat poured from his forehead. He looked back at the panel; it had come away at the top a little. It was all the encouragement he needed. Edging carefully back to the relative safety of the bar, he reached up and managed to get his fingers behind the panel. He was just about to pull when he heard a moan.

24

Nightmare. – The Dragon's Tail Hotel – Wales – 1941

The cold grey Atlantic crashed once more over the bow, each wave bigger as the ship listed and slipped ever further forward towards her watery grave. Men were screaming, faint chilling sounds from deep inside her hull, muffled by the reinforced, multi-layered steel heated by the explosions and fires from within.

He moved towards the sounds, drawn, as the compass needle is pulled north. Hopelessness overcame him as he saw the twisted metal of the bulkhead door. The screams came again from behind the mangled steel. Steam hissed from the glowing metal as each wave battled to cool the superheated structure. Water and fire in a millennial-old feud for supremacy.

He lifted the heavy fire axe. Its weight threatened to topple him, and as he heaved it high in the air above his head, he felt as if an invisible hand took hold. Together, they smashed it down on the hinge.

The men's screams paused as they heard the sound. Hopefully, they willed on the source of their salvation. The axe fell again and again. Savage blows. As he aimed yet another blow, the ship lurched, his feet slipping on the wet deck. The axe fell from his hands, and he reached forward to soften his fall.

As His hands flayed out in front of him, they landed on the searing metal. He could smell his flesh cooking as he pulled away in agony. Another wave crashed over the bow, and he held his hands high into the rushing waters like a devotee praising an all-powerful deity. More screams, this time his own.

Simon woke as the knocking at his door intensified. A long moment elapsed as he took in the unfamiliar surroundings. Instinctively, he looked at his hands. They were shaking uncontrollably, not burnt.

The knock at the door again. "Lieutenant Lewis, are you all right? Lieutenant! Simon!" Sara's voice became more and more desperate. She longed to enter the room and comfort the man, but she knew that would be inappropriate. Her aunt joined her at her door.

"Whatever is to do?" The older lady asked insistently.

"Oh, auntie, he was screaming, howling like a wounded animal. It was awful, just such a terrible sound."

The lady took her turn to knock. "Lieutenant, this is Mrs Williams. May I come in?"

Despite the question, she didn't wait before turning the handle and entering the room. The light from the hallway spread across the floor and illuminated the bed. Simon sat there, bemused, shaking.

Eleanor Williams took in the scene. The bedclothes were in disarray, but the young man was respectfully attired. Without hesitation, she moved into action. Her hand moved straight to the forehead of the boy. He was hot but not a raging fever, as she had feared. That notwithstanding, his bedclothes were soaked with sweat. He was breathing heavily, and his heart raced.

"The poor lamb." She opined to no one in particular. "Lieutenant Lewis, are you all right young man?"

Simon looked towards her, recognition finally dawning as he shook his thoughts away from the dream. "I must have been dreaming. I am sorry. Did I disturb you?"

"I should say so; I am afraid that you were crying out. It must have been a terrible dream." The woman's voice was soft, reassuring, and non-judgmental.

Now that he was fully awakened, he became embarrassed. "I am so sorry, so sorry to be such a nuisance. What must you think of me?"

"I think that you are a very brave young man who has had terrible experiences. It is only natural that you should dream of them. You are not a nuisance at all. We were just concerned for you." Her soothing voice worked its magic, and Simon began to relax.

"Thank you, so sorry, thank you."

"Have some water. Try to sleep again. Lie in late in the morning. I will make your breakfast whenever you're ready."

Simon said no more as he lay down. He felt the sheets being straightened by the practised hands of the old lady. She moved towards the door, where Sara was standing with concern on her lovely face. He closed his eyes and slept peacefully.

25

Salvation? – The Dog and Duck – East End London - 1941

Faint, ever-so faint. Had Jim imagined it? No, there it was again. The voice of a young lady. She was gently sobbing and talking softly. "Not my Joe, no way, he just wouldn't, he couldn't, not my Joe."

"Miss, can you hear me? Miss." Jim called to her gently, not wanting her to panic or move suddenly. "Miss, my name is Jim; I am an ambulance man; we are going to get you to safety. Can you hear me?" Knowing that this was a vital stage of any rescue, Jim did his best to keep his voice calm and reassuring. A person coming back to consciousness was likely to try to get up, potentially compounding an injury or setting off a fall of the timbers around them.

"He wouldn't hurt a fly, not my Joe. He'd never kill an old lady; they got the wrong man, it's a mistake. Oh my god, it's so dark in here; why is it so dark?"

Jim could hear that the young lady was coming out of her dream and was starting to be aware of her surroundings. "Miss, can you hear me? We are gonna get you out of here but for now I need you to keep very still. Do you hear me?"

"Yes." The voice was weak. "But where am I? Where is Joe and Marge?" Her voice was starting to sound more urgent.

She needed reassurance. "You are in the Dog and Duck, the pub. There has been an explosion. Don't worry we will get you out. Just stay very still for me, do you understand."

"Yes. Please hurry. I need to go and see Joe; they took him away, you see. It's a mistake; it has to be. I need to go and tell them."

"Good girl, we will get you out very soon, then you can go and see Joe. Now close your eyes for me and stay very still."

Jim pulled at the panel; it gave a little, and he pulled harder. Bit by bit, the frame released its grip on the ancient board until it finally fell away. Cautious not to shine his torch directly into it, he didn't want the sudden light to shock the girl; Jim peered into the hole. Glasses and pint pots were stacked on the shelves. Amazingly, they were all intact; they stood in rows waiting to be put to good use. Carefully, he took one at a time and dropped them into the abyss behind him. Having cleared the upper shelf, he lifted the loose board from its supports on either side and removed the glasses below.

"Miss, can you hear me?"

"Yes."

"What is your name?"

"Amber."

"I am Jim. Right Amber, I am going to shine a light. Keep your eyes closed for now. Do you understand?"

"Yes, I understand."

Slowly, Jim turned the torch towards the gap in the bar. Gradually, the scene beyond became clearer. The damage was miraculously slight. Some plaster from the collapsed ceiling was scattered across the floor but no beams, no heavy masonry, nothing that would trap or injure anyone. Lying on the dusty floor was a young woman. Perhaps 25 years old, slight, long-limbed, probably quite tall but mercifully light.

"Amber, you can slowly open your eyes now. Slowly, let your eyes adjust."

The barmaid squinted as her eyes opened. She looked at her rescuer.

"Hello Jim, fancy a pint?"

"Hello Amber, yes I do, but I don't think I have time right now." Jim was relieved that the girl was conscious and better yet, she wasn't panicking. Not for the first time, he marvelled at some people's Ability to take anything in their stride. This was indeed a remarkable young lady. "Amber, stay quite still. Do you feel any pain?"

"No, just a little stiff, maybe." With that, she began to stretch, like she was just awakening from a delicious slumber.

"Good, but please stay still just a little longer." Jim was anxious to check for any injuries before moving her. "Slowly and carefully, I want you to move your arms. If it hurts, stop straight away."

"I am fine."

"All right, I am going to shine the torch directly at you. I want to make sure nothing is in your way."

The chamber where Amber lay now became fully lit. Jim could see no blood, only a lump on her head. Satisfied that the girl was ready, he issued his instructions.

"Right, I am going to reach in. I want you to take my hand. I am going to pull you gently towards me and through this hole. The thing is that on this side of the bar, most of the floor is missing. You will need to be very careful to stay close to the bar. Do not stand up. Try to lie so that as much of your body weight is spread out on the remaining timbers."

"I am ready."

Jim reached in. Cold hands took his. Gradually, he began to pull, feeling that the girl was sliding over the floor to him. Her head came into the opening, and she smiled at him.

Jim inched backwards slowly. This time, he had to put the palms of his hands flat on the floor, just in front of his head, pushing and extending his arms until they were straight out in front of him. Then, he bent his elbows again and repeated the process. It was tortuous work. His hands slipped on the dusty surface. Bits of rubble and broken glass dug into his skin painfully. He stopped three feet from the hole.

"Now pull yourself through the hole; stay as close to the bar as possible."

In the faint light, Jim saw a head appear; it turned towards him. He reached forward and took her wrist again. Pulling gently, he managed to slide her until her head was almost next to his own. Then he repeated his own backward thrusts, just far enough that he could still reach her outstretched arms and pull her again. First, he had to brush away the glass and stone embedded in his hands for fear that they might hurt her.

In this truncated way, the pair edged along the bar. At last, his feet touched the wall.

They paused; Jim was exhausted, and Amber trembled. She could see the dangers all around her. They weren't out of the woods yet. They still had to get out of the crumbling building.

"We should rest a moment. The next part might be a bit difficult. How are you doing?" Jim asked, trying to sound as unworried as possible.

"I am fine. A little frightened. Why did you come for me?" Amber was beginning to realise the enormity of what was happening. The bravery that this man, a man she didn't know, was showing to rescue her was incomprehensible.

"It's my job, Love. Got to earn my wages somehow." Jim quipped.

Amber doubted that it was his job. He had said he was an ambulance man. Surely, this sort of thing was beyond his responsibility. A fireman might undertake such a rescue, but even then, she doubted that a few would take such risks.

"How did you know I was there?"

"Just a lucky guess. I saw how the ceiling had come down and been stopped by the bar. I thought there was a chance that someone might have survived under it."

"Looks like your guess saved my life." Amber realised that she was still in danger and, not wanting to tempt fate, quickly added. "At least for now."

"Yes, we still need to get out of here in one piece."

The mood between them turned serious for a moment. Amber wanted to tell this man how brave he was. How grateful she was. But she knew her words would not be anywhere near enough. So, instead, she turned to humour. "So, does your wife know that you spend your evenings pulling barmaids?"

"Better not tell her, eh? She'd have my guts for garters."

"My lips are sealed."

"Ready to carry on?"

"Ready as I will ever be."

Jim was about to explain what they had to do next when a dreaded sound screeched its way into their existence. Sirens.

26

A hangover – South Wales - 1941

Simon was convinced that a Fire engine, or a whole squadron of them even, with all their bells ringing loudly, were driving through his room at that very moment. The pain in his head was excruciating. The shrill noise was the alarm of his Jaeger LeCoultre travel clock. The beautiful Swiss-made timepiece had been a gift from his mother when he had left for university. Right now, he was cursing her generosity, wishing he had left the blasted thing at home and avowing ruin on those clever Swiss and their confounded, ingenious little contraptions.

The ringing stopped, but the pain in his head persisted. Climbing slowly from his bed, he pulled back the heavy blackout curtains and winced as the bright scene outside his window seared into his eyes. He poured some water into a bowl at the nightstand. It was cold and revived him a little as he splashed it over his face and head. He dressed carefully. Full Navy uniform, Sunday best—he had to look good for church.

Simon was not a religious man. He had been christened, attended Sunday school, and dutifully said his prayers as a child. But he could never really balance the existence of an all-forgiving god with some of the things he had witnessed in his short life. He was spiritual and had been interested in the religions of India. What he couldn't understand was the similarities of the major ones and yet the divisiveness, hate and violence that they all seemed to cause. Buddhism was the only one that struck any sort of a cord with his sympathies. But being a man who had been taught at least a dozen different ways to kill a man with his bare hands, he doubted that he would find enlightenment anytime soon.

He would be going to church today as part of his cover. It would be expected of an officer and a gentleman. It was also an opportunity to meet more of the locals and be seen. He hoped a light breakfast would complete his recovery from last night's excesses. Turning up for the weekly worship, looking like death warmed up, would not be good for his standing in the community. Descending to the reception, Simon could see that a lone table had been laid for breakfast in the lounge. The French doors had been swung open, and a gentle breeze blew into the room. No one appeared to be around. Taking in the view through the doors, the hills were bathed in the morning sunshine. They rose high and challenging beyond the walls of the immaculately kept garden. A few small cumulus clouds floated across the azure sky. It was a scene of peace and gentility, which belied the fact that all over the world, hatred and violence reigned supreme in the hearts and minds of men. Once again, Simon couldn't believe his luck; he doubted all his missions would be so comfortable.

Lost in the moment, Simon was startled as a small, slight lady entered the room, singing softly to herself. She, too, was surprised by Simon's presence. "Good morning, Lieutenant, I didn't hear you come down the stairs; I hope I haven't kept you waiting?"

It was the woman who had comforted him in the night; for the first time, he could look at his nurse. She was a woman of indeterminate age who stood before him with calmness and poise. Her hair was grey but still shined, carrying just a hint of its former blond hues. Her skin was wrinkled but in a way that told of a gentle, assented ageing. The lines only served to suggest that this was a face that had smiled its way through the trials and tribulations of life. Her eyes Simon knew; he had seen them before, just recently. The keen grey should have been unique, but it was again brightening another face.

"Not at all, Mrs. Williams." There was no doubt about the lady's identity. Sara had said that the owner was her aunt, and there could be no doubt that the two were closely related. "I was just admiring the garden; the clematis is quite magnificent."

"Thank you. My Grandfather planted it over a hundred years ago. He was head gardener at the estate; it's said that he was an adviser to Victoria's gardeners. When he retired, he was given this Inn, and it's been in our family ever since." Mrs Williams put down the tray she had been carrying and moved to the doorway beside her new guest. "Are you keen on gardening, Lieutenant Lewis?"

107

"My mother is a very committed horticulturist, although she has struggled with the climate in India for many years. She would love it here."

"I am sorry I was not here to welcome you last evening; I trust Sara took care of you?" Diplomatically, no mention was made of his dream, for which he was grateful.

Simon blushed ever so slightly. "Yes, she was very kind. And your regulars were very hospitable, too."

"Yes, perhaps I should have warned you that they can get quite enthusiastic on a Saturday evening." Mrs Williams smiled. "I hope that the evening hasn't dented your appetite. Will tea be all right with your breakfast? I am afraid there has been no coffee for some time."

"Tea is perfect, thank you. Actually, I am not that hungry, please don't go to any trouble." Although feeling much better than when he had woken earlier, he was still far from feeling at his best.

"Oh, it's no trouble. It's all but ready. Just do your eggs. It will take just a few minutes."

Eggs? Plural? As there is more than one. Simon hadn't seen more than one egg on a plate for years. He was about to ask for a small portion, but somehow, he knew that his request would fall on deaf ears.

The lady glided off towards the kitchen at the rear of the building, returning a few minutes later laden with a large plate piled high with food. She laid it on the table before Simon and stepped back, standing as though she intended to supervise his enjoyment of the meal, as if she was keen to watch his every bite until he had cleared the plate.

The food was monstrous in its proportions; it filled the plate, even though the disc seemed to be the size of a dustbin lid. There were sausages and rashers of bacon, it was impossible to count how many of each at this stage, as he suspected there may be more on a lower level. Mushrooms, grilled tomatoes and fried bread filled in gaps among the meat. Topping it all were the eggs, fried softly, yokes runny and no less than three of them. Simon was looking at a month's ration in one meal. His stomach was turning. He looked up from the plate to his eager hostess. She was smiling, and he smiled back. Here was a dilemma: refusal of the food would be seen as rude, he was sure. But he was far from certain that he could keep it down even if he did, by some miracle, make a dent in it. No choice, he picked up his knife and fork and attacked the plate with as much gusto as he could manage.

"Oh dear, I forgot your toast." Mrs Williams was mortified at her oversight. She whisked off towards the kitchen, returning a few minutes later with a pile of toast. "You seem to have a healthy appetite, so I brought you some extra bacon." Before Simon could object, two rashers of fatty, grease-soaked ham slid from the plate she was holding and landed on his barely depleted feast. Years later, Simon would joke that finishing that breakfast and not bringing it back during the sermon was the most physically demanding task of his war.

27

More Bombs – East End London - 1941

The wailing noise echoed around the bare walls of the building. Jim and Amber clung to each other's hands as the implications dawned on them. Another wave of bombs, hoping to reignite the fires of the earlier raid.

"Bert," Jim called out to his mate. "Bert!"

"Here, Jim."

"Why are you there? You know the rules; get yourself off down the shelter."

"What, and leave you here to have all the fun, no way, mate." Bert shone his torch at Amber. "How is it that you always manage to rescue the pretty ones?"

"Just born lucky mate, just born lucky." Jim's words faded as the explosions started to be heard. All three of them hoped that his luck wasn't about to run out.

The fresh wave of bombers was coming down at a tangent to the first, hoping to use the remaining fires as a guide to their targets. Bert could hear them getting closer as they approached from the docks. Each explosion seemed twice as loud as the one before until they were almost upon them.

Bert crouched in the doorway, pulling his coat over his head as a woefully inadequate protection against any flying debris about to come his way. Jim and Amber clung to each other's hands as the vibrations of the explosions began to be felt through the fragile building. The noise increased until it almost seemed continuous, with multiple explosions all around them. Bert could feel the shockwaves from the blasts; they rocked him backwards and forwards as he curled even more tightly into a ball on the ground. There was no possibility of shouting to each other, no hope of moving towards safety for now. The ground and walls of all the buildings around were shaking too much. All they could do was stay still, hope and pray. Each one of them lost in their own thoughts.

Amber was thinking of Joe. Where was he now? Would he be safe? Would there be an air raid shelter where he was? The injustice of his arrest riled her. She had to live and get out of here. Somehow, she would help and tell him that she knew he was innocent. He was; she felt it. Marge and Charlie would help her. Suddenly, she realised her losses. Marge had been collecting glasses and chatting with the clientele when the bomb hit. Charlie had gone to the cellar to change the Mild barrel over. They both must be dead. It seemed amazing to her that Charlie, the Cockney Calamity, could be gone. He was so big and strong. And Marge, Marge was afraid of nothing. So full of life and laughter. That they could cease to exist in a single moment made no sense to her.

She had been behind the bar on her own, she had wanted to keep busy, to take her mind off Joe's arrest. But what about Linda, where was she? Amber remembered that she had gone out the back to let the girls out. They had wanted to get away from the sailors. Maybe Linda would be all right. She liked to look out for Linda. She was a nice girl but none too clever at times. She was easily led and just as quickly duped. They shared a room at the pub. Linda was always broke, borrowing from her incessantly. Like Amber, she had no one and had come to see Charlie and Marge as her family. Perhaps Linda was alive. Tears came to her dust-clogged eyes, and she began to sob gently.

Bert was thinking of his special day. The sun had shone all day, and Brighton had been lovely. Lisa had been so pretty in her new dress. The twins in their pram. Little Jonnie insisting on pushing them. Proudly telling anyone who asked their names and how old they were. The world had seemed such a special place that day. One of love and laughter, sea and sand, ice cream and candy floss, bandstands and promenades, hope and future. Herr Hitler was only just beginning to spread his madness; nobody believed there would be another war. Nobody in Brighton that day thought of such horrors. He missed them all so much. Every day, he worked hard at the docks, and to fill his lonely evenings, he helped Jim with the ambulance. Lisa and the children were safe, staying with her sister in Cambridgeshire. Lisa helped with the farm, and the boys were now at school in the village. Far away from the east-end bombings, never far from his thoughts.

Jim was angry. The bombs always made him angry. Such a cowardly act, dropping death from the sky. So indiscriminate. They knew what they were doing. Killing innocents. He could feel the girl sobbing. The poor thing, she must be frightened to death. He thought of his own daughter. She would be about 19 now, just a bit younger than this girl, he thought. Not for the first time, he wondered where she was, what she looked like, if she was pretty, if she was clever, and if she was happy.

Jim had been a widower at just 24. His wife died giving birth to their daughter, and he had been devastated. His wife's family, supported by his mother and father, thought he was in no position to bring up the baby. His sister-in-law adopted the child but insisted that Jim promised not to see the girl; she said that it would confuse the child and that it better that she brought her up as her own. They lived in Cornwall somewhere. Jim remarried, and Emma had given him a son; they were very happy. Young Eric had passed his eleven-plus and was now at grammar school. He thought of his daughter often, as he did now, hoping she was safe and well. He knew then that he had to save this girl, Amber, this brave, pretty girl. Someone's daughter.

At last, the noise began to die away, and the trio realised that the bombers were leaving and, for now, they were safe.

"Bert, are you alright mate?"

"Oh, I can't grumble; if I did, no one would listen." Came back a chirpy reply. "How are you getting on? Are you on the whiskey yet?"

"Nah, they've got no ice, last time I drink in this boozer," Jim responded.

"You won't get served; you're both barred; look at the damage you've done to my bar." Amber joined in the banter that suppressed their fears. "Any chance you can get me out of here anytime soon?"

Bert swung his torch around the building. The bombing had stirred up more dust, and the clouds blocked any clear view he might have had. As it settled, his beam stopped on the right-hand side of the room. "Err, Jim. Bit of a problem mate. Take a butchers at the floor by the wall."

Jim turned as far as his precarious position would let him and shone his own torch towards where Bert's beam pointed.

Disturbed by the violence of the bombs, what had been left of the floor along the window wall had subsided and now sloped at a 45-degree angle down towards the cellar. It looked ready to break off altogether and join the rest below.

"Well, we ain't getting out that way." Jim racked his brains for another plan.

He and Amber now crouched on the only bit of floor left in the building. They could try to drop down to the cellar on the rope, but the rubble would be almost impossible to scramble across. Think as he might, it was all that he could come up with.

"Bert, I think I am gonna try and get down into the cellar, make my way across. Perhaps you can find some scaffold boards you can drop down so I can make a sort of bridge?"

"Sorry, Jim, take a look down there."

Jim looked for himself. "Bugger, water!" He fumed as another of his options had disappeared. "The water main must have broken; it's filling up quite quickly."

"Can't we wait until it gets a bit deeper and then swim across?" This time, Amber pitched in with a suggestion.

"Good idea, only if we get snagged on something down there, we get stuck and drown. What's more that there is the electricity mains. If the fuse doesn't blow, the water will be live, and trust me, that's a shocking way to go." Jim seemed quite pleased with his little joke, but he could sense that Amber was getting concerned. "Look, I am sorry, love. Don't worry, we'll get you out, promise, won't we, Bert?"

"Too right, mate, there's a shortage of good barmaids in London, I read it in the Daily Mail the other day. Your war work is vital. Your country needs you."

"Bert, have you got any more rope?"

"Can get some, I am sure. What you thinking?"

"Find about 40; no, make it 50 feet, get a ladder and lower it down through that first-floor window over there. Put a weight on the end and swing it like a pendulum so I can catch it. Tie the other end to something solid."

"You want me to pull you up to that window?"

"No, Bert, I want to climb up far enough so that we can swing through the window below. I just need you to hold the rope."

"What if I tied the rope to the ambulance and used it to pull you up," Bert suggested.

"That might work, but if you pulled too hard, we would get in more trouble. Let's see if I can manage to climb up first."

"Just might work. Wait there."

Bert disappeared off into the darkness. The pair could hear him shouting to a fire crew.

"While we are waiting, we might as well get ready. You will have to hold me round the neck, like a piggyback. I will have my hands full, so I won't be able to help."

"Don't worry, I can hold on. Will you be able to take both our weights?"

"No problem, I bet you are less than 7 stone wet through." Jim tried to sound confident, but as he said the words, he could feel the blood dripping from the cuts on his hands. Carefully, he removed the pieces of glass that remained in the open wounds. His right hand was the most badly damaged; he wrapped it with his handkerchief. It would have to do.

Bert appeared at the window. "I have a ladder and rope; hang on, mate."

"Take your time, mate, it's ages before the last orders."

28

A Sermon – South Wales - 1941

It was a short but pleasant walk to the church. The High Street shops were all closed, but the pavements were busy with people dressed in their smartest clothes, all heading to worship in their various locations. Simon was making for the main church, which stood level with the Hotel at the edge of the hill, on to which the town's residences clung. Being a little early for the service, he decided to have a stroll around.

The high street shops petered out and were replaced by tightly packed terraces of cottages. The road forked; the left seemed to house the more prosperous properties. Several large houses surrounded a small chapel, which was doing good business. The right option, a steep, cobbled, narrow street, led down to the Bridge. Another well-patronised chapel nestled in the gap between the houses and the picturesque river that cut through the valley. As the cobbles gave way to the tarmac of the Bridge, an Inn, closed for the Sabbath, sat in a silent vigil over the traffic and pedestrians crossing into the town from the nearby villages and farms. The tarmac surface followed the "New Road", which took an easier, less direct gradient back to the heart of the community and the church.

Steep steps brought him to the graveyard. Had they been able to turn around and rise from their eternal rest, the inhabitants would enjoy a commanding view of the valley, stretching all the way to the dark foreboding mountains in the west. A steady queue snaked its way into the church interior. Simon joined the procession; once again, he was the object of many glances, nods and knowing looks. He was quite getting used to being the centre of attention. Not wanting to push his way to the front nor hide at the back, Simon took a place on the end of a pew halfway up the aisle. The service was the usual format of hymns, readings and, of course, the inevitable sermon. The vicar, a scholarly-looking man, talked with passion but little skill about sharing our blessings amongst all of us and resisting the Temptation of taking more than our fair share. Simon wondered if the lesson was aimed at anyone in particular. He looked around for any signs of discomfort amongst the congregation; he could sense none. Nor was the vicar's gaze any clue as he looked only at his notes on the lectern.

There were a few of his new acquaintances from the last evening's revelry. Most seemed to be struggling to stay awake as the monotonous lecture droned on and on. Simon spotted Sara as she and another lady took the children away to the Sunday school. The Land girls were also present, although he suspected out of duty rather than enthusiastic free will. At last, the service concluded, and the faithful flock trudged towards the freedom of the doorway, each straining to contain their relief.

As Simon's eyes adjusted to the bright sunshine, the vicar pressed a cold hand into his and introduced himself. "Emyr Davies, very pleased to meet you. Nice to have a man from the senior service amongst us. I hear you are staying at the Hotel. I must remember to include extra prayers for our Navy at next week's service. Especially if you will still be with us?"

It was a searching statement, requiring Simon to state who he was, how long he intended to stay and the nature of his business in the area. Simon was minded about sticking to his interrogation training and just giving his name, rank, and serial number. This was good preparation for if he should ever be unfortunate enough to fall into the hands of the SS.

"Lieutenant Simon Lewis, I am pleased to meet you. Yes, I am convalescing and awaiting new orders, so I may be here for some time. It's a beautiful church, Reverend. Have you been here long?"

The man in orders smiled at the young man. "All my life, on and off, after some time abroad, I was lucky enough to be given a home posting, so to speak." Simon sensed that there was much more to that story, but this was not the time or the place for anything more than polite chit-chat. "You must come to tea one afternoon. I will introduce you to some of the community. Are you free on Tuesday? We usually take tea at 4. I trust that is convenient." Without waiting for an answer, the strange little man had moved on to greet some more of his congregation.

Many of the congregation had dispersed dinners to prepare, tables to lay, and perhaps some work on the farm, but only that which is permitted on the Sabbath. A few remained, idly chatting in the warm sunshine. Simon was not expecting to see any military uniforms; he supposed that most young men in the area would be either farmers and, therefore, protected occupations, or those who had joined up would be away. The uniform he did see was that of an Army Captain. The wearer was a man of not more than 35 years, tall, slim, and with a bearing that would have suggested he was a career soldier, even if he had been dressed in a nightgown rather than his smartest livery. He was marching, Simon supposed that he had not walked, or would he ever walk again, since his days at Sandringham, towards Simon.

"Good to meet you, old chap, Algernon Ernest Pritchard-Smythe. I know it's a bit of a mouthful; Mother was a fan of Oscar Wilde, a bloody silly name. Friends call me Ally. I am the Senior Officer at the camp just up the road. In charge of a detachment of Indian troops. Good chaps, once you get around the whole religion issues. Some of them are Christian, actually." The officer pointed to a small bunch of soldiers who were standing demurely away from the others. "Like I say, good chaps, though. Will you be with us long? Perhaps we could dine together one evening? It's so good to have a fellow officer to chat to. Most of the chaps around here only talk about farming. Personally, I don't know a scythe from a sickle. Not my thing. I say, do you play Tennis?" The monologue was produced in a single breath and left Simon feeling exhausted on his behalf.

"Yes, we must dine; that would be most agreeable."

Simon had not expected to meet Pritchard-Smythe quite so soon. Robinson and the Ministry had been concerned about receiving Simon's reports secretly. After all, letters could be opened, and telephone calls would be listened to. A radio was out of the question in case a nosy maid found it in his luggage, and he was suspected of being a 5[8] Columnist. So, an arrangement was made for Simon to pass on his reports through Pritchard-Smythe. Who in turn would telephone the reports directly to

---

[8] 5th columnist was a suspected organisation of German spies thought to exist in Britain during the early years of the war.

Robinson through a secure telephone line from his base. Simon and Smythe would meet secretly, 'by accident', on Simon's walks in the hills.

It surprised Simon that Smythe had approached him so openly, and his suggestion that they have dinner together seemed risky. But as he thought about it, he realised that Smythe was being rather clever. As both men were from a similar class—they were both military men—it might be thought more unusual if they didn't meet and strike up a casual friendship. It would also divert any suspicion if they were observed meeting out on a walk.

Simon knew that the captain's outward appearance as a dithering buffoon was somewhat erroneous. He affected the cloak of absurdity, but Simon knew from his Army records that he was an extremely capable officer. A brave and resilient soldier. His presence in the area was a happy accident. The detachment of men he commanded he had honed into a coherent and very proficient fighting unit, and they might prove useful if arrests had to be made.

'Wednesday evening would suit me best. Would it be all right if we dined at The Dragon? Our Mess chef has a somewhat limited repertoire, and whilst I do love curry, one dreams of an occasional home-baked Steak and Kidney pie. The wine cellar is somewhat depleted, I am told, but I do believe Mrs Williams has a small stock of 1929 Bordeaux; we might persuade her to let us have a bottle. Nineteen hundred hours at the Hotel, then. My treat, I insist."

Before Simon could reply, Captain Pritchard-Smythe turned on his heel and marched away towards the lychgate, his troops falling neatly behind him.

29

Don't drop me – East End London - 1941

Jim and Amber waited quietly as Bert positioned the ladder; they heard him climbing and could just make out his silhouette as he passed the ground-floor window. A head appeared through the opening above.

"The window frame and sill have been blown completely out up here, mate. The rope will be on the brickwork; try not to jolt the rope too much as you climb Jim. It looks a little loose in places." Bert's voice sounded worried.

"Well, you are full of cheering news today, aren't you?"

A short section of timber, attached to a rope, began to descend and soon extended down level with them.

"Lower it a bit more; it will need to be a little below us when you start to swing the rope. That way, I can catch the rope, and the timber won't hit us."

"Got it, mate. Are you ready?"

"Hang on. Amber, we are going to have to roll over to our right sides so we are facing the room, and I can catch the rope."

As they twisted onto their sides, Jim's heavier body was pushed further from the safety of the bar.

"Right, Bert, let's have that rope."

Bert was all too aware of the danger his friend was in, and he started to swing; as he did so, he pushed his body as far as he could through the window, trying desperately to get the cable near to the ambulance man's hands. The thirty seconds or so that it took for the momentum to build seemed like a lifetime. At last, the rope was within reach.

Jim caught the lifeline the first time with his left hand. As he did, he felt the floor below him move. It was no more than an inch, but it warned of further danger. He was about to call for his charge to hang on, but the girl had felt it too and had locked her hands around his neck.

He reached up the rope as far as he could with his right hand and grabbed the rough hemp. The pain was excruciating; it was like a wave that threatened to wash over him and carry them both away to oblivion. He desperately wanted to let go but knew he must grip harder. He had thought it impossible, but the agony increased. By the sheer force of his will, he held on until the pain subsided, and he felt he could continue.

He pulled as hard as he could, and the pair lifted off their deteriorating perch. Bracing his feet against the wall. He steeled himself and briefly let go with his left hand, the pressure and pain increasing on his right momentarily, agonisingly, until his left took over higher up the rope and relieved the torture. He shifted his feet up several inching steps before repeating the process. Agony, relief, agony, relief. Making minute progress up and across towards the window.

At last, they were within reach of their salvation. Bert called encouragement as Jim's feet came to the left edge of the window. "Do you reckon you can push off with your feet and swing through the window? I'll grab you as you do."

"I'll try anything once, don't drop us now."

Jim bent his knees and pushed as hard as he could. They swung back away from the wall.

Amber was holding on for dear life. Her head was swimming; the strain of holding on to her rescuer made the bump on her head throb. The scene around her was surreal; she could feel herself slipping into unconsciousness.

She spun upwards into the air, her body twisting as the strong hands threw her high towards the bright blue sky. She screamed in pleasure. The view before her whizzed by as blue became green and blue again. The hands, safe and secure, held her again before releasing her once more into the heavens above.

"Don't drop me, Daddy, don't drop me." She entreated.

"Never, sweetheart, never." Came the reply as she landed safely before being launched again.

"Oh, do be careful; she is so small." The voice, a voice she had known so well and missed so much now, the voice that had soothed her and had sung to her, begged the man.

"Do hush, dear. She loves it; look at her." Came the deep, sonorous voice.

Amber awakened towards reality and wished she was back in the dream. It was a dream she often had, a memory that came back to her over and over, and yet, one she never could hold on to after she woke.

"Don't drop me, please don't drop me" She whispered.

The pair swung out on the rope as Jim pushed off with his legs. Just as they reached the zenith of their backward trajectory, the rope jerked, and they fell down several feet. Jim looked up just in time to see 3 bricks falling from the window opening above. One of them grazed his right hand as it passed him, causing him to lose his precious hold on the rope. Their weights were both now hung from his left hand only.

Jim could feel that Amber was losing her grip around his neck. "Hold on Miss, hold on." He shouted desperately, powerless to help her.

"Don't drop me, Daddy, don't drop me." Her whisper. Barely audible to Jim as his heart pounded in his efforts to keep his grip.

Without warning, the weight from Jim's neck was suddenly released. Amber was no longer pulling at him. Desperately, he swung round and grasped wildly with his right hand towards his charge.

Jim felt his wrist strike the girl's arm and clutched at it with all his remaining strength. Looking down, he could see that she was barely conscious and would be of no help to him.

The muscles in his arms ached relentlessly as they were stretched taut by their combined weight, like overladen cables fated to snap. His left hand desperately clutched the rope above his head. His right hand, soaked in blood and sweat, grasped the girl's hand. The agony was indescribable, but never did he feel the temptation of letting go. How could they get to safety? He didn't know how long he could hold her, and there was no way to climb up the rope with just one hand.

Then he felt something gripping his left wrist and forearm. He looked up and saw Bert hanging down from the lower window. Precariously, all of his body and the tops of his legs projected through the opening. Jim realised that Bert was being held by Stan and another fireman.

"Can you reach the girl Bert?" He begged of his saviour.

"No, mate, can you pull her up a bit?" Bert knew it was an almost impossible thing to ask, but to his amazement, he saw the ambulance man strain and the barmaid lifting upwards toward him. "Miss, Miss, throw up your free hand."

No reaction; the barely conscious young lady swung motionless in her stupor.

"Amber, Amber," Jim called to her also. The Firemen holding on to Bert's legs and belt joined in the chorus of encouragement, as did two more of their colleagues who stood at the front door of the building watching the astonishing rescue.

Amber murmured, and her eyes flickered open momentarily. Her left hand reached achingly slowly towards the light coming from above.

"Get her, Bert. Let me go and grab her arm; I can hold on to the rope." Jim beseeched his friend. Bert hesitated, doubting that Jim had the strength left to take his weight again. "Grab her, Bert. Please just do It."

Despite a torment of doubt, Bert did as he was asked and clasped the girl's forearm with both hands. He was too far stretched to lift her, so he ensured his grip and ordered the firemen to drag him up. He felt their strength as slowly they reeled him in. His body painfully dragged over the rough masonry of the window opening. The girl's weight lifted from him as two men took the girl and completed her salvation. She spilt onto the pavement outside in an unconscious heap.

Bert turned back to his friend to help him, relieved to see that he was already climbing the rope and swinging his leg over the ledge. He took hold of his belt at the back and pulled.

Both men lay panting, battered and torn on the cold stone pavement slabs outside the destroyed building. A doctor was examining Amber. Jim crawled to her, not trusting his legs to carry him.

"Is she all right?"

"Concussion, I will need an x-ray, but I doubt there is any severe damage. What about you, mate? I better have a look at that hand."

"Nah, I am gonna get her over to the hospital; I will get looked at then."

The medical man didn't argue; he was being called by someone else, so he hurried off without further comment. Jim looked at the young lady peacefully sleeping on the pavement. Once more, he thought of his daughter. Amber stirred and was mumbling in her sleep. "Don't drop me, don't drop me."

"Never, sweetheart, never!"

30

Yet another invitation. – South Wales - 1941

Simon was following the Army officer through the churchyard when once again, he was waylaid.

"Henry Marshall, pleased to meet you, young man. Do forgive my impertinence, but are you the young fellow who has just checked in at the Dragon's Tail?"

"Simon Lewis, yes, sir, I am. I am pleased to meet you. Do you live locally, Mr Marshall?"

"In the next village, just across the river, you can see the house from here." Marshall pointed towards a large colonial-looking building that sat far enough up the hill to afford it a commanding view of the valley and Trefynydd. Spacious grounds and perfectly manicured lawns encircled the mansion. With fields below in which several horses enjoyed the sweet Welsh pasture. "I was just wondering if you would join us for Sunday Lunch."

"That is very kind of you, Mr Marshall; I should be delighted. How exactly do I reach your home? Is there a road from the bridge?"

"Ah, sorry, no. I meant at the Dragon's Tail. You see, I generally have lunch on Sundays at the Dragon with some friends. Today, it will be me, the General, and Sir Cecil Kege Le Burg. I am a bachelor, the General also, and Lady Le Burg spends most of her time in London doing charity work. So, we are all single gentlemen, so to speak, and prefer to enjoy Mrs Williams's excellent cooking and each other's company rather than dining alone on a Sunday."

"That sounds most agreeable, Mr Marshall. I guess I would be dining there anyway." Simon smiled.

"Then you must join our table. You may know that Mrs Williams will not serve alcohol on the sabbath, but she does turn a blind eye to Sir Cecil regaling us with a selection from his excellent cellar. Oh, and do call me Henry; no need for us to stand on ceremony. Although Sir Cecil likes people to use his title, I do believe that he even insists his wife uses it. Not that they converse that often. And the General is the General. I am not sure that I know his Christian name; I doubt he remembers it. Mrs Williams normally serves us at 3; we generally converge a little before."

31

A disastrous decision – East End London

Linda was a headstrong but a young lady who was not too bright. Her education had been basic; she could barely read or write. When she got an idea in her head, it was difficult for anyone to dislodge it, however preposterous or unwise it was. In service, she met Amber, and she followed her in leaving their unsuitable position. The Duck became her home. Charlie and Marge, her family. Amber her big sister, confidant, and advisor. The traumas of her childhood, of which she never spoke, were suppressed but not forgotten in the easy atmosphere and dependability of her new family. The bombing of the Dog and Duck, the loss of everyone she had loved and the stability they had provided upset the equilibrium of her existence. Her limited intellect could not make sense of the horror of her bereavement; her imagination turned to simple solutions to her plight.

The girls who had survived the bombing with her, due to the lucky chance of sharing a cigarette outside the back gate, did their best to look after her, but Her mind was made up; she thought she could make her fortune offering sexual favours to the sailors coming ashore at the docks. There was a market for that sort of thing, of that there was no doubt. Her dangerous ignorance of the brutality of such a place led her to think she could apply her rules to the services she was willing to supply.

She had been shocked by the aggression of the girls already plying their wares by the quaysides. It surprised her that they should object to her being there, totally underestimating the threat she posed as competition to their fading charms. They had laughed at her when she had told them that she was only willing to offer hand relief. Their feelings for her changed from resentment to fear for the misguided child once they realised that, essentially, that was all she was. They had reluctantly allowed her to stay, sending her to a distant corner. The pickings were slight, but eventually, her first customer came along, and her education in the reality of her new trade was swift and brutal. The man was tall, overweight, and powerful. His breath sank from the alcohol he had been consuming continuously for most of the previous 24 hours. He was on his way back to his ship, already late; he thought he might use up his remaining money on a girl. Linda explained the price and the limited service she was prepared to provide. He had other ideas, and whilst he was forcing himself upon her, he concluded that he could save his remaining money into the bargain. Linda fought with the brute but was no match for his strength and persistence. She screamed for help into the disobliging night air. As the man pawed at her body and tore at her clothes, she was transported back to her youth and the misuse she suffered by her uncle. As she had done then, she froze. No longer crying out and fighting, eyes closed tightly shut, she tried to imagine it wasn't happening to her. It was happening to some other poor girl. It was she who was enduring the pain and humiliation, not Linda.

Without notice, he stopped, and the weight of his foul body had been lifted from her. In disbelief, she cautiously opened her eyes. The man was propped against a wall, his legs barely holding him up, as another man was pummelling him with punches and kicks. It was a brutal beating, the man no longer offering any protection for himself as the blows reined in. His assailant was a younger man, as tall but many pounds lighter. He was well dressed, his stylish clothes well-tailored to his athletic body. The fight was all but over, Linda's saviour carefully picking his closing punches with the air of an artist who was loathe to complete his masterpiece. The pleasure being in the execution, rather than the result. A final swinging left hook wiped the rapist from the wall and sent him sprawling to the ground.

Linda still couldn't move as her hero strode to her. He moved with easy grace, unhurried, casual like a man taking a stroll through the majestic countryside. When he reached Linda, he extended his hand to her as though he was asking her to dance.

"Are you all right, Mademoiselle?" His accent was foreign, but his voice was calm and reassuring. Linda stared up at him, motionless and awestruck. He was, without a doubt, the most handsome man she had ever seen.

127

32

Sunday Lunch – The Dragon's Tail Hotel – South Wales - 1941

Simon could barely believe that he was about to sit down to another meal; his breakfast still sat heavily in his stomach. Although a quick nap, what his father would call "40 winks," had cleared his head, the chance to meet with some of the local dignities was too good to miss. It was a perfect opportunity to get the lay of the land and find out more about the community.

His host, Henry Marshall JP, was waiting in the lounge as Simon came down from his room.

"Ah, Lieutenant, glad you could join us. Snifter?" The businessman offered a hip flask to Simon, who politely declined. Marshall took a long draught at the pewter vessel, secreting it back in his jacket pocket just in time as Mrs Williams entered the room.

"Eleanor Williams, how radiant you look, as always. I swear you look younger every time that I see you. Is it not time that you bowed to the inevitable and ran away with me to wedded bliss?" Something about Marshall's speech caught Simon's attention. His accent was home counties and spoke of a good education. It was the phrasing that didn't ring true. The grammar was not quite right.

"Your worship, you ask me weekly, and I refuse each time. I would have thought that a man of your standing and experience would know when to give up."

"Please call me Henry. We are not in court, Eleanor. And I will never give up asking for the one prize that my heart holds most dear in life, your hand in matrimonial rapture. I will never give up, I tell you. While I breathe, I hope." The Magistrate's voice was serious and desperate in its sincerity, but there was a twinkle in his eye.

"Well, breathe away by all means, but don't hold your breath. And please, Henry, we are old friends, call me Mrs Williams."

The erstwhile lady, who had been attending to some details of the table settings, smiled with satisfaction at her rejoinder as she retired to the kitchen.

Henry winked and smiled at Simon. The discourse was clearly part of an extended exchange between himself and the landlady. Simon suspected that should the good lady accept one of the offers at any time, the gentleman would be horrified and sent into a blind panic. Equally, if the gentleman were to cease his barrage of proposals, the lady might feel somewhat slighted.

The General and Sir Cecil soon joined the men in the lounge. Introductions were completed, and, as Simon had expected, his cross-examination was started.

"I believe that you are Navy, young man and that you had the misfortune to be torpedoed." The General was to the point.

"Forgive me if I am a little coy in answering your question, Sir, but the powers that be are particularly insistent that we keep mum about such things. Suffice to say that I find myself without a ship for the moment and need to recuperate due to the manner in which I disembarked my last one." The men nodded in understanding, and the General seemed unperturbed by Simon's brush off.

"Quite right, young man, forgive me, but we are somewhat removed from the war here. We get the BBC news on the wireless, of course, but we old soldiers feel our frustration at not being on the front lines. Isn't that right, Sir Cecil?"

"Absolutely General. I do wish the military would make more use of us old soldiers. I'm sure that we can be of some good use." Sir Cecil replied, secretly quite happy to be sitting this one out.

"I'm sure the ministries will get round to it. Don't worry, general. I'm sure you'll see some action soon." Marshall assured him.

"I understand that you are commander in chief of the Welsh regiment. Is that correct, Sir Cecil?" Simon guessed that it would be a source of pride to the gentleman.

"Oh yes, but you understand that it is purely a ceremonial post." Simon wasn't sure if he detected regret or relief in the aristocrat's answer. "The General and I do have the Home Guard to keep us busy. Although we are constantly complaining that we draw the short straw when it comes to equipment. Undoubtedly, the war office doesn't think that Hitler will attack through Mid-Wales."

"I say perhaps I could help in the Home Guard whilst I'm here. I feel a little useless waiting around to get back to sea." Simon saw a chance to get more involved in the community.

"That's a splendid idea, I am sure that your attendance would be a boost of morale for the men." Enthused the General.

The meal was as generous and sumptuous as the breakfast had been. Sir Cecil had provided salmon, which his gamekeeper had caught and smoked. The main course was Lamb, again from the estate, cooked to perfection by Eleanor Williams. Dessert was Teisen Mel, a traditional Welsh cake made of honey, lightly spiced, and topped with cream.

Despite his doubts over his ability to eat another thing before the meal, Simon did justice to it. The flavours, freshness and rarity of the food tempted him into overindulgence.

As the main course was being cleared and the dessert was being served, the General offered the traditional toast to the King. Each man stood and dutifully repeated the tribute with enthusiasm. Then, in turn, additional toasts were offered. Sir Cecil warmly saluted the Navy in Simon's honour; naturally, Simon returned the gesture with his own offering to the Welsh Regiment. Eyes turned to Marshall, expecting his contribution. Standing, he said.

"Gentlemen, May you be at the gates of heaven an hour before the devil knows you're dead!"

The assembly rose and merrily repeated the toast. Marshall was an excellent host who was very generous with Sir Cecil's wine. Not that there was any objection from the knight as each glass was repeatedly topped up.

The conversation was easy-going, with much interest and many questions for Simon to answer. His carefully concocted story, based on his own real background, was comfortable for him to relay. The General and Sir Cecil were easily satisfied, both being only too keen to regale the party with their own exaggerated tales. Marshall was less forthcoming about himself, skilfully returning the conversation to the newcomer as often as possible. It was subtly done, clearly the magistrate was keen to learn as much as possible about Simon. Which left Simon wondering if Marshall was just an excellent host or if he had an ulterior motive for his curiosity.

33

Three square meals – London - 1941

Joe was settling into prison life quite nicely. It was nowhere near as bad as he had feared. The food was fairly decent. The violence, which would be the experience of many new boys, didn't come his way. The hard lads knew enough of his reputation to avoid chancing their arms in taking him on. He knew most of the East End boys. He had no enemies amongst them.

The screws treated him all right. He had thought that the charges he was facing might have tempted them into some retribution, as it had the Police in his holding cell on the night of his arrest. But a combination of them being a bit older (the younger ones having joined up) and perhaps their knowledge of the DCI, with his dubious arrest record, had stayed their hands.

Yeah, it is all right in here. He thought of the work that he had to do when he was released, and he wasn't looking forward to that. In the meantime, he could have a bit of a rest. Catch up on some reading, he wondered if they had any Sherlock Holmes books in the library.

"Get your gear, Turner, you're out of here." His relaxation was broken by the gruff voice of a prison warder.

"What you mean out of here? I just got here." Joe was none too pleased and a little worried by this sudden development. "Where am I going?"

"How the bloody hell should I know? What am I, the ruddy governor?" The officer grumbled. "Don't tell me nothing. Probably transferring you. They're moving as many as they can out into the sticks. Don't want the Luftwaffe cheating the hangman, now do we?"

Joe was led through a series of locked gates before the cheery man showed him beyond a door into what Joe assumed was the administration area. Another official took over the tour. They climbed a set of stairs and came out by a long corridor. Glass windows looked out across London, and the view was unencumbered by the usual metal bars. It seemed strange to Joe; funny how quickly you get used to something, he mused. Joe was shown into a windowless room; a table with a chair on either side were the only furnishings. The door closed behind him. Taking a seat, he waited patiently.

After half an hour or so, the door opened without warning, and the large figure of DCI Wilkinson strolled arrogantly into the room. Simon watched as the copper pulled back the other chair and sat silently opposite. Nothing was said. Wilkinson stared at Joe with all the intimidating intensity he could muster. It was water of a ducks back to Joe. He held his gaze and smiled pleasantly at the detective. A policeman stood across the doorway, arms folded. "Go and see if you can rustle up a cup of char, will you, Bob?" The request was more in the nature of an order to the uniformed man. The officer looked disappointed; he had been looking forward to the exchange between his superior and the young murderer. "Nice and strong and four sugars." All the time, Wilkinson's eyes didn't leave Joe's.

"What if they've got no sugar?" Asked the none-too-bright constable.

For the first time, Wilkinson's eyes moved from Joe's and onto the hapless man. He shifted nervously before making a hasty retreat away from the displeasure of his boss. As soon as the door closed, Wilkinson was all business. "Old Baker took the bait. He was beside himself with the thought of getting you in his clutches. Be careful, though; junior will be none too pleased. He'll hate the idea of you challenging his position in the hierarchy. He will be pissing in every corner he can find. Watch your back, son. You'll be out of here soon. Baker will send a team to pick you up. Officially, the witness who saw you leave the scene of the crime has chickened out. I am furious that my collar has wriggled off the charge. In reality, Baker has bunged me big time to get you off. You owe him your neck. He will want his pound of flesh. You'll be in on the inside. They will probably test your loyalty. Be careful; if they catch you out, the hangman will have seemed like the more genial option."

"Why, Bill, you really do care," Joe smirked.

"Seriously, son, you were a slimy little, light-fingered toe rag. But I hear you've changed your ways, and anyone with balls big enough to put themselves at the mercy of the Bakers is all right by me. Watch your back. I will keep my ear to the ground, but if things go tits up, I may not be able to help you. Trust no one. Now the copper will be back with that tea soon. Follow my lead; he's not the brightest, but he is in the Bakers pockets, so we need to put on a show for him."

"Cheers, Bill." Joe nodded seriously to the Inspector, his respect for the man beginning to grow.

The door opened and a mug of tea appeared on the table before them. "Where's mine?" Asked Joe.

"Piss off." Was the annoyed response.

"As I was saying, Turner. I will have you one of these days; you mark my words."

"Detective, you couldn't catch the clap from a two-penny whore."

"Yeah, well I might have caught it from your mother, but I only had a thruppenny bit, and she didn't have any change." Wilkinson grabbed hold of Joe by his collar and pulled him towards him until they were nose to nose. Joe could smell his stale breath, and spittle splashed onto his face as he spoke. "One day, son, one day."

He pushed hard at Joe, and the younger man fell backwards off his chair and onto the floor. Joe stayed there and smiled up at the older man.

Wilkinson spun on his heel and marched out the door; the uniform followed. "Bill, you forgot your tea." Joe called after him.

34

A Parisian saviour. – Ceylon Docks – London - 1941

Baptiste Barbeau rarely came to the docks. Most of his business dealings were conducted in more congenial surroundings. His clients of much higher social standing, girls younger and prettier, the rewards much more lucrative. A couple of Ted Baker's boys looked after the girls at the docks, but Baptiste liked to look in on them once in a while. Occasionally, it would be worth his while if there happened to be a new girl hanging around and she came up to the standards required for the brothel he ran. If he was honest with himself, he came to make sure that his girls were being looked after. Some of the Baker henchmen had a tendency to be over-violent with the ladies; he hated that.

Baptiste 'Bapt' Barbeau was born in Paris. His father, or so it was said, was an African prince and diplomat. His mother was French; she was a showgirl at times, but mostly, she was a prostitute. Other than these basic facts, he knew nothing more about his heritage. Bapt had grown up in a brothel, which had afforded him an unusual but never-the-less complete education at the hands of his 'girls'. He was a man of exceptional charm; with his striking good looks, he used them both to establish himself in Parisian society and, with it, the success and standing of the brothel. Unfortunately, his success attracted jealousy, and an altercation with a rival forced him to leave his home city. Baptiste had found himself in London starting afresh. Although he had some money behind him, he didn't have local knowledge. Consequently, He found himself upsetting another new rival; this time, it was Ted Baker. Only through his quick wit was he able to persuade his new enemy to hire him and his colossal talents.

Remarkably, Bapt talked himself out of danger and into a job. He told the gangster about how he had built his business in Paris and how he proposed to do the same in London. Only this time would he be protected by the most powerful gang in the city. He talked about how he would ingratiate his way into London society, as he had in Paris, and he would cultivate powerful 'friends' through the contacts he would make. Ted was convinced and so cautiously took Baptiste into his organisation. A suitable house was acquired, girls were selected, and new ones were conscripted. Clients were recruited subtly by word of mouth and personal invitation.

Ted Baker was impressed by his new employee, even Eddie took to Bapt, and they formed an unlikely friendship. As well as being able to befriend people of all social classes, Baptiste was particularly adept at engaging new young ladies. His method, simple but effective. Waiting at any of the major train stations, he would look for young girls arriving alone. Often, these were runaways who sought fame, fortune and romance in the metropolis. Convinced that they were bound for a career on the stage or even in motion pictures. He was also tipped off to any new girls asking for an audition at the theatres and theatrical agencies. His considerable good looks and charms were put to use, befriending and seducing the women. He preyed on the most vulnerable, those with poor educations, broken homes or those who were escaping abusive families. These were the easiest quarry for his kindness and allure. Once they were in love with him, it was amazing what they were prepared to do to remain in his good graces. The only constraint of his methods was that they were time-consuming and expensive.

When war came, the demand for their services increased rapidly. The acquisition of new young women had to be sped up. The answer to the problem was opiates. It wasn't suited if you wanted the girl to be charming, flirty and loving with the client. But for the customer who had more depraved tastes, a girl who was an addict would perform any act required.

Linda was intoxicated by the charms of Baptiste Barbeau almost immediately. After all, he saved her from her attacker at the docks. She had often dreamed of such a knight in shining armour coming to rescue her from her uncle, but that had never happened. Then he had taken her to a restaurant, wined, and dined with her. He promised her a job and somewhere to stay so that she would never have to return to the quayside.

After the meal, she felt very tired and drowsy. She completely trusted her saviour; she did not object to him taking her to the large house he claimed to be his home. She could hardly take in her surroundings as he led her through the hall, up the stairs to a small room at the top of the house. She was asleep on the bed before she was able to hear the key turn in the lock of the bedroom door.

Bapt would curry favour with Eddie by letting him be the first. He would alert his boss to the new arrival and advise him when the sedative would wear off. Eddie Baker took intense pleasure in the power of rape. For him, sex was never loving or giving. It was best brutal, humiliating, and violent.

After Eddie finished with Linda, he let Julia know that it was time for her to administer the next chapter of the initiation. Julia was an ex-nurse. Fired from her position for stealing drugs, she had fallen into prostitution. For years, she had been amongst Ted Baker's top girls. Age having caught up with her, she had found a use for her former vocation and now took care of the new recruits.

Julia let herself into Linda's room. Her soothing tones were well practiced at calming the girls. She would clean them up, tend to any injuries, and, most importantly, administer the needle.

The following days were a blur for Linda, as it was for all the new recruits. Needle, followed by unimaginable euphoria, rape (Baker's men taking turns as dictated by their precedence in the gang), another needle. It is said that addiction can take place after the very first dose is administered. Eddie found that the combination of violence, kindness and then opiates quickly became habitual, and his victim was soon craving its continuance. They were taught that willing participation in the sex led to the ecstasy of the opiate, and defiance led to the agony of its withdrawal.

Linda was swiftly led down this road to hell.

35

The first walk – Trefynydd – Wales - 1941

Monday morning, Simon woke with the feeling that he would have to work hard to make up for the weekend's excesses. He was looking forward to his first walk in the mountains. He had pre-empted the threat of another monster breakfast by asking Mrs Williams for a light meal in advance of his exercise. He managed to phrase it in such a way that didn't give offence. Nevertheless, the breakfast of porridge and toast was by any gauge substantial. Just for good measure, the redoubtable landlady made up sandwiches and cake for him to take with him for lunch. Ah, well, the extra weight would help him burn off calories.

Not feeling like much of a spy, Simon left the Inn just after 10 that morning. He tried to remember the routes that had been recommended to him by his new friends in the bar. He decided that his best bet was to climb the local mountain that gave the town its name, as it would give a commanding view of the immediate layout of the town and its surroundings.

He was greeted cheerily by the locals, some whom he had met, some strangers; all of them seemed to know who he was. It was a short walk to the end of the town, where a lane to the left took an easy gradient in the general direction of the Mountain. A mile up the track took him to a style from which an overgrown path snaked its way towards the summit. It was a hard climb. Simon was in peak physical fitness; the Major and his instructors had demanded nothing less at the spa. Also, he had walked in the mountains of India as a boy; the terrain there had been tortuous. Despite all of that he found the going hard. His legs had yet to acclimatise to the steep ground, the paths less accessible than they probably had been when more often used before the war.

It was worth it.

The mountain had slipped away from the side of a slightly more distant sibling sometime in the late Devonian period, circa 400 million years ago, or so he had read. Its summit was slightly lower than that of the more distant chain of hills that bled away into the distance. But the peak stood out from its neighbours because of its classic mountain shape. It pointed to the heavens, like the drawing of a childish imagination. A sculptured meringue of a mound, with only the very top levelled off, to create a small plateau. The path had taken him up to the base on the eastern side before cutting across the front and coiling around the back, spiralling him towards the plateau.

As he reached towards his goal, his view was restricted to the imposing wall of the mountains behind him and the path ahead, that purported to lead him ever higher into the azure of the sky. Suddenly, without warning, he reached his destination. As he stepped onto the plateau, an astonishing vista opened before him, revealing a panorama that was celestial in its beauty.

Simon tiptoed slowly across the flat surface, reticent to infringe on this breathtaking place. Each step revealed more of the view, each a new revelation of splendour. The ground sloped ever so slightly before suddenly falling away as he reached the plateau's edge. He sat and imbibed the view.

The town sat subordinately at the foot of the mountain. The inn, the church and the bridge set out in a neat soldierly row. Houses clung close to the security of these principal features, hemmed in by fields that flaunted greens of innumerable hues, overlaying the valley floor in a patchwork that spread to the east and west. A river cut across the scene. Sedate now, but mindful to roar and rage at will, self-satisfied that it, or at least its glacial ancestor, had cut a cleft through the rocks and formed this peaceful valley. Beyond the water, the ground rose again to an escarpment; a man-made scar had grazed the rocks, any ugliness now softened and palliated by nature's reclamation of man's exploitation.

White dots speckled the valley, farmhouses claiming ownership of the fields. Sheep and cattle were haphazardly placed, gorging the sweet Welsh grass, confined by neat stone walls that crisscrossed in ancient patterns. Simon gazed in wonder at the scene in a moment that was spiritual and stirring. He sat, barely moving, neglecting his purpose of mapping the land. Losing all sense of time, he had no notion of the presence behind him.

"Good afternoon, Lieutenant; it didn't take you long to find the best view in the area." A soft, chuckling, musical voice gently intruded into his reverie. Despite its placidity, Simon jumped from his seat, almost tumbling over the edge in surprise.

"Oh, I am so sorry I made you jump." The voice, concerned now at his precarious situation.

"Miss Lloyd, I am sorry I didn't hear you approach. I am afraid I was rather taken in by the view." Simon answered desperately, trying to recover his composure. He was musing silently to himself about his suitability as a spy. An enemy agent could have cut his throat while he'd been still admiring the view. He would have to up his game.

"May I join you?" Sara indicated toward a potential seat on the rock next to him. I brought lunch." She held up a package of sandwiches that mirrored his own.

"Please do; we seem to have the restaurant to ourselves." Simon was once again captivated by the girl's smile. "With plenty on the menu, it would seem." Holding up his own parcel.

Simon arranged his jacket on the rock where he sat so that Sara could also sit on it. She hesitated ever so slightly before taking her seat, the confines of the material drawing them closer than perhaps she was comfortable with. The young man blushed as he felt the warmth of her body so close to him.

"I do rather seem to have chosen a good place for lunch. Is this one of your preferred spots." Simon asked, desperate to start the conversation.

"It is my favourite spot in all the world. But then, I have not seen much of the world, certainly not as much as you, I suspect."

Simon conceded, "Yes, I have seen some very beautiful sights, but I am struggling to think of one as perfect as this." Again, he blushed as he realised that he was looking at the young lady; as he said this, he quickly turned to the view again. It had been said in all innocence, his words sincere and concerned with the countryside, but had it sounded like a tacky compliment. He needn't have worried. Sara hadn't noticed him staring, and her own thoughts were elsewhere.

"I have been coming here since I was a small child. Do you believe in heaven and hell, Simon?"

It was a strange question for such a conversation, especially so early in an acquaintance. Simon stammered to find a response, but before he could answer, Sara continued. "I used to believe that if there is a hell, then for me, it would be away from here. My punishment, if I sinned, would be for me never to be able to return to this valley. I wouldn't be able to stand that."

No answer was required to the assertion, no argument that could dispute the avowal and the pair sat in an easy silence for some time. Each of them was lost in thought, relaxed in their companionship.

"So, you must tell me all about yourself, Lieutenant Simon Lewis. Everyone in town is very intrigued, especially the ladies. If I don't provide them with some answers soon, I will be failing in my duty as the town's nosy barmaid. I will need full and accurate details with no exclusions; the smallest detail will be required. Believe me, they will want full chapter and verse." Sara's melodious voice, soft and engaging, broke the silence.

It was a voice accompanied by a smile, which would be almost impossible to refuse. "Well, really, there is not much to tell; what would you, I mean the town, like to know?" Simon's own voice filled with the mock levity of the moment.

"Now, it will not do to be coy, Lieutenant. Your public needs to know, after all you are the star man around here. People are talking of very little else, I can assure you. Perhaps if I interview you, like they do in those celebrity magazines, but you must answer my questions." Sara demanded with invented gravity, her charm so gentle and unassuming.

"All right, if you say so, Miss Lloyd, anything for my public." Simon was happy to join in the fun, but all the while trying to remember that he was there under false pretences; he was a lie.

"Good. Now, where were you born, any siblings, what does your father do, and how long have you been in the Navy? Do you have a sweetheart? Do you have hopes of a large inheritance, a heredity title perhaps? These are all things that your fans need to know Simon Lewis."

The pair fell into fits of laughter, the sound of which was as harmonious as the bird song that surrounded them in the picturesque Welsh countryside. They chatted easily, all the

141

awkwardness of their early acquaintance erased by their shared enjoyment of each other's company. They exchanged thoughts, hopes, and dreams as naturally as two people used to the companionship of a long and faithful friendship. They spoke for hours, time that flew by, seemingly in just minutes.

"Oh my, look at the time; my aunt will have my guts for garters; she will, too." In her excitement, her lyrical Welsh accent sharpened in its intensity. Like so much about her, Simon found it beguiling.

"May I escort you home, Miss Lloyd?" Simon asked gallantly. But he sensed a hesitation and realised that perhaps she did not want to share their assignation with the rest of the town. Innocent and accidental as their meeting had been, the gossips might prefer to make a mountain out of a molehill. "Or perhaps, if you are running a little late, you would be quicker than a sailor with a gammy ankle. Also, if you don't mind, I would like to take the longer path to the side, as it is less steep."

Sara looked visibly relieved, and Simon was confident that he had read the situation correctly. "Well, I am running a bit late, and I am sure you will enjoy that path; the bluebells in the woods there are just past their best but are still worth seeing. I must run; see you at dinner."

Sara skipped away, effortlessly descending the precipitous path with the ease of one who knew the ground intimately. In moments, she was gone from sight, and Simon felt the loss of her presence with regret; as beautiful as the countryside was, its splendour was diminished by her leaving.

36

The new boss – London - 1941

Joe walked through the gates and back into the real world. Except what was now his reality was a long way from the truth. He wondered where to go. Wilkinson had said that the Bakers would pick him up. No sign of them yet. Instinctively, he headed towards the east end, his old stomping ground. He had to see Amber; he was worried that he hadn't heard from her. At the same time, he wasn't looking forward to her finding out that he was going to work for the Bakers. She would be furious; there was no way to tell her the real reason; it would be too dangerous. He wanted her to stay away from him whilst he was undercover. If things went wrong, the Bakers would use her and anyone that he cared for to get to him.

He was not so lost in his thoughts that he hadn't seen the large car that followed him at a distance. It was a pretentious affair, all chrome and shine. Ted Baker was a showy git, he liked to prove to everyone he had money. The car was an American job. A Cadillac or an Oldsmobile, like the ones you saw in the Chicago gangster movies. It was a hundred yards back down the street. Any minute now, it would scream up the road, pull up alongside him, and a couple of Ted's heavies would bundle him into the back. Joe had other ideas.

He had been no more than strolling, deliberately going slow. Now, he sprinted, turning the next corner before the mobster's driver could react. Ducking down a side alley, he vaulted over the gate of a carpenter's yard.

Ted Baker swore at his driver. "Put your foot down, man; the cheeky bugger is legging it. Left, left, he went left."

Tyres screeched as the oversized vehicle struggled to grip on the tight turn. The road stretched out before them. No sign of their new recruit.

Joe quickly climbed onto the workshop's roof, dropping off the back into another alley behind. He turned left cautiously, approaching the junction with the main street. He was back where he had started, but there was no sign of Ted. He was no doubt looking down the next street, wondering where he had gone.

Joe jogged to the corner and peeped around. Sure, enough there was the chrome Goliath, stopped 50 yards further on. Two large men were reluctantly walking back to the car. "No sign of him boss."

Shouts emitted from the back of the vehicle, incoherent but unmistakably impolite and hostile to the news received. The men resumed their seats, and the car began to roll slowly forward, unsure how to proceed.

Joe crept towards the car, keeping close to the buildings and hoping not to be seen by the driver through his mirrors. When he was just 10 feet from the car, Joe marched briskly forward, opened the back door and jumped in.

"You looking for someone, Ted?" Joe was matter of fact. The ageing criminal was aghast by the sudden intrusion.

The goons who occupied the front seats tried to swivel around. Their big frames hampering any dexterity they may have had. The driver (on the left-hand side of the American imported car) had pulled a gun and was trying to aim it into the back compartment but was only managing to point it at his increasingly exasperated boss. Joe relieved the danger by grabbing the wrist of the bodyguard and pointing the gun at the ceiling of the car. He took the weapon from the hand and tossed it into Ted's lap.

"I think you need to review your security, Ted; with friends like these, you don't need any enemies. They're more likely to kill you than protect you."

Ted ignored the remark for now. "I was looking for you, you cheeky little brat."

"Well, here I am, Ted, large as life and just as ugly."

"You can say that again. I heard you have been away, Joe."

"Yes, I have been a guest of his majesty. Most congenial. Three square meals and charming company. I was just settling in when I was suddenly asked to leave. Shame."

"Yes, I heard about that. Little bird told me you had been a naughty boy. An old lady, no less."

144

"You know as well as I do that was a fit-up. I never hurt a fly."

"And yet the powers that be seemed to be certain of your guilt. Overwhelming evidence, they were saying. But here you are, as free as a songbird; I wonder how that happened?"

"Yes, I was a little mystified and then on the same day, I have the pleasure of your company."

"As much as I am enjoying this little chat, I am a busy man. Let's get down to business. DCI Wilkinson and I go back a long way. He owes me one or two favours, and I used my charm to persuade him to overlook your little indiscretion."

"Out of the goodness of your heart Ted?"

"You know me, Joe, always on the side of the little man. They say Charity is my middle name."

"Well, thanks, Ted. You are a gentleman. Do let me know if there is ever anything I can do for you. See you, Ted." Joe reached for the door handle.

"Not so fast, young man. Yes, there are plenty of things you can do for me; starting right now, you work for me."

"But we have discussed this before, Ted. You know I work alone. Thanks for the offer; it's nice to feel wanted and all that. But no thanks."

"Joe, don't waste my time. You know you have no choice. I am not asking; I am telling. You owe me, whether you like it or not, you work for me."

Joe sat silent. He knew he would have to capitulate; after all, this is what he wanted, but if he gave in too quickly, it might be suspicious. "Ted, I don't wish to appear ungrateful, but why do you want me? After all, I am not involved in the type of capers you are."

"Look, Joe, I know you have scruples about some of my business interests. You're right. I don't need you for them. I have the boys to cover them. Eddie oversees the girls and the protection. He's got it covered. The thing is, I want to expand into some new areas, and I need someone who is bright, careful and discreet."

"You going legit, Ted?"

"Not exactly, but yes, I want to move some of my money into kosher businesses. Don't get me wrong, lad, I am not going soft. You cross me..." Ted didn't finish his sentence. No need:

145

everyone knew what happened to people stupid enough to get on the wrong side of Ted Baker.

Joe nodded. "You know me, Ted; I am nothing if not an honest crook."

"Joe boy, I have watched you since you were a kid. You are careful and smart. You have a way with people. You have never trod on any toes. You haven't made any enemies. Well, except Backhander Bill, he hates you for some reason. Probably because he has never got anywhere near catching you. Until now, that is, and let's be honest, that was a fit-up if ever I saw one."

"You believe I didn't kill that old lady?"

"I wouldn't want you working for me if I thought you had."

Joe was shocked at what he heard, and it must have shown, as Ted was quick to explain.

"I know the reputation that I have, I have been working hard for a long time to build it. But have you ever heard of me harming anyone outside the game? There are no gentle little old ladies on my conscience. Everyone that I have ever had a disagreement with had it coming. Yes, I have hurt people over the years, but it is the business. They tell me that old dear you were in the frame for was beaten savagely. That's not your style. I might have believed it if she had caught you in the act; you pushed past her, and she fell. You know, an accident or something. I know you're a hard lad, but your no nutter."

Joe was seeing a side to Ted Baker that few if anyone, did. He had to admit that what he was saying rang true. His silence encouraged the gangster to continue.

"Joe, I have nutters working for me, I don't need any more."

Joe wondered if he was talking about his son, Eddie. Best not ask him that though.

"Like I say, I have been watching you. You have never had a conviction. You're as clean as a Bishop's joke. I want you to help me set up some businesses. None of my boys have the gumption for that sort of thing."

"What sort of businesses?" This was intriguing. Joe was eager to know if any of this had to do with the black market. He waited on edge, hoping he was not pushing too quickly.

"Building."

"Building, What houses and that? Doesn't sound like your sort of thing, Ted."

"Exactly, my boy, exactly." Ted smiled. Joe was starting to see that the man he had always regarded as the worst sort of thug was much cleverer than his publicity gave him credit for. It was becoming clear that this was a deliberate ploy on Ted Baker's part. A persona he had cultivated all his career.

"Look around you, son. London is in ruins. There are thousands homeless. When this war is over, whoever wins, someone is going to rebuild it. There will be contracts handed out like confetti. There will also be a shortage of builders. The profits will be immense."

"And you want to be in a position to cash in?"

"Yes, But the contracts will go to proper companies. They won't want to be dealing with unsavoury characters like me. I want you to buy up some of the older established building companies in the country. Good businesses with good track records. Only I want to do this on the quiet. I want to own them but not to be seen as owning them."

"I see where you are coming from. That will be easier said than done. We will need some good business advice."

"Yes, WE will." Ted smiled broadly at Joe. He had him reeled in hook, line, and sinker.

Joe smiled back. He was beaten, and he took it with good grace. "All right, Boss, when do we start?"

"No time like the present."

"I suppose you have the money for these purchases."

"Well, that's part of the problem. I have cash coming out of my ears, but I can't exactly keep it in the bank now, can I? That's another reason why we need some legitimate business advisors. You know anyone?"

"As a matter of fact, I just might, I just might."

"Good listen lad, I have a few things to do, and you must need to get your things together, sort yourself out. We will discuss all this in detail tomorrow night. You got anywhere to stay?"

"Not really, but I will find a guest house, no worries."

"Taken care of. I have a nice little flat in Kensington; it's yours. We also need to get you some new threads; I'll introduce you to my tailor."

"That's a bit flash thanks Ted."

"My pleasure, son. Now, can I get the lads to drop you somewhere to pick up your things?"

Joe had to think quickly. He wanted to keep his past life as separate from the Bakers as possible. That said, as Ted had told him, he had been keeping an interest in him for some time. No point in starting a lie that wouldn't hold up. "Yeah, thanks; Charlie at the Dog and Duck keeps a few things for me; any chance they can drop me there?"

"Bloody hell, lad, haven't you heard the Duck was bombed."

Shocked at the news, Joe couldn't think straight. He was silent for a long moment before he could collect his thoughts. "The Duck, bombed? Was anyone hurt, do you know?" He asked his new employer.

"I heard it was completely destroyed, full as well, they are saying."

"Poor old Charlie." Was the only reply that Joe could think of. He was really thinking about Amber. Was she safe, but he didn't want the gangster to know too much.

"Yeah, Charlie was one of life's gentlemen." Ted's comments amused Joe as he knew that the Baker's attempts to hustle Charlie for protection money had left a couple of the Baker's boys in hospital. Charlie might have been a gentleman, but he was not a pushover.

"Listen, Ted. If your driver can drop me over there, I might ask at the local Air warden's office to see if they have any news."

"All right, Joe. Come by the club tomorrow evening, and we will have another chat. Tell me about this business contact you have. Then you can move into your new gaff."

"Thanks, boss." The words felt like they might choke him, but Joe had to play the part now.

37

Good news at last – East End London

Half an hour later, having dropped Ted off at the nightclub he used as his office, the big car pulled up outside the Dog and Duck. Joe climbed out and thanked the driver. Keen to be on his own, he walked away from the vehicle, anxious that the thugs didn't see that his eyes were welling up at the sight of the old building in ruins.

Joe stood for a long time, looking at the one constant that had been in his life. He was not a fool. He could see that there was little chance that anyone could have survived, but he had to know for certain. There was a notice on the door prohibiting entry and stating that information about relatives could be obtained from the town hall or the ARP post. Knowing the area well, Joe noted the address and walked quickly in that direction. An office had been set up in the scouts' hall. Three Wardens and a couple of ambulance drivers were sitting around drinking tea. No doubt, they were preparing themselves for yet another busy night. Reluctantly, one of the wardens came across to the desk where Joe waited patiently. As he approached, recognition dawned in his eyes. There was no mistaking Joe Turner; those blue eyes were a dead giveaway.

"Hello mate, how are you? Not seen you around for a while."

"I am all right, Sid; how's that Mrs of yours? Still giving you grief about your horse being in her kitchen?" Sid Lawton was a milkman by trade, and it was no secret that he doted on his horse. One night, after a particularly enthusiastic drinking session with some mates, he had returned home somewhat the worse for wear. On checking that the horse was all right, he determined that the night was too cold for his equine co-worker to stay in the stable and decided to bring it into the kitchen. He heaped extra coal onto the dying embers of the fire and retired to bed. The next day, his long-suffering spouse had the shock of her life as she came sleepy-eyed to make the morning tea. Rumour has it that Sid and the horse kept each other warm at night, out in the stable, for some time after that.

"Don't remind me, mate, that woman's got no compassion for God's creatures."

Joe turned serious. "Sid, what happened at the Duck?"

Sid looked down at the desk, he found it impossible to meet those eyes as he explained. "Direct hit, mate. The phone lines had been down, and the warnings didn't come through in time. The sirens were only just starting when the bombs started hitting." Sid paused, embarrassed by the failure of the system. "The Duck was full. No one had any time to react. The whole of the bar area and the cellar was destroyed."

Joe fought his anger and grief. "Any survivors?"

"I'm sorry, Joe." The milkman and part-time warden could find no further words; he hated this part of the job.

"What day did it happen?"

"A week ago, Tuesday."

Joe realised the day he was arrested. It must have been not long after they took him away. He thought about the necklace he had left in Amber's pocket for her to find. He hoped that she had found it before the bomb hit. He hoped that she was wearing it when....

There was a long pause. "Thanks, Sid." Joe turned and walked slowly back to the dooor.

"Just a minute." One of the Ambulance men shouted to Joe. He had been only half listening to the conversation when he had heard the name Joe. "Sorry mate, were you asking about the Dog and Duck bombing?"

"Yes." Came Joe's eager reply.

"You must be the Joe she was talking about."

"Who, who?" Hope was beginning to force its way back into Joe's heart.

"We pulled a young girl from the wreckage. She kept talking about a bloke called Joe. Kept saying how he hadn't done it. How she had to go to him."

"Did she give her name?"

"Amber." The reply was swift; it was a name Jim would never forget.

150

Joe grabbed the man's arms and urged him for more information. "Was she alright? Was she injured? Where is she now?"

"She had a bump to the head. The Doc said she had a concussion. We took her down the infirmary. They would have kept her in a few nights for sure, maybe a bit longer. Part from that she would have been fine, I am positive."

Joe spun on his heel and raced out the door. He had to get down to the infirmary and find Amber. Pausing momentarily, he shouted back to the man, "Listen. If you see her before I do, will you give her a message?"

"Sure, I am not always here, but I tell the others."

"Tell her I am fine; they dropped the charges. I may have to go away on business for a while, but tell her not to worry. I'll see her soon. If she needs money, tell her there's some in the bank."

"I'll write it down, you get going. Go find her."

Jim stood smiling after the excited young man. Sometimes this job had its upside after all, he thought to himself.

38

Nowhere to stay. – East End London

Amber was right as rain when she left the Infirmary. The doctors had seemed quite worried by the blow to the her head, but the symptoms of her concussion had abated at last. After six days they had let her go. She was anxious to get out and find out what was happening with Joe. First, she would have to find a new place to live.

She'd had a few days to think about her options and her first thoughts were for her mates from the Duck. The girls had left, she was sure; they had wanted to get away before the sailors had got too frisky. The events of the night were hazy, but someone must have let them out the back door. It must have been Linda. Amber just had to check on her.

It was hard to look at the old building in ruins like that. It had been home to her; apart from the orphanage, it was the only home she had ever known. Marge and the Calamity were the closest thing she had ever had to family, them, and Joe. Now, her family had been torn apart. Marge and Charlie dead, Joe in prison. Linda might just have survived. She would look for her first. It wasn't that she didn't really want to find out what was happening to Joe. She worried desperately about the trumped-up charges that bent copper had slapped on him, but he was safe. At least for now. Linda, on the other hand, couldn't look after herself. She was a silly, flighty thing; who knows what trouble she would get into on her own.

Amber headed off to the scout hut, as Joe had done just the day before. Once again, Sid, Milkman, horse lover and ARW, was on duty.

"Excuse me, can you tell me if there were any survivors at the Dog and Duck?" Amber asked politely, embarrassed to interrupt the men's card game.

"Well, you are the second person to ask about the Duck. A young man was in here yesterday. Askin' after a young lady.

Name of Amber. Would that be you by any chance?" Sid smiled at the young lady; from the vibrant colour of her hair, he had no doubt about it.

"Yes, that's me." Amber was beyond excited.

"Yeah, Joe Turner was here. You were a barmaid in the Duck, weren't you?"

"Yes, yes, I was. Did Joe say where he was staying? Is he all right?"

"He's fine. There's a note here somewhere. Ah, here it is. He says that the charges were dropped. He will be away on business for a while. Oh, and there's money in the bank. He says he is fine."

"Oh, that's wonderful, that's so wonderful."

"If he comes back, what should I tell him."

"Tell him I am fine. I am looking for Linda. Then I will probably try and get a job at the Royal."

Long periods apart had always been a theme of their relationship. It always seemed to strengthen them. Make them appreciate the times they had together. If Joe had work to do it would be important, so she wasn't worried if it would be a while before they saw each other. There was no bank account, of course. When Joe had said the bank, he had meant his locker at the boxing gym. She had lost her key in the bombing, but the gym's proprietor, Raspy, would give her a spare. Amber lost no time in getting down to the gym. She only had the clothes she was standing in. She had no home, no job, no food, and no money, but as always, Joe was there for her.

The gym was in an old railway arch deep in the east end. It was run by a colourful character, the punters called Raspy. Mikhail Mihajlovic Medvedev was not an easy name for the locals to get their tongues around. Mikhail had come to London when the White Army was in full retreat in the early 1920's. He had set up the boxing gym, which was popular with the young men in the area. Mikhail would tell wild stories of his former life in Russia. He would boast of his exploits fighting the Red Army. He claimed that he had been with the Tsar's personal guard and that he had been captured defending the Royal family. Years in a prison camp followed before freeing himself from the clutches of the evil Bolsheviks, then escaping to England only when he had heard of the slaughter of his beloved Master and the whole royal family. He professed to be a close friend of Grigori Yefimovich Rasputin, the mystic and self-proclaimed holy man, a friend of the Tsarina. It was this that earned him his nickname, Rasputin. Which in turn was shortened to Raspy.

"Arrrhh, it is Amber. Is she not the most beautiful girl in London?" Raspy always spoke to people as though he was talking to someone else, someone next to him. A close confidant who must always agree with him. "This girl, she must be Russian, do you not think? Surely, she is Russian; she is too beautiful to be anything else."

"Hello Raspy, how are you?"

"I am better now that I am seeing you. This is the English expression it is?"

"Raspy, have you seen Joe lately?"

"No, Joe, not been here. I hear story that he was arrested but they have him no more the prison. This is true?"

"Yes, Raspy, the police tried to fit him up for a murder. I hear that he has been released, but I haven't seen him. You see, the Dog and Duck was bombed, so he doesn't know where I am staying."

"Yes, I hear that there was bombing, didn't I. Someone tell me, yes. Where is it that you are staying? You have place?"

"Not yet. I came to get into Joe's locker, he has left me money there. Do you have a key only I lost mine in the bombing."

"I will open, will not I? You must stay with the girls." Amber looked confused by Raspy's suggestion. "There are girls. They work factory but they have no home. Luftwaffe bastard drop bomb and they have no home. So, I make home in railway arch. Like gym. Beautiful home, very safe, very near shelter. You have friend there, err Julie. It Julie who tells me about bomb in Duck and Dog."

"Oh, Raspy, that's wonderful news. And I will pay you rent."

"Rent is not problem, no money, no rent for Girl of Joe Turner."

"Raspy, I must pay you something; I will have money; I must pay."

Raspy seemed adamant on the issue, but then he had a thought. "Julie will think that you are ghost. She told me

154

everyone dead in Duck. She will scream when she sees you, 'you are ghost' she will scream. Ghost cannot pay rent; do you not think."

The issue seemed to be settled for the moment, so the locker was opened, and Amber took from it only what she needed. Then the Russian led the way to a railway arch, three arches along from the gym.

Julie did scream and cried and then screamed again in delight at the return of her friend from the dead. When the screams had died away and the tears had dried, Julie gave a full account of the evening.

"We wanted to get away; the sailors were getting a bit too friendly. Linda let us out the back door and came and had a fag with us outside the back gate, in the alley. We'd just lit up when the sirens started; we thought we had loads of time. But then the bombs started dropping immediately, getting louder and louder. Then they hit the Duck. We was lucky as the explosion was in the cellar. The back wall of the building stayed intact. Course, the windows all blew out, but the yard wall sheltered us all from the flying glass. One of the firemen, a bit of a dreamboat he is, looks a bit like Ronald Coleman, said that I was the 'luckiest girl he had ever met', mind you he just might get lucky on Friday night when he takes me out." Julie melted into a fit of giggles.

"So, you were all safe, Linda, as well?"

"Yes, love we were good as gold. We brought Linda back here. We knew Raspy wouldn't mind. He is such a love. Hardly charges us any rent. Not that it's the Hilton, but it's dry and warm. I've been here since my old Mam's house got bombed and she went to stay with her sister in the country. She wanted me to go with her. Me in the country, imagine that. Not ruddy likely, I says." Julie giggled again.

"So, Linda is here now."

"No love, she is not. Bloody stupid little thing." Amber was beginning to worry for her young friend. "We tried to talk sense into her, honest we did. But you know what a flibbertigibbet she is." Julie was embarrassed to tell the story; she clearly felt guilty that she had not done more to stop the impressionable young girl. "Look, Amber, we couldn't stop her. She went out three nights ago, and we haven't seen her since."

155

"Julie, honestly, I don't blame you. I know what she is like when she gets an idea into her head. Where did she go?"

"She went down the docks. She got this idea into her head that she could make money, you know, with the sailors. We told her it was dangerous, but she insisted that she would just be doing, you know, hand relief." Julie made a gesture with her hand that left no ambiguity to her meaning. "She has it in her head that it's less dangerous; she said she would charge less but get through more punters."

"But she will get into trouble with the girls down there. They won't like the new competition. What is she going to do if the punters want more?"

"Honestly, Amber, we told her all this. Pleaded with her we did, ask Jenny and Jess."

39

The Inspector – Mynydd Farm – Wales - 1941

Gethin Bevan was a proud and excited man. He was proud because he was driving his almost new Morris Eight, and he was excited because he was driving it to Mynydd Farm to see the woman he had loved since he was a boy.

Gethin had grown up in Trefynydd. His father had been an auctioneer at the nearby livestock market. To his own immense disappointment, Gethin had been a clever boy and had been sent away to boarding school. The reason for his disappointment was that he would be away from Myfanwy Davies, the love of his young life. As he expected, in his absence, her heart had been won by Dai Thomas. What she had seen in the dunce, he had no idea. She could have had a much easier life with him. He had gone on to university and now had an important job with the Ministry of Food Production. He was the farm inspector for a large area of South Wales. He had a good salary, a pension, and his new Morris. What had that dullard given her? Hard work and a miserable existence. True, he had been a good farmer in his day, but his injuries from the Great War had turned him into an old man with a weak mind, a laughingstock. He was no husband for a woman like Myfanwy. Everyone reckoned he didn't have long for this world; the mustard gas he breathed in the trenches of France was still eating away at his lungs. It would not be long before Myfanwy would be a free woman, and Gethin was ready to make her his wife.

Gethin parked in the farmyard and marched expectantly to the farmhouse door. Myfanwy was waiting for him. She greeted him coldly, he didn't mind, it was her way. A front she put on for the world to see, but he knew that she loved him, that she was ready to right the mistake she had made all those years ago. She had told him as much in so many words. First, they had to make their fortune, and then they would be ready to start a new life together in Canada.

"Come through to the kitchen, Mr Bevan. Would you like tea?" Myfanwy walked quickly ahead of the inspector. "Alwyn, Mr Bevan is here. Have you finished your tea? Good, take the girls and carry on with your work. Mr Bevan and I must go over the ministry paperwork. Where is Rosie?"

"She is chopping up the tree we felled," Alwyn said with an air of resignation. It was a bone of contention for him that Rosie could weld an axe far more efficiently than he could. He was getting a little tired of the others teasing him about it.

"Good. Now away with you all. There's work to be done." Myfanwy instructed as she busied herself, making more tea.

Gethin waited for the noise of the youngsters to subside as the back door closed behind them before moving across the room to his love. He stepped up behind her and threw his arms around her, pressing himself against her back. Roughly, he fondled her sizeable breasts whilst kissing her neck passionately. For a moment, Myfanwy let him have his way. He was an unskilled lover, but she revelled in the attention he gave her. It had been some years since Dai had been capable or interested in her. She missed the days when they were first together as lovers. It was before they had married, each month had been a tidal wave of emotions, fear and guilt. Fear of being caught by their parents, fear of becoming pregnant too soon before their planned wedding. Emotions of the passion and love they had for each other. Disappointment that the relief of not being pregnant only barely hid her real feeling of regret for the child that she longed for so much. Guilt that they were sinning, breaking the word of the lord.

Gethin was trying to lift her skirt, It was time to cool his ardour, she thought. "Enough of that, Gethin Bevan; you know I will not break my vows to God. They are sacred and never to be taken lightly. I trust you will not break those vows when we are married?"

"Of course not, my love, you know I wouldn't," Gethin replied, his voice filled with hurt.

"And yet you expect me to break mine." Myfanwy admonished. She looked at his face, a mixture of disappointment

158

and shame; he had the expression of a small boy who couldn't have his way. He was such a weak and pathetic man, she thought. But he had his uses, and she needed to keep him strung along. How on earth did he expect that she could love a man like him? He was a fool, a useful fool, though. "Look darling, there will be plenty of time for that soon. I promise it will be soon, and we will have all the time and money we need to be together. Now, did you bring the paperwork and the figures?"

"Yes dear, they're here." Bevan pointed to two buff-coloured files that lay on the table; his expression had turned to that of a puppy keen to please its master. "Shall we go through them now?"

"No, let's walk over to the quarry. I want to show you the barns we have reroofed ready for the animals. We can have tea when we get back." Myfanwy wanted to get out in the fresh air. She had to admit that Gethin's touching had excited her. Perhaps she would let him have his way with her when they reached the barns. No, she had to stick to her role as a god-fearing married woman, but possibly she would let him touch her, and she would touch him. That would keep him in line; after all, he was breaking the law for her.

40

A Dockyard Search – East End London

Amber left Julie promising to return later to move into her new home in the Arches. She was convinced that Linda was in trouble. She hadn't been seen for 3 days, and that didn't bode well. The evening was approaching, and she hopped onto a bus down to the docks. It was a search as difficult as looking for a needle in a haystack. The London docks stretched for miles, but Amber had a hunch that Linda would have headed for one particular dock.

On an afternoon off, just before the war, Amber had taken Linda to see the docks. They had walked along talking about the boats. Where they were from, where they had been. What did they carry? Linda had been entranced by the romance of the place. They had bought cockles from an old lady who bore a basket seemingly bigger than it was possible for her to carry. Linda had talked about everything they had seen for weeks afterwards. Linda had particularly liked the Ceylon Docks. Amber had told her that the boats brought Tea in great quantities. Linda had speculated that all the tea in China must come through the Ceylon Docks. Amber hadn't the heart to tell her that Ceylon was nowhere near China.

The security around the dock was heavy, but the guards were always relaxed about letting the girls through to ply their trade. Only a few of the ladies had arrived. They eyed Amber cautiously as she strode towards the group.

"Piss off bitch. There's no room for you here." A tall lady, hands on hips, stepped forward menacingly. She had the air of someone who had very little, but nevertheless, she was prepared to fight to hold on to what she did have. Her dress hung from her loosely, having fitted her in former, happier times. Her make-up was garish in the early evening light. It failed to mask the harsh lines etched deep by misfortune and deprivation. Her rouged cheeks and violently red lips artlessly professed her vocation. Her friends, in coordinative attire, nodded their agreement with their spokesperson's statement. Amber didn't doubt their sincerity, nor did she doubt her own precarious situation.

"I am not here to work. Honestly. I am looking for a friend. A young girl, dark haired, my height, pretty. She said she was coming down here to work. Only she isn't meant to be here."

"What too good for the likes of us is she your friend, and I suppose that goes for you too." The spokes lady defiantly stood taller, aggressively sticking out her chin and folding her arms with determination.

"No, it's nothing like that." Amber knew that she had to be careful not to further antagonise her. "It's just that she is so young. She has no idea what she is doing, what she is getting into."

Amber felt a softening in the woman's harsh stare. Perhaps she was thinking of her own youth, regretting that no friend had ever come to save her from places like this. Her lieutenants caught her mood, each moodily submerged in their own reflections and regrets.

"When was she here? Your friend?" Asked the woman.

"Three days ago." Replied Amber, hopeful for their help.

"Dark-haired girl, you say?"

"Yes, yes, pretty." Amber bit her lip, wondering if emphasising her friend's girlish beauty was too much of a slap in the face for the well-used professionals.

"She was here." The words came reluctantly from her lips. Lips that didn't freely speak. Lips that had learned through life's hard knocks that giving out information was not wise.

"Do you know where she is now?" Amber's words were desperate and pleading.

The three girls stood motionless and silent. The two subordinates waited for their principal's decision. The leader looked intensely at Amber. Judging whether to tell. Amber waited respectfully, knowing that pushing home her point would be counterproductive.

Two sailors ambled by, idly checking out the girls. Seeing what they expected, experienced enough to know perhaps that they would look prettier later, when they happened upon Amber. Their eyes lit up like they were art dealers who had just found a Cézanne on a market stall. They were about to speak to Amber, but she stared at them, flicking her head, beckoning them to move along. The stall is closed today, boys.

"She was here." The words came slowly, hesitant, but prepared to help. "We told her to bugger off, but she was, you know, she looked lost. So, we said she could stand over there." The girl pointed; Amber looked in the direction. It was the last place in the line, the back of the queue. The other girls would get to pitch their wares to the sailors before Linda. "She kept saying that she was just doing hand jobs. We said that she wouldn't get away with that. We tried to keep an eye on her, only it was busy. She must have picked up a punter. Next, we heard her screaming. The punter was slapping her about; looked like he was ready to give her a good going-over. It happens, you know, when they don't get what they want or if they can't manage it, you know." The woman paused, thinking perhaps of times when it had happened to her. Amber waited patiently. "That's when Bapt turned up. Bapt can handle himself, and he gives the sailor a good hiding. Course your mate is grateful to him. She goes off with him. And that's that. She Bapt's girl now."

"I don't understand; who is Bapt?" Amber was frightened that she knew the answer.

"Look, girl, I know you are looking out for your pal, but you need to leave it at that. People who mess in other people's business around here get hurt."

"I must find her, please. I can pay." Amber's desperation was obvious, but the girls knew they had already said too much. Before Amber could say another word, they had turned and disappeared into the gathering darkness.

Dejected, Amber retraced her steps and took the bus back to the Arches. Nobody was at home, but a key under a brick let her into her new home. She had nothing to unpack, and the stores would all be closed now. She felt grimy and unclean, still in the same clothes she wore the night of the bombing. The nurses had kindly repaired and washed her dress. But she felt like she never wanted to wear it ever again. Washing and tidying herself up as best she could, she helped herself to a change of clothes from Julie's things. Her friend wouldn't mind, and she would make it up to her by treating her to a shopping trip. Now, she realised that she was hungry, starving, in fact. There was a chippy just a few minutes' walk away. If she were quick, she would catch it before it closed, ready for the evening's bombing. Walking through the dark streets, she wished Joe were here. He would know what to do and probably know who Bapt was. Then it hit her. Raspy might know him. Amber didn't know where Raspy lived, but she knew he drank in a little bar on a side street off the Mile End Road. It was owned by a Russian like him, and they would drink into the night, reminiscing about the Motherland. Amber quickened her pace.

41

Time passes slowly in the country – South Wales

Simon's life settled into an idyllic mix of walking and socialising in the friendly, relaxed South Wales community. He walked in the hills most days. Often meeting 'accidentally' with Sara on his travels, frequently joined by Cae, who would turn up and walk with them before slipping away back to her master's side. As old Dai's health deteriorated, her devotion to Simon increased. He dined with the gentlemen every Sunday. Drank with the farmers of an evening, especially on Saturdays. He was invited several times to speak to the ladies of the Women's Institute; the subject seemed immaterial as they sought his charm and good looks much more than his wisdom. He played tennis with Pritchard Smythe, who would take his regular reports back for transmission to Robinson and the Major. He helped with the Home Guard; the men keen to learn of the state of the war in the Atlantic. If he had been the convalescing Naval officer he portrayed, he would indeed have found the holiday extremely beneficial to his health, but he wasn't, he was a fraud, a spy. Worst of all, he was a spy who was failing. He had found no sign of any conspiracy of any kind. It was true that the area seemed to be abundant with food, with no sign of any shortages except perhaps alcohol and fruits not native to the area. He had even been able to get some petrol for his motorbike 'off ration' through Henry Marshall's friend at the local garage. Illegal, but hardly the crime of the century. He had participated in the transaction to try and engender an air of normality about his character. He wondered if he had not been working for the Major if he would have gone through with such a clear breach of the rules. Surely, his patriotism and sense of fair play would have stood in his way. But he loved to ride 'Sunflower' his Vincent motorcycle, such temptation would probably have allayed his guilt.

He had concerns about his relationship with Sara. There had been no impropriety; however, it was evident to both that they were developing feelings for each other. He worried that it was unfair, perhaps even cruel, for him to allow such a closeness to exist based on his falsehoods. He rationalised that it was part of his mission to develop any and all associations that might help him towards the information that he needed. But she had been of no help in that way, and yet he continued to selfishly enjoy her company. The only mitigation that he could call upon in his defence was that she had searched his room. The action perhaps of someone who was involved in a criminal conspiracy and was charged with finding out more about the stranger in their mists. Was she under instruction to stay close to him and delve into his secrets? Or was she just a girl interested in a man and keen to make sure that he had no skeletons in his romantic cupboard?

He was desperate not to fail on his first mission. Though both Robinson and The Major seemed quite happy for him to remain in post. There had been no recriminations from them for the lack of progress. Not for the first time he wondered if his real role in all of this was as a distraction, a misdirection as some other operative did the real heavy lifting.

42

The Infirmary and a bed for the night - London

Joe spent a long hour waiting for news of Amber at the infirmary. Eventually, he was told that she had been discharged on the afternoon of the sixth day after her admission. Joe had missed her by just a day. She had a serious concussion, cuts, grazes and bruises but no fractures. They had kept her a little longer than normal as she had nowhere to stay. There was no forwarding address. A note on the file said that she had been directed to the council offices for re-housing.

He knew he had little time to make a search for Amber. He had to get on with his mission. She would be fine, he was sure. She had plenty of friends and could look after herself. He was also sure that she would look for him. He would think of a way to get some money and a note to her.

Right now, he had to contact the Major. He had an idea of how they could further infiltrate the Baker's organisation and needed to get things in motion.

Having spent the next 30 minutes making sure that he wasn't being followed, Joe took a chance and stepped into a phone box. He rang the number Whitehall 3633. The call was immediately answered, and he pressed the A button[9].

"Hello, is that Baxter House?"

"Yes, Sir, how may I help you."

"I was recommended to you by a friend, Mr Wilber, and I wondered if you have a room for the night?"

"Just one minute, sir, I will check. May I take your name?"

"Yes, it's Turner, Joseph Turner."

"Please hold Mr. Turner."

---

[9] In the old-style telephone boxes, you were required to press a button marked A to connect the call when it was answered or the B button returned your coin if there was no answer.

Wilber was the Major's middle name. The code meant that the caller would be immediately directed to his office, or, in this case, Baxter House. The line clicked, and he knew that his call was being transferred.

"Hello, Mr. Turner, this is Mrs Craddock. Yes, we do have a room, and any friend of Mr. Wilber is most welcome. Will you require an evening meal?"

"If you might manage it at such short notice, yes, please, that would be lovely."

"We eat at 7:00 p.m. I trust you will be on time, as we cannot keep the other guests waiting. I hope you don't mind eating with the others."

"That would be most agreeable; where I have been lately, intelligent conversation was in somewhat short supply. I am sure your other guest's colloquy will be most stimulating and informative."

Through this discourse Joe had requested a meeting with his handler, Susan Cartwright. He had indicated that he had information and required assistance but that he was not in danger.

After the usual polite exchanges, Joe left the phone box and set off towards Baxter house. His route was circuitous, ensuring that he was not being followed. He arrived in the late afternoon, immediately being shown into a room and met by the Major and Susan.

"In trouble already, Turner?" the Major asked, smirking.

"No, and thank you for that vote of confidence in my abilities. Actually, things have gone rather well, and I think I have a way to get the low down on all the Baker's activities."

"Please be careful, Joe. These people are very dangerous, and you mustn't push too hard; they will become suspicious." Susan Cartwright, like many women, was very fond of Joe.

"Sue, you are so sweet," Joe smiled at Sue, causing her to blush under the effect of his hypnotic eyes, "but this is a golden opportunity. Ted Baker asked me if I had any legitimate business contacts. He is trying to clean up his business dealings and wants me to help. I told him that I might know someone. We are to discuss it tomorrow evening. I need to come up with a respectable businessman who is a little indiscreet about what he keeps in his safe."

The three discussed the details of Joe's idea well into the night.

43

Chopping Wood – Mynydd Farm – South Wales - 1941

Rosie loved chopping wood. The power of the axe as it split the solid logs was intoxicating. The skill she had developed in placing the axe head precisely in the right place excited her. She was in control, master of the powerful blade. The wood store was at the far end of the farmyard from the house, and as Rosie was lining up another log for division at the hands of the axe, she saw the back door open. Myfanwy came through into the yard followed by a small bespectacled man, who wore an ill-fitting grey suit and a bowler hat, attire designed to impress perhaps but incongruous to the setting of a Welsh farm. So, this was the inspector from the Ministry of Food. The girls had been laughing and joking about the man all week, ever since Myfanwy had announced that he was to visit. At first, Rosie had ignored their giggling gossip, but her ears had pricked up when they claimed that he was Myfanwy's lover. Looking at the man now, Rosie was even more dubious of their claims. He was an insignificant-looking man; he carried himself along with a pompous and swaggering gait, which was clearly affected. His idea of portraying his own self-importance, surely. Although Myfanwy Thomas was a lady who life had used harshly, there was no doubt that she had been, and to some, would still be, an impressive and attractive woman. She had heard tell of old Dai's good looks. Indeed, their wedding photograph on the mantelpiece showed a handsome-looking couple. If Myfanwy, notwithstanding her Christian values, were to take a lover, surely it would be a more worthy man than this one.

Rosie watched the couple carefully whilst still appearing to be engrossed in her activities. Myfanwy was marching away with her usual determined, no time to be wasted, demeanour. The little man was talking incessantly up at her whilst trying to maintain his exaggerated stride, all the time falling behind her pace.

Myfanwy stopped and pointed at the man's shoes and then the briefcase whilst clearly berating him. Unfortunately, the distance between them meant that there was no chance of Rosie hearing the exchange, but Myfanwy's bearing told of her frustration. The man ran to his car, unlocking it with clumsy fingers; he pulled a pair of boots from the rear footwell and left his case in the car. With more suitable footwear, he chased after the lady, and they both disappeared along the path that led to the fields away from the farm.

Rosie was confused. She had been told the man was due to come to inspect the animals on the farm. Duly, they had been collected together in the two fields closest to the farmhouse for his convenience. The direction they were taking took them to a part of the farm that was currently not being used, or so the Land Girls were led to believe. What was it that the inspector was going to inspect? It was time to have a nosey around.

Rosie took one of the logs and, with her knife, peeled off a splinter of wood, carefully putting it into her pocket. She sprinted across the yard to the car. Surely, she would have plenty of time; the 'loving couple' would be away for a while. The other girls and Alwyn were in the lower field and would not be back until teatime. But it was better to be safe than sorry, so she would be as quick as she could be. The lock of the Morris was easily overcome, not a good omen for a vehicle that was being used extensively by the services. The briefcase was not locked but contained nothing of interest. Rosie relocked the car and made her way to the kitchen. There on the table were two official looking files.

Rosie checked the window that overlooked the farmyard. All clear, she returned to the files and began to read the first one. It contained a series of documents, each of which seemed to detail the livestock holdings of a particular farm. There were statements about the breed, numbers, and values of the animals. Along with a checklist of inspections that had been or were due to be made. There were entries of expected yields for arable land held by the farm, along with dairy output. Each document was 3 or 4 pages long, pinned at the corner, and seemed to relate to a particular farm. All carefully typed. Everything seemed to be in order and what might be expected of the paperwork carried by a farm inspector. Although Rosie wondered why an inspector would carry all the figures, for all the farms together. Surely, when visiting a farm, as he was at the moment, he would only need the figures for that particular farm. Rosie turned to the other file. It contained carbon copies of the papers in the first file. Only these copies were covered by handwritten notes. Certain figures had been crossed through, and a pencilled figure had been written next to it. In many cases the new figure was an increase on the original. They all related to livestock numbers. At the back of the folder there were several sheets, pinned together and entitled, summary. These summaries were for each type of livestock, lambs, chickens, beef etc. and were made up of a table that showed the name of the farm, the number of beasts, the 'actual' number and the 'surplus'. The 'price to be paid' for the surplus was also stated, together with the 'expected market value'.

Rosie was in little doubt about what she was looking at, this was a plan to defraud the system of a considerable amount of farm produce. The original figures were obviously the official output from each farm. The farmers would be paid at the fixed price as stated by the Ministry of Food. The notations on the copies showed the extra production; on average, these appeared to be 10 per cent higher than the original figures. The figures notated 'price to be paid' clearly showed the value of the animals at the rate to be paid to the farmer; these were between fifty to one hundred per cent higher than the ministry rate, although some had no increase at all. The 'expected market value' was marked up another one hundred per cent, the price the conspirators were expecting to achieve on the black market.

The profits were immense. Each beast was selling for 3 or 4 times its normal value. Add to that the markup of the middlemen, the restaurants, the shops, and the butchers selling under the counter. Would people really pay 5 or 6 times the price for fresh meat? Rosie knew that not everybody would or could. A lot of people would be appalled by the very thought of this profiteering, but equally, she knew that there were enough people who would.

Rosie needed to make a note of all these details, but there was not enough time. At the 'Spa', she had been issued with a miniature camera; it was sewn into the bottom of her rucksack. It was risky but she ran to her bedroom to fetch it. There was too little time to copy everything, so she started with the summary sheets and then a random selection of the detailed notes. Whilst she was leafing through these, she noticed that on the sheets where there was no increase in production there were additional notes, in a different handwriting, in ink rather than pencil, written next to the name of the farm. The notes referred to the farmers themselves and were comments such as, 'Gryff won't participate, his wife is very religious' or 'Don't ask Thomas, his son is a policeman'. Rosie couldn't be sure, but she suspected that the writing was Myfanwy's. So, she was behind all this? Using her knowledge and friendships of local farmers she was encouraging them to falsify the numbers of their stock, selling the extras to her. The inspector was using his position to adjust the official paperwork. Rosie had an idea. Quickly, she went through the figures again; in some of the sheets, the price to be paid to the farmer was the same as the ministry rate. Could it be that these farmers were unaware that some of their herds were being filtered off into the black market? No doubt, the inspector would provide them with paperwork reflecting the number of animals they supplied. But the paperwork filed with the ministry, along with the animals delivered to the official slaughterhouses would be lower in number. The extra stock was delivered elsewhere. So long as the farmers got the money, they thought they were due, then there would be no problem. How the ministry paid the farmers, Rosie had no idea; if they received a cheque, then the difference must be made up in cash. How they were explaining that was a mystery to Rosie, but she was sure that they would find a simple enough way.

Time was marching on, and Rosie was worried that she had overstayed her welcome; as she photographed the last page of the summary, she heard her name being called from across the farmyard. She quickly rearranged the papers into the file and carefully put the folders back exactly as she had found them. Again, her name was called, louder and nearer this time, it was Dot's voice calling; she and the others were on their way back from the bottom field and finding her missing from her post at the woodshed, they would be looking for her. Having exhausted the outbuildings, they would no doubt come to the house. She had very little time and needed an excuse for being in the kitchen, a place they were not supposed to be except at mealtimes. Rosie took the wood splinter from her pocket and braced herself. She jabbed the sharp point of the wood deep into the fleshy part of her hand. Immediately, blood poured from the wound, and steeling herself again, she pushed the splinter in deeper. More blood ran down her arm; she encouraged a little more to flow by squeezing the incision, deliberately dropping blood onto her work clothes. Satisfied that the effect was sufficiently gory, Rosie stood by the sink.

"Rosie, where are you?" Dot's calls were being echoed by the others as they came through the door.

Dot ran to her when she saw her. "Oh, my giddy aunts, what have you done?" Dot was keen to help her friend but was discouraged when she saw the blood.

"Oh, it's just a little splinter. Does anyone have any tweezers? I didn't want to pull the thing out in case I left some of it in there." Rosie's voice was calm and matter of fact. As Dot and Betty were staring at the wound and looking quite queasy, Myfanwy Thomas and the Inspector returned. The farmer's wife, being used to such injuries, took over the situation. As she tended to her wound, Rosie couldn't help but smile at how close a run thing that was.

44

Pelmeni and Vodka - London

The bar was called вкуснятина (Vkusnyatyna), which meant delicious food; the locals called it Yummy Bar, although they seldom frequented it. Amber gingerly entered the noisy, smoke-filled room. The clientele were mainly men, who turned to look at her. Their loud conversations were exclusively in Russian, though they quickly hushed in the presence of the beautiful girl. Amber was used to the undesirable attentions of men in bars; this was different; the intensity of their stares, the power of their dark eyes, set in heavily bearded faces, perturbed her. There was an atmosphere of distrust. Emigrants who had cause for wariness. People who had learned the wisdom of suspicion of strangers.

A woman, short but formidable, pushed her way through the crowd and barred Amber's way. "Yeress?" The single-syllable word had become two. It was so drawn out and exaggerated that Amber could barely understand it. It was the solitary word of English known to the woman. She stood satisfied and proud of her linguistic skills.

Amber realised the futility of a sentence, so she opted for one word. "Mikhail."

The woman's face expressed confusion, a lack of understanding, and her obvious displeasure at Amber's failure to meet her own verbal standards.

Amber tried again, trying to affect the accent of the man she knew as Raspy. Just for good measure, she said it louder: "Mikhail."

"Da, Mikhail." At the recognition of the word, the gruff, tough and immovable powerhouse of womanhood turned into the most smiling, albeit devoid of teeth smiling, grandmotherly, loving, caring and maternal version of femininity Amber had ever met.

A bony hand grasped Amber's wrist and whisked her through the crowd of men. She flicked a tea towel in each of their directions, a weapon the men clearly feared, each flick was accompanied by brusque entreaties, the combined effect clearing an easy path for them.

Amber's elderly guide dragged aside a curtain, and they ducked into another room. A quieter and more genteel atmosphere greeted them. Tables surrounded by couples and families packed the space. At the far end was a large table, with just two diners, one of whom was Raspy.

Raspy stood, stretched his arms wide and warmly greeted Amber. "The most beautiful girl in London, she is here, yes?" Amber was piloted through the maze of tables and encouraged to sit. There then commenced a long conversation between the old lady and the two men. During this, the men downed several glasses of a clear spirit, assumed by Amber to be Vodka. The subject of their conversation was clearly herself. There was much waving of hands by the lady; at one point, she pinched her cheek and prodded a bony finger at her arm. The lady appeared to be pointing out the lack of flesh on her bones. Raspy seemed to be getting the blame for her want of nutrition.

"Pelmeni, Da?" The grandmother said kindly but insistently to her new friend.

Amber looked confused, so her self-elected guardian repeated her words, only louder. "Pelmeni, Da?" This time she accompanied her words with the universally recognised mime of a spoon, dipping into a bowl and then rising to her mouth, then nodding enthusiastically.

Food: The chip shop would be closed now, and Amber was indeed very hungry. "Da," she said, nodding her head, hoping the word meant yes.

The lady could not have been more pleased with herself. The evening had brought the opportunity to improve her majestic linguistic skills, a new youngster to mother and the chance to spread the word of her culinary mastery. She skipped away to her task.

"Amber, this is good friend Mischa. He Russian like me, though not much as handsome." Raspy bellowed laughter at his own immodesty. "He not speak too good English like me." Actually, Mischa Agafonov spoke several languages well, mostly those from Eastern Europe; he spoke French and German passably; his English was, however, excellent, but he was content to allow his friend, of whom he was very fond, to show off to the young lady. Raspy turned to his friend and directed a volley of Russian at him. Amber caught her own name and that of Joe several times. Mischa nodded in agreement at Raspy's statement. During the long discussion with the Russians, Amber's food arrived. The lady placed down a large, deep bowl, which steamed before her. A fork and a spoon were placed in her hands. Before she knew it, a large cloth, the lady's weapon from earlier, was being tied around her neck and hung down her front. The steam prevented any view of the contents of the dish, so in a leap of faith, encouraged by her smiling matriarch, Amber plunged her spoon into the caldron. It emerged bearing a large dumpling, which was coated in a rich sauce. After blowing away the steam, Amber bit into the large sphere. The dumpling had been stuffed with delicately spiced mince; the taste was sublime. The lady waited, her eyes questioning. Amber knew that the only way to express her delight in the food was to eat it ravenously. She gobbled up the remainder of the dumpling and immediately dived into the broth for more. The lady's delight was expressed by a little scream and the clapping of her hands. Amber did her best to smile, hampered by a mouth full of delicious Pelmeni.

Amber waited until Raspy and Mischa had finished talking and then asked. "Raspy, I need help. Do you know a man called Bapt? I think he might be involved in…" Amber was unsure how to put it, hesitating, looking for the right words. "He might be a pimp."

"Pimp, what is this Pimp? I know not this word. I do know man called Bapt. Not good man."

"A Pimp is a man, a bad man, who looks after prostitutes. He owns the girls, and they pay him."

"Arrgh, in Russia we call Kot, means chat." Raspy would often lapse into French, a language often spoken at the Russian court he had told Amber once. "Sorry, cat, you say in English, a cat that is man, er Tomcat." Satisfied that he had made the correct translation, Raspy turned to Mischa. Another barrage of Russian followed, once again lubricated by glass after glass of vodka, before Raspy turned to Amber. "Mischa, he knows this man, Baptiste. He is not good man. He very handsome man, woman like him, he likes woman. Woman will work for him. Why do you ask for such a man, Amber?" Raspy was clearly concerned that his new tenant, the girlfriend of his favourite pupil at the boxing gym, should be mixed up with Baptiste Barbeau, nickname Bapt.

Amber told Raspy and, via unnecessary translation, Mischa, the story of her friend Linda and her search to save her. When she had finished, Raspy talked at length to his compatriot.

"Amber, your friend is in danger. It will be difficult to help for her. This man, Baptiste, is not good man. He works for very bad man. They have house where men go for girls. To have love with girls. Not love in nice way, understand? These men who come for special things with girls are....." Raspy struggled for the word. "Er Elita, elite, rich, the men are rich men. They pay much money for special things with girls."

"Raspy, do you know where this house is? Who is it that Baptiste works for?"

Raspy turned once again to Mischa for the answers before relaying them to Amber.

"I know where house is, but I not tell. I tell, you will go and very danger. So better we tell Joe, Joe know what to do."

"But I don't know where Joe is. He has gone away; he may be away for weeks. I must help Linda now. Who knows what they will do to her."

"If Joe not coming, then I will take you, but it is very danger. Man, who Bapt works, very bad man."

"Who is it, Raspy? Who does he work for?"

"He work for Bratva, how say English, he works for a gangster, man called Ted Baker."

45

A runout and a cover drive. – South Wales - 1941

It would be a perfect day for Cricket. A light breeze followed the river down the valley towards the southeast. It carried along a few small clouds, but they were the only things that interrupted the picture-perfect blue sky, and they brought scant threat of rain. The groundsman, the head gardener from the estate, had been preparing the wicket for months. This would be the 42nd pitch he had laid for the annual cricket match between the Estate workers and the Town. He was sure that it would be the best yet. Constant mowing, watering and rolling had flattened the grass to an almost flawless smoothness. The recent dry weather had hardened the surface to perfection.

"You could play billiards on that wicket," he had bragged to the Vicar when the man of God had enquired about its readiness after Church the previous Sunday.

"I fancy it will take a bit of spin, but the bounce will be even. Nothing to worry the batsmen too much. We should see a few runs." He had explained.

It had been a tradition, going back many years, for the rector of the parish to take charge of the Town team. Sir Cecil Kege Le Burg, of course, presided over the Estate Team. It was a grudge match. Rivalry at its most intense. Some years the annual match had surpassed, or so it seemed, The Body Line Series[10], fought between England and Australia, in its ferocity. Although not in

---

[10] The body line series marked a low point in sporting relations between Great Britain and her former colony Australia. England's Captain used dangerous and intimidating bowling in a manner that many regarded as cheating. Such was the disgust of not just the Australians but also many in the UK that questions were asked in Parliament.

its standard of play. Neither team had ever been blessed with a batsman like Bradman or a bowler as fast as Larwood.

Simon wondered if it had been wise to agree to play for the town's team. The vicar asked him first, and so when Sir Cecil came calling for his services, he was already taken. Now, the issue was again threatening the peace of the 'friendly' match, even as the captains were tossing a coin before the start of the game.

"Gentlemen, Gentlemen, please remember your responsibilities as pillars of the community," entreated the Umpire. The General had hung up his batting gloves years ago. The wound he brought back from the Somme in 1916 had left him walking with a stick. He was no longer able to run between the wickets like he had in his youth. Umpiring the annual match had become his contribution to the cause for many years now.

Not that his inability to play now stopped him from regaling the teams with tales about his prowess as a batsman in his youth. Yarns of centuries against county bowlers and heroic last-wicket stands to win matches were somewhat dubious. Having moved to Trefynydd from Cornwall after the Great War, no one in the area could verify or dispute his claims. Nor was it generally known that the wound that had left him crippled had been gained in France, as he claimed, but from the result of falling from his horse. An accident caused by his over-exuberance in demonstrating his equestrian skills whilst trying to impress a young lady. He had been a long way from the nearest German at the time; his later contention that he had been charging a Hun trench was far from reality.

"Gentlemen, I am sure we can settle this amicably." The old War Horse continued.

Simon, who had been standing nearby, approached the bickering belligerents. "Am I to understand that your disagreement concerns my participating in the match? If so, I am happy to stand down."

"You will do no such thing young man," responded the Vicar, "You have been invited to join our team as you are staying at the Hotel, and therefore you are a resident of Trefynydd. Your qualification to play is beyond dispute."

179

"But I do dispute it, Vicar," responded Sir Cecil. "A guest in a hotel is not a permanent resident."

"And yet you claim that the 2 Indian soldiers you have drafted into your team are estate workers, rubbish Sir, absolute rubbish, I say." The Vicar was now getting more than just hot under the collar. The quarrel was starting to get out of control.

"Those young men are under the auspices of the Regiment that I have the honour to command. Their barracks are on Estate lands, which are loaned to the Ministry of Defence. What's more, a fortnight ago, whilst they had a leave of absence authorised by their Commanding Officer, Captain Pritchard-Smythe, they worked upon the estate as beaters for the shoot, for which, of course, they were paid, ergo they are estate workers." Sir Cecil's smug expression as he delivered his coup de grâce antagonised the fuming man of the cloth to the point that further words failed him. Simon seriously thought that the man was about to break the 6th commandment.

"Gentlemen, I am sure we all agree that, as there are so many of the young men who would normally play away at war, neither team would be able to have an eleven without the inclusion of, shall we say, outside help. It would be a shame not to play and maintain the tradition of the fixture, would it not?" Simon was in full diplomatic mode. The combatants both nodded reluctantly. The man was making sense; perhaps he had a solution.

Simon pressed on. "There can be no doubt that the main participants of the team should be the locally born men. May I suggest then that those of us not lucky enough to originally hail from these parts, be restricted to lesser roles in the contest?"

More nodding ensued, and the General sensed that a peaceful settlement might be possible. "What do you have in mind, Lieutenant?"

"As guests at the match, we, the newcomers, shall not bat high up in the order, let's say no higher than number 8, thereby preventing any potential expert batsman amongst us from having too big an influence on the result?"

Both mumbled consent at the suggestion, so Simon continued. "Also, we should not bowl more than a few overs each for the same reason. Of course, we will be needed in the field, but we should not occupy specialist positions, such as wicketkeeper or close fielder."

"Capital suggestions, young Sir." the General enthused. "Are we all in agreement?"

The captains both agreed, and even their handshakes were exchanged in a cordial manner, reminding them both that they were actually quite good friends.

Having won the toss, Sir Cecil decided that the estate team should bat first and so set a target, which he hoped the weakened Town team might struggle to meet. They batted steadily, accruing runs until they declared, as was customary at tea, on 125 for the loss of just 4 wickets.

Simon's contribution to his side had been 2 wickets from his bowling. His off-breaks had been studiously learned in India, where fast bowling was an exertion few Englishmen bothered with. At Cambridge, his unusual action and the difficulty it posed to the beguiled batsmen were a hit.

The Vicar had turned to his newest parishioner when he was worried about the unhindered progress of the Estate's 2nd wicket partnership. It was a good piece of captaincy as Simon took 2 wickets in 2 overs.

Feeling that he didn't want to make too big a contribution and fearing that more wickets from his bowling might upset the delicate entente cordiale that had been earlier built, Simon complained to his captain that his bowling was inflaming his ankle injury; thus, he preferred not to chance a third over. The Vicar could do nothing but acquiesce; after all, the young man was here in Wales to convalesce from his dreadful war experiences.

At tea, Simon doubted that he had ever seen such an extensive spread of food as that served by the ladies of the cricket club. There was enough to feed an army. Each lady had obviously endeavoured to outdo their neighbour. The plenty belied the rationing and privations of a Country at war, a country being choked to death by German U-boats.

Both teams attacked the spread with gusto. The abundance of food, if anything, favoured the team yet to bat, as bowling with a full stomach was not wise. Sir Cecil was inclined to agree and busied himself in limiting the intake of his key men.

The match resumed with the town team batting. They made steady progress but at the expense of a constant fall of wickets. The star man for the town was Alwyn Thomas. His batting style was agricultural, as was to be expected. His philosophy was to lunge forward to any ball anywhere near him and swing the bat as hard as he could at it. It was a successful tactic, much dependent on luck. He was dropped in the field twice. Each time, a skied hit, had the fielder squinting at the bright blue heavens, failing to judge where the ball would land and hopelessly grasping at the elusive orb as it dropped several feet away from them.

Watching on, Simon pitied the culprits. He was sure that Le Berg would be working these men extra hard in the weeks to come, especially if the Estate team lost the match.

As the game neared its conclusion, Simon found himself required to bat. He had hoped that his contribution would be small, but the fates had other ideas. The Vicar had informed him that the remaining two batsmen, apart from himself, were of very little use. Therefore, he was putting him in at number 9. As the 7th wicket fell, Simon was given urgent instructions.

"Stay in with Alwyn, keep your wicket and try to give him the strike. Young Thomas will see us home; we only need 11 more runs to win. But if you or Thomas is out, then it will be all over."

The wicket that brought Simon to the crease had fallen off the last ball of the over, but the batsmen had crossed, thereby requiring Simon to face the first ball of the new one. As Simon came out to the middle, Alwyn came to meet him.

"Just block the ball and run. Get me on strike, and we can win the match. You got it?" Alwyn turned away without waiting for a reply and marched back to the non-striker's end.

Simon took guard from the Umpire and surveyed the field. He had been watching the bowler. His medium pace was reasonable but not to the standard to which Simon was accustomed. Simon waited for the bowler. The delivery was just slightly full of a length; putting his left foot towards the pitch of the ball, Simon executed a perfect cover drive, timing the ball to perfection. The ball sped off his bat, unfortunately straight towards the fielder. Had he hit it a little slower towards the man, he might have thought about pinching a quick single, but the ball was in his hands almost immediately.

"No!" Simon shouted clearly, as he held his hand up to signal to his partner there was no possibility of a run.

Simultaneously, Alwyn Thomas had set off down the pitch, shouting as he sprinted towards Simon. "Run, Run!" Already, he was halfway towards his goal.

Simon repeated, "No, get back, get back." Simon stood his ground as it was his call as the batsman. Thomas hadn't even looked at where the ball had gone before setting off on his suicidal rush. The fielder held his nerve and calmly threw the ball to the bowler, who had positioned himself beside the wicket at the non-striker's end. The bails were removed, and the Umpire signalled out.

Alwyn Thomas stood motionless in the centre of the wicket. He seethed. Simon dared not meet his eye and pretended to be adjusting his pads as the choleric farmer strode reluctantly from the middle. As he went, He was muttering obscenities under his breath, obligingly in English, so that Simon was left in no doubt as to the gentleman's feelings towards him, the weaknesses of his nationality, and the likelihood, or not, of his mother having known his father in matrimony.

The next batsman, a gentleman that Simon could not put a name to, edged his way out to the pitch as unenthusiastically as Thomas had left it. He had seen out most of his 6th decade and appeared, from the thickness of his spectacles, to have the eyesight of a squinting mole. Simon met him mid-wicket. "I am sorry I shan't be much used to you, Sir," the man apologised meekly. "My eyesight is not what it was, too many years looking at the workings of clocks and watches."

Simon realised that he had seen the man in the Clock repairers' shop, a tiny place just off the High Street. "Don't worry, I am sure we will work things out just fine." Simon urged his partner. "Evans, isn't it? Can you run?"

"Oh yes, I used to be a very good runner," the man enthused. But that was 40 years ago or more," his more natural timidity returning to his demeanour.

"That's good. Rely on me to call a run or not. There are 5 more balls in this over. They look to be putting men back on the boundary to stop me from scoring too freely. I will only call you to run if I am confident that we can run two. So run the first one as fast as you can, don't hesitate, turn round and run straight back. Count the balls; when we get to the last ball of the over, they will try and stop us taking a single, so I will need to get it past the close fielders ......" Simon hesitated as he wondered if the horologist was understanding all this.

"Don't worry, butt; I have watched a lot of Cricket in my time. I saw Glamorgan beat the West Indians at the Arms Park in 1923. Oh, you should have seen it; the boys were magnificent they were too."

"You must tell me about that later," Simon interrupted. "Good, let's see if we can do this."

Simon took guard again. As he expected, the field had been set back. A single would be a cinch, but he needed to stay on strike, so it would have to be 2 or 4. Trying to hit a six was also an option, but as there were so many fielders on the boundary, it would be too risky.

The next ball, the second of the over, was a carbon copy of the first. This time, Simon's shot was perfectly placed. The path of the ball effortlessly dissected the field and sped away, between extra cover and long on, for four runs. Seven more runs needed.

The third ball of the over was shorter, faster, and well directed. It bounced up into Simon's ribs, and it was all he could do to fend it off with his bat. The ball bounced just in front of him and trickled away towards the leg side. A single was possible, but Simon held up his hand and called no to his partner. The watchmaker dutifully held his ground.

There were three more balls in the over. Simon's plan was to try and get the runs before the end of the over, not exposing his less able partner to the bowling. It was either that or get a single off the last ball, thereby retaining the strike. This was not the best plan, as the field would be set to prevent that.

Fourth ball. Again, it was short, fast, and accurate, but just a shade too short. Simon quickly got into position and hooked the ball with the middle of the bat past the left hand of a slow-to-react, square-leg fielder. It raced to the boundary for another four runs. Only two more were needed to level the match.

Fifth ball. A good delivery, on a length and just outside the off stump. Simon connected with the ball well; jumping up onto his toes, he managed to punch it down into the ground. The ball bounced away and seemed to pick up speed with each bounce. It went just to the left hand of the cover fielder, who took up chase after it.

"Two!" Simon shouted as he charged off down the wicket. The horologist reacted promptly and true to his word; he was a reasonable runner. Both batsmen completed the first run and quickly turned. Simon glanced towards the fielder, who was giving chase to the ball. He was just overtaking it and was dropping his hand down to stop it. If his throw was good, it would be a close-run thing. Simon hesitated a moment, but his short-sighted friend had no such doubts and had already set off on his second run. Oh well, thought Simon, "it's muck or nettles," as he scurried off towards the wicketkeeper.

The throw was good but came into the bowler's end. If the fielder had thrown to the wicketkeeper, Simon doubted that he would have made it. As it was, the myopic watchmaker made up his ground easily.

Two runs were completed; the scores were tied. A single run off the last ball of the over and the Trefynydd team would be the winners. Simon examined the field placings carefully. Sir Cecil was a good student of the game and was setting a balanced field. The options of an easy single were limited. The knight was talking animatedly to his bowler whilst being careful not to let Simon hear his instructions.

He was taking his time, and that suited Simon just fine. In fact, it was at that moment that Simon had a brainwave. Thus far his innate competitive nature had pushed him to do whatever was necessary to win the game. After the fall of Alwyn Thomas, he had thought it vital that he made sure that they didn't lose. But they weren't losing. The match was a tie, honours even. If Simon scored the winning run now, it might reignite the earlier disagreement of the captains over the eligibility of some of the players, especially him. If, however, the score remained tied, then peace would be assured. If, on the other hand, the winning run was scored by his near-sighted new friend, then the hero would be the local man, not an interloper. Or failing him the last man in.

185

Simon suspected that Sir Cecil would be asking his bowler for a repeat of the third ball of the over. Bouncing into Simon's ribs, difficult for him to get it away. The square leg and mid-wicket fielders were directed to swoop in and stop any chance of a cheeky run.

Simon was ready. As he had supposed, the ball was short and fast, and the line was also spot on from the bowling teams' point of view. Simon curbed his natural instinct to play the ball late and glance it down towards long leg for an effortless single; instead, he punched the ball down and square, directly towards the grateful fielder. "No!" called Simon, stopping the eager Evans charging down the pitch and spoiling his clever scheme.

"Over." called the General.

46

The new gaff. – London 1941

Joe Turner was at Baker's club as arranged the following evening. The doormen were the driver and his mate from the previous day; clearly, they had been demoted due to their poor efforts in following their target and protecting the boss. Joe was expected and was immediately shown through to Ted's office on the first floor.

The room was as ostentatious as his car. Parquet covered the floor in an elaborate zig-zag pattern that made the viewer almost dizzy. A giant curved desk stood in front of an arched window, which looked over the dance floor of the club below. The burred walnut tabletop was highly polished and unencumbered by any paperwork or ornament, save a white candlestick telephone and a desk lamp. The white-lit globe was held aloft by a bronze statue of a naked lady.

Joe was about to sit in one of the Art Deco tulip-shaped chairs that invitingly stood in front of the desk. "Don't get too comfortable. Let's go to your new gaff. I will show you around it, and then we can talk." Ted rose from his seat behind the desk and led the way back out the door.

When they were outside, Ted tossed a car key at Joe and instructed him to drive. He was an accomplished driver but had never taken a test and Joe wondered how much repairs would cost on a car like this. Were the Bakers complying with the law about insurance? He doubted, however, if they were likely to be stopped by the police. It was a reasonable assumption that Ted's warm friendship with DCI Wilkinson also absolved him of any of the requirements of the Road Traffic Act.

Having, after a small error, discovered where the driver's seat was situated, Joe started the car. Easing it away from the curb, he 'gunned the gas' as they said in the movies.

"Where to Boss?"

"Kensington High Street, Lloyds Bank, few hundred yards past the Albert Hall on the right."

"We robbing the Bank, Boss?" Joe asked tongue in cheek.

"Nah, I told you, son; I want you strictly legit. I own the building next door. Your new gaff is on the top floor."

They drove on in silence. Joe was meant to be impressed by Ted's ownership of a prestigious address in Kensington. It was a bit off his patch, but he knew the area well from his professional activities. Ted was showing off, and Joe was wise enough to let him. He parked the giant car on Hornton Street, just off the High Street and followed Ted as he led him down a side alley around the back of the bank building. Standing in front of a door, he handed a set of keys to Joe and stood aside as his new assistant opened the lock.

They climbed a steep flight of stairs up to the third floor of the building. Joe noticed that the stairs only led to the upper floor. Another stairway must service the first and second stories. It was a perfect place for a discrete hideaway. No neighbours would be aware of any coming or goings. The alley they had come down carried on behind the building, and he had seen at least 3 more side alleys that led off the narrow passageway. Anybody wanting to watch the occupant of the flat would need at least a team of 5 men. Joe found the key to the door at the top of the stairs, and they stepped into a small but luxurious apartment. The lights had been left on, and the blackout was in place. A fire had been lit, its effect noticeable, a little too warm for Joe's tastes on such a mild spring day. His new home had been carefully prepared for him. Today's newspapers were neatly stacked on the hall table. Fresh flowers carefully arranged in several vases around the rooms. A delicious, homely smell emanated from the kitchenette, steak and kidney pie if he was not mistaken. Very much his favourite, somewhat worryingly he felt.

Joe knew that a response was needed from him. "This is lovely Ted. You pick the flowers yourself, Boss?" He smiled cheekily at his new employer. He had to strike the right note. He had to be himself. If he ingratiated himself too much, it would seem suspicious.

"Impertinent little runt." To Joe's relief, Ted's response was smiling and good-humoured. "I got you a housekeeper. Doreen.

She worked for me for years, and she used to be one of my best girls, but she is a little past her best for that type of work nowadays. Fortunately, she is an excellent cook; she will clean, wash and iron for you. And if you have any other needs, she can take care of those too; if you don't mind a bit of mutton dressed as lamb, she certainly has the experience."

"Thanks; I think the pie will be more than sufficient."

"Right, get me a brandy, and we will chat."

Joe poured two generous glasses of the expensive and rare liquid into crystal glasses. Sitting opposite the older man, he set himself to listen carefully to the crime lord.

"I meant what I said; I want you to keep your nose clean. You work for me now, so no moonlighting. There is some petty cash for you in the box on the mantelpiece. Doreen will do all your shopping and settle all the bills related to the flat. You are to go to my tailors in Saville Row tomorrow morning and get kitted out, that will go on my account. I have arrangements with many of the restaurants around here; just mention my name. So, you won't need too much money, other than the cash in the box. When that runs out, let me know."

Joe nodded and thanked his new benefactor. Silently, he wondered what he would need to do to repay such generosity. The prospect unnerved him, but he held his tongue, letting the man continue his instructions.

"As I told you, I want to move some of my money and effort into legitimate businesses. I want you to look for ways to do that. I don't need you to be involved in any of our existing undertakings. In fact, stay away from them as much as possible. Eddie has them under control and it's best that you do not stick your nose in."

Joe had been worried about Eddie. The lad was reputed to be somewhat unstable. That was a polite way of putting it. He was a dangerous man. Unpredictable, violent, and suspicious of everyone around him. If half the stories about him were true, he was well on the way to being as mad as a hatter.

Ted seemed to sense Joe's concerns. "Look, if I am honest, Eddie is not too pleased you are joining our team. He doesn't always see the bigger picture. But he will do as I say, so keep out of his way, and everything will be fine. I will make him understand that we need to diversify the business."

"So, you want me to only be involved with legitimate businesses?" Joe pushed.

"Well actually there are a couple of jobs I need you to do for me that are right up your street."

Here it comes, Joe thought.

"I need you to break into an army depo and nick me some lorries."

"What? Nothing too risky, then." Joe didn't like the sound of this, but he knew that he would have to work off his debt somehow.

"Don't worry about it; I will give you the details another time. It's not urgent. You can have a look into it and tell me if it's a goer. Actually, I think you will find that it is simpler than you might at first think." Ted dismissed Joe's concerns and pressed on with his major requirements. "The main thing I need from you is ways to get my money into legit building firms. You said you knew someone."

Brilliant, Joe thought; he had taken the bait. "A few years ago, I did a job on a big house out in the sticks. The owner is some top accountant type who owns one of the biggest firms in the City of London. You know, merchant banking, that sort of thing. Anyway, I managed to get into the safe easily enough; there was a bit of cash, jewellery, not much to get excited about, and then I found an envelope." Joe paused for dramatic effect.

"Get to the point, son; we haven't got all night."

"The envelope contained pictures of our banker, intimate pictures, and I am not talking about with his wife."

"Dirty little bugger, some slapper?"

"No, Ted, you are missing the point. What our boy was doing was not with a girl."

"Ah, so you took the photographs, and you have been blackmailing him ever since."

"Not really. I took the pictures, and I let him know I had them; he offered me money, but I declined. Instead, he has been giving me his expert business advice. He helped me buy some properties up north, well he showed me how to do it. I rent them out and he set me right. So that I don't pay too much tax, but also, I don't pay too little."

Ted seemed a little confused. Joe explained. "You see, Ted, great minds think alike. I had the idea, like you, that I didn't want to be robbing houses all my days. Fancied a bit of a pension. I had saved money but if you just start buying up houses, the tax man might ask questions as to where it has all come from. You need to be smart and careful, but it is doable. I reckon our man could do the same for you, all be it on a bigger scale."

"Great, get the geezer in."

"I'll have a word, but you must understand that this is a very cautious bloke. You see, whilst he is keen that those pictures don't find themselves in the wrong hands, he has just as much to lose if he is found to be involved in dodgy business dealings. He only agreed to help me because I didn't have a record and if I kept his name out of it."

"You mean that he wouldn't want to deal with somebody like me."

Joe watched and listened to the gangster carefully; this was not a man to upset. Ted didn't seem too offended. He was a practical man.

"Well, you don't exactly shy away from the limelight. My man will want to keep his distance, but I have him by the Alberts, so he will do as I say. Let me sound him out."

"Alright Son. But don't let the grass grow. Ring me at the club. By the way, what did you do with those pictures?"

Joe had been expecting this. Ted would want to have a hold over this man and might not be prepared to let Joe retain control. "I burned them. There was no way that I wanted them hanging around. If anyone went through my things, I wouldn't want them to find them and think that I was into that sort of thing. So given the fact that I probably wouldn't have used them anyway, even if the gentleman didn't play along, I destroyed them, but of course he's not to know that, is he?"

Ted nodded. "Well, as you don't seem to want to share that Pie with me, I will be on my way."

Joe waited until Ted had left before picking up the telephone and dialling the pre-arranged number. He was sure that someone would be listening in, so the conversation had been carefully rehearsed.

"Coyne residence." The servant answered after the fifth ring. Joe gave his name and held the line whilst the Master of the household was fetched.

"Stephen Coyne speaking."

"Coyne, it's Joe Turner. We need to meet. I have a little business I need your advice on."

"I have told you, Turner, not to call me here." The man's voice was irritated, but more than that, there was an undertone of fear. Joe was impressed; quite the actor the Major had found for him. Remaining silent, Joe waited for the man to speak. "Alright, the usual place tomorrow, 1 o'clock. Don't be late. I will only have 10 minutes to spare you." The man tried to sound confident to wrestle back command of the situation.

Joe's response was measured: "You will have as much time as I need you to have, and we both know that, now don't we?" Joe replaced the receiver without further discourse.

47

The Lion's Den – London - 1941

Everybody who had grown up in the east end of London knew the name Ted Baker; Amber was no exception. If Bapt, the man she thought might know what had happened to Linda, worked for the Bakers, that was indeed a dangerous problem.

"We need to go to this house, Raspy. Linda must be in trouble. If this man Bapt has her, he will make her work as a prostitute. Who knows what the men there will do to her."

"You understand, this is dangerous. It is no place for you. I go, you not go."

"Come on Raspy we will talk about this on the way." Amber stood and indicated to the Russian that he should do the same.

The Russian men talked again. More vodka flowed, but this time, the men were not in agreement. Despite the language barrier, Amber picked up some of what was being said; she was sure that Mischa did not want his friend to go. The motherly figure who had fed her joined in the conversation. After appearing to be updated by Mischa, she berated Raspy before engulfing Amber in a rib-breaking hug. Tears flowed from the woman's eyes, but she seemed resigned to Amber leaving. Gently she removed Amber's napkin, before gently kissing her hands, then spinning around deftly and attacking poor Raspy with the cloth. With difficulty, the pair extracted themselves from the bar and began their journey.

"Amber, What we do when we get to house?" Raspy was not concerned for his own safety, but he was worried that Amber would take unnecessary risks.

"We do what Joe would do; we look around, and we make a plan."

With that, there was silence between them.

They walked past the house several times, carefully looking at the layout. It was a large house, Victorian with a large front garden, its gates open to the road, through which a steady stream of men in dark coats, collars turned up, and hats tilted down, made their way to the front door. There, they would ring the bell and be shown immediately into the darkened hallway. The occupiers of the house appeared to take the blackout very seriously, which certainly suited Amber's purposes.

"I'm going to have a look around the back." Amber was gone before Raspy could register an objection.

Amber walked with intent through the gates; immediately turning to her left, she hugged the inside of the boundary wall. Keeping in the shadows, she walked carefully along the lawned edging of the drive and pathway. Her route took her along the side of the building. At the rear of the house was a raised terrace that looked out onto the gardens. Music, that of a gramophone playing, could be heard coming from the rearmost room. The laughter of a party accompanied the cheerful song.

The gaiety was challenged by the sudden discordance of sirens, an air raid. Amber crouched further into the shadows as light momentarily spilt onto the garden. The French doors adjoining the terrace had been opened before the interior lights had been dimmed. In the garden, highlighted by the illegal illumination, Amber could see that Anderson shelters had been built. Shouts of rebuke emanated from the room, and the lights were rapidly quelled. A man with a torch carefully pointed to the ground, led a procession of the revellers towards the safety of the shelters.

It was a golden opportunity, and Amber made her way back to Raspy as quickly as she dared.

"Come on, Raspy, the house will be empty. They have all gone to the shelters in the garden." Without waiting for a reply, she grabbed Raspy by the arm and dragged him towards the front door of the house. As she had hoped, in the rush for the shelters, the door was left unlocked.

Cautiously, the pair slipped into the dimly lit hallway. They listened closely to the sounds of the house. Although the gramophone record's music had ended, it continued to play a rhythmic thud as the needle caught on the end of the record's groove. Otherwise, there was silence.

"Raspy, stay here and watch the stairs. If somebody comes, say you want a girl, make out you have just arrived, but there was nobody here. Speak loudly so I can hear you and pretend to be drunk."

"Where are you going?" Raspy didn't like the plan; he wasn't sure what it was, but he had a bad feeling.

"I am going upstairs to look for Linda." Amber climbed the stairs, which led to a landing, which in turn led to a corridor with doors on either side. Amber set off cautiously towards the doors, pausing at each one; she either found the rooms empty or locked from the inside. The guests and their hostess had either abandoned their activities to make their way to shelters, or they had been so engrossed that they had elected to chance the German bombs. At one door, Amber could hear the enthusiastic groans of a lady from within; either her client was skilled or, more likely, the girl was using her acting skills to maximum effect. Amber pressed on and found another staircase and more rooms. It was a similar situation, mostly empty and some locked. A smaller staircase climbed its way to the attic rooms. Just two doors, one to each side of a small landing, remained for Amber to check.

48

A cover drive – Wales - 1941

Simon and Evans met in the middle, the latter desperate for some advice from his more accomplished partner.

"I am so sorry; I don't think I will be of much use," Evans repeated. "I love Cricket, always have, just never been very good at it see. I have always dreamed of being a batsman, oh to play like Len Hutton, now that would be something."

Simon needed to get him focused. The more he thought about it, the more the idea of Evans, the Watchmaker hitting the winning runs, the more it appealed to him. He liked the man. A tied match would be perfect, but ties are a rarity in this level of Cricket, he suspected. And what would it mean for this lover of Cricket to be the local hero? Evans the batsman, Evans who scores the winning run and is carried from the field on the shoulders of his grateful teammates.

Time for some quick coaching. "It looks like the young Indian chap will be bowling." Typical of Le Berg, thought Simon, not really in the spirit of the agreement that had been made earlier. "Now he is an off spinner, you know what that is?"

"Yes, he will try to spin the ball away from me so that I edge it to the slips." Simon looked confused at Evan's answer. "You see, I am a left hander, muddles things up a bit."

Relieved that Evans seemed to have some knowledge of the game, Simon continued. "He will probably bowl 2 or 3 that spin away from you, then he will bowl one that doesn't spin, goes on straight and bowls you. You must get your front foot forward, as close to the pitch of the ball as possible."

Evans nodded; he understood the mechanics of what he had to do. He had seen it done a thousand times. He just wasn't very good at sports. In his youth, his father, who had been a good player, had pushed him to play Cricket; he had tried and tried for his father. He had practised tirelessly. His father had been patient. But he was just no good. He never got picked for the team; it just wasn't in him. Evans knew that it had disappointed his father, he would have given anything to have pleased the old man. When his father had died and he had gone through his things, he had found the old bat. Unused for many years, forgotten. Evans couldn't find it in his heart to part with it, storing it away in a corner of his workshop. The only reason Evans was playing today was that they were desperate for players. All the talented young men away to war. For a moment, he wished he was with them, then he realised it was a wicked thought; he knew how much they must be suffering. He offered a quick, silent prayer of forgiveness. He looked instinctively towards the pavilion where the Vicar looked on, waving his encouragement.

The bowler was ready. The fielders crowded around the batsman, like jackals circling a wounded animal, the smell of its blood in their inflamed nostrils. Evans felt sick. The sumptuous tea that he had readily consumed gurgled around in his stomach. He wanted to run—back to his little shop, back to his watches and clocks, with their predictable mechanisms.

He was good at his profession. If horology had been a sport, he would be a Hutton or a Hammond, even a Bradman. But no one appreciated a watchmaker; to his knowledge, no village clock repairer had ever been Knighted. He would never be Sir Emlyn Evans, preeminent Horologist, by appointment to His Majesty. Evans understood that he was panicking. He drew a deep breath and took up his stance, not ready for the little red sphere of doom that was to be pitched his way. As the ball floated through the air towards him, Evans remembered that he hadn't taken guard from the Umpire. He had seen a mark in the crease that had been made no doubt by the previous batsmen. But which stump was it for? As he stretched his right leg forward towards where he thought the ball would bounce, he had no idea where his off stump was. He thrust his bat forward at the delivery and hoped for the best.

His best was an old bat that waited some 6 inches from the line of the ball; the missile bounced and spun away harmlessly, remote from the willow of his bat and even further from the ash of the stumps. The spin of the ball even foxed the wicketkeeper, who was unable to gather it cleanly in his gloves.

Evans was startled as he realised that his back foot was out of the crease. Quickly, he grounded his bat before the fumbling wicketkeeper could remove the bails.

Phew. He had survived. Maybe he could do this? Maybe? The next ball was a repeat of the first. Expertly delivered, in exactly the right spot, spinning wickedly, zipping up and away from the bat. This time, the wicketkeeper was ready and caught the ball cleanly, swiping his gloves left and demolishing the stumps, bails flying high in the air. But Evans had remembered to keep his back foot in the crease, his toe pointed out delicately, like a ballerina. "Not out!" the General responded to the keeper's claim of "stumped".

Phew. He had survived a second delivery. Maybe he could actually do this? Maybe?

All too quickly, the bowler was ready to bowl, and Evans had to little time to bask in the glory of his survival.

For some inexplicable reason, Evans was thinking of his clocks. In every clock or watch he had ever made or repaired, he knew that the smallest adjustment was the most important. Each turn of a screwdriver must be delicate, exact, careful and made with consideration. The assiduousness that comes from trust in the knowledge of what one is doing.

Evans couldn't play, but he knew cricket. He needed to adjust, and he needed to adjust just a bit. The slightest turn of the screw, the slightest bend of the spring.

The familiar smell of the light oils of the workings of the clocks filled his nostrils. The aroma that he had smelt every working day for over 40 years. It calmed and steeled him to the task. But it wasn't machine oil he sensed; it was the linseed oil of his Father's bat. The oil had been repeatedly applied over the many years, gently with cotton wool, working down the grain endlessly, relentlessly, lovingly.

He shuffled forward on the crease, the mark left by former batsmen now firmly under his left foot. He lifted the bat up behind him. This time, there would be no prod, no gentle push, instead a full flow of his prized blade.

Evans thought about what Simon had said. Two or three spinning balls and then a straight one. He knew it would be the next ball; he felt it. The ball came and bounced in exactly the same spot as the first two deliveries. Evans was there, his foot in the perfect position. This time, the ball didn't spin but carried on as intended, travelling straight for the off stump. Evans' father's willow blade came down through a flawless arc, swept past his right leg and met the red leather missile. A glorious crack, the sweet sound of impeccable timing, rang out as the ball leapt from the bat and sailed away across the grass towards the boundary.

The blade continued its sweep until it was high above the batsman's head.

Evans, on his left knee in the victorious pose of the perfect cover drive. The bat pointed to the heavens, to his father.

Evans, the batsman.

49

Business, as usual. – London 1941

He was being followed but that was to be expected. The man stood out a mile. If he had "Ted Baker's man" written on a big sign hanging around his neck, he could not have been more obvious. Joe made no attempt to lose his tail. In fact, he was quite happy to have him tag along as a witness.

Joe walked into the Lyons Tea Shop and saw his man at a table in the corner. He made his way over, interested to see what his tail would do. For the moment, he had stayed outside. Joe sat opposite a tall man, well dressed to the point of being debonair and perhaps a little out of place in the surroundings. There were no niceties as the actor feigned irritability.

"So, what is it that you want Turner?" The actor was, in fact, the real deal. There had been too little time to set up one of the Major's usual recruits in the role. Instead, Robinson had enlisted the help of an old friend, Sir Stephen Coyne.

Coyne fitted the description that Joe had given Ted Baker. A man in the city. A man with a respectable practice. A man with much to lose. A man who would be forced to cooperate with Joe if, indeed, he had a secret that had been discovered by the thief.

"I am really not happy about these meetings, Turner. I have told you before that a man in my position cannot afford to be mixed up in your petty little schemes."

Actually, this was the first time that they had met.

"Were you followed?" Joe whispered.

"How the blinking heck should I know?" Coyne seemed to be relishing the role or perhaps he was just naturally irritable.

"Has anyone come into the café since you arrived? And did you tell anyone where you were going?"

"No one and No, of course not."

"Good, then we can be reasonably confident that if you were followed, that they haven't entered the building yet. I was followed, and I expect he will come in after a short while. Did the Major give you a plan?"

"Yes, I am to meet with you and your 'Boss' just once, where I will introduce you to an ex-employee of mine. The story is that She left my firm under a bit of a cloud, a scapegoat for the misdeeds of a senior but far less competent colleague. She has set herself up as a private financial and tax consultant. I have kept in touch and use her from time to time. I will tell your man that she will look at his situation and come up with a plan that she will run by me, although I have complete faith that it will be flawless. I will not meet with him again. There will be no paperwork in my name. I understand that this lady is one of the Major's men, so to speak. They are busy setting up an office for her. You and your man will meet with me there in 2 days' time. At noon. Here is the address." The businessman slipped a piece of neatly folded paper across to Joe.

"Good work. Now the man who was following me has just walked in; he is with a lady; she must have been following him at a distance. They seem to have anticipated us meeting in a place like this. Impressive, I almost underestimated them. Right, time for us to put on a show for them."

50

A friend in need – London 1941

While Amber was searching the rooms above, Raspy waited nervously in the hallway. He had never lacked courage, but he was also sensible enough to know a dangerous situation; his present predicament certainly rated as such. Raspy heard two men talking as they approached through the room at the rear of the property.

"Excuse, I am here for girl. You have girl for me, yes, please." Raspy walked towards the men with an exaggerated staggering gait. He slurred his words and hoped his earlier vodka consumption could still be smelt on his breath.

"I am sorry, sir, but you have the wrong idea; this is a gentlemen's private club." A tall, young man dressed as a footman did his best to affect the manners of his supposed position. He looked more like his actual trade, a doorman/thug.

"I am genteel man." Responded Raspy with mock effrontery.

"I am sure that you are, sir." The footman had taken his elbow and was gently leading him towards the front door. "However, I am afraid that you need to be recommended to us by one of our members in order to join, sir."

Raspy wanted to keep them away from the stairs. "I have invited from Member. He say come here, many nice girls." Raspy pulled away from his minder and staggered his way into the rear room before he could be stopped. "Where is girls. Where is party? My friend say, always there is party." He flopped himself down into a chair, knowing that it would make it harder for the men to manhandle him. "I need drink."

Amber heard nothing of the commotion going on downstairs. She stood close to one of the doors at the top of the attic stairs. She tried the door handle; like many of the others below, the door was locked. Unlike those, the key, attached to a small bunch of others, was in the lock. The door was locked from the outside. A design to keep somebody in the room rather than stopping people entering. She turned the key gently and silently opened the door. A small room, lit by a gas light that bubbled on its lowest setting, lay beyond the door. The room was sparsely furnished. A bed bracketed onto the floor. A small bedside chest of drawers, also fixed into place, but strangely a few feet away from the bed. A glass of water, untouched, adorned the dark wood. The floor was covered with linoleum, an unusual material for a bedroom. The window was shuttered from the inside. A rasp and padlock completed the effect of the décor. This was no boudoir; this was a prison cell.

Amber jumped as a moan emanated from below the dirty sheet that covered the bed. It came from a girl. A young girl not much more than 18 years old. She was drowsy, whimpering and writhing on the mattress. Her face was pale and bore marks of ill-treatment. Her lip was painfully swollen, and a mark above her right eye suggested she had been punched. Her arm was stretched out above her head. Her wrist was restrained by a handcuff to the wooden bed head.

Amber approached cautiously; on the drawers was a syringe out of reach of the bed. As she neared the girl, she could see that her arm was pocked with the marks of the needle. Moaning words which Amber could barely discern, pleaded for help.

"Please, please, it's time, please." Amber realised that the entreaties were not for her release or rescue but for the needle's relief.

It wasn't Linda, to Amber's disappointment and at the same time relief, it wasn't her friend. She so much wanted to help but she had to find Linda first. There was still the other room to check. Reluctantly, she turned away and crossed the hallway. The other door was also locked, this time no key. She remembered the keys hanging on the bunch in the other door. Quickly fetching them, the other key fitted, and the door swung open. The scene within was the mirror image of the first room. Same bed, same drawers, same shutters to the window. A different girl, Linda. Amber ran to her and hugged her drowsy body. Quickly she examined her arms, the right one secured by the darbies as with the other girl. As she expected there were needle marks, but less than her neighbours. Linda was weeping groggily, with no sign of her demanding the needle. Amber hoped that was an indication she was in time. Testing the handcuffs only showed that they were strongly secured. They were the standard darbies commonly used by the police. A simple key was required to unscrew the bolt that secured the hand. Amber ran to the door and took the bunch of keys from the lock; the handcuff's key was on the ring, and she soon had Linda free. Amber removed her coat and put it around Linda's shoulders. Her friend was drowsy, but Amber thought that she could walk if she supported her. She pulled her up from the bed by her arms and turned towards the door to test her theory. Linda complied and they set off towards the stairs.

As the pair passed the other room, the girl moaned loudly. "Please, I need it now. Please." Amber doubted that her cries would be heard downstairs, above the noise of the bombing. But she dare not chance it. It was a heart-wrenching decision, but there was no way to rescue the girl. It would be difficult enough to get Linda down the stairs and out through the front door without being discovered as it was. Ashamedly, she closed the door on the girl and her pleadings.

Their journey down the stairs was slow and cumbersome. As they arrived in the hall, Amber could hear Raspy's voice coming from the rear room. "He is Lord, very nice man, important man. He have drink with me and say that I must come and meet girl. I want drink. Give me drink." The Russian was playing his part to perfection. His hosts swelled in number by 2 more men who had arrived from the shelters and were having difficulty making him understand that he must leave. Amber knew she must get out and get as far away as possible. Raspy would leave soon, she was sure. He would have to before the men lost their temper with him.

Linda was tired, so Amber had to almost drag her across the hallway to the front door, just about managing to open it with one hand. She was so close, and the last thing she wished to see was someone coming up the steps towards her. Yet there he was: Eddie Baker, gangster, thug, brothel keeper, borderline psychopath, standing on the top step.

The Straight Left – The Dragon's Tail Hotel - Wales

Evans the batsman was carried from the field on the shoulders of his teammates. Simon smiled to himself; his plan had worked out splendidly. Hardly anyone congratulated him on his part in the victory; all the focus was on the glorious cover drive from the bat of Evans, and that was as Simon wanted it. Hardly anyone congratulated him except the Umpire.

"Very nicely played, young man." The General nodded knowingly, as though he had divined the plan of Simon's all along. "Very nicely played indeed."

The closeness of the result and the delight that all concerned held in Evans's success softened the earlier tensions. Handshakes and genuine congratulations abounded. The fielding team was consoled perhaps by the fact that there was still a great quantity of food to be consumed; those who had been earlier denied their fill by their cautious captain now filled their boots.

The mood was one of celebration, of triumph. The joy of a game played fairly, played as it had been played by generation after generation, played despite the obstacles, the men away. The war. No war could stop this fiercely proud community. Their hopes carried forward in their traditions and customs.

The Tea was finally depleted, and the Ladies were busy clearing away the ensuing debris. The teams and the spectators made their way in good spirits towards the pub.

'Evans the bat' held the match ball that had been presented to him tightly. Like it might disappear if he let it go, the whole thing being just a dream. He clutched onto that ball all evening, never once putting it down. He had the expression of a man in total disbelief, a man in shock. Like a man who had won a fortune on the Football pools and now agonised over how he would tell his wife, in fear that due to her strict religious beliefs and hatred of gambling, she might make him give it all back.

Only one man was not in good spirits. Alwyn Thomas was still apoplectic over his run out. Despite repeated attempts from his friends to convince him that he only had himself to blame, he was not to be persuaded. For Alwyn there was clearly only one man to hold responsible. The more beer he consumed, the deeper his resentment cemented itself into his being.

Alwyn had heard the rumours about that Toff and Sara. Adam's Sara. His best mate's girl. With poor Adam, a prisoner of the Germans. Going through God knows what. That stuck-up English prat. How dare he come here and think he can just have any girl he wants. Alwyn's hatred for Simon was now beyond all reason.

Simon had been keeping a weather eye on Alwyn Thomas. He knew trouble was coming. It had been for some time. Thomas seemed to be jealous of Simon's friendship with Sara. Now, there was the incident of the runout, which Thomas unjustly blamed him for. Alwyn was set to be the hero of the hour, his runs clinching the match until his misjudgement, but the loss of his wicket had deprived him of his glory. He would have liked to have avoided conflict with the Farmer, but somehow, he knew it was inevitable, and Simon was determined that it would be upon his terms.

Simon was at the bar, talking quietly with Sara. Alwyn bristled as he heard the young lady laughing sweetly at whatever Simon had said to her. As Simon walked with his pint back to his table, Thomas pushed his chair backwards, deliberately colliding with the object of his antagonism. The beer sloshed out of the glass and spilt on Simon and Alwyn in equal measure.

"Oy, look what you have done, I am soaked. You wanna be more careful." The angry farmer pushed Simon in his chest, forcing him backwards a couple of steps. He leaned forward towards him aggressively.

"I think the fault is yours, sir," Simon responded calmly. "You backed your chair into my path."

"Listen to the toff lads," Alwyn tried to gain the support of his friends, but they remained silently staring into their glasses. "Not content with running me out this afternoon and nearly costing us the match, now he's pouring beer all over me."

206

No one responded from any of the pub's clients, and the usual chatter had died to an uneasy hush. Not put off, Thomas pushed on with his quarrel.

"You've been nothing but trouble since you came here. Running round after Sara, what with her fiancé captured by the Hun. You ought to be ashamed. Typical English Toff, think you can have anything of ours. Well, I isn't havin' it, see. You keep your hands off her."

"Sir, I think you need to watch what you say. You slander me, and you malign the reputation of the young lady. I think you are drunk, and you need to take back your remarks and apologise, if not to me, at least to Miss Lloyd." Simon's voice was deliberately calm and quiet. The locals all strained to hear his words. The tension in the room was palpable.

The robust farmer was not pacified by his words and continued to vigorously argue his case whilst simultaneously poking a large grubby finger into his foe's chest.

"I ain't apologising to you or anyone else, mate. Question is are you gonna make me?"

"Come on, Alwyn, leave it, mate, let's all have a quiet drink, is it?" a sole dissenting voice came from one of the aggressor's embarrassed friends.

"You shut it, Owain. Keep out of it." Alwyn was quick to suppress the rebel. "Well, toff, are you gonna make me?"

Simon had hoped that he would have been able to mollify his adversary without the situation turning to violence, but it was becoming ever clearer to him that Thomas wanted a fight, and sooner or later, he would have it. Simon needed to stay in control. This was a dangerous situation, not only because the man was gargantuan but also because any trouble could have a detrimental effect on his mission. He had, since he arrived, been striving to gain the trust and respect of the community. Fighting with one of them, even if he was the local bully, might lose him some of that favouritism.

The witnesses had to be definite that Thomas had been the aggressor. Simon needed to be perceived as the unfortunate wounded party. Regardless of the outcome of the fight, Simon's actions needed to be seen as honourable. It was vital that Thomas, as the aggressor, threw the first punch.

Simon chanced his arm, "Sir, I repeat that you have slandered me, and you have tarnished the reputation of an innocent young lady. What's more, I suspect that you are less interested in preserving the lady's engagement to your alleged friend and more hoping that the gentleman might not return so you can be her next suitor."

It took a few moments for the mind of the farmer, hampered by beer but never at the best of times incisive, to work out the implications of what had been said. When the reluctant penny eventually dropped, the Titan's anger knew no bounds, and a large fist scythed through the air in Simon's direction.

It was as Simon had expected and wanted. The attempted blow was a monstrous affair. Full of hate, power, strength and destruction. But it was envisaged, anticipated, and therefore easily avoided.

Stealthily, Simon had ducked under the punch. Stepping slightly to the left and away from the source. The attacker stumbled as the momentum of the missed strike carried him around, and he lurched into the space that had been Simon.

In a moment, the Landlady, Mrs Williams, was precariously between the two belligerents. "Alwyn Thomas, I will not have fighting in this pub."

Despite the disparity of size, Thomas was cowered by the intent of the lady. Having regained his balance, he hesitated as to his next move. Simon hoped that her intervention might cool the man's temper, but that hope was in vain.

"Outside, Navy boy, outside," Alwyn shouted as he backed away from the fearsome Landlady. He turned and marched from the bar, crashing through the low doors out into the street. Simon dutifully followed, joined by the excited mob. Thomas had stridden over to the other side of the deserted street. He had pulled off his shirt over his head and was dousing himself with cold water from the tap at the monument. Simon removed his tie and rolled his sleeves up to his elbows. The crowd, which seemed to have been enhanced by nearby neighbours eager to witness the spectacle, formed a wide circle about the town square. The combatants faced each other at a distance. Alwyn Thomas stretched himself taller before hunching his back into the classic stance of a street brawler. He was a beast of a man. The hard labour of agricultural work, demanded from him seemingly since the day he could walk, had toned and intensified his muscles. Goliath arms extended from his torso like the boughs of some ancient oak, hardened by the sun, wind and rain of the rugged Welsh mountains. The limbs concluded by enormous hands, the size of rugby balls, clenched tightly, menacingly, ready to wreak havoc and destruction.

Simon thought back to his training at 'The Spa'. The regime had been intense. Barely a day had gone by when there hadn't been training for such conflicts as this. Each lesson a tutorial in the destruction of your enemy. Every class had drilled into its students the need to be first to strike a decisive blow. Be the first to maim. To strike to injure beyond recovery. To deliver force without mercy. Hold nothing back. Kill or be killed.

Simon was confident that, despite his strength and size, he could overcome Alwyn Thomas. He was trained to deal with adversaries of this size and potency, and he trusted in his training and his ability to perform as he was taught.

Precipitously, a thought occurred to him, like a bolt from the blue, a revelation, the sudden realisation that all his training, all his skills, every method that he had learned were all useless to him. He couldn't use any of them. Not one technique was of the slightest benefit to him. The Spa had taught him to Kill, kill the man before he had any chance to hurt or injure you, silence the fellow before he could give you away. But Simon couldn't kill this man. He was just a farmer. A boy with a crush on a beautiful girl and a dislike of the English. A bully, no doubt, and an asinine young man certainly, but not one that deserved to die. The man was not an enemy, perhaps he was a criminal but probably not guilty of a capital offence. Even if he was, Simon was not a Judge, Jury and hangman.

If Simon was to maintain his cover and hold on to the embryonic friendships he had made in the village, he could not hurt this man. The fight had to be commensurate with a fight that would naturally take place between two normal young men over a girl. Fights that take place everywhere in the world, all the time. Confrontations that end in a bloody nose, a black eye or a cut lip at worst.

Simon had a problem. He might have to lose this fight.

52

The Accountant's apprentice. – London - 1941

Joe was sure that the rest of the conversation with Coyne was carefully listened to, and the contents reported back to Ted Baker. Two days later, Ted took a cab with Joe to the address as arranged; the driver easily found their destination. The office was above a Hat shop in Hackney. The area was vibrant; a well-established Jewish community thrived in the busy streets. Their numbers were bolstered by refugees of their faith, the lucky ones who had fled ahead of Hitler's fury and hatred. They were a few minutes early, but Stephen Coyne was there before them. Introductions were dispensed with, and they entered via a side stairwell; the legend on the door merely said "private". Coyne led the way but stopped halfway up the stairs, turning he addressed Joe and Ted.

"Gentlemen, I am about to introduce you to a remarkable lady. She has agreed, as a personal favour to me, to help you. You would be very well advised to listen and do everything she says. She is extremely well qualified, having an exceptional mind and an insightful head for business. Had fate treated her kindlier, she would have had a brilliant career in business. As it is, she fell victim to the old boy's network through no fault of her own. She finds herself working somewhat outside the normal sphere of respectable business. She is, however, honest and trustworthy. After I have made the introduction, I will leave the meeting, and we will not meet again. You must understand, Mr Baker, that this is for your sake as much as mine. In my line of business, I and my business dealings are frequently audited. Such audits would no doubt prove embarrassing if I were advising you directly. They would also shine a light upon your activities, which might not end favourably for you. I am also extremely busy, and the complexity of your situation demands a lot of attention. Miss Hereford has agreed to work on your behalf as a favour to me, but of course, she will need to be paid; I suggest that you pay whatever rate she chooses to set. There is no doubt that she will earn it, and ultimately, it will be a price well worth paying. Are we clear, gentlemen?" Sir Stephen Coyne was an impressive man, used to setting the agenda. Joe imagined that few people argued with him. Even so, he was surprised to see Ted, a man equally accustomed to dominance, nod compliantly.

They ascended the remainder of the stairs, Coyne opening the door without knocking. They walked directly into a large room, sparsely furnished as an office. An austere-looking lady sat behind a large desk, not rising to meet her visitors; she merely pointed them towards the chairs that waited opposite her.

Joe was not surprised to see the athletic frame and quick mannerisms of Susan Cartwright staring across at them. She was dressed in a much more severe fashion than was her usual garb. Her hair worn in a conservative style, tinged a little with grey. The slight changes in her attire having the effect of ageing her. Joe knew her to be a kind and gentle soul, but this new persona was all business and lacked compassion or empathy.

"Gentlemen, meet Miss Hereford. Miss Hereford, this is Mr Ted Baker and Joe Turner. I will leave you all to get acquainted." Without pause, Sir Stephen Coyne took his leave.

The room was silent as Miss Hereford turned over some papers she had evidently been reading and composed herself to speak. After what seemed an age, during which the two criminals sat quietly waiting, like schoolboys before a fearsome headmistress, the dower lady looked up from her desk. Her eyes met each of the men in turn before she commenced an oration that neither felt inclined to interrupt.

"Sir Stephen has briefed me on your wishes, Mr Baker. I understand that you require me to help you immerse yourself in businesses that are somewhat more mainstream and, shall we even say, more legitimate than those in which you have previously been involved. Sir, I do not condone, nor do I make any judgment upon your current industries. I do not need to know the details of these enterprises except to say that I do need to know the extent to which they enrich you and your family. I will need to know, in full, all your assets, including properties, vehicles, artwork, and jewellery. Also, all your income streams and savings. Equally, all your expenditures must be detailed. I suspect that you will be reluctant to be so trusting of a person you barely know. With your permission, I will try to explain to you why it is vital that I know such details. First, let me ask, is there a particular business in which you wish to venture?"

Ted looked shocked by the directness of the woman.

Joe marvelled at the brilliance of the lady who he knew as Susan, a lady who he discerned to be an outstanding strategist but who would barely say boo to a Goose. Yet here she was, controlled, assured and dominating one of the most dangerous men in London.

"I, er, I thought I might, erm, move into the building trade."

Hereford nodded, pausing for a moment whilst apparently considering the idea. "Interesting. There will no doubt be a surge in the trade after the war. The Luftwaffe is ensuring that homes and business premises will need to be rebuilt. However, at the moment the sector has a difficulty. Manpower shortages are, I believe, crippling many companies. Wages are, therefore, no doubt correspondingly high. Cash flow must also be a factor. With these difficulties, it might just be a good time to acquire some existing firms. I take it you have the funds available?"

"Yes, I have plenty of cash available."

"And yet it is of no use to you, is it?" Without waiting for a reply, the expert continued. "You see, if you go about town buying businesses for cash, sooner or later, the authorities will notice. They will start to ask questions as to where the cash came from and, most vitally, whether tax has been paid upon its acquisition. Have you heard of a man called Al Capone, Mr Baker?"

"Yes, he is a Gangster, erm, businessman in America, isn't he?"

"Yes, he is, and he is currently serving a very long sentence in prison, I believe. Do you know what his crime was, Mr Baker?"

"Wasn't he involved in illegal alcohol? Bootlegging, they call it over there, don't they?"

"He may have been involved in illegal activity that has never been proven in court. The crime he was found guilty of is tax evasion. You see, the United States Federal tax authorities saw that his lifestyle, his assets, and his spending didn't tally with the businesses he admitted to having. Here in Great Britain our tax people are not quite as, shall we say, as enthusiastic at tracking tax evasion as in America. That is likely to change. Our government needs every penny it can get its hands on to pay for this war. When the war is over, things will get even worse because we will need to pay off the massive debts accrued by this nation. Our revenue people will be under pressure to collect from us all. They will be bolstered by returning servicemen looking for jobs; currently, they are stretched thinly, but that will change. People like me will be using all our skills to make sure that our clients pay no more tax than they need. However, in your case, the tax man might, just might be your best friend."

"You want me to pay tax, is that it?" Ted was aghast. "But why?"

"What we need to do is legitimise the money you have. The moment you pay tax on that money is the moment that it becomes above board. Here's how we will do it." Susan paused as she took a sip of water from a glass. Joe was marvelling at her performance. She had Ted hooked. "I will need to see your books for all the businesses you have. Don't worry, you won't have to part with them. The last thing that I want is for any paperwork about those businesses to be left here at my premises; that wouldn't do. You or a trusted representative will bring them here for me to peruse in their presence. I will not need copies. I will remember the relevant details and form my plans from there. If for any reason I were questioned by the police or Her Majesty's revenue inspectors, I could reasonably deny that I had ever seen them or, even if they could prove I had, that I could remember what they contained."

"Are you telling me that you can read my accounts and remember all the details? I don't believe it."

"Mr Turner, you see those filing cabinets behind you. Would you be so good as to choose any file that you like from them?"

Joe stood and made his way to three tall cabinets on the far side of the room. He opened the second drawer of the middle cabinet. Reaching in, he withdrew a beige-coloured file.

"Stay there, Mr Turner. Be so good as to read the name on the file."

"Henderson and Sons" Joe obliged.

"Ah yes, Henderson's. If you open the file, you will see a summary of their financial status typed out on the first page. Their current assets stand at £3516, 14 shillings and six pence. Last year, they would have paid tax on profits of £253, which amounts to £57, 12 shillings. Unfortunately for them, their turnover was considerably down on previous years, mainly due to a shortage of stock pertaining to the difficulty of importing. However, I have managed to negotiate with the revenue to defer payment of the tax, thus enhancing their cash flow. In fact, their turnover is not down, and we have managed to help them avoid paying tax on a considerable sum."

Joe checked the figures. "Amazing, spot on. Look," Joe said, taking the file towards Ted and offering the page for his inspection. Knowing that his Boss required glasses to read small print and was vain about wearing them, he wasn't surprised when Ted waved him away.

"Please feel free to try another."

Joe opened the bottom drawer of the lefthand cabinet and took the file at the very back. "Davis Motors."

"Assets of £2100. Stock holding £1900, 13 shillings. Money owed to suppliers £1300, 16 shillings. And a mortgage of £1700 secured against their buildings. They made a loss last year of £33 8 shillings, mitigated by unusual expenditure due to bomb damage repairs; this is expected to be recouped by a claim against the government compensation scheme."

"Correct, Miss Hereford. How many files are there in here?"

"I have 197 clients, many of whom have more than one file for various purposes. There are a total of 321 files. I will soon need a new cabinet, don't you think? Please choose another."

"You remember the details of all your clients, Miss Hereford?" Ted asked.

"Yes." Her reply was plainly stated as if it were the most natural thing in the world.

After Joe had tested her on 2 more clients Ted had seen enough and sat for a moment in thought. "You say that I would not need to part with my ledgers, that you will memorise the relevant information. You will then advise me on how to proceed. You can help me use my hard-earned cash to buy up businesses.

These businesses will then, in turn, allow more cash to be legitimised."

"Yes, that is broadly the picture. However, you must understand that there is a cost to this. I am led to understand that this is where our friend Mr Capone went wrong. Let me clarify. If you have 100 pounds cash earned from your existing businesses. You may spend it on smaller items, and no one will notice, but if you try to use it to buy property, shares in a business or even deposit it in a savings account, you do so at a grave risk of it being noticed. So essentially, it is worth very little. The techniques we will use will legitimise the money, but in doing so, you will pay interest on loans and mortgages, as well as tax, plus there are my fees. So, by the time we have processed the money, there will be roughly 50 pounds left."

"That's a lot of cash to lose, Miss Hereford."

"You may judge it that way, but you will own tangible assets. Property, businesses, and shares, all of which are likely to increase in value. Furthermore, they can't be taken away from you. I would imagine that you have your cash carefully secured."

"Yeah, no one's getting at that I can assure you of that."

"Reassuring for you, I am sure. But what if there were a fire in your building? I doubt that you are insured for large amounts of cash stuffed in your cellar. The assets you will buy will be insured. One more thing to consider. If you store your cash, as you do now, it is not making any interest. Each year, inflation eats away at the value of that cash. Inflation rates this year are projected to be over 10%. so, in a year's time, your 100 buys only 90 worth of goods. By the end of this decade, your money is worth less than 40 pounds. If we convert the cash to tangible assets, yes, you will take an initial hit, but in the long term, you will be much better off."

Joe could see that Ted was convinced but he knew him to be a cautious man.

"You mentioned your fees, Miss Hereford."

"Ah yes, I have only agreed to work on your behalf as a personal favour to Sir Stephen. I will have to devote a considerable amount of time to your situation. I can only do that to the detriment of my other clients. Under normal circumstances, I would hire an assistant or sub-contract out some

215

of the donkey work, but I judge that to be risky for both of us. Therefore, I will have to do all clerical work as well. It would look odd on your legitimate accounts if I were to charge too high an hourly rate. Therefore, you will be invoiced at my usual hourly rate, but I will be invoicing for more hours than I actually work. In fact, double. I believe that to be fair."

Ted was quick to reply. "That's scandalous. It's an absolute rip-off. Let's say one and a half hours per hour."

Joe was enjoying this. Susan was playing a blinder. Ted had made a mistake, though. By offering to pay one and a half, he had accepted the principle of paying more than the going rate. Susan was staring at the Gangster. Not for a moment did she flinch.

After a long pause, she said, "Sir, do I look to you like a used car salesman? Nor is this office a market bazaar. I have stated my rate; it is not a rip-off. I do not cheat my clients. I have been upfront and honest with you. I promise you that my services will be very valuable to you. I do not barter, Mr Baker."

Susan began to shuffle some papers on her desk. Seemly uninterested in the conversation anymore. Ted squirmed in his chair. Unaccustomed to being beaten, he grudgingly consented.

Miss Hereford looked up from her papers. "Good. Now, I will need to look at your books. If you wish to bring them to me yourself, that would be best. However, if you wish to send a representative, please make sure that the person has at least half a brain. I will be giving that person detailed and complicated instructions. It will be vital that they are carried out to the letter. Also, and I say this with the utmost respect: that person should not have any sort of a criminal record. You understand that they will be applying for loans, filing tax returns, etc. They should appear to be a respectable, law-abiding citizen."

This was the key moment for Joe's plan, the whole object of which was to get access to the Bakers' ledgers. Joe had known that Ted Baker would have been very nervous about letting them out of his sight. Hence, the elaborate trick they had played to convince Ted that Miss Hereford would not copy them because she had a photographic memory and didn't need or want incriminating copies.

Susan Cartwright, aka Miss Hereford, has an excellent memory but not near as good as had been portrayed. The filing cabinets did contain 321 files. They all detailed the accounts of varied, made-up clients. Each file had a summary of those accounts on the first page, but in fact, there were just 7 different summaries for Susan to remember, still no mean feat.

When Joe selected any of the files from the cabinets, he gave Susan the client's name. Each client name, from A to Z, was either 3, 4, 5, 6, 7, 8, or 9 letters long. Susan's memory labelled the 7 different summaries 3 to 9. So, when Joe read out Davis Motors, with 5 letters in the name Davis, she knew that the figures would correspond to summary number 5.

All Joe had to do was not pick out two files with the same number of letters in the surname.

Joe also knew that Ted's eyesight for reading was poor, so it was unlikely he would look carefully at the figures. They also gambled on Ted getting fed up long before they had exhausted the seven different options.

Now, the second gamble is whether Ted will bring the books to the office in person or entrust them to someone else.

If Ted were to come with them, copying the books would be much riskier. In such a scenario, Susan would read the pages with the ledgers laid out on the desk in front of her, pretending to read and memorise them. A man with a camera, secreted in the ceiling above, would photograph each one as she turned the pages.

If, however, Ted chose to send a representative, who would he send. His lieutenants were not normally chosen for their intellects. Even Eddie, Ted's son, was more brawn than brains. Not to mention that most would fail to qualify as respectable; most had spent some time at the hospitality of the crown.

Joe dared not put himself forward for the role; that might be pushing Ted too far too quickly. But the hope was that Ted would select him, making copying the files and discussing further action so much easier for Susan and Joe. He held his breath.

"Joe here is pretty smart, and he has a clean record. I want him to represent me, although I will be keeping a close eye on the whole thing." Ted was staring at Joe as if saying to him, 'Just you dare cross me'.

"Let us see." Miss Hereford seemed less than convinced; after a long pause where she stared at the young man as if he were a candidate at a job interview, she asked. "The first file you pulled out earlier, what was the name of the company?" Addressing Joe, she looked searchingly into his eyes.

"Henderson and Sons." Was Joe's less-than-confident reply; this bit had not been rehearsed. Sue was ad-libbing, but Joe appreciated the thought behind the cross-examination.

"And how much tax did they pay?"

"50 quid? But you said they didn't need to pay it yet, I think."

"It was 57, and the word you are looking for is deferred." Susan looked less than impressed, like she needed more convincing. "What is 7.5% of 50 pounds?"

Joe shuffled nervously in his seat. "3 pounds and fifteen shillings?" was his eventual reply, his tone was far from assured.

Secretly, Susan Cartwright was enjoying herself. She couldn't wait to remind Joe of his discomfort at some later date. "What is 24 multiplied by 12?"

Joe was panicking as he struggled to find the answer. Then he realised that 12 times 12 was 144, and as 24 was 2 times 12, the answer was 2 times 144—easy. "244." was his rapid reply. No wait, 288."

"Yes, well, I suppose we will have to make do with what's available."

Joe wondered how Susan was keeping a straight face. He knew he would be in for a ribbing when they next met in private.

"Mr Baker, I will need to see you again after I have time to examine the ledgers. Mr Turner, I will expect you tomorrow at noon with the ledgers. Please do not be late, as I will be invoicing your employer from that time on, whether you are here or not. Good afternoon, gentlemen."

With this dismissal, the accountant continued to peruse the papers on her desk. The severe lady clearly did not care for handshakes and goodbyes.

53

Captured – The Baker's Gentleman's Club, London - 1941

"Who the hell are you?" Eddie Baker Asked, clearly both surprised and annoyed that two girls were leaving his house.

Amber wasn't sure if he wanted an answer. "I am taking my friend to the hospital; she's not well." That was all that she could think of, and it didn't help.

Without bothering to reply, Eddie Baker rushed forward, spreading his arms out. He caught the shoulder of each of the two ladies, one in each hand and pushed them hard back through the doorway. They fell as they crossed the threshold, Linda sliding across the polished floor and crashing into the bottom of the stairs. Amber landed on her backside, looking up at her attacker. Baker was shouting. "Billy, Freddie, where the bloody hell are you? Billy."

"Yes, Boss, here, Boss." Billy came running into the hallway, stopping dumbfounded by the scene in front of him. He was closely followed by four men: three of them his colleagues and the fourth, Raspy, still demanding a drink.

"Who the hell is that?" Eddie was beside himself with anger. "What the hell has been going on?"

The men looked at each other, none brave enough to answer, each looking to one of their comrades to oblige the boss. Raspy was rapidly trying to think what he should do. Amber and Linda were captured, and there was little he could do about that. He considered fighting his way out. He might get the jump on 2 or 3 of them, but the odds of the other 2 waiting their turn politely were slim. He had to get away. He would feel terrible about leaving Amber, but if he got out, he could come back with some of Mischa's boys and rescue her.

"I have this girl. This nice girl. You said you have no girls. Here is one, Good for me." Raspy, determined to maintain his role as a drunken reveller, staggered towards Amber.

Billy grabbed the Russian, anxious to show that he was in control of the situation. He guided him towards the door. "No mate, she's not available. It's time you got home to your bed, old son."

This time, Raspy was happy to be shown the door; he just had to get away if he was to save Amber from these hoodlums. His ruse seemed to be working. Until just as they had drawn level with Eddie Baker, he felt the gangster's fist punch hard into his stomach; he dropped to his knees, clutching his abdomen.

"He's going nowhere." Eddie addressed himself to Billy. "Now, what the hell has been going on? Who is he?"

"Just some drunk who wandered in whilst we were getting the guests down to the shelters, Boss. He's a nobody." Billy was feeling nervous under the intense scrutiny of his leader.

"And who is she?" Eddie pointed to Amber, who was still sitting on the hall floor.

"I, I, I dunno, Boss." Billy stuttered out his shameful admission.

"You, you, you, dunno, Boss?" Eddie mocked his subordinate's sputtering reply. "I will tell you who she is, shall I?" Billy stood motionless, awed by his boss's wrath. "She has come to steal that little tart, that is who she is, come to steal our property." Eddie stared up at the trembling thug. "And this bastard." Eddie punctuated his sentence with a colossal kick, which caught the still doubled-over Raspy on the side of the head and sent him sprawling. "He was the decoy, here to distract your attention away from the fact that we were being robbed."

Billy was wise enough to keep quiet. The others followed suit; the room silent save for the diminishing noise of the bombs somewhere across London.

"Get the tart back up to her room and give her a syringe. Check on the other girl up there and make sure that they are both locked up." Eddie directed his orders to two of his men. "The rest of you get the Bolshie and red there downstairs out of sight. The all-clear will sound soon, and we don't want our guests to be seeing this pile of shit in my hallway." Once again, Eddie used his boot, hard into Raspy's stomach, to emphasise his point.

Amber was lifted under her arms and carried down the stairs to the servants' rooms. Undignified but less painful than Raspy's descent, the ruffians decided that pushing him down was an easier option than trying to carry him. The pair were then bundled into a windowless room; a small desk and two chairs were the only furniture. The sound of a key turning in the lock was the harbinger of the futility of escape attempts.

Amber attended to Raspy's wounds as best she could, but the Russian was too concussed to say much. Leaving Amber to worry on her own about their immediate future. She should have listened to Raspy and waited for Joe. Raspy had only come along because he knew that she would come alone. She had been foolhardy, and they were both now in danger. The man, the man on the steps, they had called him Boss. He was too young to be Ted Baker, so he must be Eddie, the son of one of the most feared men in London. What's more, Eddie had his own reputation. She had noticed how Eddie had dominated his men. Particularly the one he called Billy. The man was six inches taller and several stones heavier; he was no shrinking violet; he was a hard man. Amber had grown up around hard men; she knew them. But this Billy was afraid of his boss, terrified. It made her think that the stories about Eddie Baker might be true. It was said that Eddie Baker thrived on violence.

The door bursting open halted Amber's sombre musings. Billy and Freddie grabbed Raspy, forcing him to sit on a chair before tying his hands behind his back. A rope around his chest held him in an upright position, preventing him from slumping forward. Eddie Baker followed his men into the room. In his left hand, he carried a large crowbar. The fingers of his right hand were ornamented with brass. Amber recognised the weapon immediately. She had seen such a thing before; Charlie had taken one off a customer once; the fool had tried to use it on the Calamity, but the practised brawler had dodged its blows. Using his longer reach, he had pummelled the man's face before kicking his feet out from underneath him, then pinning him to the ground, he relieved him of the odious weapon. A knuckle duster was indeed a revolting item. It turned a man's fist into a hammer whilst protecting the delicate bones and joints of the hand. Eddie Baker's Knuckle duster was a custom design. Moulded to his hand, with spikes on the rings of the outer side, evilly designed to maximise the damage caused.

221

"Make her watch." Commanded the sadist to his troops. Amber was sat on a chair and held by her arms; her head pointed towards Raspy.

Eddie moved menacingly slowly towards the captive man before skipping the last two steps and swinging a colossal punch into Raspy's stomach. The rope stopped him from convulsing forward, and he screamed in pain. His attacker waited for the pain to subside before continuing.

Amber struggled in her chair, but strong arms held her in place. "Leave him alone. He has done nothing to you. I don't know this man; I came alone. I came to help my friend, that's all."

"Don't worry I will be having some fun with you very soon. Now keep the bitch quiet, will you?"

"Ha, you punch like a little girl, not a man." Mocked Raspy through gritted teeth.

Eddie swung back round to his victim and dealt a vicious blow across Raspy's face, catching his cheekbone. Blood poured from a gash that the pointed metal had opened. Eddie was breathing heavily. His eyes protruded from his crazed face, the veins in his neck and at his temples pulsed with his adrenaline-imbibed blood. Yet he was not out of control. Each blow he delivered was considered, carefully administering as much pain as possible. The cries and groans of his victim were something to be savoured and enjoyed.

The beating lasted over an hour; to Amber, it seemed like a lifetime. Finally, Eddie Baker tired and ordered his men to take Raspy away.

"He's not dead, boss," Billy stated, surprised that the Russian was still clinging to life.

Eddie looked at him wearily, then picking up the crowbar, he struck Raspy across the back of the neck, smashing his vertebrae. "I think that will do it, now, piss off and give me and the lady some privacy."

54

The slogging Ruffian – South Wales 1941

The two gladiators faced up to each other across the village square. They circled cautiously, waiting for the other to strike. Simon could see the rage in his opponent's eyes; that was good. He had been taught that angry fighters make mistakes. Thomas made the first move; a scything right hook swung dangerously close to Simon's nose as he swayed back from its path. He could feel the whoosh of air as the immense fist passed by his face. Simon realised that however expedient it might be to lose this fight, he really didn't want to. It would hurt!

Simon circled again, staying light on his feet, watching his adversary, and trying to work out a plan. Thomas attacked again, this time with a left, then a right, each big swings, both aimed at the head. Each missing as Simon ducked and dodged out of the trajectory of the swipes. With each missed punch, Thomas seemed to get more frustrated. This wasn't supposed to be happening. In every fight the farmer had ever had, ever since he was a small boy, he was the victor by some ease. His size and his devastating blows usually settled the matter quickly.

Simon weighed up his opponent carefully, sensing his annoyance. Each miss made him more desperate, each attempt less skilful and more impatient than the last. He knew that he had to avoid getting too close to the brute. Strength for strength, Simon was no match for the man. He needed to keep him at arm's length; perhaps he might tire, and Simon might get an opportunity to overcome the ruffian.

Of course, 'The Slogging Ruffian'.

One weekend at the Spa, the instructors were away, some sort of a flap on and the trainees had been left to their own devices. Bored, after the intensity of the previous weeks and months of training, Simon's friend, Joe Turner, had asked Simon to spar with him in the boxing ring. He was reluctant as Joe was a very keen pugilist and incredibly skilful. But it turned out to be a valuable education for Simon.

Joe maintained that boxing was the perfect sport. Where no man's birthright could lend him an advantage. Rich and poor could face each other in the ring on completely equal terms. Simon's education at the hands of his friend was not without a cost. The price was a black eye and several loose teeth. After several rounds, during which Simon clearly struggled to cope with his friend's aggression and skill, Joe called a halt and gave him some tips.

"Silver spoon (Joe's nickname for his well-born friend), you are taller than me with a longer reach, and yet you let me hit you anytime I want. Never stand still, keep moving and use your left to keep me at bay."

The sparing resumed with Simon trying to put in place what Joe had said. Still Joe managed to hit him without response.

"Move," Joe shouted as another blow rocked Simon.

Joe halted again. "Look, mate, it's simple; it's the Straight left versus The Slogging Ruffian." Simon looked bemused. "Are you telling me you have never read Sherlock Holmes?" Joe scoffed.

"Some of the stories certainly, but a long time ago," Simon replied.

"I think it was the story of the lonely cyclist or was it the Solitary Cyclist, anyway, no matter. Holmes is caught asking questions at the local pub by the villain. A fight ensues, and despite the man's size and weight advantage, Holmes wins by using the straight left."

Simon nodded. "That seems to ring a bell."

"Right, stand facing your opponent with your left leg forward and your right leg back, so your body is at a very slight angle to your opponent. Turn your head so that you are looking straight at the man." Joe manoeuvred Simon's body into position. "Good, now stay light on your feet and move with your opponent so you are always looking straight at him." Joe moved left and right; Simon followed as instructed. "Excellent; hold your right hand up and close to your cheek, arm bent so your forearm is parallel with your body, and the elbow points straight down. The left hand is the same. But as your body is slightly turned, the left hand is very slightly further forward."

Simon took up the stance. Joe punched slowly at his head, first with his left and then his right fist. "You see, each time I try to hit your head, the best I can manage is to hit your fists. Your ribs are protected by your forearms. The blows are cushioned, and it's hard for me to hurt you. Now, when I throw my punch, for a moment after, my head is unprotected, so you punch. Your left hand shoots out from your shoulder straight forward until your arm is fully extended. As soon as that happens, pull back your fist to guard your chin again. The straight left!"

Simon tried the technique. "Good," Joe encouraged. But don't turn your head. Keep looking at the target. Remember, always move so you are looking straight at the man."

The advice flooded back to Simon as he faced his Goliath in Trefynydd Square. Joe had made him practice for hours, and now it was time to put the theory into practice.

Thomas swung again with his right, this time as soon as the intended blow had whizzed by. As he had ducked under the swing, Simon let fly with the straight left. Stepping forward as the farmer's head stood unprotected, his weight followed his fist as it smacked into the right ear of the off-balance farmer. As Simon's fist recoiled back to his shoulder, he used the momentum to roll backwards onto his right leg, and he skipped away from the danger.

So far, so good. Hardly a killer punch, but as Joe had taught him, that was not the point. The straight left was to be repeated over and over. The cumulative effect of punch after punch, annoying the man, tiring him, disorientating him, slowing him, hurting him endlessly. Until a punch-drunk opponent would offer an opportunity for a decisive blow to be struck.

Thomas glared at his foe, wondering where the ringing in his ear had come from. Swinging again, this time with his left, it was a fearsome punch, but it was expected. Bemused, he saw his efforts miss again and a fist crash into his left eye. His head jolting back, he fought to steady himself as his feet tripped and slipped on the uneven cobbles of the street. As he regained his balance, his hands out to his side like a tightrope walker, two more jolts cracked into his face. He barely saw the punches coming as they appeared from nowhere and disappeared just as quickly.

Instinctively, Alwyn punched again. This time, his right fist came from below and arched upwards towards the mariner's chin. A classic and potentially lethal uppercut, but by the time it arrived at the target, the opponent's chin was no longer there, as if a magician's sleight of hand had spirited it away from his sight. Too late he glanced to his right, as two more straight lefts exploded from the smaller man's shoulder, like the piston of a speeding steam engine, they slammed into his right eye.

Thomas teetered again. Still swinging, he moved forward. Each time missing, each time a stinging shock snapping his head back. His neck ached from the strain imposed by every affronting jolt.

Simon moved back and gauged the weighty man's condition. He had taken enough punishment, time for the killer punch. But that was a poor choice of words. He desperately wanted to avoid seriously hurting the man. He worried that if he fell to the floor, he might bang his head on the hard ground of the village square. An impact like that might easily kill a man.

Carefully watching his antagonist, he looked to the crowd for help. Thomas's friends stood together in the halo of humanity that formed the boxing ring. Carefully, Simon circled until Thomas, drunkenly following his path, was in front of them. Simon let loose more straight lefts at the head of the giant. Each one snapping his head back and forcing him to step backwards away from the sting, back towards the waiting spectators.

Simon judged his moment and fired off two more effective weapons. This time, he followed them up with his own swinging right just as his opponent's head was still lolling backwards, exposing his chin to the incoming fist.

It was a perfect punch, landing firmly on the point of the jawline with just the right amount of momentum. The force stretched Thomas's body upright, his arms falling to his side. For a split second, his whole weight balanced on his heels before swaying over, like a felled tree, and crashing into the arms of his entourage. The men struggled to control the immense gentleman's impetus. Awkwardly, they managed to check his fall just enough to prevent the damage Simon had feared.

The crowd stood aghast; a small nervous applause broke out but quickly died away. Henry Marshall JP appeared through the audience, carrying a large bucket of water filled from the monument's ancient horse trough. Expertly, the pail's contents sloshed against the felled farmer.

To Simon's relief, the defeated 'slugging ruffian' coughed and spluttered as the cold liquid slowly brought him back to his senses. Bemused, he looked around, at first seemingly ignorant of his fate. A moment passed, and realisation dawned in his stupefied expression. His eyes met Simon's, and he nodded ever so slightly, reluctantly acknowledging the victor.

"What's happened here? Fighting, eh?" The Police constable burst energetically into the action.

"Absolutely nothing gets past your incisive mind, does it constable?" Henry Marshall despairingly quipped. "On the scene in the nick of time, as usual, I see."

The custodian of the law bristled at the thinly veiled criticism of his professional performance. "I was working on another case. I will have you know," he testily retorted.

"Another case of whisky, no doubt." An anonymous voice from the crowd contributed to the debate, much to the suppressed amusement of the spectators.

The Policeman, goaded by the comments, sought to be decisive. Looking from the downed man, his face bruised and cut, to the obvious conqueror, un-marked and clearly, to his rationale, the aggressor. "Assault if ever I saw it," he addressed himself to Simon, "I am arresting you…"

"Hold on one moment, Officer." Henry Marshall intervened. "This was a fair fight. Thomas, there, started it. He threw the first punch. He was intent on trouble, and this young man defended himself with honour. If you arrest him, then as a magistrate, he will come before my bench. In which case, the charges will be thrown out, and I will consider fining you for wasting the court's time." The Justice of the Peace clearly held little respect for the abilities of the lawman.

Several voices rose in agreement from the crowd. The constable shuffled his feet awkwardly as he looked for a face-saving retreat.

"Better get back to your case then." The nameless commentator opined, this time sending his audience into undisguised riotous laughter.

227

55

An arm and a leg – London - 1941

Joe Turner and Miss Hereford (aka Sue Cartwright) met many times over the next few weeks. With unrestricted access to Ted Baker's accounts, they were soon able to establish a true picture of the Baker family's wealth and its sources.

Plans were drawn up and presented to Ted. The gangster was totally on board with the accountant's proposals. Soon, he was releasing money, great piles of cash, to be used to purchase businesses. A fake identity had been concocted, the investments all in its name, Mr Arthur J Richmond. At least Ted was told it was a fake; in fact, the man existed. He worked for the treasury. On paper, he became one of the richest men in London. Unfortunately for him the stocks, bank accounts and shares were all signed over to His Majesty's Government.

Ted Baker believed that he was the owner of several successful and, best of all, legitimate businesses. He even had the deeds and share certificates locked away in his office safe, along with the identification papers to prove he was Mr Arthur J Richmond. Unfortunately for him, they were all fakes. The truth was that the company ownership and their profits would be going towards the war effort. Ted never saw the money again. At least his family could claim that their ill-gotten gains paid for several Spitfires to be built.

Joe Turner was the blue-eyed boy, literally and figuratively, as far as Ted Baker was concerned. He had done exactly what he had wanted, legitimising large parts of the business. Joe's successes only served to increase the distrust and hatred that Ted's son, Eddie, had for the cuckoo in the nest.

Sue Cartwright and the ministry's accountants had traced all the Baker gang's illegal business interests. They had lists of associates, employees, and business premises. They had everything they needed to bring the criminals to justice and put the father and son away for a very long time.

There remained one large stash of cash that so far Ted had kept back. Joe was sufficiently emboldened by his trusted status to ask Ted about it one afternoon as they met at Ted's office.

"Boss, there's a builder's merchant in Staffordshire. They have eleven branches, a good reputation, and sound business. However, the old boy who runs it lacks the get-up-and-go needed to take it to the next level. His son was killed at Dunkirk, and he has no one to leave the business to. Poor old bugger has lost the will to live, apparently. 'Sower pus' says we should buy it and that she needs some cash for a deposit. Says you have enough in your country account, whatever that is."

"Bit of a problem there. I have that earmarked for a very nice little earner I am working on. Tell her to Mortgage one of the other businesses or ask her if it can wait six months or so, maybe less. Actually, I wanted to have a chat with you about this one. They say you are thick as thieves, excuse the pun, with Jeff the Chef."

"Yeah, me and the Chef go way back. What's the stupid bugger been up to now? He been betting again or has he knocked up some tart." Joe's remarks were casual, but he was really concerned for his friend; he hoped he hadn't got himself into the clutches of the Bakers.

"Nah, nothing that I know of, but I think that he might have some contacts that we can use."

"What Jeff, nah, he's pretty legit is old Jeff. What sort of contacts?"

"Other chefs, restaurant owners, hotels, that sort of thing. Look, here's the deal. An old pal of mine has put some meat my way. He says that he can get me tons of the stuff for a song. He reckons that we will be able to flog it for with a tidy bit of bunce."

"Meat, what like steaks and pork chops?" Joe was suppressing his excitement. Could this be the information that Robinson had been looking for? He had to keep his cool and pretend to be ignorant.

"Yes, meat. A couple of problems. It seems that it is very fresh, so fresh that it's still mooing and bleating and whatever it is that pigs do. So, we must find a way to transport it. We have a place to keep it, but we need to find some butchers. Then we have to find people to flog it to. There'll be way too much to peddle it down the market, plus that would soon be noticed. My Pal reckons that the posh hotels and restaurants up west will pay an arm and a leg, excuse the pun again, for this stuff."

Joe laughed at the crime lord's wit, always a good thing to do however poor it was. "I see. Yeah, Jeff would know people like that. Want me to ask him?"

"I want you to set up a network of outlets for this stuff. We should get our first big shipment in six months or so, in good time for Christmas. I bought a farm in Slough; we can keep the animals there. There are buildings that can be used for an abattoir. I want you to find the customers, set up a delivery network and I want you to get some trucks together so we can collect the goods when they are ready."

"When I first started working for you, you mentioned that you wanted me to break into an army camp. Has that got anything to do with this?" Simon asked, wondering if he was pushing too hard.

"You're a smart lad, that's for sure. Yes, as I said, we need some trucks to shift the animals. It's been suggested that army trucks might be an option. Also, the farmers that are producing the animals need some army-style fencing and some Ministry of Defence signs."

"What the bloody hell for?"

"Not sure. I guess if they say they need it, then they need it; I think we should help them. Look into it. I am told that the sort of depot that stores this sort of stuff is lightly guarded, so it might be easier than you think."

Joe wasn't worried about the army depot. He was sure that the Major could set something up so that he could get the gear that was needed while he could be seen carrying out the job.

56

An unfortunate accident - London - 1941

Amber shuddered as Billy and Freddie dragged the heavy corpse out of the room, carefully closing the door behind them.

"Alone at last." Eddie sneered at his prisoner as he grabbed her by the shoulders and pulled her to her feet. "Let's have a look at what we have got, eh." He ripped her dress apart and pushed her backwards. "Urm, not bad; I know a couple of customers who will pay good money for you."

"Never, you will never make me." Amber spat out her words defiantly.

"Oh, we will, my girl, we will. But first, I think that I will try the goods myself."

Eddie advanced towards Amber, evil intent written all over his face. Amber also advanced, driving her knee hard into the crotch of her tormentor. Eddie doubled over and winced, but only for a moment before he straightened rapidly, launching a backhanded strike. His hand caught Amber on the jaw, sending her sprawling backwards. As she tried to catch her balance, her left foot caught on the leg of the chair. Falling uncontrollably, her head hit the wall first, the momentum of her body bending her neck to an impossible angle. The snap of her spine was clearly audible to her attacker.

"Shit, you bitch." Eddie Baker cursed his luck. He looked at the lifeless body and considered raping her anyway. He wasn't at all put off by the ethics of it. She was his to do as he pleased. Pointless, though, he thought. With Eddie, it wasn't about the sex. He could have all the sex he wanted from any of the numerous girls under his control. He got off on the power, the pain and humiliation of his victim. She was beyond that.

As he stooped over her, he noticed she wore a Jade necklace. "A nice keepsake." He thought as he tore it from her shattered neck.

"Billy, get your arse in here."

The door opened, Billy sheepishly peeping into the room. "Yes Boss."

"Get this bitch out of here, will you?"

"Yes Boss, oh Bapt is here, wants to see you."

"All right, send him down."

Baptiste Barbeau came into the room as Eddie was still rubbing his aching groin. "What is happening? Do you know who that man is that Billy is wrapping up?"

"We don't know, he was snooping around here with that bitch." Eddie pointed out Amber's motionless body.

Bapt didn't look at the girl; he was too concerned about the body outside. "I know the man; his name is Mikhail Mihajlovic Medvedev; they call him Raspy."

"What of it, a Rusky I suppose." Eddie was unperturbed.

"He is a good friend of Mischa Agafonov."

Again, Eddie waved away concern. "I don't care what his bloody name is or who his friends are, he was in my club, trying to steal one of my girls."

"Eddie, listen to me." Bapt was one of the few of the Bakers employees who didn't call Eddie Boss, an honorific he reserved for Ted Baker. "That man is connected to Mischa, who is one of the most dangerous Russians in London. There will be trouble if they find out you killed him. These people are dangerous."

"I am dangerous!" Eddie screamed into Bapt's face. "I am scared of nobody. They should be scared of me, right? I am certainly not afraid of some Rusky. Don't you dare question me. I am in charge here; you do as I say."

Bapt calmly held Eddie's powerful stare before steadily replying. "The Boss told us not to get involved with any other gangs at the moment. He said to us that he didn't want any trouble. No wars, he said." It was true that Ted Baker had warned his troops against disputes with the influx of people who had come in from Europe, escaping the war. Several new gangs were emerging. It was Ted's idea that if they got involved in disputes with too many other gangs, it would divert their focus and make them weaker. He reasoned that the gangs would fight amongst themselves for prominence, weakening each other so that he would remain the most powerful. If any of the foreign gangs started to look too potent a threat, then he would deal with them.

232

Baptiste, in challenging Eddie, was also reminding him that it was Ted who was the real Boss, a fact that Eddie was apt to forget, except when his Dad was around.

Eddie was fuming. He hated that Bapt, even though they were friendly, didn't defer to him like all the others. But he knew he was right and wasn't keen to get on the wrong side of his Father, not yet. For a few minutes, he paced backwards and forwards, gradually calming his temper. "What do you think we should do?" He asked, firmly bringing Bapt into the problem.

"Who knows he was here?"

"Just Billy and Freddie."

"Billy said they were trying to get the girl. The one I brought in from the docks a few days ago?"

"Yes. The Rusky was in the Hall when the boys came back from the shelter. He was asking for a girl and a drink. He was obviously diverting their attention whilst the girl tried to slip away. She said she was her friend."

For the first time, Bapt looked towards the body of the girl on the floor. When he saw her pale skin and red hair, he looked again, this time more closely. "I know this girl. She used to work in a pub. What was the name of the pub? Over by the docks. Something and a Dog, do you know it?"

"The Dog and Duck?"

"Yes, the Dog and Duck, that's it."

"I heard that it was bombed out the other week. Quite a few killed, so they say."

"That makes sense. This girl that I found at the docks, the one that they were trying to rescue, told me that she was at the docks because she had no home. She had been bombed out. There is something else I know about this girl, this girl you have killed. She is the girlfriend of Joe Turner."

"She was the girlfriend of Joe Turner." Eddie tried to sound casual, but he was a worried man. It wasn't that he feared Joe Turner, but he was afraid of his father. Eddie Baker had been told in no uncertain terms that he was not to make trouble for Joe. Ted Baker had made it more than clear that Joe was an important man for them. The work he was doing would make them all richer and safer from the law. Eddie doubted that his Father was going to be so happy that he had killed Joe's girl.

"What are you going to do?" Baptiste asked pointedly.

"We will get the boys to get rid of the bodies, and we tell no one. And I mean no one."

Baptiste nodded consent, but both men knew that the balance of power had shifted slightly. Bapt and he had become friends, but, in their world, friends were no more to be trusted than enemies. Baptiste Barbeau now had a hold over Eddie, but how and when would he use it?

57

Nothing to be ashamed of. – Wales 1941

Sara couldn't concentrate on her book. Eventually, she set it aside and let her thoughts stray. She knew which way they would head. It was her day off from the Dragon's Tail. Her aunt would cook and serve the gentlemen diners, those who always took their Sunday lunch at the Dragon. That left Sara free to help the Vicar prepare for the Sunday services and Mrs Morgan, the Butcher's wife, with the children at Sunday School. Then she would collect two plates of food from the Dragon's kitchen and take them across to the Vicarage, sharing the victuals with Emyr Thomas, father of her Fiancé and Vicar at Saint Bridget's. They would usually spend a quiet hour together before evensong. Keeping each other company and sharing apprehension for the plight of Adam, who was captured in the disastrous Norway campaign and remained a prison of war.

"Your book is not holding your interest today, child?" The Vicar had appeared to be dozing, the soft music from the radio having had an emollient effect on the nerves which always plagued him prior to his sermon and now were relieved of their burden.

His words both startled and embarrassed Sara. She had been thinking of the guest at the Hotel. Guiltily, she imagined that Mr Thomas had divined the contents of her mind. "Er, no, I normally find Mrs Christie's novels so enthralling, but recently, I find that so much talk of murder saddens me. Why do you suppose God allows so much violence in the world, Vicar?" Sara always knew that a theological question would be just too tempting to the holy man. She hoped it would cover her discomfiture.

"Dear Sara, God choose to give Man free will. He did that so that we might find our own way towards his light. It is a difficult path and to stray from it all too easy. His son taught us that we must turn the other cheek and that to forgive is divine. Thou shalt not kill, seems to me to be a pretty clear epistle. I fear too many wander from his teachings."

Sara wanted to ask, "But what are we to do about Hitler? Surely God would want us to stop him?" but she was suddenly concerned that she would bring the conversation on to an all-too-familiar and divisive subject—one over which Emyr and his son had often fought.

Adam had always been an idealist. In many ways, he was like his father. But he railed against his father's teachings, convinced that action, not words and prayer, was the only way to right the injustices of the world. He had been a communist and wanted to fight in Spain against the evil of Fascism. His father had managed to dissuade him from that course, but he had been unable to prevent him from joining the British army, even before the Germans had marched into Poland.

Her own faith was stretched to the limits by the troubles of mankind, and particularly her own battles. She realised that the thoughts she had been having since the arrival of the Naval man were sinful in the eyes of the church. But she couldn't hold them back, and what's more, she didn't want to. He was someone special. They would somehow connect to each other in a way that she had never done with Adam. She had never thought of herself as a romantic person but now she dreamed of being with this man, even though she knew little of him.

Sara and Adam had known each other all their lives. She couldn't remember a time when it was not assumed by everyone that they would be together and would one day marry. She had always thought that was what she wanted. But when Adam had joined up, and he had proposed, it had not felt like she thought it would. She knew one day he would ask her, and he knew that she would say yes. But when it happened, it felt like just any other decision, like any other outcome in her life, like what to have for tea, which dress to wear for the party, whether or not to go to Brecon on Market Day. Perhaps she had watched too many pictures. Maybe life and love just weren't like the way that Hollywood portrayed them in the cinema. Whatever the case, it didn't quite feel right to her, and by the time she began to realise it, her fiancée was away to war, captured and not likely to be home any time soon. Now, she felt trapped. She was a young girl living the life of a wife whose husband was away. She didn't go to dances with all the other girls of her age. She had no fun. She desperately hoped and prayed that Adam would return home safe and well. She felt no ill will toward him; she loved him, but not as a lover, not as the man she wanted to be with forever; more as a brother or a cousin who had always been around.

Sinfully and shamefully, there had been moments when she found herself wishing that he wouldn't return. Bitterly castigating herself when those thoughts had come, she wondered if this wearisome life she led was her punishment for sleeping with Adam the night before he had left.

58

Sore and conflicted – Mynydd Farm - Wales – 1941

Alwyn Thomas was sore, aching, and conflicted. The cuts and bruises on his face had stung as his mother had applied the iodine solution. Her scoldings and admonishments were just as hurtful. Her contention that he had let both this family and the country of his birth down by failing to beat the 'weedy' Englishman was the most wounding. She also bitterly reproached him for causing trouble that could bring unwanted attention to their activities at the farm.

What troubled him most were her instructions to him when she had finally calmed down.

"I want you to stay away from the new land and the quarry. We have some men coming in who will be looking after the extra animals over there. I want you to concentrate on the normal farm business. Keep an eye on the girls, keep them busy near the farm, and keep them away from the quarry. Do you understand?"

Alwyn was hurt by her insistence; she clearly didn't trust him. What was it she didn't want him to know? Who were these new men? He knew everyone in the area, and all the farms were short of manpower; where on earth could she have found fresh hands from? His thoughts turned to Henry Marshall. He seemed to have been around the farm a lot recently. Maybe they were his boys? Despite his mother's insistence, Alwyn was determined to find out more.

59

Nightmare – The Dragon's Tail Hotel - 1941

Still, the cold grey Atlantic crashed over the bow. Still, the men screamed from their prison behind the twisted metal door. The axe slid along the deck slowly, edging its way from his reach. He flung himself forward and grabbed at the wooden handle. His hand wrapped around it, bringing pain like he had never known. He relaxed his grip, and for a moment, the agony abated. But he knew that to save the men, he must raise the axe and strike at the hinges of the door. He doubted his strength; he distrusted his resolve. The burns were too agonising, his fervour all but gone. Tears of frustration mixed with the saltwater streaming down his face. His weakness tore at his soul and tortured his self-respect until he screamed in humiliation at his feebleness. The screams of the men, those begging, pleading cries, joined with his.

Simon woke still screaming, alone in the darkness, soaked in sweat and trembling in the fear of his failure.

60

A raid on an army depot – London - 1941

Eddie Baker could usually be found at the 'Gentleman's Club', as it was affectionately known. It was really a brothel. Joe took a cab and dismissed it at the top of the road. He wanted to get a look at the setup before he went in.

It was a nice house, large and in a quiet, secluded neighbourhood. It was sufficiently set back from the road to hide the comings and goings. There appeared to be plenty of rooms for the clients to be entertained. The perfect place for such an enterprise. Joe hated it at first sight. He had no objection to prostitution, but he was more than uncomfortable with the way the girls were exploited in places like this. What's more, he'd heard that the Bakers used drugs; he'd also heard of some of the things that went on here. Toffs with so much money and so many disgusting perversions. No, it was not his thing; there was nothing wrong with a good old honest bit of villainy, but this crossed a line.

Joe knocked at the front door. A very smart man dressed as a butler or manservant opened the door to him.

"Billy, you skinny little runt, how are you?" Joe made a mock punch at the far-from-runty man. "You still boxing, old chum, or has your trainer realised what a sissy you really are?" There weren't many men who would chance their arm by teasing Billy 'the Brick' Mason.

"Joe Turner, I heard you was knocking about. Nah, not too many of the boys left boxing, all joined up, no bugger left to fight. I heard you've decided to throw in with our lot." Billy sounded surprised by the notion of Joe working for the Bakers.

"Yeah, well, if you can't beat 'em, join 'em; that's what I always say. Shame about boxing, you were really good Bill. That right hook of yours was a killer. I hear that the army have a good set up for boxing, you should join up mate."

"I wanted to mate, but Ted wasn't too keen," Billy said ruefully.

Like many other industries, the criminal gangs were affected by a shortage of manpower. Ted had acted quickly to secure exemptions to conscription for his men through less-than-legal means.

"Is Eddie about Bill?"

"Yeah, he's in his office; come on, I will take you down."

Billy led the way down the stairs to what would have been the kitchens and storerooms of the house in former days. Eddie's office was the one-time staff dining area. He had a large desk, sitting grandly across the corner of the room. The man himself sat in a leather-lined chair that dwarfed his diminutive frame, his feet crossed and resting on the desktop, in what he imagined was a powerful and dominating pose but actually made him look ridiculous, his legs only just long enough to reach. Joe suppressed a smile and greeted his boss as warmly as he was able.

"Afternoon Eddie, how's things?" Joe went for his normal cheerful disposition, difficult when his feelings towards the man were those of disgust and loathing.

"Joe Turner, father said that you would be calling by. I have a job for you to do." Eddie wasted no opportunity to remind people of his position in the organisation. Again, Joe curbed his amusement. The job was for Ted, the organ grinder, not for the monkey.

"Yeah, Ted said that you need some army goods. Fencing and signs or something."

"We need fencing and barbed wire, enough for a 2-mile perimeter. Also, signage, you know, 'Army land, keep out' that sort of thing. There's a depot just north of Slough, which is handy coz our farm is just down the road. The idea is that you go in, nab a few trucks and load them up with the gear. Drive down to the farm at Slough; there are barns big enough to hide the trucks. Jon Glover, you know Jon, he has a paint shop over Forest Gate, he will come down and change the insignia on the vehicles. Some Welsh guys will come and pick them up after that. Got it."

"Sounds straightforward enough. Do we know how many guards there are at the depot?"

"No, we don't; you'll have to work that one out for yourself. How many men do you need?"

"I would think that 5 trucks would get us enough fencing, a driver for each and enough to help with the loading." Joe thought out loud. "I reckon 10 men should be enough."

"Alright, take Billy with you; he can tell you the best men to take." Eddie was happy issuing his orders.

The raid on the Depot went without incident; Joe managed to make sure of that by arranging through the ministry for the guards to 'look the other way'. He wanted to make sure that there were no injuries, being concerned that some of Baker's men might be a bit over-aggressive. The guards were, after all, just Home Guardsmen. So, he took the lead. Climbing the fence, he snook up on the guard house, where he overpowered the guards with their prearranged cooperation. Then he called forward the rest of the men. The trucks were loaded with fencing wire, posts, some barrels of petrol and various signs. The trucks quickly made their way to the farm, where they were secreted in two large barns.

Joe was intrigued by what Eddie had let slip, 'Some Welsh lads will come and pick them up,' is what he had said. Joe lost no time in informing the Major and Robinson; a message passed through Susan Cartwright in her role as the prissy accountant.

What both Joe and Eddie didn't know was that this was not the only raid on an army depot. Over the previous months, the Bakers had performed three more robberies. Only these raids were organised by Ted himself using only his most trusted men. The stolen goods were much more valuable and dangerous.

Ted, as always, was careful and clever. He made sure that the depots were in different parts of the country, that the type of armaments stolen was different for everyone and that they were all from different services. He knew that every robbery would be considered very serious, but he figured that each service would handle the thefts themselves. The army would not be too keen to own up to the Navy that they had lost valuable weapons, the Navy wouldn't be anxious to tell the RAF of their losses, etc. Ted hoped that by the time the authorities higher up had linked the raids together if they ever did, then it would all be too late, and he didn't think that they would be looking at his gang as prime suspects. The goods had been driven straight to a secret location in Wales, so very few people in his gang knew anything about them, definitely not Joe Turner or his own Son, Eddie.

61

An unmarked Grave. – London

The Bakers were quite adept at getting rid of corpses; they'd had plenty of practice. In peacetime it had been a quite simple matter. A boat would take the weighted body out in the Thames estuary and dump it there. They had a boatman who knew the tides and knew where to go so that the body would never come back to land. People who crossed the Bakers simply disappeared. Everyone knew it happened but, no body, no crime. Not once were the Bakers arrested or questioned. Ted Baker's legend exceeded the reality, though, as he murdered less than was generally imagined. If somebody was in debt to him, it was hardly in his interests to kill them. Beatings were much more common and effective. The occasional disappearance was enough to stoke fear; fear equalled control, and control was how the Bakers ran their business.

The war muddied the waters somewhat. The extra traffic in the estuary, Navy patrols, mines, and observation posts all made the usual option far too risky. Alternative methods had to be found. The war itself provided one possible solution. People were being killed all the time in the air raids. A body could be put into the ruins of a building, where it would be found by the rescue parties. It would be assumed that the poor unfortunate had simply been in the wrong place at the wrong time, as so many were.

There were difficulties with this, of course. The bomb site had to be recent, ideally a matter of less than a few hours old. Bodies turning up in sites that had already been extensively searched would cause suspicion. Also, the wounds had to be consistent with those of a bomb victim. Gun and knife wounds would no doubt be noticed. However, a man who has been beaten to death, like Raspy, made an ideal bomb victim. Once you have piled rubble on top of the body, it would be unlikely that a hurried autopsy would be able to distinguish an impact wound of a fist or a club from that of falling bricks.

Eddie had produced an ingenious solution for transporting a body to a recent bomb site. He had 'befriended' a man, a customer, who had a taste for attractive young women but lacked the means to pay for them. Eddie had allowed him to get into serious debt for his predilections. Leaving him in Eddie's power. The man was a gas worker, a humble but honest job. A trusted profession and a skill in very high demand during the blitz. The threat of gas leaks and subsequent explosions led to the need for gasmen to check the remains of bomb-damaged buildings before they could be searched for survivors. A gas van moving around the city was never challenged. The body was secreted in the back of the van. A suitable bomb site was selected. The gas man would approach and declare that there was suspected gas mains damage. The rescuers, including the police, were required and more than keen to retreat to a safe distance, allowing the gas worker free rein to place the body in the ruins unobserved. The man would usually have an assistant, often a volunteer, and in these cases, always a Bakers man.

At first, the blackmailed man had been extremely reluctant to take part in such a scheme, but he really had little choice. Of course, once he had done it the first time, he was in a far worse position to refuse further commissions of a similar nature.

For Raspy, Eddie decided that they should look for a site along the route from his home to that of the brothel. That way, if he had told his friends where he was going, they would assume that he had been unluckily caught up in the raid. The Luftwaffe obliged, and Raspy's body was found the next day as hoped. There was nothing to connect him to the Bakers.

Eddie Baker was not disposed to use the same method of disposal for Amber. He was keen that her body would never be found. There was one other way.

The Bakers liked to own people. People that had no choice but to do what they were told when they were told. Most importantly they knew never to speak about it afterwards, especially to the police. What made their organisation unique was the range of people under their dominion. It was natural that they should seek to recruit policemen, judges, politicians, influential and powerful people. But the Bakers knew that nearly every man has a skill, a talent or a position of trust that could be used and abused in the right circumstance. They also knew that every man had a weakness, often one that could be used against them. One such man was Harold Arnold Gordon.

Harold was a god-fearing man. He had no fondness for women or gambling or alcohol. His vices were limited to his pipe and his love of the church, where he devotedly kept the grounds. He was an unassuming man of an immutable character, someone who would normally be well beyond the grasp of a predatory blackmailer. Harold's weakness was not his own, though; it was that of his son.

Harold Junior was a sensitive boy. Clever and a talented artist, he had excelled at grammar school. But he was not a strong boy. Several childhood illnesses had left him a weak and nervous young man. He was not tough like the boys of his neighbourhood. He was subjected to regular bullying and picked on for his sensitive nature. He was certainly not naturally suited for a military career; he was not cut out for the Army.

Harold Senior had been a soldier on the Western Front during the Great War. He had survived the constant shelling, the noise, the dirt, the cold, the waiting to charge or be charged, the dread of killing or being killed, the fear. Harold had endured his trials, albeit barely, but he knew that his son could not withstand such an experience. A war, such as the one he had withstood, would consume his boy; Harold could not let that happen.

Harold Senior had heard of a man who could arrange things. A colleague of the man would arrange for the client's file to go missing from the polling register and from the conscription lists. For a higher charge, he could organise a friendly doctor to sign an exemption certificate. Perhaps inventing a debilitating disease which would release the subject from active duty. Harold used his life savings to secure the latter. When he told his son, the boy was furious and only calmed down when his father agreed that he could work for one of the rescue services as a volunteer so that he could do his bit for the war effort.

What Harold Snr hadn't bargained for was that the man he had seen, and the Doctor were both under the control of the Bakers. Ted Baker kept a close eye on the lists of people who had been helped by the scheme. At first, a gardener and groundskeeper for a church seemed to hold no prospect of advantage for them. Until it was realised that amongst Harold Arnold Gordon's duties was that he was responsible for digging the graves.

Ted Baker approached Harold with an ultimatum. He was to inform them every time there was going to be a burial. On their instruction, he was to dig the hole deeper than normal, get rid of the extra earth, and erect a platform 2 feet above the bottom of the grave. This would be covered with a thin layer of earth. If inspected before the burial, the grave would look normal, the usual depth. During the night before the service, Baker's men would come along, lift the platform, and arrange a body in the cavity below, before placing back the platform and the covering of earth. Again, any inspection would result in a normal looking grave. The real burial would take place, and the grave filled in as normal. The body under the coffin would never be found.

Harold was horrified and initially refused to be involved. Then, it was pointed out to him how much trouble his son would be in if it was discovered that he had illegally avoided conscription. If Harold Junior was an unfit candidate for army life, imagine how he would fare in prison. Branded a coward, his life would be in ruins. His mother, who knew nothing of the scheme, would be destroyed by the shame.

The fact that the Bakers would be unlikely to expose their scheme to the authorities never occurred to Harold. Under pressure and feeling that he had no way out, Howard did as was asked. But insisted that it would be a one-off. Of course, after doing the first, he was in even worse trouble; by helping to conceal a body, he was, in effect, an accomplice to a crime, the ultimate crime, murder. He also knew of the gangster's fierce reputation and feared not only for his own life but the lives of his family.

He never knew who was below the wooden platform. What manner of person they were, innocent or guilty, old or young. But he made sure that with each one, he hid in the graveyard whilst the Baker's men buried their bodies. When the coast was clear, he would stand by the hole and pray for the unfortunate below in the open grave. Hoping that by doing so, along with the words of the minister for the legitimate occupant, their souls would be ready for the judgement day. As indeed. he hoped that his own would be.

So it was that Amber's body was committed to the ground, in the sure and certain hope of resurrection, ashes to ashes…

62

Accusations at the Market – Wales - 1941

"I hear things about you, my Girl." Myfanwy's tone was harsh, and accusation coursing through every syllable of her gruff voice. "You hear what you want to hear, Mrs. Thomas. Always have and always will." Sara tried to sound confident, but she had always feared the Woman. Few in those parts would relish being on the wrong side of Myfanwy Thomas or at the sharp end of her tongue.

"What with your young man starving to death, no doubt, going through God only knows what at the hands of the Hun." Myfanwy was judge, jury, and executioner. In her hands, the scales of Justice were quickly balanced, and retribution was even swifter. Evidence and truth played minor roles in Myfanwy's judicial considerations, certainly not when rumour and gossip were much easier to come by. "And you up to heavens knows what with that, that......"

"I have done nothing wrong", Sara interjected before Myfanwy could find a well-chosen insult.

Myfanwy stared at her. That look said everything: outrage that Sara had interrupted her, distaste for her lies, and, most disturbingly, complete disbelief. Sara felt herself shrink before her accuser.

"I've done nothing", Sara mouthed, but the words fell away into silence and onto stony ground. She felt herself flushing. All confidence ebbed from her. It was as if she were transparent, and Myfanwy could see her heart. She could read all its secrets as if they were etched there on giant stone tablets. Each beat of her heart revealed more of her soul. She knew her desires and sinful thoughts; to Sara, that was worse than the false allegations. Nothing had happened; she had done nothing wrong, but Sara had wanted something to happen; that was the truth. Now, both women knew it.

"You told me to keep an eye on any strangers at the Hotel."
Sara's voice sounded desperate even to her.

"You keep your voice down; you're nothing but a Godless
hussy" Myfanwy was angry now. Sara's sins were one thing. A
thing for conjecture. Juicy gossip with the ladies at the Bridge
club. A probable source of control over her when the time comes.
She did not really care what she got up to. But now, she was
challenging her authority. Now, that was dangerous and had to be
nipped in the bud.

"You want the world to know our business?" Myfanwy glared
as she hissed her question at Sara.

"Well, you certainly don't; that's for sure." Sara regretted her
outburst as soon as it spat from her lips. She had gone too far, and
she knew it. Visibly cowering, she waited for the inevitable
consequences of her stupidity.

Myfanwy was incandescent with rage. The jumped-up little
upstart, she needs teaching a good lesson. But she was nothing if
not pragmatic. She needed Sara's information. There would be
time enough later for retribution. A dish best served cold, no
doubt. With magnificent control, she calmed herself. Her face
softened, and a sweet, benevolent smile played about her lips and
eyes.

"Now, love, we shouldn't be at each other's throats like this.
Your Mother was my best friend. You know I promised her I
would look out for you. I do not mean to judge you. Really, I
don't. I know how difficult it is for a young girl like you in this
day and age. Boyfriend away. Don't if know he's alive or dead.
No fun. All work. Then a bit of glamour comes into your life.
Good looking lad. Good background. Charming, I bet."
Myfanwy's voice was now all soft and soothing.

"He's been a gentleman. He hasn't touched me, hasn't even
tried. He knows about Adam. He has been so understanding.
Honestly, Mrs. Thomas." Sara's voice fell away again, this time
to stifle her tears.

"What do we know about the Lad Sara?" Myfanwy always to
the point.

"He says he was born in India; Parents are still out there".

"Brothers, sisters?"

250

Sara paused, thinking back through the snatched conversations at breakfast and the wonderful meetings out on the hills. "He hasn't mentioned any."

"And he claims to be in the Forces?"

"Navy. When he arrived, he was in uniform, but he hasn't worn it since. I heard him tell Joe in the bar that his boat was torpedoed. He was in the water for a while, and it affected his lungs. Said he was here to get some fresh air and exercise. Extended leave."

Myfanwy looked thoughtful. "I suppose that if you told him about Adam, you asked about his love life?"

Sara blushed again. But she couldn't lie now. "He had a girl, friend of the family. They grew up together, and there was a sort of understanding, an expectation. But she met someone else when he was away at sea. I think he felt let down but not heartbroken." Sara regretted the extra detail instantly. It told of their intimacy. Once again, Myfanwy was delving into her secrets without even trying.

"Has he been asking any questions?"

"Only general things. Nothing specific. Where things are, that sort of thing"?

"And what have you told him?"

"Nothing", Sara answered a little too quickly.

"Keep it that way, young Lady" Myfanwy's tone was back to its former harshness. Sara was dismissed.

"Remember, keep your ears open." It wasn't a request. Sara was trapped, and Myfanwy's demands had to be complied with. She knew Sara's secret and would happily shame her by telling it to everyone if she didn't comply.

Sara turned away and set off towards the bus stop.

"And your legs closed." the jibe rang in her ears and stung into her heart.

63

Nightmare.

The deck is cold and wet beneath his prone body. The axe is held loosely in his hand. The wails of the trapped men still haunt the scene, like banshees forever trapped in the torment of the sound of their own death knell. He rises from the floor and takes the axe. The pain still terrorises his weakened body, but now hope engulfs him, the hope that he can save his men.

But as hope is triumphing, the sea has its say. The axe is once again lifted high, a wave once more crashes across the deck and he is smashed into the bulkhead of the ship. Torn metal slashes at his side, piercing deep into his fragile flesh.

Simon woke holding his side, pressing at the fatal wound. Once again alone in his agony, accompanied only by his fear.

64

Worrying goings on – Mynydd Farm - Wales - 1941

Alwyn was hard pressed to keep the promise he had made to himself to find out what was going on at the new land that was attached to their farm. His mother had been keeping him busy, and it was a while before he was able to get over there and have a snoop around.

When he did, he was shocked by what he found. He approached the area cautiously as he didn't want to be seen by the new men who were working there. For all he knew they might tell his Mother or Marshall if they saw him around. The old buildings that had been there since the quarry was a going concern decades ago had received some rudimentary repairs. The larger structures had new corrugated iron rooves and appeared to have been set up as barns for animal housing, although they were only partly filled. The rough track that led into the valley from the main road to the east showed signs of repair work. The men were nowhere to be seen.

Just as he was about to venture nearer, Alwyn heard the noise of trucks approaching. They were coming from the old road from the west, along a track that Alwyn thought was impassible, clearly that too, had been made good after its years of ill use. From the nearest barn, 3 men came out to meet the delivery. They waved to the drivers who backed the 3 trucks into their allotted slots next to the barns. A car followed and parked randomly in front of the trucks. The trucks were low on their axles and obviously heavily laden. 4 men alighted from the vehicles and joined their hosts, who warmly received them; sacks were handed over, perhaps fresh food and supplies for the residents, and they all headed away to the shelter of the barn.

Alwyn carefully studied the lorries which appeared to be military, not agricultural, at any rate. The men had made no attempt to begin unloading, and there was no movement of the springs and no noise, suggesting that the wagons were not loaded with beasts.

There was laughter and shouted conversation coming from the barn, implying that the men knew each other and were happy to renew their acquaintance. Alwyn chanced, moving nearer to the trucks. Whilst he could hear the muffled sound of their merriment, he was reasonably confident that he would not be disturbed by the men. He climbed up onto the tailgate of a lorry and pulled the curtain aside. The cargo was stacked high, boxes piled up floor to ceiling. Each box was labelled with stencilled lettering. The precise meaning of the inscriptions was beyond Alwyn's knowledge, but he saw names like Enfield and Lee and numerous numbers and quantities. The young farmer had little doubt that what he was looking at was boxes of guns or bullets or probably both.

Dropping back to the ground, Alwyn slipped back to the tree line to cover his escape and hurried back to Mynydd farm. His hands were shaking, his mouth dry, his mind in turmoil. He had known that his mother had been bending the rules with regard to the animal production quotas. He knew that they had supplied unregistered beasts for Morgan the butcher to slaughter and sell. 'A little extra money for the farm, more food for our friends in the village' is how his mother had explained it. But this, what had she gotten them involved in now.

65

Ancestry – Joe's flat - London - 1941

Joe had had a hard day and night. The raid on the army depot had gone off without incident, but it had been a tense situation. He had managed to curb the over-aggressive natures of the Baker's men, but he had been waiting for something to go wrong, some innocent guard to be hurt or the police to turn up, and the ensuing battle to get messy. As it panned out, everything ran like clockwork. The fact that the Baker boys had seen him pull off such a seamless operation, which included him overcoming 3 guards single-handed, would enhance his reputation and standing with them.

They had scoped out the depot, waiting until the early hours before going in. Once Joe had secured the guards, they had set about loading the supplies into the trucks, which, one at a time, had set off for the short journey to the farm. Joe had left with the last truck, driven by Bapt. All the vehicles had made it without incident and were safely parked in the barns. Joe had then taken the opportunity to have a look around the farm. It was a large affair. The buildings were set well back from the road, in a depression in the land, causing them to be hidden from view on all sides. The farmhouse was large but basically furnished. An old wood-burning stove was the only hint of any modernity. The bedrooms and living room were laid out with camp beds; there was wood chopped ready for the fireplaces and the stove. Joe was surprised to find there was no electricity in the house; he was sure that he had seen a power line looping its way along the track from the main road. When he checked, he found that the line led to the nearest of the outbuildings. He mused as to why the electricity was needed in the barn but not the house. On looking around the barn, the answer became apparent. The building was old but had been newly renovated. Holes in the walls had been patched efficiently but without regard for any cosmetic considerations. The large doors had been rehung and opened freely. Inside, there was evidence that the roof had received attention. The room was warm and dry. The floor had been concreted, giving the interior an impression of almost surgical cleanliness. At the far end, there was a series of metal stalls clearly designed to restrain animals. Next to them, a row of hooked chains hung from a crossbeam. The chains attached to the beam on a pulley system designed for lifting and moving beasts along the shed. Below the end of the pullies, a large metal tray with a central drain had been set into the concrete. The pullies ran next to a line of wooden benches. Each of them was more than adequately lit by a large electric bulb overhead. In the corner was what appeared to be a large room built within the barn. On closer examination, Joe could see that the room was metal, lined with lead and with large steel doors. It was a giant refrigerator, like the kind you might find in the kitchen of a large hotel or in an abattoir. Ted Baker had bought himself a remote farm and built himself a slaughterhouse.

Another surprising occurrence that had come out of the operation was that Bapt had volunteered to help. Billy had put in a good word for him, and Joe was happy to have him along. But he had expected that a man such as he would consider such work as beneath him. Joe had the feeling that Bapt had wanted to be as close to him as possible. Like he was trying to get to know him, sounding him out, perhaps. Joe could think of two reasons why that might be the case. Firstly, he might be watching Joe on behalf of Eddie. Baker Junior clearly had no fondness for Joe. There was clear resentment for the fact that Ted appeared to trust him. Was he using Bapt to spy on Joe? The second possibility was the polar opposite. Bapt was wary of Eddie and wanted to cultivate an alliance with Joe. It was obvious that the loyalty of the members of the Baker gang to Eddie was founded on fear rather than any genuine fidelity. Bapt, on the other hand, seemed to have the respect of the boys. They looked to him for instruction instinctively. He was a natural leader. Whatever the truth of the situation, Joe would have to tread carefully. He thought ruefully to himself that this kind of politics and power-play was exactly why he preferred to work alone.

Joe climbed the stairs to his flat late that evening, having been on his feet for nearly 24 hours. He was ready for some of that excellent brandy that had been thoughtfully provided. He was hungry and hoped that there would be something tasty in the larder; he had no desire to go out to eat. As he approached his front door, he heard a noise from within. A cupboard door closing unless he was very much mistaken. He put his hand behind his back and felt for the cold steel of the gun tucked into his belt. He shuddered at its icy touch; he would never get used to its evil presence. He would much prefer to be without it, but he had to be practical. His life was full of danger and his enemies didn't fight fair.

Gently, slowly, he turned the lock of the front door. Its mechanism was silent; Joe had oiled it and the hinges of all the doors for just such an eventuality. He had also carefully studied the weaknesses of the floorboards in the hallway and knew exactly which ones would squeak and which ones would soundlessly bear his weight. Skilfully placing his feet, he reached the door to the living area, which was slightly ajar. Joe stood and checked his senses. The flat was warm, a smell of coal burning in the grate. Another smell presented itself, cooking pastry and meat, the sweet smell of gravy bubbling and escaping the crust, burning onto the pie dish. A soft, lyrical voice told tales of a sweet Molly Malone. A voice of an older lady but one that still carried the remembrance of beauty and innocence.

Joe pushed open the door and walked casually into the kitchen. "So, you would be Doreen?" Joe relaxed his grip on the gun as he saw that his housekeeper was alone. Although he was meeting her for the first time, even though he had been living in the flat for a few months now, he was convinced that he knew the answer to his question. After all, how many assassins would be considerate enough to make their victim a steak and kidney pie before blowing their brains out?

"And you would be Joe Turner. I'd recognise those eyes anywhere." The woman paused, shocked, clearly distracted and bemused by what she had just said. Like she had seen a ghost. Quickly, she recovered herself and carried on. "They said you were handsome; if I had known how handsome, I would have stayed back before now to make sure that your bed was properly warmed." A heavily mascaraed eye winked cheekily at Joe.

The eye belonged to a face that was worn and used but still held a hint of the undoubted beauty it had once possessed. The harsh makeup accentuated her high cheekbones and bow-shaped lips. Powder, rouge, and red lipstick expertly but lavishly applied. Her dress was tight-fitting to her slim, almost famished body. Her breasts were high and shapely as they had once been naturally, but now any pertness thanks to whalebone and the skills of her seamstress. The low-cut v of her cleavage exposed flesh enough to entice. Ted had described her as mutton dressed as lamb, a little unfair; after all, who could get Lamb in London these days? Joe warmed to the woman immediately. Not for her fading but still potent sexuality but for the warmth, humour and humanity that had clearly survived her arduous life.

"Thank you. My bed is quite warm enough." Joe smiled back.

"Well do let me know if it turns cold, I do like to please in my work" The mascara fluttered again playfully.

"Well, you certainly pleased with that steak and Kidney pie you left for me when I first moved in. Is that another one I smell?" Joe ignored the tease.

"Almost ready, just mashing the potatoes. Sit down. I'll have it ready in a moment."

"I am afraid I couldn't finish the last one. I had seconds and warmed it up the next day, but it was just too much. Would you have some with me now? Help me do it justice." Joe wanted the woman to stay for the evening. Not for her offer of intimacy, which he doubted was serious, but for her company and companionship. He liked her as a man who had been blessed with a family might warm to an aunt. Joe hadn't been so blessed, and the woman was not his aunt, but his instincts trusted her; he didn't know why. After all she had worked for Ted Baker for years, so who would know more about him and his organisation. He might well learn something of use from her.

"My luck must be changing. It's been a while since I had dinner with such a handsome young man. I better say yes before you change your mind. Just to be clear, we are just talking about dinner?" And there was that wink again.

"Just dinner!" Joe asserted firmly but not unkindly.

The pie was outstanding. Between them, they managed to make a dent in it and work their way through a bottle of wine and a sizeable amount of Ted's brandy. They talked easily about shared acquaintances and friends. They discussed the war and how all that anyone ever talked about was the war. She reminisced about Ted and the old days. The parties, the men. She was unashamed of her past profession; she spoke of it as naturally as a man might discuss his job as an engineer or a solicitor. She name-dropped some of the famous men she had 'entertained' as she put it. Sportsmen, Politicians, and, of course, senior policemen. She was a humorous speaker; her anecdotes were amusing. Joe thought that she could write a best-selling book based on her experiences, although it would be a brave publisher that named the names. She kept Joe laughing and absorbed late into the early hours despite his fatigue. At last, their conversation waned, and they sat easy and comfortable in their companionship.

Cautiously, Joe asked something that had bothered him all evening. "When we met earlier, you said that you would recognise those eyes anywhere, but we haven't met before, have we?" Joe asked earnestly, looking for the answer from behind the darkly drawn lids of her eyes.

For the first time, Doreen couldn't hold the gaze of Joe's impossibly blue eyes. She stared down at her hands, fidgeting nervously in her lap. She stayed like that for several minutes whilst she gathered her thoughts. The sirens sounded, but they both sat, ignoring their warning. At last, she looked again into Joe's eyes. "You were just a few minutes old when I last looked into your eyes. I was holding you in my arms. You were then, and still remain, the most beautiful thing that I have ever seen."

Joe sat up straight, aghast at what he was hearing. He made to interrupt, but she held a painted fingertip gently to his lips, quietening him and imploring him to listen.

"I can guess what you are thinking, but I have to tell you that I am not your mother. I wish to God that I were. I wish that I had run away with you then, taken you to my home in Ireland, the home that I should never have left. I should have run with you and brought you up as my own. We should have run from this evil city; we could have been happy. For your mother's sake, I should have taken you."

Black lines of tears streaked down her cheeks as she wept bitterly in regret. A lifetime of anguish seemed to flow, washing away at her rendered mask, revealing her frailty. Joe wrapped his

259

arms around her tightly as she cried, feeling her pain as it emanated from her in huge, uncontrollable, heart-breaking sobs. At last, the tears subsided, and she released herself from Joe's embrace. Wiping her face, she composed herself to explain. "Oh, my dear, I must look a sight." She didn't wait for an answer; her confession was years overdue, and her need to make it irrepressible. "I met your mother soon after I arrived in London. I had come from Ireland, and she was from somewhere in Scotland. She told me where once, I have it written in my diary if you would like to know. She had your eyes, those amazingly blue eyes; she was beyond beautiful. We hit it off straight away; we were inseparable. We had the same foolish, girlish dreams of stardom and fame. We had both come to London to make a career on the stage, in the theatre or shows. We both had talent, but we needed more; we needed luck, and, as it turned out, we had precious little of that. The war was on, and there were a lot of shows, but there were also lots of girls. Proper jobs were hard to find. When our luck was down, we met Ted Baker. He was a charming man in those days, good looking, on his way up. He was a ruthless, driven, determined man who got what he wanted and nothing, and no one got in his way. He took a fancy to me, and for a good while, I was his girl. You can't imagine it now but, in those days, I was quite a looker. Well, he wooed me. There was money, parties, celebrities, drink, drugs. All manner of fun and excitement. Of course, we didn't think at that time where the money came from. We were so young and stupid; we had no fear and no idea how the world could hurt us. Your mother, her name was Lorraine, became pregnant. Before you ask, I don't know who your father was. If she knew, she never told me. Ted had no time or use for a pregnant girl, and she was cast out. I went with her, and we survived on my meagre savings. An unmarried girl with a child was taboo in those days, and we hoped to deliver the baby, you, on our own. But something went wrong with the birth; Lorraine was struggling, and there was so much blood. I had to do something, so I carried her in my arms to the hospital. You were delivered, but your mother was very weak. I held you as they fought for her life. It was hopeless, and the person who I loved most in this life left us. They wouldn't let me keep you. They knew what type of woman I was, and I wasn't a relative.

They took you from me and pushed me out of the door into the street. I was in shock; I didn't know what to do. I went to Ted, and he took me back. I was ill for some time, but when I had recovered, I looked for you. I traced you to the nuns, but when I asked, they told me you had died. I should have run with you that day, Joe. I wish to God that I had just run with you."

The tears returned, this time Joe crying too, as they held on to each other.

Dawn had been and gone when Joe realised the time, he had to get over to Ted's office to tell him about the raid. He washed, shaved and pulled on one of his new suits as Doreen slept on the sofa. When he was ready to leave, he shook her gently. Her heavy eyelids blinked into life, and recognition spread across her face. Her smile was soft, gentle and loving as that of any mother for her child could possibly be.

"Well, you scrub up well, quite the dandy." Her voice was gruff from the brandy and cigarettes of the night before, yet full of pride.

"I have to go. Will you come back tonight? I'd like to talk to you some more," Joe said, his tone respectful and eager.

"Of course, we can finish that Pie. I have so much to tell you." Joe made to leave, but Doreen stopped him. "Be careful who you tell about all of this. And Joe, be careful".

Joe reassured her that he could look after himself, but Doreen pressed her point. "I mean it, Joe, be careful, you're being watched. Ted Baker trusts no one, not even his son. He is keeping an eye on you. He told me to let him know what you are up to."

Joe had expected that he would be watched, but even so, it drove home to him the danger he was in if Ted found out who he really was. "Don't worry. We will talk tonight. Everything will be all right, I promise."

Doreen nodded and smiled. For the first time in years, she had someone she could trust. For the first time since Lorraine, she had someone she could love. An honest and pure kind of love, not the kind she had sold for all her adult life.

66

Another Sunday Lunch – The Dragon's Tail Hotel - Wales – 1941

Simon was becoming impatient with his lack of progress in his investigations. It was as he had feared; the community was tight-knit. The towns folk were pleasant and polite with the stranger, but at no point could he find anyone with whom he could gain confidence. The one exception was Sara, but for reasons that he couldn't explain, he felt it prudent not to push their friendship by interrogating her about local gossip. It might be, that if he continued to have no luck, he would have to chance his arm but for now he preferred to find another way.

Simon had been, since that first meal they had had together, a regular guest of the gentlemen who dined at the Dragon's Tail each Sunday. His invitation was now presumed rather than formal. In fact, it was customary at the conclusion of each assembly, for the gentlemen to declare their intension to meet again the following Sunday. On rare occasions, a participant would pardon themselves on the grounds of some other obligation on their time; the General would occasionally be away for the weekend to visit friends, Lady Kege Le Burg would be on one of her rare visits to her home and would require her husband's attention (much to his annoyance), Marshall might be away on business. Each time, the absentee was undoubtedly regretful.

Pritchard-Smythe was also considered a fully paid-up member of the group, but his duties kept his attendance less frequent than the others. Indeed, it became noticed that Simon was the most regular attendee. With this in mind, Simon deemed it only fitting that he be the host of one of the get-togethers. He chose a weekend when all the regulars were able to attend, and at his insistence, the Army Captain was to be present.

He thought it prudent that he supply a liberal and tasteful supply of wine to oil the wheels of the conversation. Indeed, he thought it so important that he risked a message to Major Calderdale. In it, he explained that he wished to obtain for the occasion a vintage that would be considered to be rare and difficult to come by. Perhaps one that would suggest that he had used a privileged and not quite orthodox means of supply. He wished to cultivate a notion that he was prepared to bend the rules, not quite the strait-laced naval officer after all. Although alcoholic drinks were not rationed, they were in short supply. The Major came up trumps with the request, and a delivery was made to him, care of the hotel. Included with the wine were several bottles of whisky, an excellent port and some expensive cigars.

The Sunday in question was one of those dark Welsh days when the rain poured, and daylight and night were barely distinguishable. The mountains that were usually distantly visible from the dining room windows hid beneath a cloak of mist. He shuddered as he waited for his guests, watching the rain run down the windowpanes. It was a good day for his plan; none of the men would be keen to leave the party to go back out into the storm. They would be easily persuaded to consume more wine and whisky, the hope being that their tongues would be loosened.

An arrangement had been made with Mrs Williams and the fare she offered was even more sumptuous than her usual, albeit that it was difficult to imagine how she managed it. The beef Wellington was her signature dish, though she was seldom persuaded to make it due to the work involved. The wine was peerless; Simon took the role of sommelier, ensuring that each glass was never empty. Carefully he checked his own consumption whilst matching the gaiety of the others as the alcohol took effect.

The conversation took its usual course. The war was an inevitable subject, which led to the reminiscing stories of the old soldiers. When the others quickly tired of their exaggerated exploits, new topics were sought and found and exhausted. Marshall was always good for a funny story but never spoke of his own past or much about his business. Simon sought to change that and find out more of the gossip of the town. Pritchard-Smythe had been carefully briefed and took the lead; that way, Simon hoped to deflect any suspicion of inquisitiveness away from himself.

"Henry, what is it like in the magistrates court these days? Are they keeping you busy?" The young army Captain asked.

"Oh, same as usual. Never anything really exciting. It's petty stuff, really. Occasional tension between the soldiers at the barracks in Brecon and the local lads. Usually prompted by a dispute over a girl. The MPs normally handle the punishment of the soldiers, the local lads we usually bind over to keep the peace. No point in locking up a lad that's needed at a farm." Replied the Justice of the Peace.

Pritchard-Smythe wasn't happy with the evasive reply; he wanted to know more. "Nothing juicy, eh? There must be something—theft, breaking and entering, the odd murder perhaps." His tone was jovial and teasing. Come on, spill the beans, old chap."

"Happily, there hasn't been a murder that we know of since '86. Even if there had been, we are just the magistrates, we would pass it on to the Crown Court. The murder of 86 was an interesting case, though, one of a family feud no less, like the Wild West. Two families at war over a water dispute, can you imagine that, fighting over water in Wales." The men laughed as Marshall pointed to the windows awash with the rain. There was no doubt he had a way of telling a story, "Apparently, one of the farmers, years before, had dammed a stream and diverted the waterway. That dried up the stream that flowed through the others land, causing his sheep to suffer over a series of dry summers. The lord of the manor, one of your ancestors I believe Sir Cecil, forced the farmer to put the stream back to how it was. But that didn't stop the other man from claiming that the water was being poisoned. The feud went on for years across several generations. Sons and grandsons fought in the schoolyard, in the pubs, whenever and wherever they met. The local pub landlords had to bar one or other of the family's boys so that they would not meet and cause trouble. There was more consternation when one of the sons eloped with a daughter of the other family. The final straw for the murderer was when he lost his prize sheep. Convinced that it had been poisoned, the man challenged his rival on Market day in the town square. Heated words were exchanged, and punches were thrown. The wronged man pulled a knife, and that was that. There were plenty of witnesses, his lawyer cited provocation in mitigation, but inescapably, the man was hanged." The table was silent as the friends reflected on the sadness of the case.

"The thing that strikes me." Commented the General after a suitably respectful pause. "Was that the man was driven to murderous rage, not by the deflowerment of his daughter, but by the loss of his prize sheep." There was a moment's hesitation as the group considered the indecorous observation before they all broke into riotous laughter, their merriment aided by the wine.

It was a good while before the party were able to recover their decorum and continue their conversation. The General was first to speak. "In all seriousness, and please forgive my inappropriate levity, it's a sad case. What happened to the families after that? Are they still in the area?"

"I am afraid I do not know," confessed Marshall.

"I do." Interjected Sir Cecil, his voice sombre. "Of course, both families were grieving; they had likewise been subjected to a great loss. The head of each family was taken tragically away. As often happens at such consequential times, the women of the sad tale saw sense. The widows met together, arbitrated by the Vicar of the time, and they talked. They were united in grief and by the futility of the feud. They vowed there and then to put a stop to the senseless quarrel. They each bound their own relatives to forgive and forget. The young couple who had eloped were brought home, and thus, the families united. There are many descendants still living in the area, many from both lineages; I won't mention the family names, although it would be easy enough to find out if you so wished, you have stumbled upon their shameful secret, Henry. It is rarely discussed in the town and then only in hushed tones. I believe, though, that there is a strong moral of this story that we can all learn from."

The aristocrat paused and looked sombrely at each of the participants in turn, checking that they were paying the appropriate attention to his momentous words. When he continued, his voice was even more grave, to the point of being almost Churchillian in tone.

"Never!" He banged his clenched fist on the table for effect. "I say NEVER," his voice louder and beseeching, his eyes imploring his audience to take heed, "EVER, come between a farmer and his prize ewe."

The end of the Lord's sentence was barely discernible as he broke into fits of giggles. The unlucky Pritchard-Smythe had unwisely chosen that moment to take a sip of wine and consequently almost choked. Marshall, too, gagged on his cigar. The General's ageing and full bladder was severely agitated by his own hysterics, and he hastily excused himself from the table. Simon, too, rocked as laughter overcame him. It was only later that he realised that it had been some time since he had laughed so much.

It was an appropriate time for a break as the gentlemen composed themselves. The meal completed, they retired to the lounge, where a fire enticed them to sit. Arranged in their comfortable chairs of choice and habit, one or two of the assembly made mention of returning to their homes, perhaps one for the road, not too much as they had already drunk close to their fill. But having other ideas, Simon brought out the single malt. There was a distinct rumble of surprise and wonder at the quality of the offering. Generous measures were poured by their host.

"Drink freely, gentlemen." Simon adopted a pantomime of a Scots accent and held the bottle up for all to see. "Not only is this little lassie a rare beauty, but she has 5 sisters into the bargain."

Any pretence of abstinence was immediately abandoned by all. Such opportunities were few and far between; none were going to miss this one. The company visibly settled further into their comfortable chairs; they were here for the long haul. Pritchard-Smythe caught Simon's eye and winked knowingly.

"I confess that I am not satisfied, Henry," Smythe said with a mock seriousness. "There must be some crime around here; I only ask because a mucker of mine from school, who is now pretty senior in Scotland Yard, told me that they are stretched to breaking point."

"I assume much of that would be staff shortages; we had that in the last show. Remember, too many coppers going into the army." Opined the General.

"True, General, but apparently, crime rates have shot up also, which compounds the problem; of course, the authorities are playing it down. I suppose it is a town thing, especially in areas being bombed. They are a bit concerned about looting, according to Wilf." The soldier nudged the subject along.

The General and Sir Cecil were incensed and made comments advocating shooting the offenders.

"I am afraid that it is true." Henry Marshall confirmed. "There are very strong penalties available to the courts, including the death penalty. The crimes are being dealt with as quietly as possible. The newspapers are too caught up with the progress of the war, thankfully. As custodians of the law, we have been advised to consider each case on its merit. Be grateful, gentlemen, that in our little community, we have avoided Hitler's bombs."

The old soldiers still advocated strong measures. "Are you saying that you have been told to be lenient with these, these, these villains? Ridiculous. I say make an example of them." Was the Generals opinion.

Smythe commented. "My pal told me of a difficult case they had to deal with. Apparently, the leader of a rescue team had been working all night pulling people, dead and alive, from bombed-out buildings. Imagine it gentlemen, the horror of that job. Children, old people, the bombs don't discriminate, you know. As things were quietening down, the man found a bottle of brandy, miraculously unbroken, in a destroyed house. He thought of his men, who were close to collapse. He opened the bottle, and each man took a swig. Each one of them was now a criminal in the eyes of the law. Should we make an example of them General?"

The General was suitably abashed. "What happened to them?" he asked.

"The man took the blame; He insisted that his men didn't know where the bottle came from. He pleaded guilty; his good character and war work were considered in mitigation, and he was fined. Wilf said that his colleagues had a whip round to help him cover the fine, even some of the coppers chipped in." Smythe said. "You are right, Henry; I am not sure that we realise the distress caused by the bombing. People lose everything. There is a shortage of emergency housing. People have nowhere to go, no money, barely the clothes they had on when the bomb hit."

"But they get compensation surely." Insisted Sir Cecil.

"Oh, eventually, but these things take time. What do the poor souls do in the meantime? Apparently, the volunteers, the Red Cross, the Women's Institute, and such are doing a tremendous job helping people out. Gentlemen, let us hope that our small community never has to face such horrors." For a moment, Smythe's eyes stared into the distance, perhaps he was thinking of the horrors that he was sure awaited him at some point in this war. "Anyway, we have established that it has been 60 years or so since we have had a murder around here; what does Constable Blythe do all day?" the soldier tried to lighten the mood and get the subject back to local scandal.

"That's a bloody good question." Commented Sir Cecil. "What does that man do, apart from drink? The man is bloody useless; he couldn't catch a cold, never mind a criminal."

"Well, I must agree with you there, Sir Cecil. Fortunately, the mafia are not very active in Trefynydd." The General smiled. "Although we did have a missing person case quite recently, didn't we Henry?"

Simon's ears pricked up as he heard the General's words. Could this be the butcher? He looked at Henry Marshall, who seemed unhappy that that particular stone had been turned.

"Yes, we did. To be fair, Blythe did everything by the book on that one." Answered Marshall. Without asking, he reached for the whisky bottle and poured himself a large measure. He seemed agitated and reluctant to discuss the case.

"Really, what happened?" Pritchard-Smythe was playing a blinder, pushing the conversation in the right direction. Taking the role of the nosey outsider. "Who went missing?"

Marshall looked non-plussed; he sighed before answering. "Well, if you must know, we are back in the realms of local secrets and scandal. Gentlemen, I need to ask you, on your honour, to be discrete about this one. Constable Blythe had a report come through of a missing person. He investigated and then came to me for advice. David Morgan, the town's butcher, was the missing man. His Aunt had not heard from him and reported it. Ceridwen Morgan, his wife, told Blythe that her husband had joined up. Even to our erstwhile officer, that didn't seem likely; in an uncharacteristic surge of competence, Blythe dug deeper. To be fair to the man, he had the good sense to be

268

discreet about it. He couldn't find any record of Morgan signing up for any of the forces. He came to me before he escalated it. He doubted that there was any foul play; the wife is a mouse of a woman, and the son wouldn't say boo to a goose. I did a little digging of my own. It seems that Mr Morgan is a bit of a cad. It had been rumoured for years that he beat his wife. It also appears that he was leading something of a double life. He had another lady in a village on the other side of Brecon. It seems that he left his wife and son for the arms of some hussy with her own cottage and a rich late husband. Anyway, my source for all this information, a good friend to the innocent of this saga, begged me to tread carefully. She was concerned that if the truth got out poor Mrs Morgan would be destroyed by the shame. This isn't London, you understand, divorce and adultery are not so commonplace; these are God-fearing people. So as no crime had been committed, apart from the grieving lady telling porkies to the police, we let sleeping dogs lie."

Simon had been watching Marshall carefully as he spoke. This was the event that had led Robison to suspect there was something going on in the locale. Henry Marshall always told a good story; he was always amusing. But Simon detected a slight discomfort in the man's demeanour. What wasn't he saying? What more did he know? Henry Marshall started to speak again; Simon listened intently whilst trying to seem no more than vaguely interested.

"Thing is I think old Morgan had been making a bit on the side. According to Mrs Willis, my housekeeper, there's always extra meat to be had at his shop. I have been keeping an eye on that. I mean, if it's just a little here and there, then where's the harm? But recently, we have been told to be a bit harsher with any cases of black-market racketeering coming before us. The powers that be are getting a little twitchy."

"Good God, Marshall, I thought you said that there's nothing exciting happening. Murders, eloping daughters, family feuds, disappearing Butchers, it's like Sodom and Gomorrah around here." Pritchard-Smythe joked.

"Hardly that, dear boy, hardly that." Marshal smiled.

"So, are you saying that Morgan was likely to be caught selling off ration meat?" Sir Cecil asked, bringing the conversation back onto the track. Simon could have kissed the Knight.

"Well, we can only prosecute a man if he comes before our court and that's not likely to happen with old Freddie Blythe on the case. It would be interesting to find out where the excess meat was coming from, though."

"Do you have any ideas?" Again, Sir Cecil was unconsciously Simon's hero.

"Well Morgan is thick as thieves with a man called Harris, farms up towards the escarpment on the other side of the canal. Harris is not the most popular man in the area, apparently, but he and Morgan were friends. If I had to place a bet, it would be my guess that they were in league with each other. But we are speculating, and there is no real evidence. I have said too much, it must be that excellent spirit you have been pouring down our throats, Lieutenant." Marshall smiled at Simon. "Better top up my glass, young man; all that talking has made my mouth dry."

67

Who to trust. – London - 1941

Joe sat in the back of a taxi as it crawled through the wreckage of another London street on its way to Ted's office. He was replaying every word of his encounter with Doreen from the night before. He had to admit that it had been an emotional evening. Learning that your mother had been a prostitute was not a shock, hardly even a surprise, given his history. Yes, as a boy, like all orphans, he had dreamed that one day his mother would turn up. It would have all been a great mix up and he would be whisked away by his loving parents, who would live in a large country estate with horses and servants and lots of money. But Joe had stopped believing in fairytales a long time ago. Better a prostitute mother who wanted to keep him than being abandoned and unwanted, as so many of his peers had been. Siting now in the cold light of day he had to be practical and consider if everything that Doreen had said was the truth. After all she had freely admitted that she was working for Ted, that she was spying for him. She had known his mother, and she was her friend, Joe had no doubt. She was either the best actress that had ever been, or she was telling the truth. Except for Amber, Joe had never trusted anyone. His instructors at the SOE had been unequivocal, trust nobody. Trust will get you killed. But in a confusing juxtaposition the major had told him always to go with his guts. 'Which is it, guys? You can't have it both ways.' Joe's mind screamed to itself as the Taxi trundled along.

Questions sped through his mind as he contemplated the seemingly unsolvable puzzle. Why would she lie about his mother? Why would she tell him that Ted had told her to spy on him? What had she to gain from all this? She had worked for Ted Baker for years; she had been his girl, why should he trust her? She was an ageing tart who had sold herself all her life; why should he trust her? Was he being a fool, letting his orphan's need for a home, a story, and a family get in the way of his better

271

judgment? Joe saw himself as a practical man. He wasn't swayed by sentiment and emotions. He was a hard-nosed criminal turned spy. Now, who was he kidding? He knew that deep down, he trusted this woman. She had been his mother's best friend; she had loved her, and she would do anything to protect him. He was sure of it. He looked forward to talking to her again that evening. He had so many questions. He couldn't wait to tell Amber, to introduce them. He knew they would get on.

The taxi pulled up outside Ted's nightclub. Joe paid the man with a large tip added and sprang across the pavement to the closed front door. He hammered on it loudly, knowing that one of Ted's men would probably be dozing in a chair just behind it. A grumpy gorilla of a man reluctantly opened the door, and Joe skipped past him before running up the stairs and into Ted's office without knocking.

"Morning Ted, lovely day. By the way, we really should have a talk about your security. I could have been anybody waltzing in here."

"Joe bloody Turner. Am I going to regret havin' you on my firm? Look at you, full of the joys of spring. A little birdy tells me that you had company last night; seems to have done you a world of good."

So already Ted knew that Doreen had stayed the night. Had she rung him from the flat after he left, or was the flat being watched, as he suspected? One way to find out.

"Now, now, Ted. Enough of that. Yes, the lady stayed, but in the shelter in the basement. She got caught out by the early raid. We had two chaperones, the couple from the first floor flat. By the way, talking of security, if you are going to have me watched, you might choose someone I don't know. Cyril Watkins and I boxed each other in the under-16 amateur championships. I put him down in the 3rd. Being 6 foot 3, knock-kneed and with a cauliflower ear, he tends to stand out a mile, hanging around on that corner. I suppose he rang you from the call box where he spent most of the night."

"He is not knock-kneed; he's a good lad, is Cyril. Not the brightest, I'll grant you, but a hard one."

"Didn't seem that hard when he hit the canvass, out cold in the 3rd." Joe mocked. "But you're right; he's not a bad lad. Do you really need him freezing his Alberts off outside my gaff?"

"Look, if you must know, it was Eddie who put him on to you, not me. Cyril rang Eddie, then Eddie rang me to gloat about you shagging old Doreen; he thought it was hilarious."

"I did not shag anyone last night; more's the pity."

"I think that you does' protest too much." Ted was enjoying teasing his young assistant. "Look, don't take offence. I told you Eddie doesn't like you, but then again, Eddie doesn't like anybody. That said, you did yourself no harm with the way you pulled off that job at the Army depot. The boys are talking like you are some sort of genius. Bapt told Eddie that you took out the guards single-handed."

"Yeah, the thing is, Ted, your boys are generally good lads, but they lack a bit of discipline and restraint. If I had let them have a go at those Army guards, they'd have probably killed one of them. They were Home Guard volunteers, old boys. The way I see it, the Army will be a bit embarrassed about the break-in; they would most likely want to keep it out of the press. The police will not be too worried about a bit of barbed wire. They're not going to bust a gut looking for us. If, on the other hand, one of the old codgers had bought it, there'd be a full-scale manhunt on the go, with the press blowing a gasket about 'war heroes being killed in action'. It's never a good thing when a job makes the papers."

"That's good thinking. I knew you were the right man for the job. Good lad. Now get yourself off home, bet you need a rest after last night." Ted chuckled to himself.

"I told you…" Joe tried to defend himself, but Ted cut him off.

"I am only pullin' your leg, lad; keep your hair on. Besides, I told you, I don't care who you shag. It might as well be old Doreen. If memory serves me right, she knows some tricks that one."

Ted was reading the Daily Mail on his desk as he spoke, so didn't see the rage in Joe's eyes. His whole body was tensed, his fists clenched. At that moment, he could have quite happily jumped across the desk and beaten the old crook's brains out.

With a supreme effort of self-control, Joe turned and walked away. 'There'll be plenty of time for that later,' he thought to himself.

68

"We'll always remember them." - Wales 1941

Simon was pouring Marshall's drink when a loud rumbling noise disturbed the party. It was the sound of an aircraft passing overhead. The sound was not unknown in the area, but on such a filthy day as this, the gentlemen looked at each other in surprise. Simon walked to the window; the rain had abated, but the cloud stretched in a continuous blanket across the sky. As the engine noise growled every fainter into the distance, he could not make out the machine. He reasoned that it must be flying above the clouds and yet it had sounded so low.

He returned to his chair. The company had fallen silent, each man thinking of the dangers that the young men sailing above them were facing. Their reverie was broken when the front door swung open, and Sara Lloyd came running into the lounge.

Her voice was agitated as she blurted out her news. "A crash, the aeroplane, it crashed into the mountain. Quickly." She waved her arms as if directing the men to do something.

Simon was first to his feet. He took hold of the young lady's hands and sought to calm her. "Sara, tell me exactly what you saw."

Sara took a deep breath. Looking into his eyes, she fought to compose herself. "We were just coming out of Evensong when we heard a noise. It was dreadfully loud. We looked up but couldn't see anything. Then Mr Jones saw a flash of light on the mountain. He pointed to it, and we saw a red glow. It lasted only a few seconds before it disappeared. Mr Jones thinks that the aeroplane crashed into the mountain."

"Can you point to where you saw the light, Sara?" Simon asked her calmly. He led her out of the door and across the street until they could see the mountain.

"Yes, of course. Mr Jones saw it, too. He says he knows exactly where it was. He has gone to his house to get his gear; he told me to fetch as many men together as I can; he says he will lead them there."

Simon was unsure of who Sara was talking about, it must have shown in his demeanour as Sara continued. "Mr Jones knows the mountains very well. He used to be a Policeman in London, but he was born and grew up here. When he retired, he became a guide for the tourists before the war."

At that moment, a slight, older man marched purposefully up the high street, pulling on gloves as he walked. "Has Sara told you what we saw?" He asked of Simon and Pritchard-Smythe who had hastily donned his overcoat and joined them.

"Yes, can you guide us to where you saw the flames?" Simon asked.

"Without doubt. The visibility up there will be poor, but I know the way well. We need to get more men together."

"I know the way, too," Sara said determinedly. Her initial distress had settled, and Simon was both pleased and astounded by her desire to help. She pointed to the spot, and the mountain guide confirmed her accuracy.

Pritchard-Smythe must have been equally impressed with the young lady and knew exactly how she could help. The army man had a plan and wasted no time. "Sara, take your bicycle and ride like the wind to the camp. Give this note to the guard at the gate. He will take you to my Sergeant Major. Tell him to get 12 men together. I want you to guide them in the van up to that farm on the mountainside, park up there and come the rest of the way on foot. We three will go ahead from here. We will get there first and render whatever assistance we can. Tell my men to bring stretchers, first aid, torches, and blankets. They will know what to do. Hurry now."

Sara ran to the old stables for her bike. Simon returned to the Hotel and fetched his boots and torch. Within a few minutes, the 3 men were ready to get underway. The other gentlemen of the party had volunteered to join them, but each was older and naturally considered to be less fit than the younger military men. Simon wondered about Jones. No doubt he knew the terrain, but as he looked appraisingly at him for the first time, Simon realised that the man was well past his seventieth birthday. Smythe cast a look in Simon's direction as if thinking the same thing.

Perhaps aware of the doubts about his capabilities, Matt Jones smiled and marched away. "Try and keep up, gentlemen." He called over his shoulder.

Ten minutes later, both Soldier and Sailor felt suitably admonished. A tortuous pace was being set. Despite the strength and stamina that had been built into them by determined regimes of relentless training, they both struggled to keep up and marvelled at the vitality of the 'feeble' old man.

As soon as their destination came into sight, the men realised that despite their speed, their efforts had been in vain. A few small fires burned fitfully on the mountainside as aviation fuel had made torches of scattered bushes. Flames flickered in the compressed remains of the fuselage, briefly lighting the scene. Little other remained to bear witness to the events of the evening. As they stared around, incredulous at the destruction they were witnessing, each man stopped in their tracks and fell silent.

Any hope or expectation that they would arrive to save lives, that they might carry brave airmen to safety, extinguished as quickly as the flames in the damp night air. They wandered aimlessly around the strewn wreckage, barely able to discern the form or function of the tangled metal parts that remained. All other materials had been incinerated to dust and gas by the explosion. No lives left to be saved.

The men looked at each other. They knew that not only was their presence futile, but it was also intrusive to the peace of the men who had died there. They felt like voyeurs, participants in some intrusive and unwanted invasion of a sacred place. Simon and the guide fell back to the path, ready to waylay the other rescuers when they arrived. Pritchard-Smythe carefully noted some numbers that were barely visible on the remains of the fuselage and then joined his colleagues.

Jones recited the Lord's Prayer as they huddled together, waiting for the others. All that Simon and Smythe could manage, was to silently mouth the words.

When the soldiers arrived with Sara, they all returned to the truck at the farm and drove in silence back to the Hotel. They were all cold and damp. Mrs Williams busied herself with stoking the heat from the fading fire. Simon turned from the blaze, unable to bear the reminder the flickering flames conveyed.

Pritchard-Smythe was busy on the telephone, reporting the crash and advising the authorities of the position of the remains. His men lingered uncertainly in the bar of the Hotel, waiting for instruction from their Captain. Mrs Williams looked concerned at their discomfort. Simon came to the Landlady's assistance.

"Mrs Williams, some of the men will not be at ease in a room where there is alcohol. They will also wish to pray; might they be allowed to go into the snug?" He suggested.

"Of course, would they like tea, do you think?" Every fibre of the lady's nature wished to care for these strangers in her home. She instinctively felt that they would be thinking of their own homes and the dangers that they, like the brave men who had perished that evening, faced far from their families.

"Mrs Williams, I am sure they would love some tea, but bring it here, and I will take it to them when their prayers are completed."

Simon approached the men and spoke to them in a mixture of English and Arabic. They gratefully thanked him as he ushered them into the snug. Three men remained the Christians who were sometimes seen in the Dragon's Tail on a Saturday night. Simon poured them a glass of whiskey, which they happily shared.

Simon returned to his seat of the earlier evening. Sir Cecil, The General and Marshall had remained, waiting for news.

"What do you think happened?" the general asked Simon. The others looked to the younger man, aware that he was more likely to know of such things.

"It was an RAF plane, but I think the crew were Canadian." He didn't explain that he had seen the uniform of one of the airmen; he didn't want to discuss what he had witnessed. "I imagine that they were on a training flight. Perhaps they had an instrument failure; perhaps they had made a mistake with their navigation. The low cloud would have made it impossible for them to work out where they were. They would have tried to conserve fuel and hope for a break in the cloud. As time went on, they would see the sun setting and the fuel running low. They would have little choice but to gamble. They would have to lose altitude, hoping that they would break through and see the land before the light failed. With luck, they could identify where they were and look for the nearest airfield. As we know, the cloud was lower than the mountain ridge. There would be no time to pull up even if the pilot saw the hill. I doubt, I hope that he never saw a thing."

No one spoke for a few minutes, each man again lost in thought. The General was the first to break the silence. "The Canadians were magnificent in the last war. Every time that Haigh had a tricky job, he would call on them. They say that the Germans feared them the most of all our forces. We must remember them always."

There were nods of agreement as the group fell back to their silence. Pritchard-Smythe returned from his phone call. He downed the whiskey that Simon offered but declined another.

"I must be getting my men back. Gentlemen, I would be happy to give any of you a lift." The soldier offered. Sir Cecil and Marshall accepted gratefully. The General was happy to walk the short distance to his home.

When the men had left, the hotel was suddenly a very lonely place. Simon was grateful when Eleanor Williams and her Niece joined him. He had no desire to go to bed; his dreams awaited him. His taught nerves were in no condition to take them on. He wished that tonight, he would not be alone.

Sara spoke. "You say they were Canadian? They were so far from home. Why did they come so far to fight for us?"

"They came to fight for Freedom." Said Simon simply.

"They were so brave," Sara whispered. Tears slowly fell from her beautiful eyes.

"They must have been so frightened." Her aunt said in hushed tones.

"They were both." Said Simon firmly. He was a man who knew more than most about bravery and fear.

69

The truth? – London 1941

By the time Joe got back, Doreen had left the flat. Cyril, his watcher, had also disappeared, and apparently, he had not been replaced. As he was placing his keys on the cabinet next to the door, the telephone rang. "Joe Turner speaking."

"Mr Turner, this is Miss Hereford speaking."

"How very nice to hear your voice, Miss Hereford." Joe's tone was teasingly formal. He knew that Susan Cartwright, the real owner of the voice, would be smiling at his deliberately affected telephone manor.

"Mr Turner, I need your signature on some papers, and we need to discuss the Russel & Son acquisition. A half past three this afternoon would be a convenient time for me. Good morning." The line went dead, Miss Hereford, Susan, requiring no further conversation. Joe was sure that the telephone was being listened to, but what about the rest of the flat? Had they heard the conversation between himself and Doreen the previous evening? Time to find out.

Using the training he received at the health spa, Joe carefully examined the flat. He had already made a cursory inspection the day he moved in, but he had had no time to totally rule out listening devices. His detailed inspection still revealed nothing. The boffins at the SOE had been very thorough in training the recruits on the art of electronic surveillance. It was a new proficiency, and the British secret services were at the cutting edge of the technology. So, if the Bakers, and if Ted was to be believed that meant Eddie, had the place bugged, they had managed to surpass the standards to which Joe had been taught, ergo, the very best in the world. This, he felt, was very unlikely. What is more, why would they think that there would be anything worth listening to in the flat? If he were up to no good, from their perspective, surely, he would be unlikely to meet somebody there. Therefore, it would be enough to listen to his phone calls and follow him to any rendezvous'. Which is what they had been doing. Joe had been briefed that there had been an attempt to survey Susan Cartwright in her role as Miss Hereford. This had been expected and consisted of following her and listening to phone calls from the office using an operator at the Post office exchange. This they had allowed, as any attempt by the accountant to avoid such observation would have made the Bakers suspicious.

Joe relaxed, he was confident that his conversation with Doreen had been private and that he would be able to talk freely to her when she returned. All he had to think about now was what he was going to say to her. He had lots of questions for her, but how much was he going to tell her about himself? He felt absolutely that he could trust her, but how much should he involve her in what he was doing? Certainly, she could be very useful to him. She had knowledge of the Bakers organisation going back years. She was well placed to pass on misinformation that might be very helpful in misdirecting any suspicions they may have about him. He was sure she would be willing to help, but how fair would it be to involve her? He would be exposing her to extreme danger. Already, he felt that there was a bond between them; there could be no way that he would put her in peril.

As he was musing, he heard footsteps on the stairs. Just one person, light, quick and precise. The steps of someone who knew the stairwell and was making no attempt to conceal their approach. It is probably a woman, most likely Doreen, returning. Joe relaxed, sure of his instincts, but just to be certain, he held his gun in his hand, covered by a cushion, as he lounged on the sofa. A key turned, and the door swung open. The clattering heels of Doreen echoed on the tiled floor of the hallway.

"Good afternoon, Doreen; I hope you brought some more, Brandy; you drank most of mine last night." Joe quipped.

"I seem to remember that I had some help, and yes, I did bring some more. Ted has a dozen crates at the lock-up; just for your information; God knows where he gets it from these days." Doreen was smiling like a Cheshire cat. It was obvious that she was pleased to see Joe.

"Doreen love, I have to go out soon; how long will you be here?" Joe asked.

"I have brought some more veggies, so we can have them with the leftovers of that pie. I have nothing else to do today, so I will hang around here until you get back; we have so much to talk about."

"Yes, we do."

"By the way, you know that I told you that you're being watched. Only he is not here now."

"Yeah, Cyril Watkins. According to Ted, Eddie told him to watch me. Apparently, he called Eddie this morning and told him you stayed here last night. I told him you stayed in the shelter in the basement. Not that it will stop them gossiping about us."

"Oh no. My good name has been ruined; whatever shall I do." Doreen affected the accent and mannerisms of a well-heeled debutant. She was quite the actress, Joe thought. After all, she had claimed that both she and his mother were unlucky not to make it on the stage; perhaps she had been right about that. Could things have been different for his mother? "It would make sense that Eddie ordered you to be followed. Cyril is one of Eddie's boys and Eddie does like to pretend he is some gangster from the movies."

"Are you suggesting that some of the boys are more loyal to Eddie than to Ted?" asked Joe.

"Well, Eddie would like to think so, but if push came to shove, I doubt that many of them would stand up against Ted. The thing that you must understand is that Ted has always been cautious and measured; it has served him well. He has grown his business steadily. He has always been careful not to step on the wrong toes. Eddie, on the other hand, is a hot head. He feels he can take anyone on, including, if the rumours are to be believed, his Dad."

"Eddie is planning to take over from his father?"

"That's the word on the grapevine. Things is, I very much doubt that Ted won't know that. Ted Baker is many things, but he is not a fool. You'd have to get up very early to put one over on him."

"Doreen, can I ask you a question?" Joe asked earnestly.

"Of course, Joe, of course."

"How did you know who I was? I mean, I know you said I have her eyes, but was there anything else?"

"It was a few things, Joe. When Ted asked me to keep an eye on you, I thought nothing of it, by the way I haven't spoken to him today, so I will back up your story of the shelter in the basement. Anyway, I had heard of you, but our paths had never crossed. It never occurred to me that you could be Lorraine's boy. After all, I was told you had died. Although a part of me has always thought, hoped most likely, that the Nuns were lying. I thought they might have told me you were dead because you had been adopted. That they didn't want some old tart turning up at your new family home, stirring things up. I dreamed of you growing up as a gent on some country estate. Any how I never dreamed I would see you again. When I saw you yesterday in this flat, I swear to god, it was like looking into her eyes. I was shocked for a moment. I wanted to run to you then and hug you, but you would have thought I was some silly old slapper. So, I did what I usually do and flirted with you, sorry about that. I was so confused, what could I say to you, I had to be sure. Later, when we chatted, I checked some facts. I don't know if you remember but I asked your age. You told me that you had grown up with the Nuns. That you were an orphan. I wasn't going to say anything straight away, not until, I was completely sure. Then you asked me why I had said that I'd recognise those eyes anywhere, even though we had never met. Something told me there and then that I had to tell you. I knew it was you, I just knew it." A solitary tear of joy slid down her cheek.

"Thank you for telling me," Joe smiled at her. He noticed that she was less made up today, her clothes less ostentatious, and her demeanour less showy and brash.

"You are welcome. It's my turn to ask a question, Joe." Her tone was serious; she was worried he could tell.

"Fire away." Joe tried to sound upbeat, but her mood was affecting him.

"Who are you, Joe? What are you doing working for Ted Baker? You know that there are a lot of people surprised that you have thrown your lot in with them. They say it's not in your nature."

Joe knew he had a massive decision to make. He wanted to tell Doreen the truth, all of it. He didn't want her to think that he was a cold-hearted gangster like the Bakers. But his need to protect her was weighing heavily on his mind.

"Listened Doreen, things are not really what they seem. You're right. I wouldn't normally work for the Bakers, but at the moment, I have no choice. I can't tell you why right now. Please understand that it is not that I don't trust you. It's for your protection."

"Are you working for the police?" Doreen was clearly worried for Joe.

"Not exactly; it's a bit more complicated than that. I really want to tell you; I want you to be proud. Please don't ask me. Please just trust me on this."

"Oh, Joe, please be careful. You don't know Ted like I do. If he finds out that you are working against him, he will kill you. You will simply disappear. Please, I couldn't bear to lose you again."

"I am being careful, I promise. That's why I don't want to tell you anything. That way, if Ted asks you anything about me, you can tell him that you don't know; you won't have to lie."

"You're right. He can usually tell when people are lying. All right, but is there anything I can do to help you?"

"It's too risky. Everything will be fine, I promise. Listen, if Ted asks about me, tell him the truth. Tell him what you see, when I am here, what I am doing. You don't think that he knows who I am? Would he remember my mother?"

"I doubt it very much. You see, for Ted, there have been so many girls over the years. He was never very interested in Lorraine; she wasn't his type. You see most of the girls were just business for him. They came and went. He only remembers me because I stuck around. Usually, when girls get too old, he kicks them out or sends them to work down the docks. I made myself useful. I used to run a brothel for him until Eddie took an interest in it." Doreen almost spat the name of the young gangster; there was clearly no love lost between them. "Talking of that bastard. Stay well clear of him, Joe. He is a nasty little shit. More than that, he is evil. There are stories about him that would make your blood curdle."

"I take it that you don't like him then." Joe quipped.

"I mean it, Joe, watch him. He kills for the fun of it." For Doreen, Eddie Baker was not a man to joke about.

"What about the guy they call Bapt? Who's he when he's at home?"

"I don't really know. He strikes me as another fish out of water."

"How do you mean?" Joe's interest was spiked.

"Well, he seems to get on all right with Eddie overall. But I hear that they did have a bust-up. Apparently, Baptiste, that's his name, the boys shorten it to Bapt. Anyway, he doesn't like the way Eddie uses drugs and violence on the new girls. They say that Bapt ran a brothel in Paris before the Germans invaded. They say he prefers to recruit his girls the old-fashioned way and that he hates to use drugs. But Eddie calls the shots when it comes to the brothel and the girls. Bapt had the good sense to back down. It strikes me that he is the kind of man that comes up smelling of roses, whatever sort of shit he lands in."

Joe was interested in this Bapt; he would mention him to the Major next time they spoke. A man with his skills and knowledge of France might be useful to the SOE. "Got to go now; see you in a couple of hours."

"Now, you be careful, Joe. Please be careful." Doreen had hardened her heart to the world for most of her life, but now she had let Joe in without question. She loved him as much as any mother had loved a son. The thought of losing him was agonising.

"Yes, Aunt Dor, I'll be careful." Joe gently mocked.

70

Analysis – The Dragon's Head Hotel

When Simon woke the next morning, his first thoughts were of the air crash. He resolved to write a report that he could hand to the recovery crew when they arrived. He would telephone Pritchard-Smythe and tell him, it would be a good excuse for them to meet. He was anxious to analyse the conversation from the previous afternoon and report back to Robinson.

He had slept well, having finished off the last of a bottle of whisky. His head ached dully, but the alcohol had kept the dreams away; he was grateful for that.

He replayed the afternoon's discussions in his mind. Ally had played a blinder, getting the conversation on to the subjects Simon wanted.

Simon's mind ran on aimlessly evaluating the information they had gathered. So, the butcher was alive a few miles away. Could that be true? It would be difficult to check, especially without knowing an address. It had a ring of truth about it. It would explain his absence. It explained why the wife had lied about him joining up. He had disappeared from the marital home, but why was he reported missing by his Aunt? He must, in his new domestic bliss, have forgotten about the old Girl. Doubtless, the wronged wife was not forwarding his letters. Now, what about this man Harris? A loner with one friend. A farmer and a butcher, the perfect pairing for a black-market scam. Why had Morgan's letters to the ministry stopped? There had always been the assumption that the letters had stopped because Morgan had been silenced. Perhaps they had stopped because the scheme had stopped. Morgan had moved away, and Harris no longer had an outlet for his off-ration meat. All plausible, but it all seems a bit small fry. The letters had suggested a larger operation. Perhaps there is more to this Harris man than meets the eye. Simon thought that he must investigate him. Could it be that Morgan had left his wife, family, and business to get away from Harris?

One thought kept playing over and over in Simon's mind. It was something that had been stressed to him during his training. "Never trust information until it has been verified by more than one source." At the moment, he had only one source, Marshall, and there was something about the businessman that didn't ring true with Simon. He couldn't put his finger on it, but something was not quite right.

71

A far corner of a foreign field. – Wales - 1941

Sara skipped enthusiastically around the bar. Many young ladies of her age would consider emptying ashtrays, wiping tables and moping the floor to be mundane, but her work was not a chore to her. Perhaps it was the promise of the afternoon off, a walk in the crisp autumn air and the likelihood of meeting with Simon on the canal.

Their meetings had become more regular of late. The accident of their bumping into each other was only slightly contrived. That Simon would mention where his own walks were intended to take him, that Sara should choose a similar path, and that their meetings would be remote and therefore unlikely to be observed was pure coincidence.

Sara felt no guilt in the clandestine nature of their assignations. They were doing nothing wrong. There were no guilty secrets to hide. They enjoyed each other company, there was no sin in that, surely. Their discretion was simply to deny the gossips of the village the ammunition for their vile tittle-tattle.

As is often the case, their belief in their own prudence was ill-founded. Of course, they had been seen. Without question, the gossipers had taken their scant evidence and concluded that their behaviour was scandalous. Without knowledge of the charges set before them, the couple had already been found guilty and sentenced.

A harsh knock on the door stopped Sara in her tracks. The grandfather clock that stood accurately keeping its rhythm in the corner of the room gave no clue as to the caller, save the time of 12 minutes past twelve. The milkman had already been and would anyway use the side entrance, as would the other tradesmen. The postman would always enter and leave the mail on the bar. There was no evidence as to the business of the caller and yet Sara walked slowly to the door. The gaiety of her step was now replaced with sombre foreboding. Sara swung open the unlocked door. Standing on the step was her friend Yvonne, her eyes cast down, her hands fidgeting. Yvonne worked at the post office.

Sara looked in horror for the telegram that she expected to see in her friend's hands. With relief, she observed that there was no such dreaded despatch. "Good afternoon, Yvonne; what a lovely day." Sara forced a cheerful greeting. It was true that the day had beauty; the autumn sun was shining, bathing the world with a golden glow whilst failing to bring warmth; it mattered not, as the crisp air lent an intense influence, adding fog to breath and crunch to the fallen leaves. The charms of the day held no interest to the morose Yvonne, who still could not meet the eyes of her friend. She stood motionless save the twitching of her fingers, Sara silent, afraid to ask her guest the nature of her call.

When Yvonne eventually met her eyes and spoke, her voice was cracking; tears were streaming down her cheeks. "Sara, I have just taken a telegram to the vicarage." Was all the young lady could sob. It was enough. Enough for Sara to feel her heart wrench. Enough for her to know the meaning of her friend's words. Sara pushed past her and ran. Dishcloth still in hand and wearing her pinny, she raced to the manse. With each step, she divined the truth. She and Adam had only become engaged the night before he left; she was not yet his next of kin. Therefore, the telegram would be addressed to his father. She knew its contents. There was no doubting it from the look in Yvonne's eyes when they had eventually met hers: Adam Davies was dead.

Her own tears flowed uncontrollably. The cynical gossips might have cruelly suggested that they were tears of joy for her release from the bondage of her unwanted engagement. Those who loved and knew her better would say they were tears for the boy she had known and loved, in her way, since they had been small children. Were they tears of guilt, heart-breaking sadness, or relief that she might partake in a new love? If she had been asked those questions at that moment, Sara Lloyd could not have been sure she could have given an honest answer.

72

A worrying development. – SOE Headquarters – Major Calderdale's office.

Major James Calderdale had read the message several times; its contents were brief and worrying. It was a communique from Amy Percival, aka Rosie, his operative, placed as a land girl at Mynydd Farm. So far, she had been getting excellent information. She was convinced that the farmer, Mrs Myfanwy Thomas, was involved in some sort of clandestine operation. This served to back up their gamble to place Rosie on the farm. Myfanwy Thomas was known to be a close friend of the wife of the butcher who had gone missing. It seemed possible that she was involved; so far Rosie's reports were indicating that she was. This latest report was unscheduled, a brief note passed to the Army commander Pritchard-Smythe in the local pub. It read.

"Navy boy being watched closely, in danger, proceed carefully."

He would have to discuss this with Robinson, but his instincts were to pull Simon Bach, aka Lewis, out. He had yet to gather any truly useful information. His cover had always been flimsy, and it had been a tall order to expect him to gain the trust of the locals in a short time scale.

73

A job for Aunt Dor. – London – 1941

Doreen was still at the flat when Joe returned, a little later than he had planned.

"I thought you said that you would be just a couple of hours, where have you been? I've been worried about you." Doreen's words were playful and in jest, but even her acting skills couldn't keep her concern from her voice.

"What, you're going to nag me from now on? I can see I will need to be a good little boy in future." Joe mocked, but a part of him was pleased with her concern, the part of him who had only ever had Amber to look out for him, never a mother.

"Yes, you are. Now wash your hands; your tea is ready."

The unlikely pair sat down to eat, and their easy companionship warmed them as much as the bountiful food. Their conversation flowed without any impediment. The need to catch up on two decades of separation had to be satisfied.

Reluctantly, Joe turned the conversation to business. "Dor, how did you manage to get the steak for that pie? I mean, it's the best I have had since before the war. Is it legit?"

"I got it from Al down the market. Al and I go way back. He used to like to give it me up the......." Doreen paused; for the first time she could remember, she was slightly embarrassed by her former trade. Before she had known for certain who Joe was, she had been unabashed by her calling. Now they had assumed a new relationship, that of family; she was less disposed to be crude in front of him. "I mean that Al used to be a regular customer. Anyway, he let me have a couple of prime cuts, less for old times' sake and more because he thought they were for Ted, I think".

"So, it's not that easy to get hold of meat these days?" Joe asked.

"It's practically impossible to get enough for a pie like that. In theory, you can get so much on your ration, but it's usually some scrag end. If you do get what you think is prime beef, it's more likely that it came last at Royal Ascot last year, if you take my meaning."

"So genuine quality meat is hard to come by. If someone were to get hold of some, they could flog it for a tidy sum, I guess." Joe speculated.

"I suppose so. Al told me that it's a bit risky for the butcher. Their supply is pretty tightly regulated. So, the bunce would have to be good for them to take the gamble. Your ordinary customers wouldn't have the means to splash out too much; everything else is so bloody expensive."

"So, if you've some meat to flog, where would you hawk it?"

"Do you have some meat, Joe? Do I need to start calling you Farmer Joe from now on?" Doreen teased.

"Not me Dor, Ted."

"Ted?"

"Yes, keep it under your hat, but Ted reckons that he has a boatload of hooky meat coming his way later this year. Wants me to find places to knock it out for him."

"Well, Ted's no mug. If he is prepared to get involved, he must reckon that there is bunce in it." Doreen paused as she reasoned the best approach. "I reckon that when things are tight, the people who always have money to spend are the people with money." Joe looked puzzled, and Doreen realised she wasn't explaining herself well. "Look when I ran the brothel for Ted, we always felt that the most profit was to be made from having the best girls, the best looking, the ones with half a brain that could charm the punters. That the men would fall for and want again and again. We charged more for them, and the men were prepared to pay. In fact, the more we charged, the more that the men thought they were getting. Look don't get me wrong; our girls were better than your average slappers, but they weren't twice as pretty or twice as skilful, but we would charge ten times what the men would be charged in one of London's less salubrious establishments. They were paying twenty times as much for what they could easily get down the docks. The men who had money, your lords, your top businessmen, your Toffs, would pay no questions asked. Look, rich people are never poor. Your ordinary Joe, excuse the expression, might have to tighten their belts when the economy is struggling but rich people always have money. If you want to knock out your sirloins, you want to be punting it to posh gaffs that have clients that can pay. And make sure that you don't undercharge. Especially when you have them hooked. Once their clients are used to getting what they want, they will pay more to keep getting it."

"Doreen, you have hidden talents. You should be a captain of industry."

"Well, it is true that I have worked under a few of them." Doreen's quick humour came out before she remembered her newfound bashfulness. "Do you want me to help you find some punters?"

"No thanks. I have a contact who can give me an introduction to that world." Doreen looked disappointed. "There is something that you could help me with."

"Anything Joe." Doreen's smile returned to her lips.

"I told you about Amber?"

"You did, Joe; she sounds lovely. I just can't wait to meet her. I suppose she will be all right about me. I mean, she won't judge me?"

"Nah, she's not that type. Salt of the earth is old Amber. She will be happy for us. She, too, has no family that she can remember. She will be delighted to have a new aunt."

"Oh, I do hope so. Are you going to marry her, Joe?" Doreen felt emboldened to be direct.

"We always used to avoid talking about marriage. We used to say that our future wasn't certain enough. But I nearly lost her when the Dog and Duck was bombed. I realised then that none of us can be certain of what fate may hold for us. As soon as this business with the Bakers is done and dusted, I am going to ask her to marry me."

Doreen screamed with excitement and hugged Joe ferociously.

"Hold up, she hasn't said yes yet." Joe managed to say despite being half crushed.

"Ah, get over yourself. You are just about the most handsome man I've ever seen, and I have seen my fair share. Now, who could refuse you? Have you got a ring yet?"

Extracting himself from Doreen's grip, Joe went to the bedroom and returned with a small jewellery box. He flipped open the lid to show her. Inside was a simple silver ring with a single jade stone.

"The last time I saw her, I gave her a necklace with a matching stone. You see, the stones are the colour of her eyes."

Doreen resumed and intensified her hold.

When he had released himself once more from her clutches, Joe continued. "Thing is, we haven't seen each other since the bombing. I don't want the Bakers knowing anything about her. I have been so busy I haven't had time to track her down. I know she was safe after the bomb. An ambulance man told me he had pulled her out of the wreckage. I looked her up at the hospital, but she had already been discharged. I know she is a resourceful girl, she'll be fine, but I do want to get a message to her. Dor, do you think you could look her up for me? Give her some money, tell her I am all right, and I will be in touch with her soon. Tell her not to believe any of the rumours about me, especially to do with the Bakers."

"Of course I will Joe. Don't worry, Ted will never find out. I come and go as I please these days. He never notices what I'm up to. But where will I find her?"

"I keep a locker in a Gym. I always leave a bit of money in it for emergencies. Amber has a key and will go there and leave me a message. The Gym is run by a man called Raspy, a Russian. Do you know him?"

"No, but I have heard of him."

"Raspy is a good man; if she went to see him, he would have looked after her. She will be safe."

"Give me the address of the gym and a note for Amber. I will find her."

74

A Town in Mourning - Wales

It was a sombre time for the people of Trefynydd. First was the loss of one of their sons, Adam Davis, who was killed in a German prisoner-of-war camp. The details of his death a mystery, the full facts remaining unknown until after the end of the war. His was the first name to be etched onto the monument in the town square for the latest conflict, joining those who had made the ultimate sacrifice in the war to end all wars a generation before. A name that didn't make it onto the cenotaph was that of Dai Thomas. He died the same week as the news came through about Adam, though his life had all but ended in the trenches of the western front.

The town went about its business as usual, but its joy and vigour were missing, especially until the funeral for Dai and a service for Adam had been observed. Simon kept himself very much to himself for the period of mourning. He attended the funeral; after all, he had known Dai; they had chatted often in the pub, the subject exclusively dogs. Indeed, without any formal bequest, Cae, the dog that had been beside the old man for years and who held the honorific of being 'the best working dog ever known', came to live at the Dragon's Tail Hotel, giving her devotion to its young barmaid and its only guest. She slept in the old stables with the motorbike and was ready each morning to walk in the hills with her new master. She was generously supplied with her victuals by Eleanor Williams, who did so in remembrance of her Master, that fine young man she had seen marching off to war years before. It is said that Eleanor was known to offer a bowl of chicken to any canine visitor of the Hotel for years afterwards, so much so that it became a ritual of the establishment, even when the foundation of the tradition had long been forgotten.

For a while, Sara avoided meeting Simon on his walks; he understood, and it seemed to be the respectful thing to do. Whilst he missed her company it did afford to him more freedom to roam freely in search of any criminality. Taking up on what Marshall had said about the man Harris, Simon took several walks around the man's farm. He even bumped into him on one occasion. The farm was a shambles. It seemed that the man had never married and after his parents had died and he had inherited the business, he had struggled. He seemed to lack the business acumen needed. It appeared to Simon's admittedly inexpert eye that it was an enterprise on its last legs, perhaps only surviving due to the subsidies and stability of the Ministry of Food's pricing. Simon ruled out Harris as a person likely to be running any sort of a serious criminal conspiracy in the Black Market. Indeed, Simon was surprised that Marshall could have thought Harris to be involved. Was that a poor judgment on the part of the JP, or was it a deliberate misdirection?

Having searched most of the immediate vicinity of the town, Simon set himself to wander further afield. One such hike took him past the mountain that rose immediately above the town and onwards to the mountains beyond. Having gained their summit, he spurned the usual route along the ridge to the west, instead heading along another ridge that led to the northeast. He had been advised against this path by his friends in the bar. He found that it was true that the path was less obvious, the way tricky to the point of being precarious. But it wasn't insurmountable, and he wondered if the advice he had received had been given in good faith to protect his safety or to keep him away from the area. After a while, the track became easier, the ridge well-defined and easy to follow. He fancied that it would lead him to a view of the valley beyond. From his studies of the pre-war maps, he remembered that there was a long-time disused quarry in the region. As he neared the point where he suspected the vista would open to his view, he came across a fence.

It was a modern barrier, crisscrossed galvanised steel, taller than him by 2 or 3 feet and topped with coils of barbed wire. It was a solid construction, not designed to contain livestock; a creation of half its height would be sufficient for that. Its design was surely aimed at keeping out intruders. The barricade was new, of which he had no doubts. It was built right up to the edge of the ridge; the ground fell away so steeply there that an attempt to skirt around it would be hazardous to the point of suicide. To the other side, it ran down the hillside in a gentle arc as far as he could see. It was climbable; the students at the spa had learned a technique for scaling the barbed wire, but Simon did not have the right equipment with him. In the centre of the wire, at head height, was a plain and unambiguous sign. Its legend read: KEEP OUT – MINISTRY OF DEFENCE.

Simon was disappointed that his route was blocked, he had been looking forward to seeing the view in that direction. He was about to turn around and head back, but something didn't feel quite right about the fence. He studied it again. On the face of it, all looked well. Indeed, it was a tidy job, as they said, in this part of the world. Considering the uneven terrain and the remoteness of the spot, someone had made a nice job of it. In the last few years MOD fencing had popped up all over the country, miles of it, probably thousands of miles of it. Simon had seen a lot of it from both sides. It was often erected hurriedly, time being at an absolute premium. He doubted that he had ever seen a better job than this one.

Something else was playing on his mind. Before he had left for his mission, he had carefully studied maps of the area issued by the MOD. It was true that Wales, particularly the Brecon Beacons, was an area popular for training infantry, particularly elite units. But most, if not all, of that land was over to the west. What's more, he had heard Pritchard-Smythe complaining one day at Sunday lunch that he had to take his men 20 miles from base to a training exercise. He was bemoaning that his own base didn't have enough land for anything but drill exercising. He explained that live fire was not allowed so close to town. What would the MOD want with the land in the valley? Simon determined that he would ask the Captain about it at the earliest opportunity.

75

Missing - London

Doreen had never wanted to do anything half as much as to find Amber for Joe. She just couldn't wait to meet her. However, she had to be careful and waited until the following evening before she set off to the east end and the address that Joe had given her for the gym. She wanted to make sure that the Bakers would not notice her absence. Ted had some function planned at the club, which both Joe and Eddie were required to attend. So, it was unlikely that she would be seen in the east end. If Ted had seen her that night, he would barely recognise her; once again, she had toned down the exuberance of her attire. She now had the garb of a respectable housewife, stylish, conventional, moderate. The effect was astonishing; she was a different woman. A woman who had dropped the garish costume of a painted lady, a uniform designed to shield her from the indignity of her life. She was a woman ready to leave that world behind and find the person she could and should have been. A woman who was finding her true beauty was not enhanced by cosmetics.

The gym was closed, and there was no answer to her persistent knocking. It seemed strange as a weekday early evening would be prime time for people to be at the gym. As she was wondering what to do, a lady came walking down the cobbles of the darkening road. She smiled at Doreen as she passed. It was an unexpected and novel experience for Doreen; most 'respectable' people would normally avoid making eye contact with her. Her changed persona was having curious side effects. Doreen smiled back. "Excuse me, you wouldn't by any chance know where I can find Mikhail, would you?"

"Mikhail?" the lady was perplexed. "Oh, you mean Raspy."

"Yes, that's him. A funny name." the two of them laughed politely together.

"Actually, he hasn't been around for a couple of weeks. He hasn't even been opening the gym; shame 'cause my sister's lad used to go there. Did him a world of good it did. 'Course he's joined the army now, off to North Africa he is. Oh, bugger, I'm not supposed to say that am I? You won't say anything, will you love?"

Doreen smiled her agreement to be discreet at the gossiping lady.

"Do you know where I could find Raspy?"

"I don't. We have been really worried about him. He just disappeared."

Doreen made her excuses and departed from the lady before she gave away any more information useful to the enemy. She was desperately disappointed; she had stumbled at the very first hurdle in finding Amber.

76

Fence, what fence – The Dragon's Tail Hotel – Wales – 1941

Simon and Prichard-Smythe had developed that habit of dining together once a fortnight at the Dragon's Tail. It was innocent enough that two men of the same class, both officers, would strike up a casual friendship. Of course, it meant that Simon could pass messages back to Robinson and the Major, although they were careful about discussing anything other than Tennis, fishing, and news of the war in general. An overheard conversation about Simon's mission would be disastrous.

The bar was empty on the next occasion that they dined together. That was not unusual for a mid-week evening. The local farmers were a hard-working lot and whilst they would be enthusiastic revellers on a Saturday night, the demands of the farm would generally limit them to just a couple of pints on other nights of the week. Those who had sought to quench their thirsts on that particular evening had done so and retired to their beds early. Sara was visiting the vicarage, and Mrs Williams was busy tidying her kitchen.

"Tell me again where this fence is." Asked Ally as he sipped his beer.

Simon explained in detail the route he had taken and where he had come across the barrier.

"And it had MOD signs?" He further enquired.

Simon nodded.

"You are sure about this."

"Oh, for God's sake, man, I think I know what a fence looks like, and I have seen enough MOD signs to know that this was either a genuine one or a bloody good facsimile." Simon regretted his outburst; he realised that his friend was apt to tend towards caution. "I say I am sorry, old man; it's just that after all this time, this is the first thing that I have come across that stands out as out of place."

"That's all right, old chap, and for what it's worth, I think you are onto something. I very much doubt that there is ministry land up there. If there were, I would have been told about it. Even if it is hush, hush, I would have been warned to steer clear. I think someone is trying to keep people from accidentally stumbling on a little secret that they've got going on up there. I'll pass it on to the powers that be, shall I?"

"Please and tell them that I will get back up there and find out what's beyond as soon as I can."

"The thing is, old boy, I have a message for you from the Major." Pritchard Smythe looked a little sheepish about passing it on.

"Go on." Simon picked up on his friends' reticence.

"They have received information that would suggest that you are compromised. Certain parties are convinced that you are a ministry spy. Calderdale thinks that it would be safer to pull you out."

"Not bloody likely; I am just about getting somewhere with this mission. Anyway, what information and from whom?"

"Don't ask me, old boy; remember, I am just the messenger."

"Yes, well, I am not pulling out just yet; you can tell that to the Major." Both men were quiet for a while; Simon was thinking hard. "Look, tell the Major I am staying put, partly to follow up on this fencing and partly because I have a good idea where this information is coming from. If I am right, then for me to pull out now might very well compromise that person. Tell the Major to stick that in his pipe and smoke it."

"Alright, I will tell him, but do you mind if I phrase it a little differently? Anyway, be careful going to look at that fence. I got the weather reports this morning, and the next few days look filthy. Hell of a storm is on its way by all accounts."

77

On the Scent – London's East End - 1941

Disappointed as Doreen was, she wasn't about to give up on her quest to find Amber. She had a hunch that finding the man known as Raspy would help her. She was delayed by the fact that she hadn't seen Joe for a while. He has obviously been busy and had not been at the flat when she had been there. She hadn't been able to ask if he knew where Raspy hung out. She thought about leaving a note for him but who knew who might have access to the apartment and might see it. Joe has been clear about his desire for as few people as possible in the Baker organisation to know about Amber. That need for discretion also ruled out the telephone. Her patience exasperated, she decided that she would have to do a bit of sleuthing. Her brain was not what she was known for, but that was only because she had hidden her intelligence for years. The men she mixed with didn't like intelligent women, they certainly didn't like intelligent whores. She had a keen and incisive mind; she revelled in the chance to use it for a change.

So how to find this man Raspy? She could hang out around the gym and see if he turned up. It didn't feel much like a plan. After all, the gossiping woman had said that he hadn't been seen for a while. She seemed the sort who would know, the sort who would be aware of most things going on in the area. She could go and knock on a few doors in the immediate neighbourhood. Ask if anyone has seen Raspy. It's what the police do in the movies. But then again, the police had the right to do that. What chance would she have of neighbours giving out information about one of their friends to a complete stranger? If there was one thing that Doreen knew about, it was men. She reasoned that most men have a favourite drinking place. She might face the same sort of obstacles regarding people not wanting to give out information, but the good thing about asking in a pub was that there would be mainly men there. She had a lifetime experience of manipulating men. But where did Raspy drink? It was likely that Joe would know, but she couldn't wait until he was around. This Raspy character, Mikhail, was Russian, an immigrant. People who had come to the sprawling metropolis of London tended to reside or at least socialise with others of their culture. To Doreen, as a girl from Cork, she understood the need to hear a familiar accent. It must be even more important for a person from a foreign land to speak with someone in their own language, especially those people who have left their homeland for distressing reasons. This war had created plenty of those. So Raspy would gravitate to a Russian bar or restaurant. That thought made Doreen smile, Mischa. It had been some time since she had seen Mischa; she had to admit that he was one of the few men from her checkered past that she missed.

78

Nightmare.

The only warmth he can feel is that from the blood leaking from his side and onto the waterlogged deck. His hands still tremble with pain, the burns tormented by the freezing water. The realisation that he is dying doesn't disquiet him. His only concern is his failure to help his men.

His heart is raging in his chest, and with each beat, he can feel the warmth in his side. The certainty of his plight strangely consoles him; his regret is those helpless souls. Perhaps he could have one last try. He finds he can kneel. Miraculously, he is standing. Wondrously the axe is smashing into the hinge. Blow after blow is managed until the hinge breaks and the door cracks open. He jams the rear of the axe into the gap and strains with all he has left to free the door. Behind it, he can hear the men, hope in their voices, as they clamber to join in the battle against the twisted metal.

Astonishingly, they are free. He issues orders for them to get to the boats, refusing their help, and then once more, he is alone—alone with the metal, the steam, and the waves, alone with the pain.

Simon wakes alone. He, of all men, knows what it is to be alone.

79

A vodka hangover – London - 1941

Doreen Fletcher could take her booze; it had been a prerequisite of being successful in her profession, but this morning, she felt the effects of her previous night's drinking only too clearly. It had been a long time since she had seen Mischa; their time together had been one of the happiest of her life. She had at one time, high hopes that he might be the one who would rescue her from her debauched life. Hopes that rapidly faded when his wife turned up from Russia. Still, that was a long time ago, and she did not bear a grudge. Although it was funny to see him squirm a little when he realised who this woman was that had turned up at his bar asking after Mikhail. Doreen had thought about turning up in her previous wardrobe but that side of her was gone since she had met Joe. Her new garb allowed her to blend in much more effectively in her new role as a sleuth. The only time she 'dressed' up was when she was due to meet with Ted; she didn't want him to notice any difference in her.

Mischa, over repeated shots of vodka, had told her of the night that Amber had visited the bar. How she had been asking after a man called Bapt, that she was looking for a friend and that she and Raspy had left together to seek out the man whom she believed knew of Her friend's fate. It was not good news for Doreen; of course, she knew who Bapt was; she knew he was an associate of Ted Baker. Why, even just the other evening, Joe had been asking her about him.

Mischa was concerned to hear that Raspy had not been seen for some time. The two of them worked out the dates of Raspy's last visit to the bar and the last time he was seen matched, but they had too few solid facts to work on. Both knew that if Raspy and Amber had been foolish enough to confront a member of the Baker gang, then the outcome may well have been unfavourable. Mischa was keen to help his friend, and Doreen knew that if something had happened to Raspy, then he was likely to want revenge. She also knew that revenge Mischa style was not going to be pretty.

Doreen needed to think about what to do next. She managed to persuade Mischa to wait before taking any action, at least until she had found out more. The Russian was no fool, and whilst his honour would drive him to seek retribution if his friend had been harmed, he was wise enough to serve that dish as cool as it needed to be; thus Mischa had agreed to wait to hear from Doreen,

As she nursed her hangover, Doreen faced a dilemma: Should she involve Joe or find out more for herself first?

80

Who is that man? – SOE Headquarters – Southern England - 1941

Robinson swilled the whisky around in his glass; he was deep in thought, and eventually, he spoke to the major. "I think, James, that there is more to this case than meets the eye. I know I've been the one who has been talking about black market meat and food but I'm not sure if there's something else going on here as well. This man Marshall interests me, I can't tell you why, but I have a feeling about him. We might as well get Simon to keep an eye on him if he is disobeying orders and refusing to pull out."

Major Calderdale knew his boss too well; there was something that he wasn't telling him. "Robinson, I've been working with you a long time; what is it about this Marshall that interests you? On the face of it he's just an ordinary businessman, JP, doyen of the community, I think you know something about him but you're not telling."

"All right Major, during the last war, we were tracking a man who was working out of Switzerland. He was setting up all sorts of arms deals, moving money for people, arranging illegal business deals between English firms and the enemy, that sort of thing. Generally anything where he could make money from the war. We thought we'd caught up with him when he did a deal supplying the Irish Republican Army with weapons that had originated from Germany. We were close to tracking him down, but somehow, he was always one step ahead of us. Eventually, he contacted us asking for immunity if he told us where the IRA had stashed the weapons. We never met with him; everything was done through letter and the occasional brief telephone conversation, but true to his word, we found the weapons. Then he just disappeared, and we never heard from him again. Most people thought that he'd gone to South America, but I had Intelligence that he came to the UK and that he was hiding in plain sight. My boss told me to drop it as we had other fish to fry at that time. The thing is, he used to call himself the Colonel; what if he's given himself a couple of promotions to Marshall? The other thing is what Bach told us he said at the lunch. His toast, 'May you be at the gates of heaven an hour before the devil knows you're dead!' It was an unusual thing to say. The last time I heard that expression was when I spoke on the telephone to 'the Colonel' 25 years ago. I thought it a strange thing to say then, so I had people investigate it. Apparently, it is a traditional, if not informal, Irish saying. But the information we had on this Colonel was that he was born in the far east, no connection to Ireland other than arms business with the republicans."

Major Calderdale thought carefully about what Robinson had just said; he was not convinced. "You think that this Marshall is the same man as the one who was dealing arms to the IRA during the last war. That's a bit of a stretch based upon a toast at a luncheon, isn't it?"

"No doubt you are right, but you know what it's like when you get a hunch about something. It's probably just a coincidence, but I think we should bear it in mind. After all, we have been wondering how this whole thing pieces together: the butcher in Wales, the Gangsters in London and Fergus McDowell, our rogue Irish republican. We don't even know if these things are linked. Maybe they are, and this man Marshall is the connection."

81

Years in the planning – London - 1941

Doreen still couldn't speak to Joe. She also knew that until she had more information, she wasn't sure she wanted to involve him. Approaching Bapt directly was a risky option, as would speaking to anyone in the Baker gang, except there was one person who would know and with whom she had unfinished business.

Julia Davis had been her successor at the Brothel. She had taken over when Doreen had refused to inject the new girls as Eddie had instructed. Doreen knew her to be a sadistic and vindictive woman. Who revelled in cruelly treating the girls who she was supposed to be looking out for. It would be Doreen's pleasure to get one back on her. The trouble was, once she had 'spoken' to her, there was no way that she could be allowed to return to the brothel and inform the Bakers that Doreen had been asking questions. Doreen had a plan.

Years of working for the Bakers had left their mark. She had hoped that the exposure to the naked cruelty and inhumanity of their methods wouldn't change her. She had fought an internal battle against becoming the type of person they were. It had been a fine balancing act, as any compassion shown was likely to be seen as weakness. Doreen had wrestled to keep her humanity but knew now that she would have to become the person she had despised; she would have to deal with Julia with no mercy. She battled with her conscience, but in the end, she knew that she would do anything for Joe and, by extension, for Amber. If there were any way of saving her and Joe's friend Raspy, she would. Once she had spoken to Julia, there could be no possibility of it coming back to her or Joe. Julia would have to be silenced.

Doreen knew something of Julia's habits; she knew that on a midweek afternoon, she liked to go to see a matinee at the cinema. It meant a few fruitless afternoons waiting for her to turn up, but Doreen was prepared to sacrifice her time. The patient hunter waiting by the water hole for the big game. When Julia arrived on the fourth afternoon of her vigil, Doreen was ready and waiting. She had seen her quarry enter the cinema and knew that she had just enough time to arrange things. She had made sure that she had change for the telephone, so her call to Mischa was made minutes later. True to his word, his boys were on hand, and she met them in the side street by the cinema as planned just half an hour into the feature film. Doreen returned to the side door of the cinema, the one used for the moviegoers to exit, and she waited once more.

Julia was distracted when she left, the film had been a real tearjerker. Her favourite kind, with her head still full of romance, she was suddenly brought back to reality as a strong hand grabbed her arm and marched her down the empty side street. She made to struggle, but as she did so, the hand-spun her viciously, her high heels teetered on the rough cobbles, her balance gave out, and she fell in an undignified heap onto the hard floor. She looked up at her assailant in shock.

"Dor Fletcher, what the fuck are you doing?"

"You always did have a foul mouth, Julia. We need to chat." Doreen calmly explained.

"Get lost; what have I got to say to you? You're just a fizzled-out old slapper; wait till I tell Eddie about this." Julia was trying to stand, her pride hurting more than her scraped knees.

"Hey, less of the old." Doreen quipped as she smashed her fist into the side of Julia's cheekbone, sending her back to the ground, this time too dazed to get back up.

The Russians, who had very much been enjoying the altercation between the two ladies, stepped forward, hauled the woman to her feet and carried her to the van. Julia's resistance completely quelled, and she was thrown into the back without complaining. A short journey brought them to Mischa's warehouse, where she was equally unable to resist as she was tied carefully to a chair.

As she waited for Julia to regain her senses, Doreen searched her victim's bag. She had been carrying a handbag, slightly larger than average and somewhat dated. Unusual, Doreen thought, as she knew Julia to be very vain, obsessed with fashion. The reason for Julia's choice was clearly for practicality. The bag was capacious, it's volume easily enough for its vile contents. Even though Doreen knew Julia to be a fanatically cruel woman, she was still surprised that she was carrying with her the tools of her odious trade. In the bag were two cases, wooden construction, leather-wrapped, and velvet-lined. The hinged boxes had a simple locking mechanism. They contained hypodermic needles in one and glass vials in the other. The drugs that were used to enslave the girls and the means of administrating their poisonous venom.

As Doreen was making her gruesome discovery, Mischa arrived. He was keen to find out what had happened to his friend. He was also a little intrigued to see how Doreen proposed to persuade this woman to cooperate.

"Mischa, how lovely to see you! How is your wife?" Doreen smiled sweetly, unable to resist the temptation of teasing her former lover.

Mischa winced as if the barbed comment had actually stung him physically. He was confident that Doreen didn't require an answer, so he asked his own questions. "Did everything go smoothly? No one saw you take her?"

Doreen felt a little ashamed of herself. After all, Mischa was helping her; without him, things would have been much more difficult, if not impossible. "Yes, everything went smoothly. Your boys were good. Thank you, Mischa." This time, her smile was sincere, with maybe a hint of regret. Doreen showed her Russian ally her discovery.

"I hate this shit. It is filth. The people who sell this are worse men alive. Why she have this?" Mischa asked.

Doreen explained the method of controlling the young women so they would participate in the depraved sex that Eddie Baker offered his clients. She knew Mischa to be a ruthless man who was no stranger to crime, but she could see that he was genuinely disgusted by what he was hearing. "Would any of these boys know how to inject her with this?" Doreen asked, indicating Mischa's men.

Mischa asked his men, one of whom sheepishly answered. Mischa was nonplussed that the man seemed to show some expertise in the hateful practice. However, after some discussion, his mood lightened, and his respect for the man was apparently restored.

"This man was training to be medical man before he left Russia. Here he volunteers in ambulances, he speak English good." Mischa proudly extolled the virtues of his man.

"Good, have him ready with the needle; tell him to wave it about so she can see it, but don't give it to her until I tell him. I need her to be fully focussed while I persuade her to cooperate." Doreen was businesslike and determined. Mischa had always regretted that she had refused to be his mistress after his wife had turned up. Women, he would never understand them, then again; perhaps he should have been honest with her from the beginning. Maybe he could have had his cake and eaten it, as he believed the English would say.

82

The Storm – Wales - 1941

Simon mused about his mission. All the indications were that the land beyond the fake MOD fencing was being used, but to what purpose and by whom? He had to get up there and have a look, but the weather worried him. True, the rain, wind, and particularly the low cloud on the peaks would mean that he was unlikely to be seen. But he was no fool; these hills were not to be messed with in poor weather. Much more experienced hikers and climbers than he had been claimed by the vagaries of the mountain weather.

He dressed as warmly as possible whilst allowing for the free movement of his limbs. His gear had so far been reliable, but he had a feeling that today would be the ultimate test. Just to be sure, he packed extra socks, gloves and a warm jumper into his rucksack. The bag bulged with the additional bulk of an old horse blanket that he had found in the stable. He descended the stairs and made his way through the bar; there was a small contingent of early drinkers making use of the free time afforded them by the weather.

"You going out in this son?" Enquired one of the older of the clientele, with barely contained disdain.

"What's the matter with you, Elwyn? It's hardly raining. Nice walk in the hills will do the boy good. Blow the cobwebs off, isn't it?" Pitched in another of the group. The rest seemed to agree and gave their blessing to the adventure.

"Don't see any of you out there working in this lovely weather, now do we?" The original dissenter was not convinced, his words mumbled and not meant to be heard by Simon. "Which way are you heading, lad?" He asked.

"I thought I would head on up the mountain. Keep it short today." Simon replied, concealing his true intent of walking to the ridge beyond.

Simon thanked the men and walked to the old barometer that hung on the wall by the doorway. He tapped the instrument; its needle shuddered a fraction as it gave its answer. 'The glass is falling,' thought Simon. This time, it was his turn to shudder as he thought of his dreams.

Cae looked up hopefully at him from the fireplace. "Perhaps you should sit this one out, old girl," Simon suggested. If she was truly disappointed, she hid it well, returning to her curled pose by the heat.

The door swung shut hurriedly behind him, denying him both the heat of the room and the last comments of the men. "Bloody English chump, freeze 'is nuts off. He will, too. Serves 'im right, pokin' 'bout in other people's business." Was accepted by all as the most pertinent of their remarks.

Simon set himself an arduous pace, he was determined to get up and down before the worst of the storm struck. As he powered on, he pondered on the attitude of the men in the bar. He knew it was a foolish venture, and he was pretty sure that their local knowledge of the mountains would agree with that. So why were they so keen for him to go? Were they hopeful of his demise? It certainly seemed that way. He had noticed that Alwyn had been sat with the group but had not been his usual opinionated self. However, there was little doubt in Simon's mind that he was behind the sentiment. He was also now convinced that there was something going on in the valley and that some of the locals were keen to keep the truth from him. He doubted that they had it in them to kill him to keep their secret, but it would seem that they would not be shedding too many tears if an accident were to befall him. If he was right, it meant that he had failed in his mission. They had seen through his cover and suspected him to be the spy that he was. Apart from his discovery of the fence, he had nothing to show for his efforts. He wondered now if his mission had been a questionable one from the very beginning. His cover feeble, the reason for his presence in the area dubious. Had Robinson underestimated the criminals, or did he have some other plan in mind?

As he climbed, the temperature fell, and the rain turned to sleet and then to snow. The conditions worsening with each step it seemed. He had learned the path well and used his compass to

314

keep on course at each deviation of the track. At the shoulder of the mountain, he skirted around its side, ignoring the temptation of climbing to the peak. The wind had picked up, and he had no intention of finding out how powerful it was at the top. Locating the faint path that led away towards the hills beyond, he pressed on, almost running. His breathing was fast, and the ice-cold air convulsed his lungs, causing him to pant like a dog. He knew that he was losing heat that way, but his muscles demanded oxygen, and he hoped that the strenuous pace would be enough to keep him warm. His fitness was at an all-time peak, and he revelled conceitedly in his strength.

As Simon found the level path, the weather deteriorated further, as the valley beyond gave unfettered access to the storm's path from the west. He marvelled at the intensity of the wind as it blew with the seemingly rancorous purpose of blowing him from the ledge, thereby keeping the mysteries of the mountains from human knowledge. He crouched and forced his legs to push his body against the tempest, occasionally falling flat on his face as the gusts abated without warning. A cruel trick, with the evident design of mocking this derisible mortal, who persisted in his unwanted imposition here.

Simon walked into the fence, its grey steel covered with frost and snow and perfectly camouflaged in the driving blizzard. Despite the indignity of the collision, he was relieved to have made his goal. Crouching at the base of the obstacle, Simon tied his rucksack to a post in the fence before pulling out the blanket. His object was to throw the blanket onto the barbed wire at the top of the fence, allowing him to slide across it. But as soon as he made to do so, he realised the futility of trying. The wind would not allow such a feat.

He had to think of another way. As he was grappling with the blanket, the wind threatening to rip it from his hands at any moment, he realised that if he held it in front of him, when he was turned face-on to the storm, the wind secured it to his body. He pulled the coarse material across his chest and held the top in his teeth. He gripped the fence, thankful for his gloves on the frozen metal, and started to climb. His heavy boots prevented him from getting his toes into the holes, so he had to push the soles of his feet hard against the wire, pushing his bottom out and holding on for dear life with his arms fully extended. When he reached the top, he inched his feet up to as close to his hands as he could. Then he waited for a gap in the gusts. As soon as he sensed the wind easing just a little, he launched himself up and forwards, diving so that he landed on top of the barbed wire, the blanket under him and partly protecting him from the spikes. Reaching down, he grabbed the fence on the other side and flipped over. His feet landed hard on the ground, his backside following painfully a moment later. The barbs of the wire had gripped the blanket, preventing it from blowing away. He quickly tied the corners to the wire to hold it in place for his return journey.

Simon found himself on the top of a ridge that led away to the northeast. The wind ripped at him, the ice it carried, trying to tear the skin from his face. The ridge was no place to be in this weather. He fell to his knees in frustration as he knew he could not go much further. He crawled forward as near to the edge as he dared, trying to look down. Surely, the fence was there to prevent unwanted visitors from getting onto the ridge and getting a clear view of the valley floor below. He felt his way to the edge. Tears stung his eyes, the blinding blizzard closing them to the secrets of the abyss below.

For a moment, just a few seconds, the tumult hesitated as if the wind drew breath, pausing to gather its strength before renewing its terrifying tantrum. Simon could see the valley floor. The old quarry workings had flattened out the ground below. Several large buildings, remnants of past endeavour but surprisingly well maintained, dotted the terrain. Corrugated iron topped the ancient walls, and new timber added support where needed. Several trucks stood parked in a neat row by the side of a rough but well-maintained road.

The view evaporated in a moment as the storm took up its ferocious scream.

Simon was sure that there was no more to be learned from his adventure and it was time to make a strategic retreat. He crawled his way to the fence and reversed his acrobatics over its top. Wanting to hide all potential evidence of his presence, he pulled at the blanket in an attempt to release it from the wire. It tore a little before coming away, Simon just managing to hold it as it tried to fly away across the mountain. He stuffed it into his pack and set off, retracing his steps.

83

Torturous – London - 1941

Julia was coming around; she would have done better to have stayed quiet and pretended that she was still unconscious. Instead, she began a tirade at her captors. "Do you know who the fuck I work for? Have you any idea what he will do to you?"

Her ranting was quickly quelled as Doreen's open hand connected with her face. It was a hard slap, Doreen putting plenty of weight behind it and making sure to drag her nails across the girl's cheek as her head twisted away. Four deep scratches glowed red on the shocked victim's face. Doreen's hand stung, but boy, did that feel good. Before Julia could continue her protests, Doreen advanced towards her, holding a pair of heavy pliers. Julia squirmed back into her chair, unable to pull away her tightly bound hand as the pliers locked onto the nail of her wedding finger. Julia's nails were long and perfectly shaped, ironically their length allowing the tool to establish a firm and relentless grip. A product of hours of filing, polishing and painting, Doreen knew those nails to be the conceited woman's pride and joy. In one harsh, decisive, vicious movement, the nail was pulled from the finger. The shock of the event delayed the reaction; for a few seconds, all the victim could do was stare at the finger and its missing nail. Once the realisation set in, the screams and tears began, accompanied by her foul recriminations and threats.

Doreen had seen Ted torture men. In most cases, there was little need for violence. The victims were ready to talk to avoid the pain that they knew would be coming. Ted's reputation saw to it that there was, in effect, no need for him to hurt his victim. Except, of course, he couldn't be seen to go lightly on someone. His reputation had to be maintained, plus retribution satisfied. Doreen realised, however, that she didn't have the luxury of such a reputation. Her victim, Julia Davis, might not believe that she would have the stomach to inflict any such pain or damage.

Therefore, Doreen concluded, she needed to act first before asking the questions she desperately needed the answers to. Now she had to decide if she should start asking or if she deliver more pain and humiliation. She had no idea what to do; this was, after all, her first, and she hoped last, torture session. No option but to wing it. Doreen clamped the pliers onto another nail.

"Please, no, please. What do you want? Please, I am sorry. What did I do? Please, please." Julia seemed to want to cooperate, but Doreen was still wary.

"There was a man who came to the Brothel, a Russian man. What happened to him." Doreen demanded. Julia looked surprised, her brain working hard to make sense of what was happening. What was the Russian to her?

Doreen sensed that Julia was delaying, working out what to say. She needed her to be more spontaneous, that way, she was more likely to get the truth. Slowly, she started to pull on the nail. This time, it would come away much more slowly and painfully.

"Wait, yes, there was a Russian; he came to the house." Julia sobbed as she felt the pliers let go of her nail.

"What happened to him?" Doreen's voice was firm and left no doubt in anyone's mind that she was determined to get answers.

"I wasn't there. I promise I wasn't there." It was hard to be sure that Julia's sobs were genuine or if she was delaying.

"But you know what happened." It wasn't a question but a statement.

"Yes, I heard about it."

Doreen could sense that Julia was delaying; she was trying to avoid telling the full truth. Time for another nail, she concluded. No swift movement this time. Even the hardened Russians winced as they heard the tearing sound as the nail came away from the flesh, even above the screams of the victim. Doreen's stomach turned; it took all her willpower to stop herself from throwing up. Only her steely determination to find Amber stopped her vomiting and pushed her on. She slowly selected another nail and took up the strain.

"Wait, wait, please, I will tell you. I will tell you." There could be no doubting the sincerity of her willingness to cooperate this time. Without further prompting, she continued. "I was in the shelter; I swear I had nothing to do with it." A slight pause caused Doreen to increase the pressure on the latest nail. "Wait, please, the sirens had sounded, so we had taken most of the guests down to the Andersons. When two of the boys went back to secure the house, they found this Russian bloke, pissed he was. Demanding a girl and vodka. Then Eddie turns up and has a fit because there's this bimbo coming down the stairs with one of the new girls, trying to help her to escape she was." Julia was panting; with her effort to supply answers and stop further pain, she was out of breath. This time, Doreen left her to recover a little before she prompted her. "Eddie was going mad. He reckoned the Rusky was distracting the boys while the tarts made a break for it. You know what he's like; he went off on one. Beat the man to death he did. Billy said it was brutal, out of control, he said."

"And the girl? What happened to her? Where is she?" Doreen screamed, desperate to know.

So, it's the girl that she is interested in, Julia was starting to piece things together. Her hesitation nearly cost her another nail. "Wait, Wait. Eddie was going to use the girl in the house. He sent Billy to get me to bring the needle, but you know that he likes to break them in himself."

"He raped her?"

"No, well yes, he was going to, but apparently, she struggled; he pushed her, and she fell and banged her head. Billy said it snapped her neck."

Doreen's pain was greater than any other dished out in that warehouse that day. Fingernails can regrow, but she would forever feel the loss that hit her. The loss of a loved one she had never met. How could she ever tell Joe? She struggled to hold back her tears; she had to stay focused; she still had answers to find.

"Eddie killed her?" She sought confirmation.

"I don't think he meant to, but yes."

"Was Baptiste there?"

"I don't think so; no, he wasn't. I remember he had gone up west that night, but when he came back, he was furious, laid into Eddie apparently."

"Why?"

"Because of who she was, the girl."

320

"Who, who was she?" Doreen asked, but in her heart, she didn't want the confirmation of what she already knew. She wanted it to be someone else.

"It was Joe Turner's tart, the redhead, used to work in the Dog and Duck."

Julia's description of Amber was ill-advised; Doreen had heard enough; her right hand, still holding the pliers, smashed into the hapless woman's face. Breaking Julia's cheekbone and several of her own fingers. The pain would have been excruciating if she had felt it over the agony of her broken heart.

Mischa sensed his former mistress's pain and took over; he had questions of his own. "What did they do with the bodies?"

Julia was confused; the blow had knocked her half senseless. "What?"

"The bodies, what did Eddie do with the bodies?" Mischa shouted.

"I, I don't know."

Mischa wasn't happy with the answer and took the pliers from Doreen's hand.

"Wait, please, I don't really, I don't. Why would I know that?"

Mischa took hold of one of Julia's remaining nails. "Take your best guess. What is their usual way?"

"Bomb sites, they dump them in bomb sites." What was left of Julia's nerves was long gone now, and she sobbed pitifully.

Mischa turned to Doreen. "I don't think she know more."

"Then she is no fucking use to anyone, is she?" Having made her observation, Doreen punched her again, this time with such force that the chair toppled over. To Mischa's amazement, she used her already damaged hand, further injuring it. He marvelled that Doreen showed no sign of any pain; it was as if she didn't even feel it. On the contrary, Doreen's pain knew no bounds.

"Get rid of her."

Mischa nodded and waved to his men, who untied the beaten woman and bundled her back into the van. The Russian had agreed to arrange for Julia to disappear. But he didn't like murder unless it was absolutely necessary. Instead, he had booked for her to go on a nice leisurely cruise. Mischa had just completed a business transaction with a ship's captain whose freighter was in port. The cargo had been delivered on time and Mischa had paid

321

handsomely for the service. However, when he did business, he always believed that a bonus was a good way to conclude the deal. It left all parties with extra satisfaction and encouraged the possibility of further business. Mischa knew that where the captain was headed, an English rose, even one whose petals were somewhat wilting, was a valuable commodity. Plus, he was sure that she would be very popular with the Captain's crew. Julia Davis's former career as a pleaser of men was about to experience an unexpected swan song.

As Doreen was leaving the warehouse, debating whether to walk or take a taxi back to the flat, Mischa offered her a lift. She politely declined; her feelings for him had never completely gone away, and she didn't want to test her willpower, after all, what would his wife say? Walking along the road, the van carrying Julia to her future stopped next to her. The young Russian, the one who was a medic, climbed down from the passenger seat and walked over to her. She smiled at him sweetly, wondering what he wanted to say to her. "Miss, I don't think that you know." He hesitated as if he was not sure if he was betraying a secret.

"Know what?" Doreen prompted keenly.

"I don't think that you know that Mischa, his wife, his wife she died. It was some time ago, maybe ten years. She died, he on his own since. I don't think that you know." The boy turned and got back into the van, which promptly sped away.

"No, I didn't know, I didn't." Doreen's words were lost in the roar of the engine.

84

Lost and Found – Wales - 1941

Taking note that the wind was raging from the northwest, Simon judged that he was better advised to take the path around the mountain that then descended on the southeast side, which would be protected from the storm by the mountain. It was a longer and slower route but safer and easier going, although still not without discomfort. The wind was reduced, but the snow fell steadily, hampering his view and making his footing hazardous.

It was well after dark that Simon trudged down the road towards the welcoming lights of the town. He had been out for over 5 hours; he was tired and cold to his bones. A hot bath called to him, followed by a beer or even a whiskey.

He swung open the bar door and trudged into the congenial warmth of the smoky room.

"Lieutenant, thank the lord you are safe; I was so worried. But where is Sara?"

Simon stood aghast, "Sara? What do you mean? Sara was not with me; she went to Brecon today, didn't she?"

"Oh, lieutenant, she went out looking for you; we were so worried. The boys should never have let you go out in this; they know very well how dangerous it can be on the mountain." The bar's clientele all looked sheepishly into their glasses, avoiding the accusing glares of the landlady.

"Mrs Williams, I realised that the storm was picking up, so I kept to the lower path. I walked round the back of the mountain and took the southern path back, as the wind was gentler there. I am not a fool, Mrs Williams; I knew better than to climb the mountain. How long ago did Sara leave?"

The landlady looked at the grandfather clock that stood sentinel by the lounge door. "She must have got the half past three bus from Brecon that would have got her here at just after four o'clock. So, she has been out for just about an hour."

Simon barely waited for the lady to finish before he was out the door. This time, Cae didn't wait for an invitation. The old dog sensed that she was needed and followed closely at her new master's heels.

Delaying only to collect a torch from his motorcycle panniers, for the second time that day, Simon headed for the mountain, this time to save a life. He castigated himself for the deception that he had encouraged when he had led the men in the bar to believe that he was going up the mountain. Sara must have been working on that presumption as she had followed his path, fretting that he had not returned and must be lost. If only he had taken the same path back down from the mountain, surely then he would have run into her, and they would both be safe.

Simon had thought that the conditions had been bad earlier, but the storm had reached new levels of ferociousness. The sun, unseen on that day in Wales above the scudding clouds, had already set unobserved. Dusk was a fleeting memory as night had wrapped her dark cloak over the valley and the mountains. The wind brought the snow, driving almost horizontally to the ground. The torchlight only just managed to light the scurrying flakes as they passed its feeble beam. Vision beyond the sweeping squalls was a wild hope. Pointing the torch downwards allowed only a perception of the ground for a few feet ahead. His progress painfully slow, hampered by the barbarous wind and the necessity to stay on the narrow path, Simon bawled bitterly at the storm. His hope was dying with each step, and desperation overwhelmed him. It was a futile quest. The storm was winning. All possibility of finding Sara on the mountain dissipated.

As his steps faltered, unexpected salvation reached out and piloted him onward. At first, Simon couldn't understand what was happening; Cae was running towards him and then turning and slowly walking away. As the drifting snow engulfed her, she turned once again and returned to his sight. This time, she barked as she walked determinedly into the storm. Simon caught on at last and struggled to keep up. Directing all his focus on the tail of the remarkable animal, he upped his pace, trusting in his faithful friend. His passage vacillated between the reassurance of following Cai's unrivalled instincts and moments of near panic when a squall of snow took her from his sight. At times, the expedition seemed impossible; the elements seemed affronted by their insistence to carry on, raging with the cruel intention to send them into derisory retreat. He couldn't believe that he was walking on the same path that had afforded him such pleasure, such beauty on recent warm summer days. The gentle breezes had been soothing and fragrant then. Now, the storm, with all its reminders of the horror of his dreams, traumatised him more than anything ever had before. He shook with terror, his legs weak like a newborn foal, tears streamed from his eyes, and his heart raced incessantly. But if Simon had of weakened, and fallen short in his resolve, then surely the obstinacy of Cae would have kept him going.

She was magnificent. An animal, who of an evening in the pub, would lie close to the fire to placate her rheumatoid old bones, now she ran like the prize-winning pedigree she had been. She covered two, three, maybe four times the distance that Simon did. She chased ahead into the storm, sniffing the violent wind for clues. Finding the secure path and hastening back to her man, guiding his way. Without her, he would have been lost in minutes. He would have strayed from the path, perhaps stepping into the mossy ground, sinking knee-deep into its mire. Dying there, freezing in that unforgiving terrain.

He was now completely lost, but for his faithful ally, he had tried to count his steps, estimate the time that had elapsed, and work out the distance travelled. But all the normal rules of navigation were useless. There was no way back for him; the only clue would be the direction of the wind, but that would not suffice as an accurate benchmark. Without Cae, there was no hope for him or Sara; without his best friend, all was lost. His clothes were sodden, and the snow that had stuck to his coat had melted by the heat escaping from his body. The water seeping through the seams in the material. More snow had frozen on the cloth as his body heat subsided. He had been shaking uncontrollably, but now this had stopped; his laboured breathing had slowed, and he felt confused and drowsy. He was snapped out of his stupor suddenly by Cae's barking. He had stopped walking and so she jumped up at him, compelling him to carry on. Simon recognised that he was beginning to suffer from Hypothermia. When he had walked in the mountains of India, the guides would speak often of the dangers of the cold. They told of how quickly a man can succumb to its effects. When a man was affected in such away, his remaining life would be measured in minutes. Simon shuddered again, this time from fear.

In what seemed to him to be an unachievable effort, he strode forward, each step an agony of willpower over his fatigue. Cae was barking again, this time an uncontrolled cacophony of noise as she raced backwards and forwards to him. She ran to the side of the path, and Simon followed in unquestioned obedience to the canine.

Sara Lloyd had strayed from the path as the weather and the gloom had closed in around her. She had stepped on a tuft of grass, her foot slipping from it and into a wet bog. Her weight, falling forwards, had put an intense strain on her knee, as the lower part of her leg was held firm in the watery vice of the mire. She screamed out in pain as she fell on her face. Thin ice cracked beneath her as she sunk into the water-soaked moss below. In a scrambling effort, she managed to pull herself to firmer ground, where she lay crying as she realised that her knee could not support her weight. There would be no way for her to carry on and look for Simon and no possible retreat to get help from the town.

Cae licked her face and barked at her immobile body. Simon fell to his knees next to her, praying to a God whom he despised for a sign of life. A faint pulse filled him with joy and his own sufferings vanished in his newfound hope. He pulled the pack from his back and took from it all that was of use, discarding the rest. He put both the gloves and the socks onto her hands, not having the time or the dexterity in his frozen fingers to remove her boots. Her coat was wet through, so he tore it from her, replacing it with his spare jumper and wrapping her tightly in the horse blanket. Simon swung her body onto his shoulder and rose painfully from his crouch. Cae needed no instruction and was already leading the way down towards the town. The wind now behind him, Simon expected to be grateful for its assistance in pushing him forward, but at times the gusts were too much and threatened to topple them over. Carrying Sara, it was much more difficult for him to see his footing. The batteries of the torch had weakened, diminishing the already paltry light it gave. It was a race against time; Simon imagined that with each second, the cold was drawing life from her, so he marched on. All thoughts of his own ordeals were banished from his mind. It had taken Eleanor Williams some time to convince her clientele that they should join the rescue effort. Each man knew the dangers, and while they battled with their consciences, they argued that the attempt would be futile. At last, they had been persuaded when Matt Jones had come into the pub. Jones, a retired policeman, had been an accomplished mountaineer in his younger days. Before the war he had guided groups of tourists around the mountains. Since the start of hostilities, he advised the army on mountain navigation and survival. When the situation had been explained to him, he had jumped into action. He had run home to his cottage in the town and brought back as much gear as he could find. He insisted that each man should be properly kitted out. With stout boots and warm clothing. He had rope so that they could be tied together for safety. He had doubts about the success of the mission, promising that they would try; he also warned that he would not risk the lives of the volunteers in any reckless manner.

The party had barely made it onto the mountain track when they came across the miraculous sight of an old farm dog leading a man carrying a motionless body. As they relieved Simon of his burden, he collapsed to the ground, exhausted.

Simon woke in the warmth and smoky atmosphere of the Dragon's tail bar. It was a moment before he realised where he was. Mrs Williams swiftly reassured him that Sara was safe. The doctor had been called and had tended to her. She had badly strained her knee, but otherwise, she was uninjured.

"The doctor said that she wouldn't have lasted much longer out on that mountain. You saved her life, young man." Elanor Williams smiled gratefully at Simon.

Simon looked towards the fireplace where Cae was curled, warming her aching bones, as she did most evenings, as if nothing had happened. "Not me, Mrs Williams; I didn't save her." He nodded towards the dog. "I didn't save her."

Simon thought on old Dai's words. 'Best working dog, I ever saw, won prizes too, best-working dog ever.'

327

85

My enemy's enemy – London – a West End Bar - London

Joe Turner had been spending a fair amount of time with Baptiste. The man had been very useful in Joe's efforts to set up a trading network for the new enterprise. Joe had originally taken Baptiste along for a meeting with a French restaurant owner in the west end. He figured that a fellow French speaker would be able to smooth the way and he had been right. Bapt had charmed the woman. She was eating out of his hands almost as soon as they had sat down in her office. It turned out that Baptiste, in his time in London, had befriended many of the Maître d' of the best establishments of the city. They trusted him and were delighted with the service that he and Joe promised to supply. It was clear that maintaining pre-war standards was a badge of honour for these people. Any slip in quality was out of the question for them, even if there was a war on. That they were preparing to break the law was not in consideration. After all, such rules were there for the ordinary people; their clientele couldn't be expected to eat spam and Woolton pies[11].

Bapt had used the project to escape the brothel and Eddie Baker's odious practices. He also wanted to get closer to Joe Turner. Bapt could see that change was coming, and he was anxious that he should emerge on the right side of it. It struck him that Turner was a man to watch, possibly one to be close to when things came to a head.

Joe and Bapt were sat in a bar in the west end. The place was moderately busy; it was too late for the pre-dinner drinkers and

---

[11] Woolton Pies were a recipe that was published as an alternative to meat-based pies. It was made using vegetables freely available. It was named after Frederick Marquis, 1st Lord Woolton (1883–1964), who popularised the recipe after he became Minister of Food in 1940.

too early for the after-show crowd. They'd had a successful day. Flogging hooky meat was like shelling peas; Joe's expression had confused Baptiste's understanding of the language, but when Joe had explained, he found it very funny. The two men had begun to become friends. They had shared the stories of their upbringings and found common ground. Baptiste had told of his hate for the Nazis and his desire to revenge his country and free his people from the German occupation. Joe found himself agreeing with the Frenchman on this and many other subjects. The only missing ingredient needed to cement an alliance was trust, however trust was a rare commodity in their world.

"How did you become worker for Bakers?" They'd had a few drinks, and Joe noticed that Bapt's usually careful English was coming apart a little.

"Let's just say that Ted can be very persuasive when he wants to be."

Bapt wasn't satisfied with that answer, and, buoyed by the drinks, he pushed for more. "People say that you didn't want to work for them, that you resisted. Is it true you murdered old lady?"

Joe was intrigued as to why Bapt was asking such questions. It was bold of him; they were not the sort of questions he would expect. Joe considered pretending to be offended, telling the man to mind his own business. He had to stick to the story cooked up by Susan Cartwright and DCI Wilkinson. Joe decided to play along, trade a little information, and see where Baptiste was leading.

"No, I didn't murder anyone. The police tried to fit me up." Joe could see that Bapt didn't understand. "They tried to say that I had committed a murder, but I hadn't. The police had a trumped-up case against me, and if it had gone to court, I would probably have hung for it. Ted Baker used his influence with the coppers, and the case collapsed. Of course, then I was in his debt. That's how I came to be working with him. To be fair I don't mind it, it's easy work."

"You aren't a man who is a gangster. A crook, yes, but not a violent man, not a man who enjoys violence. Am I right?"

"I can handle myself, but I don't go looking for trouble if that's what you mean. Anyway, I could ask you the same question: why are you with the Bakers?"

"I am a man in a strange town. I try to do businesses but when you don't fit in, when you are stranger, you have to bow to the king of the town. I work for Bakers, or I work against them, it is obvious, even to a stranger, that this is not good idea."

Joe nodded; he was making sense despite the alcohol.

"You like Ted Baker?" It was a very direct question, and Joe thought that things were getting a little too honest.

"I didn't before I got to know him. Where I grew up, everyone knew his name, everyone respected him, and if they were sensible, they feared him. I never knew him, now I respect him, and I would never be so foolish as to cross him. No reason for me to."

"And Eddie, what do you think of Eddie?"

"What is this? Why are you asking me these questions? Who are you asking for?" Joe was less than comfortable. Bapt spent a lot of time with Eddie Baker. Was he trying to trick him into saying something against his boss? Was he Eddie's stooge? If he was, he wasn't doing a particularly subtle job of it.

"I hate Eddie. He is a cruel and dangerous man. You know that he intends to get rid of his father and take over the businesses?" Bapt direct again and now very serious, sober even. Like he hadn't touched a drink all night.

"I'd be a little careful about who you go around saying that to if I were you, old chum." Joe tried to sound casual; had the drunkenness just been an act?

"I am worried man Joe. There will be trouble, and I don't want to be on the wrong side. How is it you say it? There's trouble in the air."

"Why is it that you think I know what to do?" Joe Asked earnestly.

"I think that you work with Ted, and I work with Eddie. When there is trouble, we could warn each other, we could look out for each other."

"And why should I trust you?" Joe Asked.

"Of course, why should you? Why should I trust you? You need a reason to trust me, no? Well, I will give you a reason. You

330

will trust me because of what I will tell you now. If when I tell you, you do not believe me, maybe you will kill me. This is chance I take."

Joe was aghast. He had no idea where this was going, but the man was sincere; he believed that. Joe felt he had no choice but to listen and see where this went. Perhaps it would lead him deeper into the Baker organisation and give him more information to work with.

Bapt drew a deep breath and started his tale. "I told you that Eddie is an evil man. I do not pretend that I am saint. I have done many things wrong. I hope, though, never to be the man that he is. Eddie has told me that he will take over and that he will make me his second in command. He is waiting, though. There is a business that his father is making. One that Eddie does not know too much about. He says that it is a very profitable one. He doesn't want to miss out on it, so he is waiting until it is set up. He did not say what the business was, but I think that it is this business for which you are working. He says that I am to be ready next month. Is that when the animals start to arrive?"

"I honestly don't know, but it is possible," Joe admitted.

"There is another thing, Joe, he doesn't like you. He says you interfere in his businesses. He is worried that you move money for his Father. That you make money safe from the police. Eddie is worried that the money will be lost to him, his father has told him nothing of where the money has gone. With his father dead, the only man who will know will be you, Joe. I dread to think of what Eddie will do to you to get his hands on it."

A realisation struck Joe. Ted Baker hadn't been moving his money just to clean up his act. He had been doing it, so his son couldn't get to it. The crafty old bugger, Joe thought to himself. Of course, Ted must have realised that his son was out to take over. He knew what Eddie was capable of. By stashing away the loot and not telling his son, he was insuring himself against Eddie acting against him.

"There is one more thing that you should know. I tell you this hoping that you will realise that I had nothing to do with it. Joe, some weeks ago, I found a young girl at the docks; I took her to the brothel. I hate doing this, but it is my job. I hate it because of the way that Eddie treats them. I did not know then who the girl

331

was. I swear this, Joe. I know now that she is called Linda and that she used to work at the pub, the Duck and Dog."

Joe's blood was running cold. He could sense that there was more to come, and none of it was going to have a happy ending.

"One evening, I was in the west end; when I came back, it was late. I found Billy; he was wrapping up a body. I knew the man; he was a man they call Raspy. He was a friend of yours, no?"

"Yes, Raspy and I go way back," Joe said automatically.

"Joe, Raspy had come looking for the girl Linda. Eddie had caught him, and he beat him to death."

Joe interrupted. "But why was Raspy looking for Linda? He didn't know her, did he." Joe's brain was a fog, running subconsciously slowly so it need not come to the conclusion he feared.

"Joe, Amber had brought him. They came to look for Linda together. I don't know how they knew she was at the brothel, but they came to get her."

"What happened to Amber Bapt?" Joe grabbed the Parisian by his jacket lapels and spat his words into his face. "What happened to her." His screamed words echoed around the empty barroom.

Bapt caught him around the shoulders as Joe's legs gave out from under him. It was as if he had drunk a bottle of whiskey, and he had only just realised it. Joe was muttering, sobbing, paralysed by the shock. Bapt led him from the bar, making excuses for his 'one too many' friend. A taxi whisked them swiftly to Joe's flat. They were inside and Bapt was pouring some brandy before Joes senses returned.

"What happened to her?" No screaming this time, just Joe's calm voice and the click of his pistol as he pointed it at Bapt.

"Joe, I wasn't there. It happened when I was out, you must believe me."

"What happened to her?" Joe lifted the pistol and aimed at the messenger's head.

Bapt fought his nerves, and as calmly as he could, he told the truth. "Joe, Eddie killed her. He beat Raspy, and then he tried to rape Amber, but she fought back; in the struggle, he pushed her against the wall, she fell, and her neck broke. She must have died instantly."

Joe lowered the gun and tried to process the words he had heard. It was unreal. He couldn't believe what he was hearing. It couldn't be true. Baptiste took a swig of the brandy and waited for his friend to speak.

"How do I know that is what happened? How do I know that it wasn't you that killed her?" Joe surged forward and thrust the pistol against Bapt's head. "How do I know." He screamed.

Neither Joe nor the trembling Baptiste had heard the door open nor the footsteps across the tiled hallway.

"How do I know?" Joe screamed again as he forced Bapt to his knees, the muzzle of the gun painfully pressed against his temple.

Joe felt a gentle hand on his, and a soft voice was talking to him. "He's telling the truth, Joe. It was Eddie. Joe, He's telling the truth."

Joe looked down into Doreen's kind eyes as she took the gun from him and sat him down on the sofa.

86

Entente – Dragon's Tail Hotel – Wales - 1941

Simon was settled into a chair by the fire, which he shared with Cae. The old dog snored gently as if nothing had happened that evening. Simon's nerves were stretched tight by the danger that they had faced; he knew that even if he managed to sleep, the memory of the storm would bring about his dreams. Unable to face such terrors, he had fetched the last bottle of the Major's whisky from his room and was seeking oblivion with its powers and the captivating effects of the fire's glow. He had imagined that everyone had left the bar and that Sara and Mrs Williams had gone to bed. As he stared at the flames, he became aware of a presence just behind him. He turned to look over his shoulder; there stood the imposing figure of Alwyn Thomas. Simon started, at first suspicious of the giant's intent, but something in his manner suggested that he harboured no ill will.

Alwyn spoke. "I err, I." It was clear that he wanted badly to say something, but what little eloquence he possessed had deserted him. "I just wanted to say, I mean err." Once again, the words he needed slipped his grasp.

"Sit down, Alwyn." Simon's words were firm but kind. As the farmer sat, Simon rose and fetched a clean glass from the bar. Placing it on the table before him, he poured a generous measure of the whisky. The gesture seemed to say it all. It said that Simon understood what it was he wanted to say. That words were unnecessary.

Alwyn Thomas nodded his thanks for the spirit and the implied understanding. He took a large swig at the liquid, coughing softly at its unaccustomed harshness. As if its effects were instantaneous, his large body seemed to relax visibly. He took one gentler sip before he managed to find his words. "What you did was very brave." It was all he could manage.

Simon struggled for a response.

"You saved her life." The farmer pressed.

"It was my fault that she was out there. I should never have gone out in that storm today. Besides, I would have died of exposure if it wasn't for old Cae. Your Dad was right about her."

"He was, wasn't he." The farmer laughed. "All the times he used to go on about her, 'best working dog I ever saw'," The boy's imitation of his father was true to form. "She were a good dog, but she would only work for him, until tonight that is."

"I would have liked to have seen her working when she was in her prime, it must have been something to see."

"You should go and see Geraint Ryland's bitch, over at Cwm ty Gwyn farm. She is related to Cae. They say she will be odds on at the next Welsh show. Geraint has always had good dogs. He would be happy to show her off to you; he's a good man, is old Geraint. I could call him and arrange for you to go over."

It was a generous offer enthusiastically proposed. Simon got the feeling that the young man wanted to make amends in some way. But more than that, he felt he wanted something else. "I would like that, thank you." Without asking, Simon poured more whisky into both their glasses, a simple gesture that invited his new friend to talk for longer.

"I wanted to say sorry to you for the fight." Alwyn's words cascaded quickly from him as if from blessed relief.

"That's alright, I did run you out after all." Simon smiled good naturedly, his hope that the remark would be taken in its intended spirit.

Alwyn smiled back. "We both know that it was your call, and I was to blame. Besides you won us the game, you played well."

"We both know that was down to Evans the bat." Simon countered.

Alwyn chuckled. "Of course, I had forgotten about that; I mean, it's not like he has reminded me about it every time I have seen him since." The chuckles turned into laughter for both men.

"Has he told you about the time he saw Glamorgan beat the West Indies?"

"Has he? Every single ball bowled, and every run made. Did you see that he has mounted the ball from our match on a stand and now displays it in his shop window."

"I have seen it. He deserves it. It was a fine shot."

335

"It was, too."

The pair settled into an easy silence. It occurred to Simon, for the first time, that this man was not the brute that he pretended to be. Nor was he the dunce that people made out. Now that he was communicating properly with him for the first time, Simon could see that his slow mannerisms were more from a considered way about him rather than any lack of intellect. He didn't suppose that he had enjoyed much in the way of schooling or that if he had, he would have benefited much from it. In a way he was much like Pritchard-Smythe; they both acted in the way in which they were expected to, the difference being that Smythe used it to his advantage. His almost comical, stereo-typical buffoonery hid the incisiveness of his mind, which might otherwise have put people ill at ease. Thomas was different in that he was playing the dunce because that was what he had been told he was. Simon could imagine his mother casting him in such a light, perhaps his teachers too. He hoped that for the young man's sake, there would be someone in his life, one day, who would believe in him.

'All the world's a stage, and all the men and women merely players.' Simon mused on the quote; he thought it was Shakespeare, but he could never remember from which play. It certainly applied to him; here he was acting out another scene with no script, just constant ad-libbing.

"I spoke to Sara; she told me that I was wrong about you. That you had been a gentleman. I was wrong to think that you wanted to take her from Adam. I am sorry." Alwyn's apology burst into the silence.

"That's alright; you were just sticking up for your 'butty'. I admire that."

Alwyn smiled at the Englishman's use of the Welsh slang. "Where did you learn to fight like that?" It had clearly been a question he was longing to ask, and it fell from his lips involuntarily.

"You had never been beaten before in a fight, had you?" The farmer shook his head. "You're a strong man, Alwyn. Those punches of yours are incredible; if you had connected with just one of those, you would probably have knocked me into the middle of next week, but I used your strength against you. I can't imagine that any of your previous fights had lasted too long. Most would have been over after your first punch had landed or you had wrestled your man to the ground." This time, a nod confirmed Simon's conjecture. "I was taught to box by a very good friend. I used to spar with him. He was so quick that I barely ever laid a glove on him."

"I know that feeling," Alwyn interjected, laughing at himself.

"Did you notice that when we fought, I did not try to hit you at first?"

"That's right, you didn't. I hadn't thought about it until now, but you just kept dodging out of the way. Not very sporting of you, old bean!" This time, Alwyn mocked Simon's very English accent to amusing effect.

"Sometimes fighting is as much about not getting hit as hitting. Every punch you threw, you put everything you had into it. Commendable but also none too wise, if you don't mind me saying so." Again, a nod indicated that Alwyn was willing to listen and learn. "Every punch you threw was a big effort. Inevitably, it became tiring when you kept missing. Also, it showed me where I could punch you. After each missed blow, you were vulnerable, off balance, and your head was unprotected. The more you missed, the angrier you got. Never fight angry. Stay calm, watch your opponent, and try to anticipate what they will do next."

Alwyn nodded. "Sounds like good advice, perhaps we could have another go, see how I get on now." A big smile spread across his tanned face.

"Not bloody likely. I got away with it last time, but I wouldn't like to chance my luck again. Next time there's a fight, you're on my side, right?" Simon raised his glass, and the new friends drank to the idea.

"I am going to join up." Alwyn spat out unexpectedly.

87

Grief. – London, Joe's flat

Joe Turner took another slug of the strong liquor. The fiery liquid burnt at his throat, but it was the only sensation he could feel. The rest of him was numb. He knew now that he had to complete his mission. He had to stop the trade that threatened to destabilise the war effort. In doing so, he would put an end to the evil crime empire of the Bakers. Most of all, he would put a stop to Eddie Baker. His grief would have to wait until later. The most pressing matter for him now was for him to decide who he could trust. In a pivotal moment of realisation, Joe understood that he didn't care. If he was going to bring down the Bakers, he needed help. He had to take a chance.

Doreen had just finished telling him everything she had learned from Julia. She was a little bit hazy on how she had persuaded the woman to part with such information, but Doreen was certain that what she was telling him were the facts. Baptiste had also gone over his story of the night that Raspy and Amber had died. It was time now for Joe to tell some home truths.

"Dor, you asked me once who I was, well now it's time that I told you. You know that I am a burglar by trade, a good one as it happens. In peacetime, it was a trade that I was happy with. I knew on some levels that it was wrong, but I justified it by stealing from toffs that could afford it. When the war came, I wanted to join up, but I wasn't sure what I could do. Then, I met a man who gave me a job working for the Government. I guess you could say that I am a spy of sorts. You see, my talents as a house breaker are quite useful to the war effort. But the case I am on now, why I am here, is they wanted me to find out what the Bakers are up to. The government want to know how and why a criminal gang like the Bakers is getting involved with the black market, in particular the trade in black market meat. That's why I am working for the Bakers Dor; you were right. Under normal circumstances, I wouldn't touch them with a barge pole."

Doreen smiled, relieved that her Joe was not willingly a Bakers gangster.

"You understand." Joe paused, looking intensely at Baptiste Barbeau. "That what I am telling you is a Crown secret, that if you divulge any of this to any unauthorised person, you will be committing treason. If you cross me, then you are also crossing the British Government. Under war regulations, the punishment is death, even for a foreign national. You told me, Baptiste, that you hate the Nazis; well, if you help me, you will be helping the war effort, and when this is over, I know a man who will be happy to put your talents to good use in defeating those bastards. Will you be able to go back to the brothel and carry on as you were? I need you close to Eddie; let me know what he is up to. But be careful. If he finds out any of this, then he will kill us both."

"This is no problem; do we wait for Eddie to move against Ted?" Baptiste was clearly relieved that Joe believed the truth that he had told him. Now, he was excited that he would be working for him. It meant a lot to him that his life would be taking on a new meaning.

"We wait and see. Doreen, do you think that Mischa will help us? I mean you said that he wants revenge for Raspy, but how far do you think that he will go?"

"I know that he cared very deeply for his friend. He is a very loyal man. I think it is time that I go and speak to him." Doreen's words seemed to carry a meaning lost on Joe, but he trusted her. He was glad she was on his side.

"Bapt, you have been spending a lot of time with me. Did Eddie ask you to?" Joe asked.

"No, I had a feeling that you were a man to watch. I wanted to find out more about you."

"Right, now the worry is that if Eddie has noticed you spending time with me, he might get suspicious. I want you to go back to him and tell him that you think I am working for the police. Tell him that you overheard me on the telephone, anything."

"But Joe, he will kill you." Doreen pleaded with Joe. "It's too dangerous."

"She's right Joe." Baptiste also seemed scared for his friend.

"Look, Eddie wants to kill me anyway. You making him more suspicious of me will make very little difference. What it will do is give you credibility with Eddie. He will trust you more; with any luck, he will tell you more about his plans."

88

Which service? – The Dragon's Tail Hotel - Wales

So, this was it, Simon thought to himself. This was the main thing on the Welshman's mind: whether he should join up or not. He wondered what to say.

"Why did you choose the Navy?" Alwyn asked. It seemed obvious to Simon that he was unsure which service would suit him best.

Simon had to think quickly; after all, he hadn't chosen the Navy. "I thought about the army, but I wondered if I would be able to kill a man, you know, up close. I am terrified of heights, so the RAF was out. That left the Navy, and as I had sailed a bit and thought I could be quite good at navigation, I thought it the best of a bad bunch. But you won't be called up, correct? As a farmer, you are a protected occupation, so why do you want to join up?"

"It's just that…." Once again, the man's eloquence seemed to abandon him; he fumbled for the words. "It's every time I go out in Brecon, I see people looking at me and thinking, why isn't he in uniform? He's a coward. Hiding behind his protected occupation when other young men are doing their duty. Nice cushy life for him, far from the bombs. Out in the fresh air. Making his fortune while the real men are fighting the fascists."

Once the words had come there was no doubt that they were opinions passionately held. Simon let the man settle as he sought his own response. "Army, Navy or RAF?" He asked eventually.

"I don't know. I have never flown so I don't know, and I guess I haven't got the right schooling anyways. The same goes for the Navy. I went on a fishing trip from Barry one summer holiday, but I was sick as a dog, so I suppose it's the Army. I can fight, even better if I were taught how."

"No doubt you would make a good soldier, just one problem."

"What's that?" Alwyn sounded offended.

341

"You're too bloody big. Yes, you would be good in a toe-to-toe scrap with Jerry, but imagine you running across no man's land. I'm a terrible shot, but I reckon that with a rifle, I could drop you from 200 yards out. What's more, you would be the first one I would shoot; I'd prefer to slug it out with one of your smaller comrades than a giant like you."

"So, I am bloody useless for anything. How the hell am I supposed to do my duty, like you?"

The last two words were telling Simon thought. "Like me?" His incredulous reply.

"Yes, like you. Look at you; you're a bloody hero. You're doing your duty, not hiding behind your mother's skirts on some comfortable farm a million miles from where the war is being fought."

"Perhaps we could swap. You could go to sea when my ship is ready, and I can stay here and run your farm." Simon spoke quite seriously, and Alwyn wasn't altogether sure if the sailor was being sincere. There was a pause as Simon seemed to consider the proposal, and Alwyn waited for him to continue. At last, Simon spoke again, and this time, there was no doubt about his opinion. "The problem would be, of course, that I know nothing about farming. I would probably try to milk the Heffers or the Bulls or some such thing. I'd overwater the crops or be late harvesting. As for you, I am not sure if you would get the ship out of the harbour without wrecking it, or you would get lost in the Atlantic. I doubt that the Admiralty would see you as a hero if you did that old boy." Both men laughed as they imagined the ridiculous prospects, but when Simon continued his tone was serious and unambiguous. "Every day, there are ships, men, fighting their way across the Atlantic. The ships are full of vital supplies, armaments, fuel, and perhaps most importantly, food. Every day, those ships are being sunk in great numbers. Men are dying, and cargos are lost. If things carry on as they are, we could lose this war. Not because we are not brave, or we are not resourceful or clever, but because we will starve. Hitler is trying to starve us into surrender. His U-boats are winning, and there is not much we can do to stop them from sinking our ships. But you can do something, Alwyn Thomas, you can do something." Simon had pulled himself forward to the edge of his chair and was staring the young man directly in the eyes; the farmer held his gaze and was captivated by the sincerity and passion of what Simon was saying. "You can do something; you can bend your back and use all your knowledge. You can work your fields, you can tend your flocks, you can sow seed, you can harvest, you can maximise your yields. You can make every acre, every inch of ground productive. You can fill the stomachs of the factory workers; you can feed our armies. When you do your job, our ships won't need to sail to bring our food because the food we need is here in Wales; it's here in your hands, and it will grow by the sweat of your brow and the bend of your back. We need you, Alwyn Thomas; this country needs you and Dot and Betty and Rosie and all the men and women on the farms. Without **YOU**, Hitler and his evil win."

By the time he had finished there was the glimmer of a tear in the eyes of both men.

"Bloody hell But, it's like listening to Churchill when you get going isn't it." Alwyn laughed, but there was more than a nod of gratitude in his voice. The message was well received.

Simon poured the remains of the bottle equally into their glasses. The old clock chimed a single warning of the late hour.

"Blimey, by the time we have finished these, it will be time to milk those heifers and bulls." Alwyn laughed.

"Need a hand?" Simon asked, sleep wouldn't come easily, and he could use the exercise.

"Aye, thanks, why not? It's about time you did some honest war work."

89

Time for a Bollocking – London – Accountant's Office

Joe climbed the stairs to Miss Hereford's office slowly. He was in no hurry to face the music. He knew that he had overstepped the mark when he had included Baptiste, Doreen and potentially a gang of Russians in his plans. He was confident that the Major and Robinson would be livid when he told them.

Joe reached the office door, knocked and entered without pause. "Miss Hereford, how radiant you look today. I swear that you look younger every time that I see you. Is it true that you have a portrait in your attic that ages in your stead? Tell me what manner of wizardry you use to beguile me." Joe had taken the lady's hand and was kissing it repeatedly.

"Enough of your flirting, you two. We are busy men and don't have time for your childish games." The Major was trying to sound gruff, but as always, he was quietly amused by Joe. Miss Hereford, aka Sue Cartwright, was also pleased and would have been quite happy for Joe to continue his flirtations.

"Report, please, Mr Turner." Robison was to the point, as always.

Joe bit his lip and took up his story. He told his superiors about the progress with the black-market business. They had just about got to the bottom of all Ted Baker's assets and were ready to move the final ones to safe accounts. He explained about the murder of Raspy and how he had found out from Baptiste. Joe didn't mention Amber; he didn't want them to think that he was too emotionally involved and remove him from the case. He told them that he had recruited Doreen and Baptiste. The Major interrupted him at this point.

"This woman, Doreen, you trust her." Asked the Major, as always ready to probe with the pertinent question.

"Yes, sir"

"May I ask why?"

"I am sure you can, Major, if you like." Joe thought it best to be as flippant as usual.

"Turner, I swear one day I will pull that cocky little tongue from your mouth and shove it......" James Calderdale remembered the presence of a young lady and checked himself. "Why do you trust her."

"Sorry, boss. Gut feeling really. She's sort of an old family friend, long story. She also wants out of working for the Bakers, especially Eddie. She has given me good information; she's stuck her neck out already."

"Tell me about the Russians." Commanded Major Calderdale.

"Well, Sir, before the war, they were a lively bunch, I can tell you. They had quite a business going; next to the Bakers, they were probably the biggest fish in the murky little pond. But something seems to have changed them. You don't hear about them like you did. I am told this Mischa can be trusted. He wants an eye for an eye for Raspy. I'd say whatever happens, sooner or later, they will be calling on Eddie Baker."

Robison joined the debate. "You're quite right about these people. Before the war, Scotland Yard had a beady eye on them. They seem to have settled down, as you say. Of course, most of them are anti-communist, White Russian they call themselves, loyal to the old Tsar. We think that they are conscious of their position here. They don't want to make too much trouble for the British authorities; after all, they have nowhere else to go in Europe if we kick them out. In fact, they might be only too happy to help with the war effort. You see, as much as they hate the commies, they also detest the Germans. After all, many of them were fighting against them in the last show. They are a complicated lot, but they may well have their uses. Keep your ear to the ground, Turner. We need to keep an eye on them."

Joe was busy working out on how it was physically possible to keep an eye on someone when you've got your ear on the ground when the Major snapped him from his musings. "And what about this Baptiste?"

"Again, he has stuck his neck out by telling me about the Russian's murder. He wants out as well; the fact is he never wanted in. He also wants a chance to get stuck into the jerries. He's Parisian; he wants to get back there. I thought you might quite fancy him for one of your little adventures over the channel."

"Did you now, and have you any other suggestions for how I should run my affairs?" The Major sarcastically asked.

"No sir, by all accounts, you seem to be doing a fairly decent job, under the circumstances, that is." Joe smiled and winked at the now incandescent officer.

Sue Cartwright was having the utmost difficulty not to laugh out loud, even Robinson was struggling to hide a smirk. Having gained control of himself, he deemed it wise to take over the interview before his colleague lost it completely.

"Turner, how do you propose to handle things from here on in?" Robinson asked.

"Well, sir. It seems to me that the black-market scheme is ready to be put into action. There seems to be some secrecy over exactly when; old Ted is being quite coy about the date of the shipment. It would appear that it will be quite sizeable. You should see the operation at the farm in Slough; there'll be some improvement in the grub at the Spa once we have confiscated that little lot, I can tell you. Rumour has it that Eddie will move on his Dad as soon as the shipment arrives. He will then come after me for the money he thinks his Dad has hidden away. I guess we move in and close them down then."

Robison nodded his agreement. "Sounds about right, only we are anxious to keep a lid on this little lot. A public trial of the Bakers might not lead to the discretion that is needed. So please bear that in mind."

90

Nightmare

The wind blew, one wind, one hellish wind. It raged down the Welsh valley with a hostility that could not be fathomed by the humble God-fearing people of the town. Rattling the windows of the old buildings, it fought against the defiance of the solid stone of the houses. It sought out the vulnerability of the flimsy glass, the gaps in the decaying wood and the cracks in the old stone.

Occasionally, it subsided, pausing like an old orator fumbling for a new way to convey its tired, antiquated argument before returning to its familiar bluff and gusto, devoid of any subtlety or reason. Might of nature against the obstinacy of the manmade structures. The wind secure in the knowledge that one day, having time on its side, it would overcome, as nature always did. As attested to by the many ancient ruins of the surrounding countryside, remnants of long-lost and forgotten civilisations.

Simon shuddered at the power of the gusts. They shook the very earth beneath him and further weakened the faltering courage within him. Inevitably, his thoughts turned to the storms of the seas and oceans. His fears forced his mind to dread the dreams that would undoubtedly ensue, those that would haunt his soul, obliging him to confront the hopelessness of the fight humanity made against the sea and the terrors that lay beneath.

Dread of such nightmares kept him awake long into the cold, dark and lonely night.

But sleep he must have, so once again, he awoke screaming. Holding his unharmed hands in front of his face and searching his side, in vain, for the life-threatening tear in his skin that had been cruelly inflicted by the torn metal of the ship.

Every time the dream was so real that he was sure he felt the pain and was always amazed that he was in one piece, warm and safe in his bed.

91

No more – Mynydd Farm – Wales

Sara had made her mind up; she was sick of the deceit, and she was sick of being bullied. As she strode along the road to Mynydd farm, she rehearsed what she would say, first to Myfanwy and then to Simon. If she had any chance of being with Simon, she had to be honest with him; she prayed that he would understand.

When she arrived at the farm, she avoided the front door; Sara knew that the farmer would be in the kitchen. She also knew she would be alone. The Land girls had gone to the market in Brecon and would return via the pub; it would be late evening before they were back, and Alwyn would be with them. She knocked on the kitchen door but didn't wait for a reply before she marched in. The formidable Mrs Thomas stared at her, annoyed by the rude interruption.

"Myfanwy Thomas, I have come to tell you that I will no longer be your stooge. You have no hold over me now. Adam is dead, and half the village thinks that I am sleeping with Lieutenant Lewis, so your blackmail will no longer work on me. I am going to tell the Lieutenant everything I know about what you are up to here at Mynydd Farm." Sara's voice was calm and determined. She had never felt so confident.

"And what is it that you imagine that 'we are up to' here at Mynydd farm? Are we Fifth columnists, do you suppose?" Myfanwy mocked, but was there a slight edge to her bravado, a trace of doubt?

"You are dealing on the Black market. You are keeping extra animals, probably over by the old quarry, if I am not very much mistaken. Rumour has it that you are having an affair with the Ministry inspector. Is that how you are fiddling the books? The prim and proper, bible bashing Mrs Thomas. Have you no shame?" Sara was guessing mostly, the rumour of the affair was just the idle chatter of the land girls, but she could see by the shock in Myfanwy's eyes that she had hit a nerve.

"You wash your mouth out, Sara Lloyd. I am doing no such thing." Myfanwy countered, but she lacked conviction. The power she had held over the girl seemed to be slipping from her hands.

"Myfanwy Thomas, I am going to find Simon Lewis and tell him everything I know. If he is a Ministry spy, as you fear, then I have given you fair warning. If he is who he says he is, or you are as innocent as you claim, then no harm done." Before there was any prospect of a reply, the Barmaid was striding from the kitchen and marching across the farmyard. As she did, a car, followed by a truck, sped into the yard. The car swerved to miss the young girl before screeching to a halt. Four men climbed out and stared at Sara. The truck had also stopped, and a dozen or so men dropped from the tailgate onto the ground. After a moment's silence, Sara was subjected to a cacophony of catcalls and whistles. A passenger from the car stepped towards her. "I am sorry if we scared you miss. I do hope you won't hold it against me. My name is Fergus, and you are?" the man held his hand out to Sara. His accent had an unmistakably Irish lilt. Sara paused, not knowing what to say or do. Something about the man frightened her; his eyes were cold and calculating. He looked at her with hunger and desire, like a man might look at an object he wished to own. Sara spun on her heel and ran from the farmyard, the shouts and taunts of the men ringing in her ears as she raced away towards the mountain.

Myfanwy witnessed the confrontation and hurried over to Fergus McDowell. "Mr McDowell, I presume. Nice to meet you; I am Myfanwy Thomas. I wonder if you might send a couple of your men and ask them to catch that girl and bring her back here." She asked as dispassionately as she could, not wishing to alarm the man whom she knew to be dangerous.

"And why would we need to do that, Mrs Thomas?" Fergus asked.

"She may make trouble for us. I will explain later."

"I think you better explain now." The Irishman signalled, and 2 of his men joined him.

"It is probably nothing, but there has been a Navy Lieutenant staying in the village. We thought that he might be here to spy on us, but we aren't sure. The girl was keeping an eye on him for us,

349

but she seems to have developed an attachment. She is threatening to tell him all she knows, which is not very much, but better safe than sorry."

"Connor, Liam, get after that girl will you and bring her back here. Don't hurt her, and boys, keep your hands to yourselves and any other parts of you that might be interested in her for that matter."

"Blimey boss, have you fallen for the cailin? Why, you only just met her, so you have." Connor teased.

Fergus McDowell didn't bother to answer; he merely stared at his subordinate, who quickly got the message and hurried away after the girl.

"She is headed for the mountain; she must be going to meet him," Myfanwy said to no one in particular.

"Connor, if she meets anybody, bring them back as well," Fergus called out.

As the assembly watched the pair set off in pursuit, another car pulled into the yard. From it stepped Henry Marshall. "Fergus, old boy, how are you? I trust you had a good journey. It's good to see you, old man," Marshall said warmly as he strode towards his old comrade, offering his hand.

"Marshall." Replied the none-too-happy Irish man. "Would you mind telling me what the fuck has been going on around here?"

92

Baptiste tells all. – London – Baker's Brothel

Baptiste returned to the brothel later that same night. Business was evidently slow, or all the clients were in the bedrooms; there was certainly nobody in the lounge. He wandered over to the drinks cabinet and poured a large brandy. As he sipped at the drink, he heard footsteps in the hallway. He turned as Eddie walked into the room.

"Where have you been?" Eddie demanded suspiciously.

"Up west with Joe. We have been talking to restaurant owners that want the hooky meat." Bapt's French accent is incongruous with the east-end slang. "Eddie, I need to tell you something."

"Yeah, what is it?"

"Joe made a phone call today. We were in a restaurant; we had been talking to the owner about the meat; I had gone to the toilet, and when I came back, he was on the telephone at the bar. He didn't see me coming back, and I hid just out of sight; I heard the end of his phone call. He was arranging to meet someone. When he finished the call, he went back to the table where we had been sitting. I waited a minute or two before I joined him. When I sat down, he said that we should call it a night; he said I should take the car as he could walk back to his flat from there. I followed him on foot. He didn't see me. He walked towards his flat at first but then took a turn away from his route. Ten minutes later, he was walking along the river. I couldn't follow him because it was so open along the riverbank. So, I went up onto the bridge. I could see him from there; a man was walking beside him. They were talking, and I think that Joe gave him something, maybe a note. They were walking very slowly before they stopped; Joe turned around and walked back towards me. The man walked the other way. The man, he was a policeman."

Eddie was intrigued and asked. "Was he in a uniform?"

"Of course not," Bapt replied.

"How do you know he was a copper?"

"They are the same here as in Paris. I can see them from miles away. He was definitely a policeman of some sort. Anyway, who was he, and why had Joe met with him so secretly?"

Eddie, with his suspicious mind and hatred of the 'cuckoo in the nest' that was Joe Turner, was willing to believe Bapt's tale. He wanted to know more. "Why did you listen to him on the phone?"

"I knew that there was something about him that was not right. I didn't know him before he came to work with your father, but the rumours were that he always worked alone and was not the sort to be involved in an organisation like yours." Baptiste skilfully used his wording. Implying that the gang was his and that it was his father that had been deceived by Joe Turner, and not himself. "Why now has he agreed to work for Ted? Why is he making a big secret of what he is doing?"

"You are right, of course. I don't know why Dad has always been so taken by him. He's just a jumped-up little thief, a housebreaker. What good is he to us?"

Baptiste knew that Eddie had believed his story and decided to press his point. "What is he doing for Ted? I know that he has this meat business, but there is something else he won't tell me about. Do you know what it is?" Bapt challenged Eddie, hoping that his pride would make him reveal what he knew.

"Of course I do." Bapt smiled to himself; his ruse was working. "Dad said that he wanted to buy up some legit businesses with the spare cash we have got lying about. He said that we needed someone who didn't have a criminal record, and he rated Joe as the man for the job."

"So, are these businesses going to be in Joe's name? Does he trust him that much?"

"No, they're in a false name, a fake identity. Dad has all the deeds; he keeps them in his safe."

Baptiste wondered how Eddie knew this, did he have a spy in Ted's camp, he was intrigued but thought better of asking him, just yet. "But Joe could be skimming something off the top of the milk, no?" Baptiste's command of cockney idioms was impressive for a man so new to the country.

"Of course, he could but Dad is usually very careful about such things, and I doubt that Joe Turner would have the balls to cross my Dad. Once I am in charge, I will get the Deeds and things put in my name. I will make that shit do it before I kill him."

Baptiste was beginning to wonder if Eddie Baker was out of his depth. His father was obviously aware that Eddie was plotting against him. He'd moved his money to stop his son from getting it. What other measures had he in place to stop his crazed offspring?

93

Capture – The mountainside above Mynydd Farm – Wales

Simon had told Sara where he was intending to walk that day. She wasn't wearing a watch, but she knew from the shadows cast by the low midwinter sun where, at this time, she was likely to find her would-be lover. She set a lively pace, unaware that she was challenging the two Irish men that followed her.

Connor and Liam were country-bred like their prey and used to the difficulties the steep ground posed. They were taken aback by her pace, but the unhindered visibility of the crisp and clear winter day and the fact that their quarry knew nothing of their pursuit and, therefore, made no attempt to hide from their sight meant that they were content to follow her at a distance.

Sara spotted Simon coming down the path that descended from the ridge to the west of the mountain. He was a mile or so away. By going off her path to her right, she could cut across the angle and meet with him. Their combined pace brought them together quickly, Sara emerging from the bracken and surprising him. What surprised him even more was how she flung herself into his arms, holding him tightly around his neck, her tears dampening his collar.

"What on earth is the matter," Simon asked as he loosened her grip and sat her down on a large bolder beside the path.

"Oh, Simon, please forgive me. I have done a terrible thing; I had no choice, really, I didn't." Sara was close to hysteria.

"Sara, you are not making any sense. Please start at the beginning and tell me what has happened."

Sara took the handkerchief that was offered her and dried her eyes; she took several deep breaths and set upon a monologue telling Simon everything that she had done since he had arrived at the Dragon's Tail, how she had searched his room, steamed open his letters. Listened to his phone calls. How she had questioned him, asking him about his life, not as a friend but as a spy who would pass on all his secrets. When she was finished, her eyes were cast down, so she failed to see the smile on his face.

"So, you think that I am a spy and tell me, who do you think I am working for, and more to the point, who are you working for?" Simon said jovially; his best chance of maintaining his cover was to try to make the whole thing seem ridiculous, he reasoned.

Sara looked up at him. "I know it seems far-fetched, but they think you are a spy from the Ministry of Agriculture. You see, they have some sort of a scheme going on where they are underreporting their livestock. They're nervous about being caught, and when you turned up, they made me keep an eye on you. I didn't want to, but they blackmailed me. When I got to know you, I told them how ridiculous it all was, but they insisted that I continue to watch you."

"I have to say it is a bit of a blow to one's ego to learn that you were watching me for somebody else. I thought it was because you liked me. I reasoned that you searched through my things because you wanted to know if I had a wife, or a sweetheart stashed away somewhere. What a chump I have been."

"Oh, I do like you, Simon." Sara protested. "In fact, I think that I love you."

Her words hit Simon like a hammer blow. Of course, he had suspected that she was developing feelings for him, but her professing them to him made him ashamed of his deception. That he should hurt a sweet young girl in the course of his mission was unforgivable. Still, he had a job to do; there would be time for regrets later.

"Sara, who made you spy on me? Who is it that is running the black-market scam?"

Sara hesitated; she had been so resolved to tell him everything, but the full implications were beginning to dawn upon her. These were her people, her friends, and her neighbours. She had grown up with them. If she gave them up to the authorities, would she ever be forgiven by the community? Would she ever be branded as a traitor, a tell-tale? Myfanwy Thomas was a cruel and domineering woman, but she had been

355

her mother's best friend. Life had treated her harshly, but was that mitigation for her actions, Sara couldn't decide. Whatever the case she had gone too far now to turn back, she owed Simon an explanation.

"It is Myfanwy Thomas from Mynydd Farm. She is the one who has been blackmailing me to spy on you. There must be others involved, though."

"Her son Alwyn?"

"I don't think so, probably not. Alwyn does anything she tells him, so he has probably played a part, but I cannot see him as being an organiser."

"Who then?"

"I don't know. The Land girls on the farm have been gossiping about Myfanwy; they say she is having an affair with the Ministry Inspector. I think that they might be keeping some animals at the old quarry. And there is one other thing, something that has only just happened." Sara hesitated, gathering her thoughts.

"What is it, Sara?" Simon prompted.

"I was just down at the farm now, telling Myfanwy that I wanted no more to do with her schemes. There were some men there; they just arrived as I was leaving. They were strangers; I had never seen any of them before. Simon, I think that they were Irish."

Simon was trying to think quickly. He remembered what Robinson had said about the Irish; could it be that his fears had some foundation, that the Irish republicans were involved in the black market here in Wales? He had to contact Robinson and the Major.

"Come on, Sara. We need to get back to the Hotel and call the authorities." Simon rose to his feet.

"Ah, you won't be doing that, lad, I am afraid. Put your hands in the air, high where I can see them." A loud voice called from the bracken behind him. Simon turned to see two men who were standing barely 10 feet away. They had probably heard everything that they had been saying. One of the men was holding a pistol, pointed at Simon, the other a shotgun trained on Sara. "If you move, lad, Liam here will blast the head off your girlfriend. Be a shame that, she is a pretty one. Oh, and don't be in any doubt, he won't miss. Liam is good with a shotgun;

hunting rabbits is the only way we get any meat these days in Ireland. Now, lie on your face on the ground if you would."

Quickly and efficiently, the men searched Simon; they had done it before. They were careful not to present Simon with any opportunity to fight back. Each one covered the other as they conducted their examination. The threat posed to Sara was constant, designed to put off any thoughts Simon might have of taking a chance. In just a few minutes, they were being marched towards Mynydd Farm.

94

The Battle of Slough – London

It was just before 7 am that the telephone rang in Joe Turner's flat. He wasn't surprised when he heard Ted Baker's gruff voice at the other end of the line. Few people rang his number, and he was by far the most frequent caller.

"Right, Turner, we're on for the delivery tonight?" Ted barked without prior pleasantries.

"Blimey Ted, you're up early; what's this about a delivery?" Joe sounded sleepily confused.

"The bloody animals, you know, the meat you have been flogging for the past few months. I need you down at the farm to take an inventory as the loads come in. You will be there most of the night, so get some kip now and get over there later this afternoon."

"Crikey Ted, how much have you got coming?"

"There'll be 15 trucks arriving at staggered intervals. I got my lads going over to Wales; they should be nearly there by now. I am driving up in the car now to see them loaded up. But I'll set off before they do, and I'll be quicker in the car, so I will get back to the farm before them. I want you there ready.?" Ted sounded excited.

"Have you got any boys at the farm to unload the wagons?" Joe Asked.

"Yeah, I've got a couple of farmers and a couple of our boys, plus you. The driver of each truck can help, and as more arrive, you will have more boys. Make sure you count the animals properly as they come off the trucks, I don't want any light-fingered toe rag helping themselves to Christmas dinner."

"Alright, governor, I'll be on top of it."

"An' listen, Joe, not a word to Eddie about this; I don't want him or any of his hooligans anywhere near this lot, you understand."

"Got it, boss. I have an appointment with sour face about some deal she wants to set up this afternoon, so I'll keep out of Eddie's way today."

Ted ended the call leaving Joe thinking hard about his last request. Eddie had barely been included in the scheme; indeed, Ted had been secretive about the whole thing with everyone. But for Ted to say that he wanted Eddie and his boys to be kept in the dark about the delivery today was another thing altogether. Joe wondered if Ted might be feeling a bit vulnerable, with most of his men away collecting the livestock, it would be a good opportunity for Eddie to make his move against his father. If the rumours were right, Eddie had his finger on the trigger, and he was itching to pull it. It seemed to Joe that it was for this reason Ted didn't want Eddie to know about the delivery.

Joe had to wait until office hours before he picked up the telephone receiver again and dialled Miss Hereford's number. After three rings, his call was answered, but before the recipient had a chance to greet Joe, Joe jumped in impatiently. "Hello, is that, Miss Hereford?"

"Yes." Was the curt and dry response.

"Good morning, Miss Hereford. This is Joe Turner. I am just calling to confirm our meeting this afternoon. I seem to have forgotten the time. Was it 2 o'clock?" Joe Asked without his usual repartee.

Sue Cartwright knew from Joe's words that he needed an urgent meeting, or at least a telephone conversation, with Robinson and Major Calderdale. "Actually, Mr Turner, our meeting was set for 11 o'clock this morning, and, as I have said on many occasions, I expect you to be on time. I will see you promptly at 11. Good morning." The call rang off.

Even in his excited state, Joe couldn't help but smile. His colleague was having the time of her life playing the prissy accountant.

Joe was on time—in fact, he was early—but even so, both the Major and Robinson were waiting for him. As the three men and Sue Cartwright sat down, the tension was palpable. They all knew that the mission was coming to a head. This was what they had been working towards.

"The livestock is arriving tonight; I have been instructed to be at the farm this afternoon." Joe gave his report. "But I have been told that I will be there most of the night. There are to be 15 trucks arriving at intervals. I am to make an inventory and supervise the unloading."

"Are only Ted's men involved, not Eddie's?" Asked the Major.

"It seems so; of course, technically, they're all Ted's men, but he will be using the ones who are closest to him, the ones he trusts. He is definitely trying to cut his son out of the deal. The word is that Ted Baker is not as green as he is cabbage-looking." Joe saw the look of exasperation on the Major's face at his colloquialism, so he explained. "Ted is as sharp as a, as a, well, he is not slowing down in his old age, let's put it like that. He will have sworn all his people to secrecy, as he did with me. It's a brave soul that will ignore Ted Baker's wishes. So, it is unlikely that Eddie will know about the delivery."

"In which case, tonight is not the night to move in on their operation." Robison intervened. "Not if Eddie and the rest aren't going to be there. I will put the army unit on standby, but I think we need to wait before we shut down the operation. I want to get the whole gang; there's no point in nabbing Ted with his hand in the cookie jar if Eddie Baker gets off Scot-free. Get back to us as soon as you can and let us know the numbers of the livestock. Also, see if you can find out about the next shipment."

95

Not happy – The Dragon's Tail Hotel – Wales

Alwyn Thomas had sat nursing his pint in the bar of the Dragon's Tail Hotel for over an hour. The amber liquid, normally anticipated and craved on a Saturday afternoon, held none of its usual allure. His mind was in turmoil; it had been since he'd had that chat with Simon Lewis on the night of the storm. He had spoken that evening of the need to produce food for the army, of feeding the workers in the factories. How men were dying at sea to bring in food, and how he, Alwyn Thomas, must work as hard as he could to grow food to replace the cargo being sunk. He had said that without his work, the nation would starve, and Hitler would win. But Alwyn knew something Simon didn't, a shameful truth as he saw it now, he knew that his mother was cheating the system. She had been holding back food and selling it on the black market. He had always had a feeling that what they were doing was wrong, but he would never dream of disobeying his mother. She had always known best, and he had eased his guilt by not thinking too much about it. He had reasoned that what they produced was a drop in the ocean; it couldn't possibly make any difference in the overall scheme of things. But now his eyes had been opened. He had a job to do for his King, country and for freedom and he had been failing. He pushed away the pint and dropped from his seat on the barstool. As he strode purposefully from the bar, he shouted that he 'would be back' to his friends, who sat shocked at his departure.

His long legs stomped purposefully back to his home. He was spotted as he came through the gate, and his mother met him in the yard before he could enter the kitchen.

"What are you doing here?" Myfanwy demanded in the language of her birth. Her son's expression worried her; she had never seen him so determined-looking before.

"Mother, what is going on?" he answered in Welsh instinctively, following his mother's cue. As he towered over her, he spotted the vehicles in the yard. One car he recognised as belonging to Mr Marshall; the others were strange to him. By the truck, he saw some men. They withdrew from his sight, but he could see their feet under the body of the lorry.

Myfanwy ignored his question. "I told you to stay in the village. I need you to keep the others out of the way this afternoon. Here is some money: treat them to some food and drinks and keep them entertained. I don't want to see any of you until later tonight."

"It's wrong, Mam; It's wrong what we are doing. Lieutenant Lewis says that there are men dying in the Atlantic trying to bring in food and that we should produce as much as we can." The young farmer didn't have his new friend's way with words, and his inability to express his convictions frustrated him.

Myfanwy Thomas slapped her son hard across the face with her hand. "So, you have more respect for some English toff than you do your own mother now, do you? I will not have you questioning me Alwyn Thomas. I know what is right and wrong and I tell you what to do. This is my house, and you will obey me. 'Children, obey your parents in the Lord, for this is right. Honour your father and mother that it may go well with you and that you may live long in the land.' Ephesians 6. This is the fifth commandment: I have taught you to obey the ten commandments. Now do as I say now; we will talk about this later."

Alwyn Thomas turned away and walked back towards the gate. His face stung, and his mind was spinning; he had no idea what to do. Who were the men at the farm, and why did they try to hide from him? Why had his mother blocked his way into the house? What was he to do? He checked his watch; the girls would be arriving on the bus from Brecon soon. He had promised to meet Dot at the Dragon's Tail. He had to tell someone; he had to confess his immoral secret. Dot's friend, Rosie, seemed to be level-headed; she might know what to do. He would tell them both he decided. As he set off at pace towards the village, a movement caught his eye away to his right. He squinted his eyes towards the mountain; he had excellent eyesight over distance.

His eyes trained to seek out his flock across the wide expanses of the hillsides. What he saw shocked him. There were four figures coming down the track, two by two. The first two were a man and a woman. The woman was a slight figure; she walked with a light gait, and she was unmistakenly Sara Lloyd. With her was a young, tall man; he too was thin, and he walked with the slightest of limps. Alwyn was less sure, but he was prepared to assume that it was Simon Lewis. The two men behind he did not know. They were shorter than the Lieutenant, bulkier. They walked with less confidence than the young couple. Less used to the path, or perhaps their footwear less suited. There was a constant distance kept between the two groups as they made their way towards the farm. As they crested a rise on the path, they were, for a brief moment, silhouetted against the clear, pale blue winter sky. One of the men was holding something long, parallel to the ground. It was pointed at the backs of the couple. In the Welshman's mind, there was little doubt that the object was a shotgun and that the couple, Simon and Sara, were the prisoners of the men.

96

The adversaries - the brothel, London

At the same time Joe was meeting with Robinson, Baptiste was in Eddie Baker's windowless office.

"It's happening tonight." Eddie was beside himself with excitement. "The old man is bringing in the livestock. I am telling you, it's the opportunity of a lifetime. We strike tonight." Eddie was chuckling to himself; Baptiste had never seen him look so happy.

"What do you mean boss?" Baptiste asked uncertainly.

Eddie was only too happy to explain. "Dad has arranged to collect the animals and meat from Wales tonight. The stupid old man has made a mistake, he thought that I wouldn't find out. But he has always underestimated me. You see, he is using his boys to ship back the livestock; 15 vans there is going to be, so there will only be 1 maximum 2 men in each." Baptiste looked for the significance of what Eddie was saying, but he wasn't making any sense, "Don't you see, Dad is usually surrounded by his men. Tonight, most of them will be in the trucks. The trucks aren't driving together in a convoy; they will arrive at intervals. So, as each one arrives, we will be able to kill the driver, then unload the cargo and wait for the next one. Dad is coming first in his car, probably with 3 or 4 of his lads. If I take 15 of our lads, we can easily overpower them, probably won't even need that many. They will be surprised because he thinks I don't know about tonight. He's sworn all his lads to secrecy, even that moron, Joe Turner. Dad has told him to be there waiting".

"You want me along, boss?" Baptiste was hoping he did; he needed to be if he had any chance of saving Joe's life.

"Nah, you stay here. We have some important people in tonight, and I want you to look after them; you're good at that."

"What you gonna do with Joe Turner?" Baptiste couldn't help but ask.

"I am going to kill the jumped-up bastard. Very slowly, I am going to torture him, and he is going to tell me where he has put all the money for Dad. But before he dies, I'm going to tell him how I raped his little bitch. He'll die knowing I fucked her to death." Eddie Baker's laughter sent shivers down The Frenchman's spine.

97

Taking no chances – Mynydd Farm – Wales

Fergus McDowell had listened to and watched the confrontation between mother and son from the doorway of the farmhouse kitchen. He couldn't understand the language, but it was clear from their body language that things weren't right. The boy seemed to be at odds with his mother's wishes. On top of the revelation of the possible presence of an English spy in the area and the young girl's apparent defiance, Fergus sensed trouble. He was a careful man; he had to be in his game; he had already stuck his neck out enough as it was. His bosses knew nothing of his schemes; in the republican army, it was not wise to keep secrets from the leaders. But if he pulled off his plan, he would be a hero in Ireland. If he failed, he was a dead man. So, he wasn't about to take any chances at this late stage.

"Is everything all right, Mrs Thomas?" Fergus asked as the farmer returned to the kitchen.

"Oh yes, everything is just fine." Lied the woman.

"Only your boy there doesn't seem so happy."

"Oh, you know how these youngsters are these days, he was wanting some money to spend in the pub. I have asked him to keep the land girls away this evening whilst we conclude our business, and the cheeky bugger said he didn't have enough money."

"Does he know about what we are doing?"

"Oh, very little. He knows we have a few extra cows, but I have told him nothing more. He's a good boy but not the brightest, I am afraid." She lied again, Fergus thought.

Fergus laughed along with the lady. "Well, he looks like he'd be a good worker, big lad you reared there, Mrs Thomas." The pair laughed politely together. "I'll just be checking on my boys, make sure that they aren't up to no good."

McDowell walked across the farmyard to where his crew were waiting. "Michael, Thomas, come here, would you?" he picked two of the hardest of his men. He knew them both and recognised that they would not be squeamish about what he had to ask. "Boys, did you see the young lad that just left?"

"Aye, we did. His mother gave him a right slap. Did you see it?"

"Take the car and go after him. Be careful not to make too much noise as you leave; I don't want the mother to see you go; I will distract her. I think that he has got cold feet, and he could ruin everything. I need you to stop him before he gets to the village. Give me your guns; you can't risk shooting him; the shots will be heard. Bury him somewhere he won't be found, and make sure the grave is deep; we can't risk a fox or something digging him up, so take your time. When you have finished drive back to London, there won't be time to catch up with us. I will contact you there in a few days. Are we clear?"

The men looked happy with their assignment, which was much more exciting than herding a load of cattle.

98

A warning is needed. - London 1941

Baptiste had to wait for Eddie to leave before he could do anything. He was expected to stay at the brothel; he had to stay put until he was sure that Eddie would not be coming back. His hand hovered over the telephone in Eddie's office, but He distrusted the device; after all, how had Eddie obtained all the information about the delivery tonight if not from the telephone? He must have someone listening to his father's calls and no doubt a microphone or two in his office. As he deliberated over his best course of action, some papers on the desk caught his attention. They were copies of the deeds for the farm. Eddie, or one of his men, had obviously liberated them from Ted's office. There were plans of the building work that had been carried out on the outbuildings and a map of the area showing the fields belonging to the property. He grabbed one of the plans and the map; they might be of use for what he had in mind.

There was very little time, but he had to warn Joe. He wondered if he could call Joe's flat from a telephone box, but he was confident that Joe's phone was bugged, too. He had no choice; he would have to get there in person. But first, he must change. He had a feeling that he would be running around in muddy fields before the day was through, and his Saville Row suit was not fit for that.

To Baptiste, it seemed to be the longest journey of his life. He was forced to take a cab because Eddie and his boys had taken all the cars. Traffic and diversions caused by bomb-cratered streets slowed his progress, so he was convinced that he could have walked the route quicker.

Eventually, he made it into Joe's street. Baptiste could wait no longer and having thrown a handful of change, far exceeding the metered fare, he leapt from the vehicle as it crawled along; he ran the rest of the way. He was about to bang relentlessly on the door but realised that he didn't want to bring attention to himself.

He knocked softly. There was no immediate answer, so he knocked a little louder and held his ear to the door. He could hear a vacuum cleaner, its noise getting louder and quieter as it was pushed backwards and forwards, almost certainly covering the noise of his knocks. He tried the door handle, and to his relief, it opened.

Baptiste walked into the flat and followed the noise to the living room. There, Doreen was singing to herself, her song drowned out by the din of the machine. At that moment, she saw Baptiste and was about to scream out when she realised who it was. She responded to his urgent signals to be quiet. Doreen made to turn off the cleaner, but Baptiste indicated to keep it on. He drew close to her, and taking directly into her ear, he asked where Joe was.

"I don't know" she mouthed back at him. The Frenchman held his finger to his lips and flicked the switch of the machine. In the deafening silence he indicated for Doreen to follow him. The pair walked quickly from the flat, Doreen grabbing her coat on the way out. Baptiste looked about as they scampered down the road; he couldn't see anyone watching. On balance, he doubted that Eddie would have anyone covering the flat when he knew that Joe was expected at the farm. Baptiste dragged Doreen into a pub, and they sat at a table just inside.

"Do you know where Joe is?" Baptiste's urgent and worried voice concerned Doreen.

"He left me a note. He said that he was going to see the accountant, that he had been instructed to go to the farm this evening, and that he would be there all night. He was going to eat on the way, and so wouldn't be back at all this evening."

"Doreen, Joe is in danger; Ted has gone to Wales to load up the livestock. He has taken all his trusted men with him. He is meeting Joe at the farm. The thing is, Eddie has found out. He sees that Ted will be vulnerable, so he is going to make his move against him. He will kill Joe; he intends to torture him to get the details of the money that Joe has been investing for Ted, and then he will kill him. We must warn Joe. Both Ted and Joe don't know that Eddie has found out about the delivery tonight; they won't be expecting anything."

"But how can we warn Joe? Do you know where the accountant's office is?" Doreen was fraught; she was beginning to panic.

"No, he never told me." Said Baptiste despairingly.

99

Time for Tea – Mynydd Farm – Wales

Myfanwy Thomas was making tea in industrial amounts. She had fetched out the large metal teapot that the ladies used for the cricket matches. The Irish lads had already worked their way through one pot and were into draining the refill. In the kitchen their leader was talking to Henry Marshall as they waited for her to bring them their refreshments.

"I take it the financials are all sorted, Mr Marshall." Asked the Irishman.

"Yes, I had telephone confirmation yesterday that the transfers have been made. As soon as Mr Baker arrives and we have had our tea, we can go over to the quarry and begin the loading." As if conjuring up his presence, the men heard a truck and a car drive into the farmyard. Marshall went to the window and confirmed that it was the large American car of Ted Baker. "I am afraid we might need some more tea, Mrs Thomas."

As McDowell and Marshall went out into the yard to meet the Londoner, there was a disturbance amongst the Irish men. Through their midst came the young couple and their captors. "We found them on the mountain boss, having a right cosy little chat they were." Shouted Connor.

"Well done, lads; take them in the kitchen and tie them up."

Ted Baker, who was standing by his car, looked troubled; it was his turn to ask exactly, "What the fuck was going on."

100

Insurance – The accounting office-London

Baptiste and Doreen might not have known Miss Hereford's address, but Eddie Baker did. His men had been watching the office for some time, and that day, they had further instructions. They observed as two men arrived that morning, followed by Joe Turner. An hour later, Turner left, and the men followed shortly after, leaving just the lady they knew as Miss Hereford in the building. It was the opportunity they had been waiting for, and they took it.

One of the men went for the car that was parked two streets away. The other two marched up the staircase and kicked their way through the door; ready with handguns, they quickly had them trained on the redoubtable lady.

"Come in, it's open." Susan Cartwright said cooly as the men gestured for her to stand. She didn't; she just sat implacably, surveying the men and working out her next move. She thought about her own gun in the drawer of her desk, but even if she got a shot off, she would be unlikely to be able to shoot them both before they fired at her. Her odds weren't good. "Who are you, and I hope you are going to pay for that?" she asked the taller of the two men matter-of-factly, whilst pointing at the shattered door frame with her right hand. Involuntarily, the men's eyes looked to where she was pointing, not for long, just a split second, but long enough for her to grab a paperknife and secrete it up her jacket sleeve.

The man didn't reply except to tell her to stand and keep her hands where he could see them. Slowly, she complied with his request. Her hands she placed on the desk in front of her as she stood, her right hand covering a paper clip that lay on the desktop. As she did, she was thinking quickly about who these men were. They must be working for Eddie Baker. There was no reason for Ted Baker to wish her harm, not unless he had found out who she really was, surely, they had been too careful. On the other hand, Joe had been certain that Eddie wasn't ready to move against his father. The men were getting impatient with her and were becoming angry.

"You are coming with us; Eddie Baker would like a word." The man sneered.

"Please tell Mr Baker that, unfortunately, I have prior appointments this afternoon, but if you ask him to telephone the office, I will happily make some time for him next week." Sue, despite her heart pounding in her chest, was maintaining her part as Miss Hereford, prissy accountant, to perfection.

"I am afraid Eddie Baker is not the sort of man to wait. We have a car outside; you will calmly and quietly get into it. If you scream or make any trouble, then we will shoot you. NOW MOVE!" The man insisted.

Sue doubted that they would shoot her on the street outside. It's a busy place with too many witnesses. As the three of them descended the stairs towards the street, She imagined herself driving her high heel into the man's foot as they walked towards the car; she would stab the other man's leg with the paper knife, with both of them temporarily incapacitated she could run to the police station around the corner. As if divining her intentions, the men closed in tightly on either side of her. The taller one, who had done all the talking, grabbed hold of her right elbow and painfully prodded her with his pistol, which was covered by the coat he carried across his arm. The other man had his gun shoved hard against her lower back. Sue was forced to abandon her plans and had to be content with the tools she had been able to conceal, hoping that they might be useful later. She was grateful that she hadn't been searched, careless of them, she thought, but then again, why would anyone search a middle-aged lady accountant? What would they expect to find? A pair of knuckle dusters and a flick knife?

"Where are you taking me?" Sue demanded as she was bundled onto the back seat of a large saloon car, followed closely by her captor.

"You'll see." The talkative one replied.

'Yes, I will see', Susan thought to herself. She hadn't been blindfolded, so they weren't worried about her knowing where she was when they got to their destination. They weren't concerned that she could lead the police back there at some later time. Only two reasons that she could think of why that might be. Either the place would be known to her already and obvious, or she would never be leaving that place.

101

Interrogation – Mynydd Farm – Wales

Fergus McDowell was enjoying punching the bound Englishman, but he knew he was wasting his time.

"He won't talk, not a man like him." Opined Marshall.

"Oh, he'll talk eventually; they all do, but I agree we don't have time for this now." The out of breath Irishman acknowledged.

"So, what do we do?" Ted Baker was the one to ask the question all three of them had been thinking.

After a moment or two's thought it was Henry Marshall who had the answer. "As I see it, we don't know whether this man is a spy or just a man in the wrong place at the wrong time, let us assume the former for now. From what your men told us when they captured them, the pair were just about to go to the village to inform the authorities. So, he hadn't had time to pass on his knowledge to his masters. If these two disappear then we have nothing to fear, for now. We will move the goods as planned tonight. Fergus, if you wouldn't mind taking the Lieutenant with you, I am sure that your people will be able to find out who he really is. Mr Baker, I am sure that you will be only too happy to take the lady and find her some suitable employment in one of your establishments. Your son will now doubt ensure that she speaks to no one. Mrs Thomas and I will take a little cruise with you, Fergus, just in case there is a reaction from the authorities. Assuming that all is well, we will be able to return in a month or two and prepare the next shipment."

"What about Alwyn?" Myfanwy Thomas jumped in, concerned for her son.

"He will be fine; you can leave him a note saying you are taking a little holiday with me. If the police come calling, they will find nothing. There will be no evidence of any crime. The animals will be gone. The inspector will say nothing; he wouldn't dare. If they do start poking their noses around the place, we will hear of it and know to stay away. It will be the end of our little scheme, but we have made a nice profit from this first shipment; maybe it is just best not to be too greedy. If all is quiet, we can return and take up the good work."

"Won't the couple be missed?" asked Ted.

"If the man is who he says he is, then people will assume that he and the girl have run away together. There's a lot of that sort of thing happening at the moment, I understand."

"And if he is an English spy?" asked Fergus McDowell.

"Well, your people will find that out when you question him, won't you? Then you will have to lie low in Ireland for a while. Myfanwy and I can make our own plans, Canada perhaps. Mr Baker, so long as you hide your livestock carefully, you will never be connected to the case. If he is a spy, I am convinced he only knows what the girl told him today, and he hasn't had time to pass that on. I repeat, there is nothing to point the authorities to this farm."

Though his face was bruised—he had taken quite a beating— Simon was conscious enough to hear the conversation. Marshall was right; he had failed to find any evidence of a criminal scheme in the area. He had failed miserably in his mission. Unless the Major and Robinson had something else up their sleeves, they would never hear from Simon Bach, aka Lieutenant Simon Lewis, ever again.

102

Time to call in a favour – A pub in Hackney, London

With no way to warn Joe about Eddie's plans for him and no possibility of stopping him from going to the farm where Eddie and his boys would be waiting for him, a pimp and a former prostitute, Joe Turner's best friends in the world at that moment, were at a loss for what to do.

"So let me get this straight." Said Doreen after some minutes of quiet thought. "Eddie and his lot will be waiting at the farm. They will overpower the men that are there, probably just a few of them and not hard men. First to arrive will be Joe, who will be walking into a trap; he will be on his own, and we don't even know if he's armed. So, he, too, will be overpowered. Next up will be Ted. He will arrive later in the evening and has just a few men with him, 3 or 4, I think you said. Eddie, on the other hand, has 15 men, and he is the odds-on favourite for that fight. If he uses the advantage of surprise that he has then maybe he can overcome Ted's men without any bloodshed, not that that would concern Eddie too much. After that, the lorries carrying the livestock will start to arrive. We think that they will arrive one at a time, with an interval between each one. There is a maximum of 2 men to each truck so they can be easily subdued one at a time." Doreen paused.

Baptiste considered what she had said and then nodded his agreement with her assessment.

"Do you think that Eddie will kill Joe straight away?" Doreen asked, her voice breaking as she considered the unimaginably terrifying thought of losing Joe.

"I think not. Eddie likes to savour these things; he will want to take his time. Also, he wants the money and that might mean getting account numbers and information such as that from both men. I think that he'll want to wait at least until all of the shipments have arrived. By then, all of Ted's men will be out of

the picture, and Eddie will feel in control. Then he will start to…"
Baptiste paused unwilling to say what would happen next; he
could already see a tear in the corner of Doreen's eye; he didn't
want to worry her further. He needn't have worried, desperately
upset as she was. Doreen Fletcher was made of sterner stuff, and
she knew that crying now would not help. After all, Joe wasn't
dead yet, and if she had anything to do with it, he wouldn't die
today; there had to be a way to save him.

"I need to telephone Mischa; do you have any change?"

With a handful of coins clutched tightly in her hand, Doreen
ran to the corner of the street and made a call from the telephone
box. While she was gone Baptiste studied the maps and plans of
the farm. By the time she arrived back a few minutes later a plan
was already forming in his mind.

"Mischa is on his way. He can get together maybe 15 men;
they will be armed mostly with pistols, but he has one man who
has a rifle and is a crack shot." Doreen blurted out her news.

"That's Good; how long will it take?" Asked Baptiste.

"He said he would be here in half an hour, three quarters at
most."

"That's good, but I think I should get out to the farm straight
away. I can survey the ground and see what is happening, how
many men Eddie has, things like that. Here are the plans for
Slough Farm. Tell Mischa to take the turning off the main road
here, well before he reaches the farm." He pointed to the map.
"He can get to the farm along this smaller road here; he must stop
here. I will meet him there, and we will arrange what to do. I
think we must wait until all the trucks have arrived. Otherwise,
we will have more men turning up, not knowing which side they
are on, and it will get messy. Tell him they must stay out of sight
and be quiet. With luck, they won't be expecting anyone else to
join their party, so we will have a surprise on our side."

103

A slogger turned pugilist – Wales - 1941

Alwyn was halfway down the road to the town before the two Irish lads caught up with him. He heard the car coming from a distance. Very few cars used the road, so he surmised that it was probably one of the vehicles from the farmyard. The question on his mind was what they were doing coming this way; something told him that they were looking for him. The road was narrow, so if they did mean him harm, it would be easy for them to run him over. Alwyn started to run; he knew that just round the corner, there was an embankment that he could climb, he had to make it, or he was convinced that he would be in serious trouble.

He made in in the nick of time, as he scrambled up the bank, he felt the rush of the car as it skidded along the edge of the road. It came to a halt 30 yards down the track. The doors of the car opened, and two men stepped out; they walked back towards him with menace in their every stride. Smoke from the exhaust pooled around their legs, giving their approach an eerie and evil effect. Alwyn dropped down onto the road from the bank and set himself to face his assailants. As they drew near, one of the men pulled a knife from his boot and crouched in the classic pose of the street knife fighter.

"Now be sensible, lad, you are to be coming with us now." The pair had decided that it would be easier if they kidnapped the man and found a suitable burial place. He was a big lad, and they didn't fancy the extra effort of lifting his body in and out of the car. "We won't be hurting you; no need for any unpleasantness."

Alwyn was surprised by the heavy Irish accent, and he was not convinced of their professed friendly intentions. "Fucking typical of a paddy, too cowardly to fight a man fair and square, he has to hide behind a knife." Alwyn taunted.

"So, the sheep shagger wants a fair fight, does he." The man lowered the knife a little.

"What are two Irishmen not enough to take on a single Welshman?"

"All right, it will be just as much fun to beat you to death as stab you." He put the knife back into its scabbard in his boot."

Alwyn stood as tall as he could, trying to intimidate the men as much as possible. But the words of the man had chilled him to his bones. It was clear to him that his instinct not to trust them had been wise; the men intended to kill him. Alwyn had been in many fights, brawls, and schoolyard scraps. There had usually been a winner and a loser, but the loser would suffer little more than a black eye, a broken nose perhaps; he had never been in a fight where the loser would lose his life. The men were smaller than him, lighter but they had the air of hard men, men who are used to such struggles. What was it that the Englishman had told him about fighting, he desperately tried to remember. He knew for certain that he couldn't wade in with swinging punches as was his usual style. He needed to watch and wait for them to make the first move.

He didn't have long to wait. The first man stooped and charged forward at him; his arms spread wide, intent on wrestling him to the ground with a rugby-style tackle, his colleague no doubt ready to apply his boot when he had fallen to the floor. Alwyn, using all his experience of the Rugby field, stepped to the right and braced himself; as the attack came in, he too stooped and leading with his shoulder, he smashed into the head of the man. The momentum of his attacker added to the impact, and he bounced off, sprawling into the embankment by the road. Quickly Alwyn turned to face the other man, just in time to skip back as a swinging right swished towards him. In a moment of clarity, Alwyn saw his chance, remembering what the sailor had done to him; he saw the Irishman's head unprotected right in front of him. He struck out instinctively, his left fist darting out from his shoulder, a punch with a fraction of the power of his habitual scything clubs, but effective, smashing into the side of his head; the man staggered, his hands dropping. Alwyn stepped back with the momentum of the return of his punch; he waited, he watched. Still stunned, angered by the unexpected blow, his foe came at him again. This time, a left hook swung towards him. He swayed back, waiting for the punch to fly harmlessly by before rocking forward and unleashing his newfound weapon. Once again, a perfect straight left found its target. The Irishman rocked this time Alwyn didn't wait; he could see the man was dazed and was in no way able to avoid the thunderous right hook that caught him square on his cheekbone. There was a sound of breaking bone, and the man fell backwards to the ground.

Alwyn spun to his left in time to see the first attacker rising from the embankment. This time, the man was on him in a second, and Alwyn had barely enough time to put up his hands in defence. From close quarters, the blows came raining in with impossible speed. Alwyn held his arms close in beside his body; his fists held up, protecting his head. The assault was relentless; his muscles ached from the pounding, each punch a stinging blow against his arms, He desperately wanted to straighten them, to ease the agony, but to do so would expose his ribs and head. The Irishman maintained his assault, the rate of his punches slowing ever so slightly but still dangerously threatening; Alwyn pushed forward against his enemy, trying to limit the power of the blows by lessening the distance between the two of them. It became a test of strength, of resilience, of stamina. Alwyn gritted his teeth and bore the pain, waiting desperately for a break in the assault. It came after what seemed like hours; the man took a backward step. Alwyn's weight and strength had forced him to retreat ever so slightly; the moment the punches paused, he was ready, and his left fist flung forward blindly. It barely connected, but his hand was back in place, ready to protect himself against the next onslaught. This time, the punches were slower and less powerful. They petered out quickly, and the next straight left flew from Alwyn's shoulder. It connected solidly. Another followed immediately, and a third smashed into the jaw. The Irishman backed off, and it was Alwyn's turn to take the offensive. Leading with his left fist probing out ahead of him, he forced the man back, his foe's feet staggering and stumbling on the uneven ground. Alwyn was cautious, reluctant to chase the man, nervous that he might lose his own footing which he sensed would be fatal. The gap opened between them, giving Alwyn time to look around. The second man had gained consciousness and was trying to rise from the floor. Not wanting to take any chances,

Alwyn took two quick paces towards him and kicked his head like it was a rugby ball.

It was now one on one. Alwyn liked his chances more and more. It was clear that his opponent was tiring, the cockiness of his demeanour had evaporated, and he was plainly in awe of Alwyn's strength. Then, in a moment, everything changed. The Irishman smiled and reached down to his boot, his hand returning holding the knife.

"Now, you would be a little bit naive, I am thinking, if you thought that there was such a thing as a fair fight." His face was contorted by a cruel smile; he started to laugh.

Alwyn had never fought a man with a knife, and he didn't like the idea of the large blade slashing across his face. His opponent was catching his breath, taking his time before his imminent attack. He was stood at the edge of the road his back to the embankment; Alwyn was in the middle of the road. In the circling of the exchanged punches, he was now nearer to the car than his assailant; the doors of the vehicle were wide open, the engine ticking over smoothly. Without any further hesitation, Alwyn sprinted for the vehicle. Surprise and a 10-yard start were on his side, but he was a big man; he was not made for speed. It felt like he was running through treacle as he strained to reach the open door in time; he could hear the footsteps of his enemy, much quicker than his own close behind him. He jumped into the vacant seat and slammed the door behind him. He hammered his foot down on the clutch and jammed the gear lever into first. As he felt the gears crunch into place, the door flung open. To his horror, the knife, large, shining and menacing, seemed to float by his side. The man pulled it back then it came flying towards him. He floored the accelerator, slipped the clutch, and the car lurched forward. The blade sliced into the flesh of his shoulder before embedding itself in the leather of the car seat. The door ripped from the hand of the man and slammed shut as the car sped off down the road.

Alwyn raced the car forward a hundred yards. In the mirrors, he could see his attacker standing, raging after the escaping vehicle. Alwyn braked hard to a stop. He stared at the man in the mirror, for a moment uncertain what to do. They had tried to kill him; perhaps even now, they would follow him and finish the job.

He looked down at the unfamiliar gearstick as he selected reverse. He twisted in his seat and revved the engine. The man had been right; it was naïve to think that there was such a thing as a fair fight. The gears screamed as the car raced backwards, covering half the distance before the man could react; by the time he was three-quarters of the way, his nemesis was leaping for the bankside, but he was too late, and with a sickening crunch, the solid metal of the heavy vehicle swept the man up in its path. His body, for a moment, seemed glued to the back window, then it slid slowly down until it disappeared, and Alwyn felt an almighty bump as the rear wheels rolled over the body. Alwyn brought the car to a standstill, the enormity of what he had done hitting home. At the same time, his fear, the icy cold panic he had experienced at the sight of the knife, was still uppermost in his mind. He had to escape the scene; there might still be danger. Once again, he found first gear and lurched the car forward, the drive wheels spinning on the blood-soaked road before bumping over the body.

In a daze, blood pouring from the cut in his arm, muscles aching from the pounding punches of the fight, he fought down the bile that bubbled in his throat until he swung the car into the stable yard of the Dragon's Tail Hotel, screeched to a halt, swung open the door and vomited on the cobbled ground.

104

The forward Scout. – London - 1941

Baptiste left the pub and then remembered that he didn't have any transport. A cab out to the farm near Slough would be unlikely; he doubted he could persuade any cabbie to drive him on a one-way 30-mile trip to the country. He thought about stealing a car; he had done it before, but if by any chance he was stopped by the police, his chances of saving Joe would be gone. Then he had a thought, if Ted and his boys had left for Wales earlier, there might be cars left in the car park at the back of Ted's office at the club. He decided to chance it; he knew most of the Baker's gang, so whoever was holding the fort at Ted's club wouldn't object to him borrowing one; he was sure he could produce a plausible explanation. It was a short taxi drive over to the club; unusually, there was no one at the door, which was unlocked. Baptiste made his way cautiously up the stairs to Ted's office, where he found Billy Mason and a gentleman he didn't know. Billy was looking embarrassed, and the other gentleman was kneeling in front of Ted Baker's safe, carefully listening to the door as he twisted the combination dial.

"What's going on, Billy?" Baptiste asked.

Billy shifted from foot to foot, his eyes looking down, unable to meet Baptiste's gaze.

"Billy, what are you doing? That's Ted's personal safe and who is he?" Baptiste's concern was much more about what Billy was getting himself into rather than any affrontery he felt on behalf of Ted Baker.

"Bapt, Eddie told me to do it. He told me that I had to get this man from the station. Bring him here, an' he was to open the safe. Then I was to take him back to the station; then I was to take the contents of the safe to Slough farm. Eddie said that his Dad had told him to get the stuff from the safe." Even though Billy hadn't the brightest of intellects, he could see the flaw in the story.

"Billy, if Ted had wanted his son to get the stuff from the safe, he would have given him the combination, not brought in a safecracker from out of town." Baptiste pointed out.

"I know, but what was I supposed to do, Bapt? Say No to Eddie?" Billy asked helplessly.

Baptiste had to concede that Billy had a point. What was Eddie up to? He obviously wanted the paperwork badly, badly enough to bring in an out-of-towner, probably paying him a small fortune; why? Baptiste thought he knew why; so that he had the deeds for all the transactions that Joe had been arranging for Ted. He wanted to ask them about each and every one. He didn't want to miss out on a single deal. That must be it. Interesting that he wanted the paperwork to go to the farm and not back to his office at the brothel. Baptiste had assumed that Eddie would bring Joe and Ted back to his home patch. Then it dawned on him, What better place to 'question' them than in the abattoir that had been built at the back of one of the barns at the farm. No one around, no concerns about anybody hearing the screams and an easy clean up afterwards. No blood stains on the carpet.

Baptiste pulled the younger man to one side, out of the hearing of the safecracker, who was steadfastly carrying on with his work. "Billy, do you know what is happening, what Eddie is up to?"

Billy nodded nervously. "Eddie is taking over from his Dad." The young man didn't look at all happy.

"Billy," Baptiste said gently, "what are you doing here? You're not a gangster like these men. I know you are a hard man; I would not like to fight you, not in a boxing ring anyway. But I reckon I would beat you in a street fight; why? Because I wouldn't worry about killing you, I would fight dirty. These men are like that. You are not; you are a good man. Do you want to work for Eddie Baker after Ted is dead?"

"I have no choice; I owe him." Billy, all 6 foot 3 inches of muscle and brawn, was close to tears.

"Because he paid for a Doctor when your Grandma was sick?" Billy looked shocked at Bapt's words. "Yes, I know about that. This is the way they control you. Men like Eddie and Ted Baker always have a way to control people. Would your grandma be proud of what you do for these men, Billy?" Baptiste waited a moment for his words to sink in before continuing. "Eddie is going to kill Joe Turner, Billy." Again, Billy looked shocked at Bapt's words. "That's right. He is going to kill his own father, and then he is going to torture Joe to find out where Ted's money is hidden. Then he will kill him. One day, he will kill you, Billy. You will say the wrong thing or do something that upsets him accidentally, and then he will kill you. If he is willing to kill his own father, he will not care about killing you, or me, or anyone."

"Are you going to try and stop him?" Billy asked incredulously.

"I am going to try and stop him from killing Joe. Joe is a good man. I know that you think so. He likes you, too. He told me. He told me how you boxed with him at your gym when you were younger. He said to me you had the best right hook he had ever seen."

"Do you want me to help?" Billy asked uncertainly.

"I want you to be safe. I don't want you to get killed today. Are you armed, Billy?"

Billy nodded and showed Baptiste the pistol in his coat pocket. "Eddie made sure that everyone had a gun yesterday. He said we had to always carry it."

"Have you ever fired a gun?" Baptiste asked.

Billy shook his head. "I know how to load it and about the safety."

"Billy, I am not going to tell you what I am going to do, not because I don't trust you, but because if you don't know, then Eddie can't make you tell him. Do you understand?" Billy nodded. "Take the papers from Ted's safe to Eddie, as he asked. If you don't, he will wonder what has happened and become suspicious. Where did he tell you to meet him exactly?"

"In the kitchen of the farmhouse."

"Right. Once you have delivered the papers, try and get out of the house. Say you need the loo; the outhouse is just behind the kitchen. If you go there, you should be able to walk to the trees without being seen, so long as you keep the building between you and the kitchen window. I will meet you, if for any reason I am not there, wait. If you are spotted, don't pull out your gun. If it is one of Eddie's men just say you were going to the trees to take a leak, tell them the toilet is blocked. They're not going to be suspicious of you. If it is someone you don't know hold up your hands, don't try to fight, say my name, my full name, 'Baptiste'. Do you understand?"

Billy looked crestfallen. A man in turmoil, unsure of his future and what he should do for the best.

"Billy." Baptiste's tone was calm but insistent. "Joe can help you; you must trust him. He is a man that can get you away from all this. He is a man that can save you. We must help him; we cannot let Eddie kill him."

Baptiste turned away. Opening the drawer of Ted's desk, he found a key with a Jaguar emblem on the keyring. He searched the other drawers and discovered what he was looking for: a revolver and a box of bullets.

At that moment, the door of the safe opened, and the cracker kneeled before it with a self-satisfied smirk. Baptiste pointed his newly acquired gun at him, and the smile quickly fell from his face.

"Sorry, you are going to have to delay your journey home for a few hours. Billy, tie him up, please. Let him go to the WC first, though. It might get messy otherwise." Baptiste was worried that the man might have had an arrangement with Eddie Baker to contact him at the farm by telephone. Better to be safe rather than sorry, so he intended that the man should be kept out of the way until after the evening's events had unfolded.

105

Alwyn tells all to Rosie - 1941

The Girls, Dot, Betty and Rosie, had just arrived at the Dragon's Tail Hotel, having caught the bus back from Brecon. They were still busily removing their coats and chatting about their purchases from the Market. The side door of the bar flew open, and the staggering frame of Alwyn Thomas fell through it. Dot screamed as she saw the blood streaming from the wound in her lover's arm.

The clientele of the pub stood and sat frozen in horror; just two of the assembly moved into action without hesitation. Rosie was by the injured man's side and, despite his size, had pulled him onto a bench that sat beneath a nearby window. As she was stripping him of his coat and tearing away the sleeve of his shirt, she was joined by Eleanor Williams. The landlady had grabbed a bunch of tea towels as she had ducked under the bar, and she was pressing them against the wound to slow the bleeding.

"He's lost some blood, but the wound isn't deep. We should get him to a Doctor as soon as possible." Eleanor had seen many such injuries in her work in the first war. Two of the men in the bar set off to the Doctor's surgery.

"It's a knife wound, isn't it? Who did this to you, Alwyn?" Rosie asked urgently of the farmer.

His friend Owain had shoved a pint of beer into his left hand and the giant was happily taking his medicine.

"I'm all right; I'm all right." Dot was smothering him with kisses, and her hugs were more of a hindrance than a help. "Rosie, I need to speak to you in private." He cast his eyes towards the men who stood around, all keen to hear what had happened.

"Mrs. Williams, can we take him into the snug? He needs peace and quiet while we wait for the doctor," Rosie asked.

The Land Lady obliged, seating him in a comfortable chair, oblivious to the threat of blood staining its fabric.

Once out of the intrigued clientele's hearing range, Alwyn told his story to the four women: Dot, Betty, Eleanor Williams, and Rosie. For a man whose life had been threatened, who was suffering from blood loss, and who was drunk with adrenaline, he was remarkably composed. Rosie asked a few questions for clarification; otherwise, there was no hesitation before she began to issue orders.

"Betty, you can drive right." A nod from the land girl confirmed. "Take Alwyn and Dot to the Army camp; use the car Alwyn took from the Irishmen. Ask to speak to the commander, Captain Smythe. Give him this note." Rosie began scribbling in a small notebook she took from her bag. "They have a camp sick bay there, I believe, and a medic. They can see to your wound, Alwyn. Tell the Captain everything you just told me." Rosie tore several pages from the book, folded them and gave them to Betty.

"What are you going to do?" Asked Eleanor, concerned for the impressive young lady.

"Oh, I am off for a ride."

106

Jaguar or Delage? - 1941

The SS 100 Jaguar was parked under a canopy at the far end of the club's car park. It was a beautiful 2-seater open sports car, elegant and powerful. The long bonnet housed the 3.5-litre engine, which it was claimed would propel it beyond 100 miles per hour. It was Eddie's favourite car, but Ted wouldn't let him drive it because he said he was a terrible driver. It was one of the many ways that the father would humiliate his son. In France, Baptiste had driven a Delage D8; it had been a gift from one of his female admirers; it had been a very generous gift, but then again, he had worked hard for it. He had been upset to leave it behind when he had been forced to quit France in a hurry. As he reached the outskirts of town in the Jaguar, he opened the throttle and compared the two vehicles. The Delage had a bigger engine and was more powerful, smoother perhaps, but the Jaguar was a lighter vehicle and, thereby, much quicker. Baptiste wondered to himself which he preferred; it was like deciding between two lovers, he concluded, and why choose if you don't have to? He revelled in the thrill of the speed, and in no time at all, he was racing down the Great West Road towards the turn-off for the farm. As planned, he slowed and took an earlier turn in advance of the farm and instead of the wider, well-worn road, he approached the farm from the East on an underused farm track. After a couple of hundred yards, the track split; the right-hand fork took the traveller through a farm gate, and thickly wooded land, into the open grazing land of the farm, between two large barns, finally arriving at the farmyard to the rear of the stable block. The left fork was even less used, it led to ramshackle, rotting buildings long since abandoned and being consumed with each season by the woodland. Baptiste drove as far as he dared into the woods before abandoning the Jaguar and backtracking on foot to the gate.

He concentrated and recalled the map of the farm. He had to admit that it was a brilliant location for such a clandestine operation. Despite being less than a mile from the busy highway, to all but the most determined observer, the buildings and the land of the farm, were hidden from view from every direction.

Baptiste walked north from the gate back towards the main highway. Just before he reached it, he turned left from the track and started to climb the gentle incline. The ascent steepened as he curved his route ever westerly until he reached the summit; the Great West Road was to his back, and an uninterrupted view of the farm before him. He dropped to the ground, keen not to be seen by any vigilant sentry, and he surveyed the farm and firmed up his plans.

He dropped back down to the road; then he descended towards the base of the hill until he reached a small wood that tied the two hills together. By walking south through the trees, he came out just behind the outhouse. He skirted to the right and could see the kitchen window, but from that distance, there was little detail to see. He had to get nearer. Taking a chance, he edged to his left until he could no longer see the kitchen as his view was blocked by the outhouse; thereby, he, too, couldn't be seen as he ran swiftly across the grass and flattened himself against the brick of the building. He slid along the wall and peered round its end until he caught a view of the farmhouse. At this distance he could see much more, but even so, he could only just make out the figures of men in the room. He had to know more about who was in the room and where they were, if Mischa and his men were going to storm the building, they had to be careful that they didn't kill Joe as well.

Bapt heard the kitchen door open; he carefully took a quick look to see what was happening. He was just in time to see the door close again as a man walked towards the outhouse. Baptiste couldn't make out his features. He was large, but then so were most of Eddie's goons. He didn't panic; the man was probably just about to use the facilities. He was confident that he hadn't been seen. He heard the footsteps of the man on the gravel footpath, then the hinges of the toilet door creak as it was opened and then closed again; he heard no sound of a lock. Baptiste stood still with his back against the wall and waited. He considered rushing in through the door and slitting the man's throat. He felt the knife in his pocket; it was nothing to him to do this. He felt sure that his adversary would be off guard, he could be dead before he had managed to stand from his seat. Then again, many of these English men seemed to like to stand to do their business; better yet, his lifeblood would be gushing from him without him even seeing his executioner. Baptiste decided that there was no advantage to killing the man. Indeed, he would be missed; a search would take place, and his body found, that would complicate things. Baptiste was convinced that their best policy was to delay their involvement until as late as possible. As things stood, there were three dogs in this fight. The first dog was waiting to surprise the second, and neither of them had any notion of the third. That was to his advantage; it wasn't time yet to join in; what he needed now was information so they could be ready to act when the time came.

As he mused, he heard the door of the lavatory open again; he held his breath. The man turned right out of the door and was walking away from him towards the woods. He was a large man, well over 6 feet tall. He walked with a slow, lumbering gait; he trod carefully, evidently not wishing to make a noise. He was casting furtive glances to either side and seemed to pay particular attention to the barns where most of Eddie's men were congregated. Baptiste dreaded him turning round as he had nowhere to hide; the man could not help but see him. He thought about charging at the man, tackling him to the floor and ending his life swiftly, but the chances of him doing so without the man crying out were slim. The man was nearly at the woods when he paused briefly; he stood briefly looking at the barns again; he removed his Trilby hat and ran the fingers of his left hand through his hair. It was a gesture that Baptiste knew very well, one that he had seen many times. Undoubtedly, the man was Billy Mason. He turned back towards the woods and disappeared from sight in the darkness of the trees.

Casting a quick glance at the rear of the farmhouse, Baptiste followed the same path and entered the woods at the same point as Billy had done. When he was out of sight of the barns, he chanced a whispered call. He didn't fancy falling over Billy in the gloom and prompting him to swing out wildly with his killer right hook.

"Billy, Billy, it's me, Bapt."

"Bapt, over here." Was the hushed reply.

Baptiste gestured to Billy to be silent and follow him deeper into the woods. When he was sure that they were out of sight and sound of both the farmhouse and the barns, he stopped, and both men sat on a fallen tree trunk. Baptiste was aware that they didn't have much time. It must have been already five minutes since Billy had left the kitchen. He needed to get back before his prolonged absence was noticed.

"Billy, who is in the Kitchen?"

"Eddie has Joe, as you said, and there is a woman, no idea who she is, but Eddie said they weren't to be harmed, at least not yet, he said." Billy excitedly spat out his news.

"Is Ted there yet?"

"No, but they are expecting him; they think in an hour or so, they are all hyped up about that."

"How many of them are there, Billy?"

"I am not sure; when I got there, I saw a bunch of the gang waiting by the barns; I think there might have been more of them inside; I don't know."

"That's all right, Billy. Now tell me exactly the layout of the room and where the people are."

Billy described the room, and his account matched the plans that Baptiste had memorised. The kitchen was large, and the hub of the home as was traditional on a working farm. A large table stretched along its centre, filling the space. At the far end was a range, which gave both heat to the room and provided the cooking facilities. It backed onto the fireplace in the Parlor, which was the room behind, the door to which was in the opposite corner to the back door. A large window-lined the outside wall to the left of the table, with a sink and workspace below it. There was a smaller window next to the door on the rear wall. Two doors stood next to each other at the beginning of the right-hand wall; the first smaller one led into a larder, and the second was the door to the hallway and the rest of the house. Billy described how Joe had been sat with his hands handcuffed behind his back in the middle of the table with his back to the sink; the lady was sat on his right-hand side nearer to the door. Billy had been stationed in the corner by the larder door. The back door was patrolled by Phil, one of Eddie's crueller lieutenants, whilst Eddie was at the far end of the room pacing up and down in front of the warmth of the Aga.

"Is anyone else in the room?"

"No, there are some men in the room at the other end of the hallway. They are waiting for Ted to arrive. They will jump his men from behind as Ted walks into the kitchen from the hall."

"There is a plan in place for when Ted arrives?"

"Yes, Eddie will hide in the Parlor, I am to be in the Larder, Phil outside the back door. We jump out and grab Ted when his men have been shot in the hall."

"They seem very confident that Ted will come in the front door."

"You ever known Ted Baker to use the back door, just not his style."

"Who is this lady?"

"I don't know, never seen her before but Eddie has been asking her questions about money and accounts and stuff. She hasn't uttered a word, as cold as a fish she is, and it's driving Eddie crazy, I can tell you."

Baptiste had all the information he needed. "Billy, I need you to go back to the house."

"You gotta be kidding, mate. I am out of here; it's all going to go to hell in a handcart round here, and I want to be miles away when it happens."

"Billy, if you do a runner, you're as good as dead. If Ted comes out on top, he will think you helped Eddie; if Eddie wins, then he'll be mad at you for buggering off. Your only chance is to help me to save Joe. I have a plan; I have help coming. If you do as I say, you can be rid of this life. You can join the army; you can box again. It's the right thing to do, Bill, you know it is. Think about Joe."

Billy 'the Brick' Mason was an honest crook. He hated violence, especially the cruelty of the sadism brandished about by the Bakers. He wanted desperately to live an upright life, the life his Grandma had wanted for him. In the end, he knew deep down that it would be better for him to die trying to escape the Bakers than carry on in the sewer that was their world.

"All right, Bapt, what do you want me to do?"

107

The ride of her life – Wales - 1941

Rosie ran to the old stables and pulled the cover from Simon's bike. She had no doubts that she should be able to start the machine even without the key; it was a simple matter of wiring the ignition cables together. She looked around the stall for something to wear. The dress she had on would be no protection at all against the cold winds of the ride that she had in prospect.

Simon's long wax coat hung from a nail, and in the corner, rolled up on the floor, she found an old pair of dungarees. The clothes were several sizes too large, and they weighed heavily on her. Her only problem now was her inadequate footwear, and there was nothing she could do about that.

The bike was bigger and heavier than the ones that she was used to racing at Brooklands, but she was excited about the prospect of riding such an advanced and powerful machine. Just as she was preparing to push the machine off its stand, she put her hand into the coat finding the keys for the motorcycle.

She unscrewed the petrol cap and examined the petrol level, which was almost full. Simon had obviously prepared himself for a fast getaway. Pulling out the choke, she kicked down on the starter, and without hesitation, the monster roared to life. There was no time for delay; she had to find out what was going on at the farm, and she had to do it without being seen. Pulling out through the archway of the old hotel, she turned right down the main road, away from the direction of Mynydd farm. She rode as hard as she dared; the headlight was heavily shaded due to the war restrictions and cast an inadequate glow on the road ahead.

This is some machine; she thought to herself as she tore down the road. After a mile of heading west, she found the turning on the right to a small lane that she knew climbed up towards the mountain. She had walked up the lane several times, but now the bends came at her in rapid succession. The cold rubber of the tyres struggled to grip on the rough and loose surface of the country track. She fought her desire to ride too quickly, the power of the machine threatening to spin the rear wheel away from underneath her. The lane came to a t junction; she braked hard, then threw the machine into the tight left turn.

This new road would take her to the west again and then zigzag around the base of the mountain. It was an inadequate road for a machine of this power, but she had to find out what was happening at the farm. After 10 minutes of careful riding, she pulled up next to a footpath that led to the summit of the hill.

It was a short but difficult climb on foot, not helped by her flimsy footwear. On completing her ascent, she was able to see the town below her to the South and, turning to her left, down onto the farm lit dimly by the rising moon.

A large truck was parked in front of the farm building; two men were smoking cigarettes and shuffling their feet as if waiting for their comrades inside. Rosie had a dilemma; did she try to get closer to the building to find out what was going on? But she knew that if she did this, she would put herself further from the motorcycle, and she would need to follow the vehicles if they left suddenly.

A light shone from the doorway as two men emerged from the house. One of them shouted to the sentinels by the lorry. Rosie couldn't hear what was said, but she saw them lower the vehicle's tail gate.

More people came into sight. The first was a lady; from her figure and gait, Rosie was sure that it was Myfanwy Thomas. Then, a younger lady stumbled forward from the doorway. Behind her a man in dark clothing was grabbing her arm and pushing her forward. Another man followed; he looked nervously from side to side as if looking for an escape route. He, too, was ushered from the farmhouse by his own personal escort. Rosie was sure that it was the Naval officer who was staying at the Dragon. One of the Major's men, as she had long suspected, but why hadn't he left town? She had warned them that he was blown. Now, he was in real danger.

The girl was manhandled into a car that was parked in the farmyard. Simon was directed to the lorry, where he was made to climb up into the back. The two vehicles set off in convoy, with another larger car, down the driveway to the road. Rosie could just about make out their dimmed lights as they headed away from her, down towards the main road.

As she was about to turn away, to get back to the bike, the car turned left off the road. Rosie was confused. They were heading straight into a field. To her knowledge, there was nothing that way. The field was unused. Alwyn had said that it had been left to fallow, not used in years as the soil was stoney. To her surprise, the vehicles had no difficulty crossing the ground. Despite the recent rains, there appeared to be little mud; even the large car, which was much more suited to town driving, sailed across to the far side before disappearing through a gap in the trees and into the old wood that lined the eastern border of the farm.

Where were they going? Rosie hesitated, unsure how to proceed. Without knowing where they were going, she was lost. Then, faintly, she could just about make out the lights of the vehicles as they came out from the trees further up the hillside. They turned left. They had joined the old road, the one she had seen on the ancient maps that she had studied, the road that, decades ago, serviced the quarry.

Their suspicions had been correct. The plotters were using the old quarry land. It would take her an age to get back down to the main road and follow them. No, she would have to ride around the mountain and along the old drover's track. It would take her above the quarry; she could cut across and have a good view of the old workings.

Stumbling down from her observation post, she was soon back at the bike. She had left Vincent in gear and pointed downhill. Vaulting onto the machine she kicked up the side stand as she pulled in the clutch. They rolled, slowly at first but quickly gaining speed, until sure that they had enough momentum, she clicked on the ignition and dropped the clutch. The back wheel snatched at the chain and spun the engine through the intervening gears. Electricity and volatile petrol combined in glorious combustion, exploding the machine down the track.

Rosie roared out loud with pleasure. A less skilful rider would be frightened stiff at such a ride. The rough terrain, the road tyres too smooth, the overpowered engine, the night sky just barely allowing enough moon to light the road ahead. But Rosie was not afraid. She had felt fear many times, fear was not fun, and right now, she was having so much fun. The bike was responding; it was as though it was revelling in her experienced touch. If it had been capable of human emotions, it would have surely felt guilt at preferring her practised dexterity over that of its clumsy first lover and owner.

The track levelled off as it curved along the ridge that joined the mountain to the series of hills that bent away into the distance. It was an ancient road used for centuries by the herders who had brought their livestock from the north to the markets of Trefynydd and Brecon. Unused now, replaced by the new lower road that had been carved through the valley by the machines of the modern age.

The path was smooth and level due to the geology. The rock has worn smooth by the ministrations of winds and rains for millennia. But legend told a different tale. There had once been two families, it was said, their names long forgotten, who had feuded; they lived on opposite sides of the hills and had kept apart but had cursed and sworn death upon each other. Then, as fate was apt to do, the young son of the Trefynydd family had met with the beautiful daughter of the family from the North. Of course, inevitably, they had fallen in love and arranged to run away together. On the night that they had agreed to meet, the girl, heartbroken at leaving her mother, had told her of their plans. The father overheard and forbade his daughter to leave the house. But the headstrong girl had jumped through the open window and run towards her lover, waiting in the hills.

Her brothers and father gave chase, but as they climbed, a terrible impenetrable mist descended. The young man waited on his horse at the prearranged spot. He saw his love in the distance just as the fog took hold. It was the last that anyone saw of her. It is said that the young lover never gave up on finding her and rode up and down the ridge, looking for his love, until the track was worn smooth by the hooves of his faithful steed.

Free of mist this evening and illuminated by a moon that shone ever brighter in the clearing winter sky, Rosie tore down the lover's trail until suddenly she came to a fence that cut across the track. It was built right up to the edge of the cliff on one side and stretched away into the distance on the other. There was no way around it; there was no way of telling how far down the hill the fence stretched. She would have to go through. For a moment, she considered ramming it with the bike, but it looked pretty strong. Even if it fell, the barbed wire could do all sorts of damage to the tyres. Rosie had no tools with her; she was losing the convoy. The conspirators would get away, and the poor Navy lad was in deep trouble.

108

The Cavalry arrives. – London - 1941

Baptiste waited until Billy had got back to the Farmhouse without incident, and then he made his way back the way he had come to the gate on the east side of the Farm. All was quiet when he reached the place set as the rendezvous with Mischa and his men. Baptiste looked around carefully. There was not a soul to be seen. Eddie's men were clearly focused on the western approach to the farm where Ted and, later, the convoy of trucks would arrive from their trip to Wales. Mischa was late; he had expected that they would be here at least half an hour earlier. As the minutes slipped by, he began to worry that they wouldn't show up. Perhaps they had got cold feet and had decided that a war with the Bakers wasn't in their best interests after all.

"Good afternoon, waiting for someone." A heavily accented voice chuckled from behind him. Bapt spun on his heel, but no one was there. The voice laughed again, louder. Batiste grabbed hold of his gun, searching for the source of the voice. "Be careful, my friend. It is not yet time for us to announce to our hosts that we have arrived for their party."

A dark figure emerged from behind a tree to Baptiste's left. It was a heavily set man in a dark, heavy coat. He held his hands out to the side, showing that he was unarmed. He walked slowly towards Baptiste, stopping only when Baptiste had turned to him and his pistol was lined up on his stomach.

"Please not to shoot, it would not be wise for either of us."

The fingers of his left hand fluttered ever so slightly; a signal so faint that Baptiste didn't notice it at all. Before he knew it, 6 guns were trained upon him, as men appeared like ghosts from the trees around him. An astonished Baptiste lowered his gun. He felt no fear as he realised that if these men had wanted him dead, then he would already have drawn his last breath and felt the knife slice through his unsuspecting throat. Instead, his overriding feeling was that of admiration and astonishment at the skill of these phantoms. He fancied himself as no fool and equal to most men. But his natural environment was the city; in the bars and back alleys of the metropolis, he was king. These men, who had flanked him so easily, were a different breed. They were guerrillas, soldiers that could move through any terrain undetected, silently infiltrating their targets and carrying out their objectives. He wondered how and why these men had acquired such skills.

"Mischa Agafonov, I am Baptiste Barbeau. I have been expecting you, but I see that you have been here for some time." Bapt spoke in Russian, one of the many languages he had learned from both the customers and staff of his business in Paris.

"I am pleased to meet with you, Monsieur Barbeau. I understand from Mademoiselle Fletcher that you are a man to be trusted." Mischa answered in French.

"I think that we both have the same interests; we want the same things. We both desire the safety of the same man. Perhaps it would work best for all if we spoke in English." Baptiste suggested.

Mischa nodded in agreement. "That is good; all my men speak English well." As he spoke, he pulled from his pocket the map and plans that Doreen had given him. "I understand that you have a plan."

"I have some ideas, but I see that you and your men are the experts."

"Please tell me what the situation is."

Baptiste, using the documents, showed Mischa the layout of the farm and the house. He explained who was in the room, who was expected, how the shipment of animals would arrive, and Eddie's plan to wipe out Ted's men one at a time as they came.

"I think that it is best that we wait until all the trucks have arrived; I don't believe they will harm their hostages until all Ted's men have been killed. We should be ready to move in then."

Mischa looked at the plans, concentrating hard and thinking about what Bapt had said. "I agree. We will have our men ready to move if something changes, but otherwise, we wait. Let these men kill each other if that is their wish; it will save us a job later. When we move, we will have to be quick. Their men will be off guard; they will be celebrating their success. The problem will be attacking this room." He pointed to the kitchen on the plan. "This is dangerous for our friend Joe, and this lady if she is a friend also. A stray bullet could easily kill them."

Baptiste smiled. "I have a plan for this."

109

No need to take offence. - Wales

She put down the stand on the Vincent and leapt off. Walking up to the fence and kicked it in frustration, screaming out a series of profanities that would shame a docker. Looking back at the bike she noticed the panniers that hung on each side of the bike. "Toolkit, that's it," Rosie said to herself excitedly. Rifling through the bags revealed nothing of any use before Rosie remembered that some bikes come with a toolkit under the seat. She felt around, looking for a hinge or a catch, when she realised that there was a tray that slid out like a drawer. She smiled in triumph as a pair of 6-inch pliers lay in front of her on the tray; what's more, they had a wire cutter.

It was no easy job; the pliers were new, and the cutting blade was sharp, but the wire was strong. Soon, her hands were bruised by the pressure she had to apply to the metal handles. She needed more leverage. She looked hopefully into the tool tray. There were 2 hexagon box spanners, probably for spark plug removal. Wrapping a piece of cloth torn from a rag in the tray around each of the handles, she found that she could jam the box spanners onto them, effectively making them a few inches longer. It was enough to ease the work. Cutting from the very bottom all the way to the top of the fence, she was able to bend back a section, allowing enough room for the bike to get through.

Rosie rode on hard until she estimated that she was above and a little to the north of the quarry. She stopped and walked over to the ridge edge, and looked down into the valley below.

To the south, the ground steadily sloped away from the ridge she had just ridden along before suddenly dropping hundreds of feet. A wide area had been flattened at the bottom of the cliff. Formed by the workings of quarrymen a hundred years ago. A stone chimney stood despondently like a gravestone, marking the demise of the industry of the men. Nearby a few buildings of the old plant remained surprisingly intact. New iron sheeting sat across the ancient stone walls forming a makeshift but serviceable roof. A road extended away from the site into the valley, forking into opposite directions half a mile in the distance. Recent, albeit rough, repairs had been made to the road. Upwards of twenty large trucks stood around the yard. Some, low on their axles, were clearly loaded. Whilst the others queued for consignments.

Rosie was amazed by the scene. This was a bigger operation than she had imagined. As she stared down at the loading of the wagons, she guessed at the numbers in each vehicle. How much was each beast worth? Surely much more on the black market than the price paid by the government. Cattle mooed, half-heartedly complaining as they reluctantly idled up the ramps into their carriages. Rosie counted the vehicles. 29 in total, a mixture of military and agricultural lorries. At that moment the cars and the lorry arrived from the farm. The lorry joined the queue to be loaded. The cars parked in front of a group of people. Orders were issued and bodies scuttled off, some to help with the loading, others climbed into the cabs of the idle wagons.

At length, the loading was completed. The last vehicle, the one from the farm, seemed to take the remains of the livestock. As the tailgate had been lowered, a man jumped down from the back and attempted to run from the scene. It was a futile attempt at escape. His laboured running suggested that he was injured, his captors caught him with ease. He was knocked to the ground, and 3 of the men aimed kicks to his body as he writhed on the floor. He was then hoisted up by his arms and dragged up into the truck. Out of her view, Rosie did not see him again as the remaining animals were loaded.

When the loading was completed, shouted instructions could be heard across the still valley before the whole scene exploded into a cacophony of noise as thirty diesel engines cranked into life.

The first of the vehicles, the cars, headed off down the track before turning to the right at the fork in the road. It was closely followed by a truck. Another of the lorries followed but took the opposite fork. Then, there was a pause before the next two vehicles set off. Again, one took the right turning, which led to Mynydd farm and the main road, the other turning left, bound no doubt for a westerly road. Another delay, which Rosie timed at exactly a minute before the next pair set off. Rosie had to decide what to do. She would have to rely on a series of suppositions that were no more than guesses.

She reasoned that the procession that was heading towards Mynydd farm and the main road was ultimately bound for London. The Major had said that they knew the likely destination of the livestock, and they had that end covered. As she couldn't follow both convoys, she would have to trust the fate of Sara and half of the contraband to Joe Turner.

The westerly travelling traffic's destination was less than certain. Could it be that they were bound for a boat to Ireland? But the exact embarkation port was not known, so it was down to her to follow them. She also felt she had to try and rescue the sailor. There was no doubt that he was a British officer and that, in the hands of Irish Republicans, he was in major peril.

Next, she had to consider which route they were taking. She pictured the map in her mind. Would they take the old coach road towards the Pembrokeshire peninsular? Join up with a ship from one of the major ports at Milford Haven or Fishguard. They could go to the south coast ports at Carmarthen or Swansea. She doubted any were suitable; they were all busy places. No doubt full of military traffic. Security would be tight; they would need a quiet quayside. Also, if they were headed that way it would have been quicker to drive down to the main route via the farm, like the others.

The fact that they were heading west seemed to indicate that they were headed cross country. Avoiding the major roads and population centres, heading for the west coast, where any number of small havens could dock a ship relatively discreetly. The crossing to Ireland would also be shorter from there. Rosie thought that she would just about be able to scramble the bike down through the tracks to the road that wove its way westerly; the road she was sure that the convoy must be taking.

With no time to waste, she set off on the bike. It was a harsh ride that threatened damage to her and the machine, but she was confident that she could meet up with the road and find where the motorcade was joining the route. The delays each truck was enduring would give her a chance to make up the extra few miles of her more circuitous route.

It was a blessed relief when the track led Rosie and the Vincent to the tarmacked road. By her reckoning, she must be some 2 or 3 miles southwest of where the old quarry road would join the Builth Wells Road. Riding swiftly as she dared for 5 minutes, until she estimated that she must be near the place where the lorries would turn in from the right. She pulled over at the crest of a hill, killed the engine, and looked with anticipation at the road ahead as it snaked down into the valley below. The silence and stillness of the night, after her frantic ride, was deafening. The ribbon of the tarmac was clearly visible in the moonlight. But the hillside to the right was covered in a blanket of trees that absorbed all light. The blackness of the forest hid utterly any signs of the side road that Rosie was sure must be there.

After what seemed to be an age, but logically couldn't have been more than a minute, she heard a diesel engine. A moment later, a dark shape emerged from the forest just 150 yards ahead onto the tarmac. It had been a close-run thing; a few extra seconds of riding would have left her on the road in front of the convoy. As it was, she was confident that she had not been seen.

But which vehicle was it? And how many more were due to come this way? Her best guess was that 3 lorries had set off this way before she had left the hill above the quarry, and her journey was maybe 5 or 6 miles longer. Allowing for the Vincent's extra speed, even over the rough terrain, she guessed that it was the 4th or 5th in the procession. Assuming that the loot was being split 50:50 between London and Dublin, as she was sure that it must be, there would be 10 or 11 more to follow.

There was no real way of knowing how many more lorries would come this way. So, she counted off the seconds, and, as expected, when she had reached 64, the next lorry leapt clumsily from the darkness of the trees. Rosie reset her count, this time reaching 58 as the ensuing lorry emerged onto the moonlit asphalt. The cavalcade continued for 7 more vehicles, making 9 that she had seen join the road. It must be soon that the last would pass her. As each new vehicle materialised, she expected the new count to exceed 60, making it the last. The timings of the gaps had been consistent. The shortest had been 55 seconds, the longest 66.

When, at last, her latest count reached 70, she began to prepare herself for the chase. She waited until 90 before she set off in pursuit. Rosie had been tempted to wait longer to ensure that it really had been the last truck. Just in case there hadn't been a delay at the quarry or on the track. But each extra second's delay put her further behind the convoy.

More guesswork was required. The strict manner in which they had set off at 60-second intervals, to her, indicated that they wanted to avoid being noticed as a procession as they passed through the towns and villages en route. Therefore, they would want to maintain that discipline by keeping to a uniform pace. Allowing for the divergence of performance of the various engines, Rosie expected that on the better roads, the lorries would cruise along at 30 miles per hour. A mile every 2 minutes.

So, in the 90 seconds she had waited, the last van had covered three-quarters of a mile. If she maintained a speed of 40 mph, then the 10 extra miles per hour, or a mile every 6 minutes, would allow her to catch the tailender in 4 and a half minutes. Crucially, the van would have travelled 2 and a quarter miles by then. From her memory of the map, that was well before the first major crossroads, which was some 15 miles or so further on from her current position. All good in theory, but 40 miles per hour on a country road at night, without the luxury of using her headlights in case she was spotted in the mirrors of her prey, was not without risk. But what was life without a little danger?

Rosie rode for 3 minutes at the required speed before dropping off her pace a little, not wanting to come upon her quarry too suddenly. After what she estimated to be 6 minutes, Rosie got her first glimpse of the truck 200 yards ahead. As it rounded a bend, it was lost from sight again. It was not seen again until a series of bends had been navigated and a straight section of road revealed its steady progress.

Closing the gap to around 150 yards, Rosie set her speed to match that of the lorry, and she settled in for the journey to the first crossroads. The road twisted and turned but broadly followed a north-westerly direction. Which would bring them to the Irish Sea midway up the Welsh coast. At these speeds, she was in for a journey of 4 hours or so.

Comfortable in the more sedate pace of the ride, Rosie began to hatch her plan.

110

Ted Baker is expected. - Slough

Mischa's men spread out across the farm perimeter whilst he, his sniper and Baptiste made their way back to the wood at the rear of the outhouse. Taking up a position that commanded a good view, they settled in for a long wait. There was tension in the air; there always is when men wait to kill or be killed. Baptiste was calm, but at the same time, he was excited. He felt that for the first time in a long time he was doing something that was worthy, that was meaningful. It felt good, and he hoped that if Joe Turner kept to his word, it would be the way he could get home. Back to his family, to his city, then he could use his skills to help drive out the evil of the Nazis from France.

The stout Russian sat beside him, and as if divining his thoughts, he asked. "So, you worked for Eddie Baker and now you turn against him. Doreen says that you are to be trusted; she knows a thing or two about people, so I believe her. But you interest me, Baptiste Barbeau; why is it that you can be relied upon."

"Well, that's a long story." Replied the Frenchman.

"We have a long time to wait; what else shall we do? Play cards?"

"That would be less of a gamble than telling all my secrets to a man with a small army that can appear from nowhere and could probably disappear just as quickly." There was a humour to his voice, mingled with a respect for the man's obvious power.

"Do you have any cards with you?" asked the Russian with a smile.

"No."

"Then we talk." The smile was still there, but the man's manner was insistent.

Baptiste talked; he told of his life in Paris, why he had left, the circumstances of his enforced employment by the Bakers, the brutality and malignant reign of Eddie Baker, the things that were practiced at the brothel, and his loathing for the depravity that he had become a part of.

"I think that we are both men that have committed crime," Baptiste said as his story was coming to its conclusion. "We have lied and cheated, killed when we had to. But I think that, like me, you have done what you needed to do to survive. Eddie Baker is a different kettle of fish; as these English say, he kills to watch a man die. He rapes not because he desires a girl; there are many girls who would lie with him because of who he is; no he rapes to have power. He wants to see them humiliated, debased, controlled. He tortures, not to punish, or to get information, or to establish his power; he tortures to enjoy another man's pain." Baptiste shivered, not from the cold winter air but from the thought of the things he had seen.

"I have known such men." The Russian said after a moment when both men reflected on what Baptiste had said. "Such men are best squashed like you might stand on a cockroach. When he is dead, you will take his business?"

"No, that is not why I am doing this. I want to return to France. The man I killed in Paris, his friends are dead now. The Germans killed them and the Policeman who hunted me also. It will be risky, but I think that I can return to my home, to my girls there."

"What will you do there?" Mischa was intrigued.

"I will run my business as I did before. I will make friends as I did before. Powerful friends. I will make friends with the Germans. They will come to my girls because they are the best in Paris. I will befriend them; they will tell me information, or I will steal it from their briefcases as their minds are elsewhere. I will send the information to the British. Now that the Americans are coming, there will soon be a fight to liberate France from those scum. When the time comes, I will slit their Ayrian throats as they lie in the beds of my girls. Or I will send them home to their wives, without their cocks and balls, a warning never to defile France again." There was a passion and an energy in Baptist's voice that convinced Mischa of his ability to achieve his aims. "And what of you, my friend? What brings a man with a small army to fight a London gangster? Is it just love?"

411

Mischa smiled and nodded in admission. "Yes, I do it for the Lady. For me she has been the only one. But I was married, a marriage that is arranged; to break such a marriage would have been dangerous, and dangerous men would have been angry. I had no choice then; perhaps now I can help the woman I have always loved. Also, there is my friend. He was my friend in Russia, he was my friend here in London. He saved my life, and he helped me to come here when there was nowhere else for me to go. He was a loyal man, and he tried to help his friend; his reward was to be beaten to death by Eddie Baker as he was tied to a chair. This is the action of a coward, not of a man. Tonight, I swear, he will die."

Baptiste had no doubts about the Russian's sincerity. "Tell me about Russia; how did you come to England?"

"I was a very young man, really just a boy when I became a soldier. The village where I was born was near the border, and the Germans came without warning. They stole everything. They raped, and they killed. We were just peasants; we had little, but they took everything anyway. I escaped and ran for my life. I came across a Russian army unit and joined them. I learned quickly; I was small and quick and agile. I would run into their camps at night and cut throats and be gone before any alarm was raised. I was 13 years old when I killed my first man; by the time I turned 14, I had more kills than I had had birthdays; by the time I was 15, I had lost count. The war dragged on, and men died. I was promoted over and over. I led men not because they sewed stripes on my arm but because I knew what to do, and the men followed me; they trusted me. Then there was the October Revolution, and the traitorous Bolsheviks surrendered to the Germans. The war was over, but the civil war began. I fought with the White Russian Army, and I fought the communists. I fought them everywhere. In Siberia, in Slovenia, in Finland, everywhere they took their foul poison. Everywhere we went we were betrayed, too many of our leaders argued amongst themselves, there was no unity, too many factions. All the time, the communists grew stronger, and we grew fewer in number. In the end, it was no good; I had to leave, and I was a marked man. I came here with many of my men. We settled here into a quiet life; we have jobs and businesses. We do not make trouble; the

English have been good to us. But we all swore that one day, we would return to our Motherland and oust the communists. So, we train, we teach our sons how to fight like we fought. The men you see here are ready to fight. They will fight against the Germans when the time is right, and though Russia fights alongside Britain today, there will come a time when the British and the Americans will see Stalin for what he is, and then my men will fight again beside the British."

It was a remarkable story, and Baptiste was full of admiration for the man. As they sat in wait, the quietness of the night closed around them. The silence was disturbed only occasionally by a passing car on the great road to the north of them. Each engine noise heightened their senses as they anticipated Ted Baker's arrival.

111

Sorry Darling – Wales - 1941

There were no surprises at the crossroads; the lorry continued on the north-westerly road. A good time for a little more fun on the Vincent. Rosie knew that the road they followed would bring them out to the next town, some 15 miles ahead. But there was an alternative, a smaller road that linked together several tiny hamlets nestled on the banks of a river. This road re-joined the main road 5 miles further on. Rosie banked left and took to the substitute way. She twisted hard on the throttle, glorying in the sound of the V twin as growled its pleasure at being let off its leash. They had one aim: to get as far ahead of the truck as they could. Rosie gambled on the quietness of the hour; using all the road, she threw the machine hard into the bends. Trusting that there would be no traffic coming in the opposite direction. In a little over 8 minutes, they approached the junction of the main road. Holding back a little, out of view of the traffic on the main route, she waited and watched. After 30 seconds or so, a lorry passed. A military truck, not the tail-ender she had been following, but the vehicle ahead of it in the procession. She waited 15 seconds and then joined the road behind. The road swung to the right, and she watched the lights of the truck disappear. Rosie, in turn, rounded the bend; as she did so, she slowed before banking hard right and jamming on the rear brake. The wheel locked, and the back end of the bike began to slide on the smooth tarmac. Rosie stood up on the footrests. Waiting for the precise moment that the bike slid sideways along the road, she jumped from the machine and ran along with her forward momentum.

"Sorry, darling." She whispered as the Vincent scraped along the road, sparks flying as metal parts left ruts in the tarmac. The bike came to rest 30 yards further on, the back wheel spinning as the engine continued to idle until the carburettor was starved of petrol, and it spluttered to silence.

Rosie ran back towards the bend, pulling the heavy overcoat off and flinging it onto the floor in the middle of the road. Quickly, she headed towards the bike, tearing at the overalls she was wearing and her dress underneath until they were ripped and somewhat revealing. She dropped down a few feet from the downed machine, lying on the ground. The hope was that the coat would be the first thing spotted by the driver of the following lorry. With luck, it would jolt him out of any stupor that he had fallen into on the long and monotonous drive. The next thing he would see is the bike and the body lying prone next to it. Then he would stop. At least she bloody well hoped he would stop.

112

Ted Baker arrives. – Slough Farm

Ted Baker dozed as the big automobile rocked him gently along the comparatively smooth Great West Road. The earlier part of the journey had been less pleasant; the winding Welsh roads had not been to his liking, but all in all, it had been a good evening so far. The business had been settled successfully. The sale of arms to the Irish had turned a very healthy profit and more than covered the outlay for the animals. There was the worry of the Naval officer that they had caught snooping around the farm. Was he a spy? The Irish lads would find out; he was confident of that. If he was, how much did he know and more to the point, how much had he fed back to his masters? What could he know? That a number of animals had been gathered together and shipped off somewhere. Doubtful, he would know where they came from; even more unlikely, he would know where they were going. If he had been able to report back to his bosses, all they would find is some empty barns and a pile of shit. No evidence led back to him or the Irish; the British authorities would have a hard time proving anything against the Welsh farmer. They might have to change the gathering point for the animals, which might complicate future deliveries, whilst they let things settle down, but he had plenty to be going on with. Plus, he had the girl, not to his tastes, but he was sure that she would be a nice little earner in Eddie's house. In a week's time, all she would care about was her next needle, so she wouldn't be telling anybody about livestock shipments; she wouldn't even remember where she came from. The Irish lads will take care of the Sailor, so the locals will all assume that the two of them have run away together. It's nice bit of juicy gossip for the ladies at the next Women's Institute meeting, no doubt. He had a nice little set-up for the animals at the farm in Slough. Joe and Baptiste had plenty of willing customers chomping at the bit for the produce. He was a sound acquisition that Joe Turner; he'd done a good job setting up the kosher businesses; he's got a good head on his shoulders, that lad. Who would have thunk it, the elderly gangster chuckled to himself, Ted Baker, Master Builder and Gentleman Farmer. The girl was sobbing persistently beside him on the large rear seat; it was annoying; how was he supposed to get any kip? Just as he was about to ask the lads to bung her in the boot, his driver spoke. "Er Boss, we are just coming up to the Farm turning now." Ted sat up in his seat. He couldn't see a thing. The road outside seemed the same as it had for that last hour. He congratulated himself that his farm was so well hidden from view. They could come and go as they pleased, and nobody would spot the animals being housed and butchered on his land. The big car turned and bumped along the less-than-smooth side road. Another turn took the big cruiser onto a track full of potholes and deep ruts. The car's suspension struggled over the unbefitting terrain, the passengers being tossed and thrown about, the underside of the cumbersome sedan scraping noisily on stones. The driver pulled up in front of the farmhouse beside a smaller car, Joe Turner's. A light shone invitingly through the curtain of the Parlour window. Nothing to worry about; it couldn't be seen from the road, so there would be no meddling ARP warden sticking his nose in, but it was probably better not to be the target of the Luftwaffe; better have a word with Joe about it. He would get Doreen to knock up some black out curtains, Ted thought.

Ted pulled himself arthritically from his seat and out into the cold night air. He grabbed the girl and dragged her snivelling after him. He pushed open the heavy front door of the house and marched through the hall and down the short passage to the kitchen, his men struggling to keep up with him. The door was ajar, and he could feel the warmth coming from the dimly lit room. He pushed on the door, and it swung open to reveal Joe Turner sitting at the table in front of him; he shoved the girl into the room ahead of him and stepped through the door.

"I hope you've got the bloody kettle on Turner." Ted bellowed. As he finished his sentence, he understood that something wasn't quite right. Next to Joe at the table was sat a prim, austere lady, who sat with her hands on the table in front of her. It took a second for recognition, but he realised it was Miss Hereford, the Accountant.

Ted heard the distinctive click of a revolver being cocked, ready for firing, and his son's voice. "Hello, Dad, chilling evening, isn't it?" Ted turned to the voice and saw the gun held inches from his face. Almost at once, there were two gunshots from the hallway behind him, followed by the thump of bodies slumping to the floor. There was a rush of feet and a third, and then a fourth shot rang out as the lives of his men were extinguished. He felt something being pushed into his lower back and his left arm being grabbed just above the elbow. He was dragged backwards and pushed down onto a hard kitchen chair. Hands quickly searched him, but he seldom carried a weapon, and the men knew that.

Ted refused to look at his son, who was laughing gently to himself. "Good evening, Miss Hereford; I trust my son has been a convivial host in my absence." Ted addressed the demure bookkeeper.

"Quite so, Mr Baker, quite so." Replied Sue Cartwright, aka Miss Hereford.

"Miss Hereford would you be so good as to help the young lady to a seat." In the confusion of the ambush, Sara had fallen to the floor by the door and had subsequently been ignored.

"Of course, Mr Baker." Sue rose from the table and gently did as she was asked, doing so without asking their captor's permission.

Joe was impressed with them both. Ted must have had the shock of his life but was remaining calm, and Sue was doing a tremendous job; she had been sensible enough to stay in character and to say nothing to the constant barrage of questions that Eddie Baker had thrown at her, much to the young gangster's annoyance.

At last, Senior addressed Junior. "I don't know what you think you are doing, young man, but I won't forgive this. When my men arrive, which they will do soon, you will be begging for that forgiveness. In fact, best for you if you start begging now."

Eddie Baker had still held the gun pointed at his father. He smirked at the old man's words as he walked slowly in short, backward steps to the warmth of the range, never turning his back to the room; he lowered the gun. Only now was he fully confident, with Phil and Billy holding guns on the captives and the length of the table standing between him and his father.

"My boys are looking forward to your men arriving. If the weather had been warmer, we could have sat in the farmyard and watched them come, one at a time; then, you could have seen what happened to them, one at a time. As it is you will hear it from here. You will hear each truck arrive one at a time. You will hear each one back up to the barn. You may hear the sounds of the animals as they are unloaded. You will definitely hear the shots, as your men are dealt with. One at a time you will hear your power slipping away."

Joe was watching the encounter with interest. Eddie had clearly rehearsed the speech and seemed pleased with his oratory. For a moment, a fleeting moment, perhaps for the first time in a long and bloody life of crime, Ted Baker seemed defeated. He realised his mistake, he had been betrayed, he had assumed the loyalty of his men, but one had revealed his plans. He had left himself vulnerable, he had underestimated the boy. In truth, he had always held him in disdain, weak and slow, bent on cruelty, mistaking it for strength. He was not the son he had wished for. For years, he had mocked and teased the boy, hoping it would steel him. Instead, it had just fuelled his weaknesses. Ted Baker had never been bettered, and he knew that he could get under his offspring's skin; what else could he do but try and push him into a mistake?

"How long have you been practising that little speech? All day is my bet, in front of the mirror. All your own work? Nah I doubt it, you were never much good at school. Parents' Day was an embarrassment. You only passed your exams because I found out the Headmaster had been fiddling with the boys at his previous school. Funny, he was so keen to help that he wanted to give you top marks, but I told him not to; no one would believe you could do anything other than just scrape through. It's all you've managed all your life."

Joe was impressed; Ted Baker was staring down the barrel, but he wasn't prepared to give up just yet. It was clear what he was trying to do. Joe laughed along with the older man, hoping to add to his son's chagrin.

419

"Shut up, shut up," Eddie shouted, pointing his gun again, this time at Joe. Interesting that his anger wasn't directed at his father, thought Joe; the shrinks could have a field day with this lad.

Ted carried on. "Why have you captured us? Why not just kill us? After all, if you showed my dead body to the men as they turn up in the trucks, they are hardly likely to make a fuss. They will throw their lot in with you. As it is, you are about to kill half of our men. You'll be weak, and every gang in London will know it. I'll give it 6 months before one of them tops you."

"Shut up."

"I know what he's up to." Joe intervened; he was addressing his comments to Ted, ignoring Eddie as though the gangster wasn't even there. "He wants the money that you have been investing. So, he is going to torture us, but he will wait until all the trucks are unloaded. He'll gather all 'his' men together and string us up in that abattoir you had built; he'll have them watch as he tortures and kills you. He thinks that will ensure the men's loyalty to him. You know, like a rite of passage, the king is dead, long live the king, that sort of thing. I don't think that he's thought about how few men he will have left. You sure he's your lad Ted? Wasn't a mix-up down the hospital, was there?"

Eddie was silent, but it was obvious he was struggling to control his temper. Joe was gambling on Eddie, waiting to kill him. Hoping that something might happen in the meantime, that he could somehow escape. He was eager to put the man off his guard, but it wouldn't be wise to push him too far. Whatever might have happened at that moment, fate intervened, as the sound of a Lorry was heard coming down the driveway.

The room was instantly noiseless; every individual was listening to the progress of the truck. The low squeal of brakes as the vehicle was met by the men, instructions mutely given, waved gestures indicating where to back up, friendly and good-humoured, crunched gears as reverse was found, engine growling and gearbox screeching the unmistakable scream of reverse, before the clicking of the handbrake ratchet and the dying of the engine, clicks of a door opening, a thud as a man jumps to the ground, the slam after him. Then, once again, silence.

Only Eddie stood at the window and watched across the farmyard. A macabre spectator of the hideous cabaret.

420

Joe counted off the seconds; he knew that if he didn't, it would seem like hours. He counted steadily, one thousand, two one thousand, three one thousand, trying desperately to emulate the perpetual pace of a ticking clock. He reached 34 when the first shot was heard. It was dull, distant, muffled by the wooden walls of the barn and the thick stone of the house, but nevertheless unmistakable, and jarring to the tense nerves of all present. Thirty-five one thousand, Thirty-six one thousand, Thirty-seven one thousand, shot number two. Softer this time, quieter, perhaps the muzzle pressed against the man, skull bone and brains mollifying the murderous blast.

Again, stillness engulfed the room. Everyone knew the implications of the sounds. They waited for news from the barns, but none came. The longer they waited, the less assured Eddie's smirk became. It's time to play more mind games, thought Joe.

"I wonder who shot who?" Joe asked to no one in particular.

Eddie took the bait. "Obviously, my men shot the driver. I have 10 men out there; if the driver had shot first, there would have been many more shots. One man less on your side, Daddy." He taunted.

This lad is not a full shilling, Joe thought to himself. He was treating the whole thing as if it was a game. What's more, he was swinging between being overconfident and having nagging doubts. Joe knew it was a tactic that had its risks, but he could see no other way than to gnaw away at Eddie's insecurities.

"Or maybe the shots were fired in the air, making you think that the driver has been shot. Maybe your lads bottled it. Maybe they've seen sense and switched sides. Maybe they are waiting for you to go out and check, and then they will blow you away."

"Shut up, Turner."

"I am not telling you your business, mate, but I would go and check if I were you."

113

Curiosity killed the cat - Wales

Terence O'Hare was tired. The loading of the animals, the tension of being in enemy territory and the dull pace of the driving were all having an effect on him. The old man in the passenger seat, Sean, was no help. He had dozed off almost as soon as they had joined the smoother roads. Terry fought his own fatigue and longed for the journey to end. The steering wheel was heavy; he pulled hard at it as they rounded yet another bend. Quickly, he was snapped out of his reverie when he spotted the body on the road. He braked hard and swung the truck hard to the left to avoid hitting it before he realised that it was just a coat. As they came to a stop, he saw the real body a little further ahead.

Sean had woken at the sudden change of direction and speed. "What the….?" He hadn't finished his sentence but just stared, open-mouthed, at the scene ahead.

A motorcycle lay on its side near the ditch at the edge of the road. The body of the rider lying just before it. An accident, no doubt, but Sean was suspicious. Terry reached for the door handle, but Sean grabbed his arm.

"No, son, drive on."

"We can't; someone is hurt, and it looks like a girl. We should help," Terry was adamant.

"You know our orders, no stopping. We should just drive on; what if it's a trap?"

"Away with ya, who's waiting out here to ambush us, a lass on a motorbike?"

"The bloody English bastards, that's who."

"Look, I will just see if she is dead or not; cover me with that shotgun of yours."

Without waiting for an answer Terry had jumped down from the cab and was marching towards the girl. As he neared, he slowed his pace and took in the scene, his hand clasped the revolver in his pocket.

It was a girl, her clothing was torn, ripped by the road as she had fallen from the bike. She wasn't moving, save her chest was rising and falling, her breathing heavy and ragged.

He crouched next to her. As he did, she groaned and stretched a little. The buttons on her overalls were all undone, and the dress she wore under them was torn. Her movement parted the clothing, and her right breast peaked through the rent in the fabric.

Terry, convinced that she was unconscious, edged closer to her. His right hand, still holding the gun, he used it to steady himself as he reached towards the girl. Carefully, using his left hand, he lifted the clothing, baring her breast. The girl didn't move, still breathing heavily as if in a deep sleep. Emboldened, Terry slid his hand under the cloth and touched the bare nipple.

"I usually insist that you wait until our second date before you get to do that, lad." As the voice whispered from the still unmoving girl, Terry felt something hard push against his groin, and he heard the unmistakable click of a revolver being cocked.

He looked cautiously down, confirming that a gun was pointed at him and in a most inconvenient place. He was off balance. His gun hand was on the ground, and any attempt to raise it to shoot would be a long and cumbersome affair compared to the speed and ease with which the girl could just squeeze the trigger and blow his manhood away.

"I see that you are rather attached to what I am aiming at. As it seems to be the thing that does all your thinking for you, you had better do as I say and avoid having it blown off." Rosie's voice was calm and still a whisper. "And just to be clear, when I say blown off, not in the way that you would like. Now, very slowly, you can move your hand."

"Now, are you sure now, miss? Only you seem to have been enjoying it."

"Don't flatter yourself, mate; it's bloody cold out here, that's all. Now you are going to put on a show for your mate over there. Slide your gun away and help me to my feet. Shout over to him to come and help. Only don't try anything, cause little as it probably is, I will shoot it clean off." Rosie's voice was full of menace.

"Hey, it's not little; it's big enough to fill a pram." Terry joked, trying to sound calm, but this girl meant business, and he knew it.

Terry slowly rose to his feet with Rosie holding onto his arm. All the while, the gun stayed firmly pressed against him. They started to shuffle towards the truck. "Call him," Rosie instructed.

"Hey, Patrick, would you give me a hand here please. The lassie is hurt, so she is."

Sean had watched nervously from the cab of the lorry. Now Terry was shouting at him, but why, oh why, was he calling him Patrick? He'd known the boy all his life. Suddenly, the penny dropped, so he had been right—it was a trap after all. He checked the shotgun and opened the door, keeping the gun down, out of sight of the girl.

Rosie and Terry saw the old man jump to the ground on the far side of the truck. As he came round the front of the engine, Terry took his chance and threw himself onto the ground, away from the girl. The shotgun came into view as the old man raised the cumbersome weapon to fire. Rosie reacted and took aim. As a race, it wasn't a fair one; it was like a greyhound against an old lumbering scent hound; there was little doubt who would get the hare. Before the barrel of the shotgun was a quarter of the way to being aimed, the first bullet had left Rosie's pistol. A second projectile followed an instant later. Sean, the old lumbering scent hound, never knew that he had lost. The first shell hit him mid-forehead, snapping back his head so that his throat received the second. What brains had been left intact by the impact of the first followed the second out of the back of his head. He was dead before his legs collapsed from under him.

Rosie spun round to where Terry was on the ground, reaching into his boot for his knife. "I wouldn't if I were you. Hands behind the back of your head."

"You killed Sean, you bitch, you shot him."

"I thought his name was Patrick. Yes, I shot him, and he hadn't been groping me, so you might want to be a little more civil. Now kick your boots off."

Terry stared at her dumbfounded.

"Boots off, now."

424

Terry complied, and the knife spilled to the ground as his right boot came off.

"On your feet."

Terry slowly stood.

"Now drop your pants."

"So, you do like me? I knew it."

"Sure, I like you enough to not want you running off or taking a kick out at me. So, pants down and leave them round your ankles."

Terry undid his belt. For a moment, he thought about pulling the belt quickly from the loops of his trousers and whipping it towards the girl. But his slight hesitation was accompanied by the clicking of the revolver as the girl cocked it to fire. He looked up at the girl, who was smiling at him with an expression that seemed to say, 'You really are dumb, aren't you?'

Bitch!

"Good, now turn round and walk to the back of the truck."

Terry shuffled along as best he could under the restraint of his trousers. Stones on the rough tarmac dug into his stocking feet but he thought better of complaining. The bitch didn't seem to be in a sympathetic mood. Slowly, he reached the back doors of the lorry.

"Open it."

There was no lock, just a bolt passed through an eye that held the door lever in place. Terry pulled on the heavy door and swung it open with all his strength. If he had been hoping that Rosie had been standing in the path of the door, he was disappointed. This lass seemed to confound him every time; she had read his mind and carefully stepped back away from the danger. As Terry looked up into the back of the van, a large boot appeared from nowhere and caught him square in his face. The impact knocked him backwards and onto the floor. The sound of his nose breaking was almost as loud as the earlier gunshots.

Above him, in the doorway of the lorry, stood the English spy, looking down at him.

"You're really not having a good day, now, are you?" opined Rosie, laughing as the Irishman tried to stem the blood rushing from his nose.

Simon looked towards the girl ready to take the fight to her.

"Easy sailor, I come in peace." Rosie moved around so that Simon could see her. "Major Wilbur sends his compliments."

Simon stared down aghast; it was the land girl. Rosie. So, she was one of the Major's people, after all. "How is Major Rider? How thoughtful of him to send such a lovely saviour for me." The exchange of two of the Major's Christian names, without mentioning his surname, confirmed to the operatives that they were on the same side.

"Well, actually, my orders were to save the animals. He said that you were big enough and ugly enough to look after yourself."

"Hmm. Sounds like the Major's level of compassion."

"Don't be too down on yourself. I think he just fancies a nice T Bone."

"Well, thank you anyway; it's much appreciated. But they have the girl, Sara, from the hotel. They are taking her to London."

"Yes, I know, we have that end covered, so I understand. Joe's down there."

"Yes, I a little birdie told me that he was involved. He will get the job done."

"Oh yes, Joe knows how to take care of a lady." Rosie's voice sounded whimsical, and Simon wondered if the two had worked together before, but this was no time for chit-chat.

"Well, thanks again; I had no real wish to travel to Ireland with these people."

"You might want to wait to look at your bike before you get too grateful."

"Why? What has happened to Sunflower?" Simon keenly asked.

"Sunflower, you call a machine like that Sunflower. Why? No, forget it, tell me another time. We have a job to do, and don't worry about Sunflower; I can make her like new in no time at all."

"Good. What's the plan?"

"Actually, I have been kind of winging it so far. But we need to catch up with the rest of the convoy." Rosie explained what had happened and what she knew about the conspirators and their scheme. As she did so, they bundled the injured Irish man into the passenger seat in the cab of the lorry, having tied his hands behind his back first.

"Can you drive?" Rosie was concerned by Simon's injuries.

"I am fine. I think I have a couple of broken ribs, but yes, I can drive the truck."

Rosie explained about the speeds and gaps of the lorries in the convoy. If Simon put his foot down, then they should be able to catch up with plenty of time before the next crossroads.

"You set off now. As soon as you see the truck ahead, back off to make sure they don't see you, and cruise at 30mph. I will deal with the body, don't want some poor farmer coming across that in the morning. I will follow on the bike. I will find a telephone box and ring the major, get fresh orders. I will catch you up."

"Do we know where they are headed?" asked Simon.

"No, we don't." Rosie turned to the unhappy Celt. "How did you know which way to go? You must have had a map, right?" she questioned her captive.

"Go to hell Bitch!"

Rosie grabbed the already broken nose of the man, twisting hard on the shattered gristle. Terry screamed and spat out more oaths along with the blood, which, unable to flow past Rosie's firm grip, was now pouring down the back of his throat.

"He won't tell you, his kind don't. Some sort of badge of honour thing." Simon advised as he tried to avoid the splashing blood. "Might as well kill him."

"You're right. What do you reckon the chances are of anyone coming along this road before dawn?"

"Pretty slim. Push his body into the trees, and it will be months before he is discovered. Bullet to the back of the head. Can I do it?" Simon looked enthusiastic at the prospect.

"No chance, he's mine. And no, I think kneecaps and elbows. He'll bleed out before anyone finds him. Painful and slow; Couldn't happen to a nicer guy."

The duo's act worked its magic. "No, wait, wait. Sean had the map. He was probably still holding it when you murdered him." Terry spluttered out his words in his desire to save himself.

It was good enough for Rosie. So, she punched him hard on the side of his jaw, knocking him unconscious. She ran over to the body and, sure enough, found a map stuffed into his coat pocket. She brought it to the light cast by the lorry's headlamp. It confirmed her theory of a small harbour mid-way up the west Welsh coast. She noted the name and memorised the simple route before giving it to Simon, along with the rebel's gun she had found in the road.

As Simon set off in pursuit of the convoy, Rosie dragged the old man's body into the trees; she would give the approximate position to the Major, who would no doubt send a party to clean up.

The bike was heavy, but her exercise on the farm and knowledge of the correct technique required allowed her to right it without too many problems. Some petrol had spilt out, but there was more than enough left in the tank for her purposes. Once again, she rode hard as she looked for a roadside red box. This mission had been so much fun, farming, pubs, beautiful countryside, motorbikes, torturing lecherous men, it just didn't get any better than this.

The next village supplied what she needed. She rang the usual number and gave out the number from the plate on the wall of the phone box. She hung up, waiting just 30 seconds before the receiver rang and the Major's dulcet tones echoed out down the line. The girls and Alwyn had got hold of Pritchard-Smythe, so the Major had been alerted.

Rosie gave her report of what she had seen. Robison was patched in on the call, and the 3 spies discussed tactics. A plan was hatched. Rosie set off once again in pursuit of the convoy. She couldn't be too far behind.

A few minutes later, Rosie caught up to and passed Simon in the truck. Stopping a little further on, she hid the bike in some bushes beside the road and flagged down Simon in the lorry. As she opened the door of the cab, she motioned to their captive, who had awoken from his imposed nap, to step down from the lorry. When he was a little slow to do so, she held back her fist, ready to punch once more. The Irishman suddenly moved with surprising dexterity.

"He's not much use to us now that we have the map, plus he smells. It's time to say goodbye, I think." As she spoke, Rosie pulled out her pistol and started checking it.

"No, please, please......" Terry had no doubt that the girl was capable of putting a bullet in the back of his head. But He realised that his pleas were pointless. So, he cut short his outburst and tried to maintain his dignity.

"Better save him for the Major; he will want to 'question' him later," Simon interjected. With the emphasis that the Englishman had put on the word 'question', Terry began to wonder if the quick action of the single bullet was still an option. The Irishman's life temporarily lengthened he was treated to the hospitality of riding in the back with the cattle, much to Simon's satisfaction. He wondered if his former captor was familiar with the concept of Karma.

"Would you really have killed him?" Enquired Simon as he tended to his own wounds, Rosie now driving the cumbersome vehicle along at what seemed to be impossible speeds.

"Ask his mate Sean, or was it Patrick" Replied the seemingly disinterested Northerner.

A short while later, they saw the lorry ahead in the distance. Cutting their speed, they settled into a long and uneventful journey.

114

Bapt and Mischa see the lorry arrive. – Slough Farm

The arrival of Ted and his party, followed sometime after by the first truck, was witnessed by Baptiste, Mischa and his men. Things happened much as was expected, the only surprise was the girl who accompanied Ted. Who was she? Her presence in the kitchen might complicate things. However, she seemed to be his prisoner, so she was not someone who would be likely to interfere in Baptiste's plan, but she was another person in the firing line, a potential casualty. The shots in the farmhouse were clear and loud at the short distance of their observation post. Probably, Ted's bodyguards were being dispatched, but they would find out soon enough.

Baptiste was able to see the man jump down from the truck and be marched at gunpoint into the barn. Without thick stone walls to surround them, the sound of the gunshots from the barn was louder to the men outside. They were able to hear raised voices just before the first shot, though they couldn't make out what was said. They could only imagine a man begging for his life or cursing at his executioner.

Shortly after, a man left the kitchen and ran over to the barn. He emerged just a few seconds later, followed by a colleague. They walked quickly over to the house, but at the last moment, the first man exchanged some words with his comrade and diverted his course towards the outhouse. He opened and closed the lavatory door but didn't enter. Instead, he stealthily slid around the back of the building before jogging across the grass to the cover of the trees. Baptiste met Billy 'the brick' Mason and led him, as before, deeper under the cover of the woods.

"Billy, this is a friend; he is here to help," Baptiste explained as Billy started at the sight of the stranger. "Who is in the room?"

"Ted is sat at this end of the table, Ted's bodyguards were killed by Jimmy and Arthur, they went over to the barn. I think they are the ones that killed the driver of the lorry." Billy was panting loudly; he was having difficulty catching his breath. Bapt doubted that it was due to the jog across the grass; Billy kept in good training. He was obviously upset by the violence and the momentous events that he was witnessing. Bapt let him be for a moment; although time was tight, the last thing he needed was for Billy to lose his nerve.

"It's alright, mate, take your time." The Frenchman soothed.

"There's a young girl, came in with Ted. She is crying all the time; she looks like she is in shock or something. I don't know who she is."

"Where is she sitting?"

"At the far end of the table, near Eddie. Eddie is just pacing up and down all the time by the fire. I think Joe is trying to wind him up. Ed is close to losing his rag, I can tell you."

"You and Phil are in the same places?"

"Yes."

"So, who is it that has just gone into the kitchen?"

"That was Arthur. I was told to go and get him. You see Joe was winding Eddie up, told him that he reckoned that the boys weren't killing the truck drivers, that they had jumped ship, and they were on Ted's side all along. You know what Eddie is like, he don't trust no one. He told me to tell Arthur and Jimmy that they had to cut a right ear off each of the men when they had killed them and to bring it over to the kitchen. You know to prove they is dead and that. I can tell you Arthur wasn't happy. He's worried that the next truck might turn up early."

"Alright Billy this is what you must do."

115

Oh, I do like to be beside the seaside - Wales

Simon had been following their progress, marking off the villages as they passed them by. When they arrived at a T junction and turned left as per the arrows drawn on the map, the pair began to discuss their options. Rosie told Simon about the Major's orders. "He is arranging a detachment of troops to be ready to stop the ship leaving. However, they could do without a battle taking place in some sleepy Welsh port. So, we are to try and secure the vessel and cargo, by quieter means. Then call in for further instructions. The army will seal off the town. Stop anybody going in or coming out, once they are sure that all the trucks have arrived. They think that the loading will take some time. So, we have a bit of leeway."

"What about this truck? They will be looking out for it. How many men do they have."

"15 trucks; I don't think that everyone had 2 men. Maybe 15 to 20 men."

Together, they hatched a plan, after which they were silent, perhaps because each of them knew it was far from perfect and so much could go wrong.

Rosie and Simon arrived at the seaside village more or less on time. As they approached, Simon having taken the driver's seat, they saw the other trucks lined up along the quayside, each waiting their turn for loading onto the cargo ship docked in the harbour. As they expected, 2 men were waiting for them as they joined the harbour road, and they signalled for them to join the queue. The guards barely looked towards the lorry, so Simon and Rosie's disguises were not tested. They looked at each other, relieved as their truck parked in its allotted place. For Rosie, it was time for yet another costume change. She removed the heavy overcoat and an old tatty trilby that was left on the seat, presumably Sean's. She was now just down to her dress. She managed to repair the front fastenings by use of her hair clips, which she had removed so that her hair fell freely around her shoulders. However, she still left as much of her cleavage on show as she dared. A last-minute tucking up of the skirt allowed her to show off her legs, always her best feature, if she said so herself. Now, what to do about her shoes? She wanted maximum effect and wished that she had worn her higher heels, but still, she would have to make do.

"How do I look?"

Simon appraised her thoughtfully. "A little tarty for my tastes, but I suppose that's the look you are going for." He smiled.

"Oh yes, I forgot, you go for the girl next door, innocent country barmaid look. How's a girl supposed to compete with that? And after all we have been through together."

Without waiting for a witty retort, which was just as well as Simon was struggling to come up with anything, Rosie climbed down from the cab, careful to keep out of sight of the guards. They had stayed in position; she wondered why, as all the trucks were here now. It then dawned on her that they were lookouts for any unwanted, if unlikely at this hour, visitors. She slipped behind some old crates that lined the road and made her way back towards the sentinels' unseen. When she had passed them, she stepped out into the road and strode towards them. Rosie walked on her tiptoes, mimicking the effect that high heels would have on her legs. In the dim light, she hoped that the men wouldn't notice. She was sure that they would be looking further up her legs. She swayed along, the gait of a girl who had been in the pub all evening and had come to the docks looking for business. As she neared the men, she could tell that she had their full attention. The ruse was being accepted. They obviously had spent enough time in seafront places such as this for them to accept that a lady of her profession might be part of the scenery.

"Hello, boys, don't suppose you could spare a lady a fag, could you?"

The boys, flustered by this unexpected potential pleasure, hurried to supply her needs. As they clambered to find their cigarettes in their pockets, they simply didn't know what hit them. Rosie chopped the edge of her right hand into the throat of the man standing on her right. It was a brutal blow, a favourite of her trainer at the Spa. She knew she had caused a lot of damage. The man's instinct was to clutch at it as he tried to breathe through his broken windpipe, with limited success. Before his comrade had taken in his distress, he had his own problems, as Rosie's right foot dealt a disabling blow to his groin. With both men subdued, it suddenly occurred to her that she wasn't sure whether she should kill them or not. Would the Major want to question them? Simon arrived, having slipped away from the truck on the far side, creeping towards the scene of the skirmish in case he was needed.

"What did they say to upset you?"

"They didn't have the right money," Rosie explained without emotion. "Do you think we should kill them?" She Asked coldly, in a manner that someone might ask if you want sugar in your tea.

The man with the aching testicles must have heard and made to rise; he had been kneeling, clutching at his pride and joys. Simon's turn to use the Spa's favourite weapon. He chopped the man on the back of his neck, rendering him unconscious.

"On the basis that it is easier to tie them up now, in case they are needed, and kill them later, if they are not, than it would be to do it the other way round. I suggest a stay of execution." Simon spoke like he was conducting some sort of scientific analysis.

"Ohh, you don't 'alf talk nice," Rosie said adopting the accent and pose of a street girl, which fitted well with her attire.

The other guard was still clutching his throat, gasping loudly; he was beginning to panic. Rosie knocked him out, his distress quelled, and his breathing became more relaxed. With the two gentlemen tied up and hidden behind the crates, the duo hatched their next moves. Starting at the back of the queue, they positioned themselves on either side of each truck. Then, stealthily working themselves along the sides of each one, they flung open the doors in unison, holding their handguns out, ready to subdue the occupants of the vehicle. In each case, they found the cabs empty. When they neared the front of the queue, they could see that the men had been required to load the livestock onto the ship. As they watched, they realised that stealth was no longer an option. All the enemy were involved in loading; as such, they were all relatively close together. Little chance that they could be picked off quietly, one or two at a time.

"We better go and see if the cavalry has arrived." Suggested Simon. Nodding, Rosie led the way as they slunk back into the shadows and made their way towards the main road. As they walked, they chatted for the first time in what would become a long and adventurous friendship. They discussed the Spa and the Major. Compared acquaintances. Admitted difficulties and shared specialities.

"I told the Major that they were on to you, did you know?" Rosie asked the question that had been playing on her mind for a while.

"Yes, Calderdale suggested that I should leave Trefynydd." Replied Simon. Rosie knew that Robinson and the Major didn't deal in suggestions; they gave orders.

"So why didn't you? You must have known it was dangerous; did you know about the Irish and the London gang?"

"I had a hunch. I was sure that Henry Marshall was not what he said he was. I also thought that he might be Irish. Something about his grammar, his connections to horse racing and one or two things he let slip. As for the London side of things, Robinson told me early on that Joe Turner was working on the case. He led me to suppose that there was an organised crime gang involved. As for leaving, I figured that the info about them knowing I was spying on them must have come from another operative they had in place. I thought it might be you. You're bloody good, by the way. I wasn't sure it was you until I saw you from the back of that van earlier. By the way, thanks for saving me." Simon smiled sincerely at the young woman, whom he was beginning to respect very deeply. Rosie returned his smile but said nothing as she waited for his answer. Reluctantly, not wanting to in any way highlight his own bravery, Simon carried on. "If I had left, then it would have looked odd. They would have had their suspicions. Eventually, they would have concluded that I had been tipped off. Then they would be looking out for the informant, that may have led them to you. I figured that they wouldn't move against me until they were ready to ship the goods, so I was safe until then."

It was Rosie's turn to nod her thanks. Simon was right. He had left himself in harm's way to protect a fellow operative. One that he didn't even know. He had risked his life for her and for the mission. This was a man she could work with, a man she could trust.

116

Crunch time – Slough Farm

As Billy and Baptiste started their walk across the grass towards the kitchen, they were just in time to see Arthur running back to the barn to get ready for the next truck. Billy knocked on the kitchen door in the prearranged way and pushed open the door. He pushed Baptiste into the room, holding his gun to the side of his head.

"Bapt, what the fuck are you doing here? I told you to stay at the Brothel." Eddie was angry; things weren't running as smoothly as he had wanted.

Baptiste made to answer, but Billy clipped him on his head with his gun. "I caught him snooping around, Boss," Billy said confidently.

"He was doing what?"

"You see, Boss, I was just off to the Khazi when I saw something moving in the trees. I went to have a look, and I clocked someone scarpering. So, I chased after them and low and behold, it's only Bapt. I grabbed him, but he slipped away and tried to leg it, so I let him 'ave a right." Baptiste's left eye was beginning to show the bruising that gave credence to the story. "I heard you tell Bapt to stay at the House an' why did he run away? I searched him, and he had this gun." Billy held up a pistol for Eddie to see. "I thought it was a bit dodgy, so I brought him in for you."

"Good thinking, Bill, well done, son. I will deal with him later. Sit him down."

"But Boss, I was just coming to help out." Bapt's deliberately lame excuse for his presence at the farm only further angered Eddie. For a moment, Bapt thought he was going to be shot there and then. Only for the next truck to arrive and divert the crazed gangster's attention.

Billy pushed Baptiste down onto a chair next to Ted and directly opposite Sue. "I'll tie him up, boss, just in case." He

437

volunteered but Eddie was too engrossed in the events of the yard, so Billy carried on. He pulled the Frenchman's arms behind the chair and got to work with a rope. With the deliberate placement of the new prisoner, neither Phil nor Eddie could see his hands from where they were stationed. Billy tied Bapt's hands loosely, although he made a grunt as he pulled hard on the knot; it was all for the show as Billy had tied a bow, slipping the end of the rope into the captive's hand.

Sue Cartwright was thinking along similar lines. With 2 of the captors busy looking out into the yard and the one called Billy busy tying up Baptiste, she reached to her left and slipped the paperclip into Joe's right hand. Then she shifted her chair back slightly so that when the guard in the corner returned to his duties, he would not be able to see Joe's hands. All Joe had to concentrate on was waiting for Eddie to be distracted or on one of his marches across the end of the room.

Joe looked across at Baptiste, who was staring at him. Bapt checked that the guards were still looking away and chanced a wink at Joe. Joe nodded. Batiste lifted his head backwards as if pointing towards Billy behind him. Joe lifted his eyebrows questioningly; Bapt nodded and winked again.

'So' Thought Joe. 'Batiste has a plan, and Billy is on our side. What could possibly go wrong? I just need to remember what they taught me at the Spa about how to open these bloody handcuffs.'

Joe kept up his slow and deliberate wind-up of Eddie Baker. However, it became harder and harder to stay positive and confident as after the arrival of each truck and the following gunshots from the barn, Arthur would run across the yard bringing the trophies as he had been instructed. As the night wore on, the row of bloody right ears became a gruesome sight across the kitchen table. They marked the time and the progress of the transfer of power from father to son. They counted down to the moment when Eddie Baker would start his inquisition of the prisoners around the table. Joe shuddered at the thought. He was a brave man, but he knew the methods Eddie would use would get him what he wanted. He also knew that once he had that information, he wouldn't stop. He enjoyed it too much. Joe thought that the worst part would be watching Sue being brutalised. As if reading his thoughts and sensing a weakening of Joe's banter, Eddie Baker started on a wicked and barbarous diatribe to his captive audience.

"I expect you are wondering what is in store for you all when the last truck arrives and is unloaded. Not long now, just 5 more trucks, 5 more ears and the collection will be complete. Then it will be time for you to tell me where all the money is, Father. I expect you will be reluctant, but you know the methods I will use; after all, you taught them to me. Although I have a few new ones of my own, which I think you will appreciate. I think that you will be 'questioned' together. Stripped bare first, the indignity and feeling of being defenceless is a massive psychological blow against any prisoner, so I am told. Especially for you, Miss Hereford, I think that it has been some time since a man saw you naked, if ever. Imagine all my men looking on. How will that feel? Perhaps I will let them have some fun with you; they're such a horny lot. I might even have you first; I bet you're not too bad underneath those frumpy clothes. And what will you be thinking, Joe Turner, when you watch me raping her? Will you be thinking about me with your lovely Amber?"

Joe pulled against his restraints. His face was red with anger.

"Arh, you don't seem surprised by that, angry but not surprised; someone has told you, I see. Was it our friend here, Baptiste? Yes, I think it was; you two have been thick as thieves recently. Is that why you are here tonight, Bapt? To rescue your friend, and how is that going?" Eddie laughed demonically. "I would imagine that you told him gently, broke the news with care and compassion; perhaps you lied to him and told him that she died quickly, with no pain and no disgrace. Yes, you will have done that to ease the pain of your friend. But we both know the truth, how she begged for her life. Oh, the things she was prepared to do to save her own neck. She seemed to be enjoying it too. Such an enthusiastic young lady. Shame about her demise, a tragic accident, really. Anyway, back to the present. You see, my kind father here has built the ideal place for us to chat. It has these big hooks and winches and all sorts of ropes and things. There are lots of very sharp knives and choppers and all sorts. It's supposed to be for the animals, but they won't mind if you have a go first. My boys will hang you upside down in a nice

439

little circle; that way, you can watch what I am about to do to you. Helps with the anticipation. Of course, if you are first, then it's a nice surprise."

The noise of the next truck entering the yard distracted Eddie, driver number 11, who was on his way to his demise.

Joe looked at Baptiste, wondering what he had in mind and when he would make his move. Baptiste shook his head. ' No, that's not what happened,' he seemed to be saying. Then he nodded his head slowly and blinked deliberately and calmly, 'Patience, all is in hand.'

Then it struck Joe that Bapt was waiting for the last truck. He didn't know what would happen then, but he had to be ready when it did. With renewed vigour, he worked away at the lock of the handcuffs with the paperclip. Sue Cartwright could see from the corner of her eye Joe's endeavours and was concerned at what would happen when he was successful. She had also seen the discreet gestures Baptiste had made towards Joe. She reached forward with her right hand and started to drum her fingers on the oak tabletop like a frustrated client impatiently waiting for a shop assistant to parcel up her order. Her nails were sharp and harsh against the wood. When the lock suddenly gave way, to Joe's imagination, the click was as loud as any of the gunshots that had rung out that night, but Sue's ruse seemed to have worked. She carried on her agitated gesture for a few seconds more before folding her arms and making her own nod towards the Frenchman, 'We're ready when you are.'

117

The Marines - Wales

In the distance, along the main road, Rosie and Simon spotted a roadblock. It hadn't been there when they had driven along the road not long before. The cavalry!

They walked in the middle of the road, holding their hands out where they could be seen. When they were challenged, they shouted in turn. "Major Wilbur, Major Rider."

A minute later, they were meeting with a Marine Captain. "Matthew Brown, very pleased to meet you. I understand that you need a little help. Only too happy to oblige."

The captain was young for his rank. But everything about him told of someone who had not risen through the ranks purely by accident of birth. His accent, Simon thought midlands, probably Nottinghamshire, was earthy, suggestive of humble origins. His eyes were bright and intelligent whilst steely and determined. He was handsome, thought Rosie, 'now he might get his hands inside my dress on the first date,' she mused guiltily to herself.

"You're a commando unit?" Suggested Simon as they shook hands, surprised. "Funny to find you in a backwater like isn't it?"

"Yes, we were posted to a town 20 miles in land of here a couple of weeks ago, just told to stay alert and that we might be needed."

"Robinson and the Major guessed that they would ship from somewhere along this coast." Suggested Simon.

"I got a call earlier. My orders were to allow the convoy in and then secure the area. We got here before those chaps arrived. They came in at minute intervals, the last one was a little late, I assume that it was your good selves, but once there were no more for 10 minutes, we closed in. We evacuated the village. Told the villagers that a mine had drifted into the harbour. They have been moved to a village 15 miles away. So, if there is any gunfire, it probably won't be heard. By the way, the harbour master wasn't at home, so it's likely he is in on this."

"How many men do you have, Captain?" Asked Rosie.

"10 men, my NCO and me. I have access to some more if required. There appear to be 19 enemy combatants as far as we were able to count off as they arrived. That includes a man who met them as they arrived. Possibly, that was the harbour master. Then, of course, there is the ship's crew. If the men that we have seen came over with the ship, as we suspect, then they would make up most of the ship's company. However, it is likely that the ship's master, the engineer and a couple of crew, possibly juniors, stayed back to prepare for sailing. So, I would hazard a guess that we are up against 25 men who are likely to fight.

Rosie looked around at the men on the sentry. They were fit and alert, constantly checking the road in both directions. She surmised that 12 marines would be overkill.

"Good, we are to secure the boat, all their men; it is vital that nobody gets away. Then check in for orders."

"Yes, pretty much my orders." Agreed, the Marine.

The captain gave Rosie and Simon the layout of the town. All-access to the harbour had been secured, including the footpath that led down from the cliffs. A plan was hatched between the new comrades. Captain Brown was impressed that the two spies both insisted on playing their parts. Brown's men worked their way down the road towards the ship; by keeping near to the shadows, they managed to get close without alarm. Rosie and Simon followed directly behind. In position, they watched the loading. As one vehicle was completed, it was driven away by one man to the back end of the queue. Another came to fetch the next from the front. The vehicle was driven forward to the ship for its passengers to be shepherded off the truck directly onto the ramp into the ship. Men on the ship kept the animals moving, herding them into the hold.

Three of the captain's men were dispatched off to the beach carrying a rubber-inflated boat. They were to silently row to the end of the quay and move in and onto the ship at the arranged time.

Three more were to come down the path from the cliff and attack the vessel from that direction.

Two men were to stay back, securing the entry road to the harbour and rounding up any of the enemy if they tried to get away.

That left 2 men, the NCO, Captain Brown, Rosie and Simon, to make the main assault on the gang. The six of them made their way to the lead truck and waited in ambush for the unlucky soul who came across to collect it for unloading. Having silently overpowered the man, one of the marines jumped in up front, and the rest climbed up into the back. Without hesitation, which might have raised suspicion, the driver swiftly manoeuvred the vehicle into position. As the unwitting dockers lowered the tailgate, the invaders jumped swiftly into action. Subduing 6 more of the enemy.

No noise, no casualties, although the surprised men might contest that, pointing to their sore heads, bruised chins and one broken arm. Although, with hindsight, they would probably count themselves lucky given the obvious abilities of their attackers to inflict harm.

Captain Brown looked to the bow of the ship. There, as expected, he saw one of his men signalling toward him. The marine holding up his hand with 4 fingers raised. A comrade, holding 5 fingers aloft, stood at the stern. 16 men down.

Rosie and Simon had ushered out several of the cattle from the truck and were herding them towards the ramp onto the ship, 2 abreast. One of the marines quickly followed by Simon and then Rosie, jammed themselves in between the reluctant beasts as they slowly worked their way onto the ship. As they arrived on deck, the marine jumped out from the camouflage of the animals and struck out at one of the loaders. It was a vicious punch that would have rendered any ordinary man insensible, but this was no ordinary man. Firstly, he was well over six feet tall, probably nearer seven, thought Simon as he watched the contest from the safety of his vantage point in the herd.

The marine's punch had no doubt been aimed at the man's chin, but surprised by his height and hampered by his own diminutive stature, he had barely reached the middle of his chest with the blow. Which had bounced off with little or no effect on its victim. The heavily bearded giant grabbed his attacker and threw him to the floor. Simon was reminded of his dust up with

Alwyn and was minded to lend a hand but thought better of it as he had his own battles to win. He and Rosie set about two more of the enemy with relative ease. They were joined by the others as well as two more men, one from each of the parties' bow and stern. The remaining loaders were overpowered with reasonable ease, save the gargantuan defender, who was still locked in combat with the marine.

Simon made to assist the smaller man, but the captain grabbed his arm and held him back. "He'll not thank you." Advised the man's commander. His comrades stood and watched, making no attempt to intervene. Bets were whispered between the men, which seemed to be based on how long the contest would last rather than who would win.

The marine had suffered several blows from the giant. Each of which would have halted a lesser man. But the persistence of the titan and his failure to be bowed by the stinging blows from the armoury of the professional had only succeeded in increasing the determination of the bantamweight. But at last, the bigger man was tiring. The decisive blow came when he failed to dodge a savage kick, which caught him full on his kneecap. In his hampered state, no longer able to move freely away from his assailant's blows, he was easy pickings. A swinging left hook finished the contest and sent the colossus sprawled onto the deck of the ship.

Twenty-one men were taken, and not a bullet was fired; Simon was rightly impressed. Just as the thought occurred to him, he felt the wake of a bullet pass by his ear. The shot struck the shoulder of the victorious Marine, who was still dusting himself down. As more projectiles followed, the peace and quiet of the night was a thing of the past.

The party of boarders all flung themselves for cover, save two men who bravely grabbed their wounded colleague and dragged him to safety. The others drew their weapons, but none returned fire, reluctant to give away their positions by doing so. Whispered communications were issued as the men fed back information as to the whereabouts of the shooter. The fire was coming from the bridge of the ship. A structure that was one storey from the deck, a mere 50 feet to the stern of their position.

Simon, being careful not to let the marksman have a second chance of blowing his head off, moved forward until he was next to the Marine captain.

"There can't be more than a few of them left," Simon whispered in Brown's ear. "The ship's captain, the harbour master, a man called Marshall, civilian, who I would say wouldn't be up for a shootout and Fergus McDowell, the leader of these men. Unfortunately, he would be the sort of romantic who would see himself as a hero going down in a blaze of English bullets. Of course, there may be others."

"Do you want to see if you can talk them down? Seems to me that we could take their position quite easily but not without casualties. Major Calderdale seemed anxious to avoid that, and we don't want to upset the Major now, do we?"

Simon was inclined to agree. Having made sure that he was out of sight, he began his discourse.

"Marshall. McDowell." Simon shouted; instantly, a bullet ricocheted off the metal bulkhead that he was crouched behind. "Come on, Fergus, give it up." Another shot pinged off the metal. "We have all your men. They are all safe." Simon thought it best not to mention the unfortunate demise of Sean, lying in a ditch in mid-Wales somewhere.

"Go to hell, you English bastards." Shouted McDowell, punctuating his words with random shots.

"We have orders to stop this ship from leaving. We also have orders for as few casualties as possible. If you give yourself up, I promise you and your men will not be harmed."

"Sure, and we all know we can trust the English now, don't we." Two more shots rang out before the gun clicked on empty. Fergus McDowell reloaded as quickly as his shaking hands would let him.

As he did so, Henry Marshall pleaded with him. "Come on, man, give it up. We don't stand a chance."

"Shut it. I will not let no English man get the better of me." Shouted the irate gunman as he let off two more rounds from the reloaded gun out through the open bridge window.

"Don't be a fool. Did you see those boys down there? They are professionals. They took your men without firing a shot. Not one single shot. You are outnumbered. Surrender before you get us all killed." Henry Marshall, who was crouched down at the back of the bridge, his arm around the sobbing Myfanwy, implored the crazed rebel.

"I told you to shut up, or there will be a bullet for you." Fergus waved the pistol at the couple, who cowered back into the corner of the room. "Surely you don't trust these bastards; they'll hang you for sure; you might as well die here, fighting."

"They said they won't harm us; you heard him say so." Myfanwy sobbed.

"She's right, Fergus. Why do you think that they didn't come in here, all guns blazing? My guess is that they won't want this getting out. They won't want trials. They won't want newspaper reports about the IRA stealing food from ordinary British people." Marshall said thoughtfully, as he spoke, he was beginning to see that there might be a way out of this for him.

"Yes, I can see your game. You'll be quite happy to turn traitor. Anything to save your neck from being stretched. Now shut it, or the next bullet is for your Welsh tart."

On the deck, the raiders could hear the raised voices but could not make out exactly what was being said. Captain Brown spoke to Simon and Rosie.

"There is only one shooter, and judging by the way there was a pause in his fire, I would say he has just one gun. We can test that by getting him to fire 4 more shots, we will see then if there is another pause. Keep him talking and distracted. Wind him up if you can. I am going to get a couple of my boys to work along either side of the deck and behind the bridge. They can climb the steps and be ready at the doors. When we count off the 6th shot, they will go in."

Simon resumed his negotiations. "Fergus, there is no way out for you. As things stand, you have committed only minor crimes, but if you shoot one of these men, then it's the gallows for you."

Four more shots rang out into the night. Simon kept up his dialogue, determined to test out Brown's theory. Standing up, he held out his hands and beseeched the man. "Fergus, you can trust us. Throw out your gun, and I promise you will be safe." Simon was shouting slowly, drawing out his words. He could just about make out the shadowy figure of Fergus McDowell through the open window. He seemed to be fiddling with something but there was no gun and no shots, at least for now.

"Go to Hell, you English bastard." Simon fell to the floor as a gun accompanied the words coming through the open window. He was just in time as 2 more shots whizzed over him.

Meanwhile, Brown had wasted no time; two of his best men had been briefed and were already at the foot of the Bridge steps. Their comrades opened fire from several directions, each carefully aiming to miss their target and any of the bridge's inhabitants. The covering fire ceased, and the enraged McDowell responded indiscriminately until, once again, his pistol clicked empty.

Under the cover of the noise, the two assailants had mounted the stairs. In time to hear the empty clanks as the hammer of the pistol fell on the vacant chambers, they arrived at the doors, which, without hesitation, were crashed in under their heavy boots. Before the luckless Celt could respond, he was overpowered and pinned to the floor.

Simon, Rosie and Matthew Brown arrived seconds later. The occupants of the bridge were all lined up against the rear bulkhead under the calm supervision of the two Marines.

"Time to place a call to the Major."

118

The Last Truck – The woods behind Slough Farmhouse.

Mischa, like everyone else at Slough farm that night, had been counting off the lorries as they arrived. When the fourteenth had driven into the farmyard, his men jumped into action. There was no need for him to say anything to them at that point. Instructions had been given earlier and every one of them was in their correct place. They would all carry out their role without question; he would bet his life on that. In the battles to come across Europe, that would be exactly what he would do.

A detachment of his men had congregated at the side of the road just as it turned off from the Great West Road towards the farm. They had been concealed in the trees, but as soon as the fourteenth vehicle had passed, two of the men went with torches and waited in the middle of the track. The rest lingered in the trees, alert, watchful, tense, ready to strike.

They didn't have to wait too long; the last vehicle was early. The driver was perhaps a little too eager, his foot just a little too fervent on the accelerator. As he turned into the country road, he slowed to a crawl, anticipating the potholes and ruts that would surely be waiting there. He was thinking about the beasts in his van; it had been a long journey for them, and they would be tired and thirsty, and the last thing they needed was to be thrown around if he drove too fast. Consequently, he was able to stop easily when a man stepped in front of his truck and waved a torch in his eyes. The engine's noise died to a low rumble, a relief after the unceasing reverberation of his constant speed along the highway. He heard a voice shout an instruction, but he couldn't make it out. His eyes were blinded by the glare of the torch. He had his hand on the door handle, ready to jump down and find out what the problem was when the door was wrenched open. A strong hand grabbed his jacket, and he was pulled from the cab. He landed in a heap; before he could object to his treatment, a hand clamped itself onto the top of his forehead, fingers dug agonisingly into his eyes, and his head was jerked back, a blade flashed before him, blood spewed from his throat and pooled into one of the potholes he had been so anxious to avoid.

His body was dragged to the roadside and laid, with a degree of respect, amongst the trees. His height was assessed, and the most suitable double was chosen. Wearing the dead man's jacket and hat, the Russian, two colleagues crouched down in the passenger's foot well, with the rest of his comrades packed into the back with the animals, drove on towards the farm. He drove in as he had watched the others do, swung his lorry in a wide arc across the yard and backed up to the doors of the barn as had the others.

It was Arthur's turn to kill the driver. He and Jimmy had taken it in turn; the fact that he had won the toss and got to go first, along with there being an odd number of trucks, meant that he got the last one, one more than Jimmy. Jimmy had backed him up by taking his position at the passenger side, ready if there were two men. This had happened on three occasions. Arthur marched forward to the driver's door and swung it open as he had done before, seven times before. Each time, it had been easy. The driver had not been expecting any trouble; he had thrust his gun into the man's face and ordered him to get down from the cab, hands where they could be seen. He had stepped back as the man complied before jumping forward as soon as he was on the ground and spinning him around to face the truck. After a quick search, some of them were armed, and most had knives. Then he marched them into the barn. At the far end was the animal slaughter area. Fresh, newly laid concrete, with a steel drain in the centre, designed to easily wash away animal blood, just as efficient for humans. The first one had been different from the others; the victim had no idea of what was coming, Arthur had shot him in the back, and he'd fallen forward exactly in the centre, over the drain. His second shot, just to make sure, saw his brains blasted over the new floor. The ones after that were more exciting. As the men approached, they would spot the blood, then see the bodies; as they had piled up, no attempt had been made to hide them, and then they would panic. Some begged, some cursed, and some made a futile attempt to rush him. All met the same fate.

Number eight for him, plus the two passengers he had earlier dispatched, this would be his tenth kill of the night. He would be a legend in the gang. Revered, feared, respected. This time, things were a little different. As the door opened, the driver held up his hands, good as gold. But only to make space for his comrade, who was crouched in the footwell, to rest his arm across the driver's lap, then fire off three shots, quickly one after the other. Not that Arthur saw it, but Jimmy was coming in for similar treatment. Three shots in quick succession were fired by the third man in the packed cab. All six shots hit home; they were fired almost instantaneously, and the noise was immense.

As the first shots were fired, the back doors flew open, and the Russians fired at the men waiting to unload the animals. Four more of Eddie Baker's gang were killed before they could get a single shot off. Six men were killed in the opening salvo. They were the first of the battle of Slough farm.

Across the yard, from the trees behind the outhouse, Mischa's men opened fire on the farmhouse.

119

The interrogations. - Wales - 1941

The main body of prisoners was being held under the guard of the Marines in the hold of the ship. The principal characters were imprisoned in the Village Hall, from where they were to be brought in turn to a room in the Post Office, where they were to be questioned. It was also from the Post Office that a call was made—it was a long call—to the Major and Robinson. Each of the party was given their own special instructions in turn.

Rosie was up first; her instructions were issued quite quickly. Her job was in the engine room and hold of the ship. After which, she was to help with the interrogation of the prisoners.

During her call, Pritchard-Smyth arrived with a detachment of his men. On the way, they had collected the body of Sean, the night's only casualty, and the slightly damaged but magnificent body of the Vincent V Twin. Smythe had already received his orders from Robinson, and his men had made a number of arrests in Trefynydd. He and his men were now to assist Captain Brown, after which they would return to Trefynydd to tidy things up.

Captain Brown was charged with reloading the animals, petrol, weapons, and ammunition discovered in the hold back onto the lorries. More of his men were on their way to drive the consignment to London.

Simon's instructions were long and detailed. He was to interrogate the prisoners.

Simon spoke to each of the prisoners in turn. First up was Henry Marshall.

"What's your real name, Marshall?" demanded Simon.

"Well, now, I have been Henry Marshall for a long time. I have had several *nom de plumes* in my time. Really somewhat of an interesting story. I am sure your bosses would like to hear it, but I suspect that we don't have time now."

"We will get to the truth; it would be better for you to cooperate." Simon tried to sound as threatening as he could.

"Oh, you misunderstand me. I have no desire to hide anything from you. I appreciate that I am on a sticky wicket, as you English would say. I am perfectly happy to help. Indeed, I think you will find that I can be of great help to you and your masters. You see I don't have any loyalties to this lot. And I have a great deal of information and contacts that you could put to very good use for your war effort."

Simon's dislike of the man, the mistrust that he had felt since they first met, was never stronger than at that moment. He was a mercenary. A soldier of fortune who would sell to the highest bidder without guilt or conscience. But what he said stirred an interest in Simon; he had a feeling that he could be used.

"All right, as you say, we don't have too much time. Tell me how you became involved in all this. And if you are not English, Irish, I suppose!"

"Actually, I was a child of the Empire, like yourself. Only I was born to a Portuguese father and a Chinese/English mother in Singapore. My father worked for the British embassy out there. Unfortunately, I was orphaned young and brought up in a Catholic monastery by Nuns. Irish, ladies mostly, hence my propensity to slip into a grammar that would suggest that I hail from the Emerald Isle. That and the fact I have spent quite a bit of time in that fair country. I have fended for myself ever since leaving Singapore on a freight steamer, working my passage when I was just 14. I landed in Ireland, was a jockey for a while. Made money on the track, lost even more money on the track. Made more money again smuggling guns for the Irish Republicans. Made even more money by telling the British where those weapons had been hidden. When that got to be a rather hot profession I left and travelled. I ended up in Switzerland and got involved in banking. Made business contacts with people from across the continent; people you understand who had need of discreet banking services. When I made my pile, I took it to Wales. Changed my identity and set up as a respectable retired businessman. Even became a Justice of the Peace."

Marshall paused momentarily. He seemed to be enjoying baring his soul. Simon waited patiently; there seemed to be no need to prompt his guest.

452

"All went well until I made a few unwise investments, mostly on the track again. One never really gets the thrill of racing out of one's blood once you have the taste for it. I found myself a little embarrassed for funds. A solution usually comes up, I find, and so it did, so it did. I noticed that there seemed to be no shortage of fresh meat to be had in the area. The butcher in the village was most cooperative if one fancied a steak or a nice joint. Then he suddenly disappeared, you will remember that we gossiped about him on one of our boozy Sunday afternoons, his son taking his place. He was reported missing, but not by his wife, some aunt of his apparently. The family claimed he had joined the army. The local bobby, a useless man, as I am sure you noticed, investigated but came up with nothing; he suspected the wife but had no proof. I told him to let sleeping dogs lie but did a bit of digging and found no trace of him joining up. The wife was thick as thieves with the lovely Myfanwy Williams. I have always had a way with the ladies, and Myfanwy does have a certain charm in a rustic sort of way. I am sure you know the story of her husband. Sad case, I am sure. But here was a not unattractive woman, virtually a widow, and running a nice little side business from her farm. Long story short, I wooed her. She thinks that we were going to run away to Canada together with the proceeds from this little enterprise. She let me in on the business. I had confronted her about the death of the Butcher, and it turns out it was the wife who had stabbed him. Self-defence, by all accounts, nasty sort, beat her relentlessly. I never had any time for chaps that use the whip excessively, if you take my meaning. Anyway, Myfanwy had helped her get rid of the body and came up with the story of him joining up. I squared things off with the local Police, and they accepted the story on my say-so. Once I was in on the business, I could see its potential. The area's inspector of farms was an old school friend of Myfanwy's; he was cooking the books to show that the farm had less livestock than it actually had. The extra could then be then sold on the black market at a considerable premium. Myfanwy, at my suggestion, persuaded him to do the same thing for some of the other farms he inspected. All we had to do was to collect the extra beasts and secrete them away until needed. I was amazed at the numbers available, far too many for the local market. So, I used my contacts in London and Dublin to expand our client base. But then you turned up, and we thought that the authorities were suspicious. We felt it best to make it one big shipment, then lie low and see if we were right. I had contacts who were able to provide me with details of minefield layouts for the Irish Sea so that our route in and out of Wales would be safe. Another thing I am sure that your bosses would be interested in. I am sorry that you were in the way. I thought that I had put you off the scent. If it had been left to me, I would have just knocked you over the head and left you to it. But you know how these republican chaps are; they seem to hold a grudge. Sorry, no hard feelings, I hope."

Simon had lots of hard feelings. But now was not the time to discuss them. If half the things that Marshall claimed were in any way the truth, then he really could be useful to Robinson. Not that he believed everything that Marshall had said. For one thing, he wondered about the timings. Had Marshall found out about the murder of the Butcher as he claimed? Had he been in on it? Had the Butcher died at the hands of his wife, or had he been silenced? Henry Marshall still had a few questions to answer. But Simon suspected that he was one of those people who always came up smelling of Roses.

Next to be interviewed was Myfanwy Thomas. She was reluctant to talk until Simon threatened her with her son.

"I think it better that you cooperate with us Mrs Thomas. Your son is in serious trouble, wouldn't you think?" Simon probed.

"Don't you threaten my son. He has nothing to do with this. He is a good boy and does what I tell him. He knows nothing of the business. Anyway, what's he going to get? A fine, they could send him to prison, but I doubt it; he is needed for the war effort."

"I think you underestimate the seriousness of his and your crimes, Mrs Thomas. You have colluded with a foreign enemy of His Majesty's government, a terrorist organisation, in a time of war. The punishment is Death by hanging."

"It was nothing to do with him. It was me, I tell you. When I tell the court that they can't hang him, not if it was me. They can hang me."

"You don't seem to understand. There will be no court trial for you, we can deal with this under war legislation, no jury, just a judge. There's also the matter of the murder of David Morgan.

When we find the body, Marshall has told us where it is, by the way, then your son will be charged with his murder. I think we can make a pretty good case for that, don't you think."

"You English bastards. You know he had nothing to do with that. You would frame him for something he didn't do."

"Yes, we would. It seems to me that your good little boy isn't as innocent as you would have us believe unless you are prepared to tell us the truth, the whole truth and nothing but the truth."

Myfanwy Thomas did tell the truth, well, mostly. Her story basically backed up what Marshall had said. The only exception was that she claimed that she had killed David Morgan. She claimed that he had threatened her; she stabbed him in self-defence and buried the body on her land. No one else knew of it.

Simon begrudgingly respected the lady. She was prepared to cover for her friend. She was willing to do anything she could to protect her friend, her friend's son, and her own son. Even to the extent of putting her own head in the noose. There seemed to be honour in that as far as Simon was concerned.

"But I don't understand why you got involved in this business. Don't you see that you were helping the nazis?" Simon was still aghast that people like her would not be fully behind the war effort.

"You English and your wars. It's all you think about. Like it's a bloody game. But you forget that its people like us that do the fighting, do the dying, do the suffering." Myfanwy was in full rant and shouted over Simon as he tried to interrupt. "You met my husband; god bless his soul. He went off to fight one of your wars; look what you did to him. He died in that war; he was never the same man. Do you think I get a widow's pension? No, they said that he was fit to work. You should have seen him as a young man. He was ten times the man of any English toff like you. It would have been better if he had of died. You killed him with your war. You told us that it was the war to end all wars, and yet here you are again, ready to send my Alwyn and his mates to their ruin. How many more generations will you destroy with your blood lust? You always ask us to pay the costs. Farmers in Wales have been trodden under your policies for generations. We can barely scrape together a living. Before the war it was cheap imports, impossible for us to compete with. Now, you want us to

455

increase production and feed the nation, but you pay a pittance. You talk of fighting for democracy, for freedom. What freedom do we have? Who voted for this war? Did we have a say? We are the ones working our fingers to the bone. Why shouldn't we make a little on the side? You can bet that the so-called English gentry will be filling their pockets on the back of this latest slaughter."

Simon said nothing as the wrathful lady was led from the room. He had some sympathy for her stance, but he wondered if she knew how hard things were for the people in the cities of Britain. The bombs falling, the livelihoods destroyed, people killed and maimed, the long hours in the factories, followed by nights of volunteering, with barely enough to eat. There were no sumptuous teas being served at cricket games in Manchester. No mountainous breakfasts are being enjoyed in Birmingham. The workers of Sheffield had no fresh eggs on the menu of their work canteen. Perhaps Myfanwy Thomas producing a little extra, distributed to the people of her community was understandable, forgivable, but a ship full. A ship the likes of which were being blown out of the water by the evil of Hitler's U-boats. There was no justification for that. It was greed. Plain and simple as far as he was concerned. That she had been influenced by Marshall, he had no doubts. The man was more than capable of taking a woman's opinions and twisting and magnifying them to suit his own covetous ambitions. Simon thought that this war would leave any number of people, including himself, to look at their own actions and wonder if they were completely innocent of self-centredness. And yet there would be some, the likes of Marshall, who will lose no sleep from the guilt of their avarice.

Fergus McDowell was less chatty. Apart from a few choice words that he had on the subject of Simon's nationality and his legitimacy, he refused to talk at all. The only thing that Simon got from him was when he asked him about Ted Baker and his gang. Robinson had briefed Simon on the London end of the operation when they had spoken on the phone. He wanted to know if McDowell and Baker had been working together or if they were just two separate customers of the Welsh-based scheme. McDowell had reacted when Simon mentioned Baker's name. He was clearly surprised that Simon knew about them.

Simon thought hard. Marshall had boasted about London and Dublin contacts. So, was it Baker who was the London contact? Robinson and the Major would be asking Marshall about that and other things, no doubt.

The Harbour master was the classic case of a local official who had been tempted or bullied, or both, into looking the wrong way when instructed. It appeared that he had looked the wrong way on many occasions over a number of years when boats, goods and people had come in and out of his harbour. When Simon told him of the contraband that was involved on this occasion, particularly the armaments that they had found, he seemed genuinely shocked. He visibly shook when he was told that he was an accessory to smuggling guns for the IRA; he seemed to be well aware of the penalties involved.

Last was the ship's captain. He, too, claimed to have been coerced into providing his services. He feigned shock at the suggestion that he was working for the IRA. Professing no knowledge as to the activities of his employers.

Just as he was finishing with the captain, Rosie arrived from her duties on the Ship. Simon briefed her on the discussions with the conspirators.

"Quite an operation then." Acknowledged Rosie as the two of them drank tea and discussed what was to happen next.

120

The fifteenth Ear. – The kitchen - Slough Farm Near London

The tension in the kitchen was at its most fraught as the fifteenth and final lorry was heard to arrive in the farmyard. Joe was convinced that Baptiste had something up his sleeve, but of course, he had not had the luxury of discussing it with him. All he could do was to be ready and help as best he could.

At first, everything seemed to be the same as the previous 14 arrivals. The same engine noise, the same squeal of brakes, the same crunched gears as reverse was found, engine growling and gearbox screeching the unmistakable scream of reverse, before the clicking of the handbrake ratchet and the dying of the engine, the same clicks of a door opening. This time, an eruption of noise, pistol shots, unfeasible to count how many, 3 or 4 thought Joe, but very loud, so possibly some shots were simultaneous. What was certain was there was no delay from the stopping of the vehicle to the start of the firing, as there had been before. The shots had taken place at the truck, the drivers returning fire perhaps, impossible for Joe to know. Any thought of him working it out was quickly forgotten as the kitchen descended into a torrent of chaos.

The window at the end of the room shattered, spraying glass across the room. Bullets hitting the ceiling. The sound of an intensive salvo striking the brickwork around the window. The room was under a sustained attack.

Mischa had instructed his men to open fire as soon as shots were heard from the last truck as it pulled up outside the barn. The salvo was started by his sniper, a man called Anatoly, who had been with Mischa since the Great War. Anatoly had crawled out across the grass towards the kitchen. It was not that he wanted to get a closer shot; if he had wanted to, he could have hit men in the room from hundreds of yards away. He needed to get near so that the trajectory of his shots would be upward into the room.

The idea was to break the glass but for the bullets to go harmlessly into the ceiling. Mischa had been very clear about that; he didn't want any stray bullets hitting anyone. It was not often that his old comrade had asked him to miss deliberately. Anatoly was somewhat offended by the task, but he knew his old commander too well to doubt that there was an excellent reason for his orders. The Russian marksman could see a man at the far end, nervously walking backwards and forwards across the room. As the bullets started to fly in the farmyard, the man was to the left, so Anatoly put 3 bullets into the right-hand corner of the room, then dropped back to higher ground, ready for further orders.

The rest of Mischa's men started firing at the walls surrounding the kitchen window and through the windows in the rooms above and to the side. Anybody in the kitchen would think that all hell was letting loose, and a serious attack was taking place against them.

As the bullets started flying, Baptiste was ready. He had slipped the ropes from his hands, thanks to Billy's deliberately sloppy knots and had grabbed his gun from his belt behind his back. Bapt knew that once 3 bullets had passed through the window and into the room, no more would. He rose to his feet, knocking over the chair behind him. Eddie had flung himself into the corner in an effort to avoid the bullets; Phil, however, seemed less shocked by the attack and had his gun in his hand, waiting for a lull so he could return fire. Bapt thought him the greater threat to his plan, so he swung his gun left and fired at him twice. Both shots hit home; the first hit his left shoulder, and the second hit his side and passed through his left kidney. He slumped to the floor against the door.

Baptiste swung his gun back towards Eddie, but the gangster had recovered from his initial shock; he had raised his gun and was aiming it straight at him. Bapt knew he would be too slow, and his adversary would get his shot off first.

Joe had crouched as low as he could when the first shots had hit the window, then he had seen Bapt jump up. The Frenchman seemed unperturbed by the prospect of being shot by the bullets being rained down on the house. It was clear that Bapt knew there was no threat; the shots were a diversion and that the serious work of overpowering the gangsters would have to be done by those in the room. Joe saw that Bapt was aiming for Phil by the back door. It was obvious to him that his job was to take care of Eddie. He dropped the handcuff from his right hand, the restraint now only attached to his left wrist. He pushed back from the table, his chair spilling over behind him, and he spun towards Eddie, who was aiming his gun at Baptiste. Joe sprung at the gunman; using all the power he could create from his legs, he pushed off and drove headlong towards him. As he hit his shoulder, driving into the midriff of his foe, he heard the gun go off.

Baptiste watched as Joe launched himself at Eddie; he knew that he would be just too late. He saw the muzzle flash of the gun and felt the impact. It was like nothing else he had ever experienced. A punch, but one magnified many times over. The projectile hit his right shoulder, just missing the socket, piercing through his shoulder blade and hitting the wall behind him. The impact threw him backwards and sent him sprawling, tripping on his discarded chair, his temple hitting the wall; he landed in a twisted tangle on the floor at Billy's feet, insensible.

Joe's rugby tackle sent Eddie crashing back against the kitchen range, his left hand landing on the hot stovetop as he tried to steady himself. Joe grabbed hold of his right wrist and held it into the air to prevent him from firing off another shot. The two grappled with each other for supremacy in what they both knew to be a life-or-death struggle. Sara, still cowering in the chair next to the deadly battle, screamed before falling to the floor and crawling away into the corner. Still holding his adversary's arm high in the air, Joe arched his spine, craning his head away from his foe; with devastating effect, he used all the power of his back and neck to whip his forehead into Eddie's unprotected face. Blood spurted from his smashed nose, temporarily blinding both men. Joe's hand slipped on Eddie's wrist; it was now free to bring down the gun onto Joe's head. But before he could react, Joe unleashed a series of vicious punches into his stomach and ribs, doubling him up in pain. Groping for the arm and hand that held the gun but still blinded by the blood, Joe grabbed his man by his jacket, threw him across the tabletop and dived on top of him to try to restrain him.

Eddie's gun fell from his hand and slid across the wood towards his father. Ted Baker saw his opportunity, and putting his hands on the table, he pushed himself up, crouching forward; he was about to reach for the gun when he felt a searing pain in his left hand, which he could no longer move.

Sue could only witness the scene as the Frenchman had shot the guard in the corner behind her and then had been gunned down; Joe and Eddie now fought savagely to her left. Like the older gangster, she had seen the gun fall loose, but it sped at a diagonal across the table, moving out of her reach towards Ted Baker. She saw him make his move to grab the weapon; when she remembered the letter opener, using all the force she could muster, Sue Cartwright, aka Miss Hereford, prissy accountant, stabbed the silver spike through Ted's left hand, pinning him to the table. His natural reaction was to grab at the source of his pain, involuntarily giving up on his quest for the gun, which slid off the table and out of reach. He stared in horror at his hand, securely nailed to the solid oak; he turned to his assailant just in time to see her standing and unleashing a merciless right hook, which hit him just below his left eye and would have sent him collapsing to the floor but for the restraint of the letter opener. It was probably the best punch of the night.

Billy 'the brick' Mason witnessed it all and was now the one remaining person in the room who was armed. In a daze of confusion, he held his pistol pointed in the vague direction of each event and was now aiming at Joe Turner as he struggled with Eddie Baker on the tabletop. Joe had managed to grab Eddie's right hand and bent it up behind his back, but still, the sadist squirmed against the restraint.

"Shoot him." Cried Eddie Baker to Billy, who stood dumbly holding the gun. "Shoot him." He screamed again.

Billy was a loyal man; he had worked for Eddie Baker for 3 years now, and he had done as he was told despite the loathing that he had for the life he led. He had been a part of things that he was so ashamed of and revolted by, all because of the debt he felt he owed. He was not afraid to admit that Eddie Baker frightened him; he had obeyed him without question because of his fear. Now, what was he to do? Joe Turner was a good man; everyone knew that. He, like them all, had been amazed when

461

Joe had joined the Bakers. Bapt had said that he should trust Joe, that Joe could get him out of this life. Did that mean that Joe was working for the police? Was that what was happening? He had done as Baptiste had asked but now, he wasn't so sure. What was happening outside? Who was shooting? Was it the police or the army? They would surely arrest him, he would go to prison, maybe even hang.

"Bill, put the gun down. Everything will be all right. You will be fine, I promise you. Billy, I am working for the government. There is nothing going to happen to you, I promise." Joe's voice was calm and soothing. He could see the conflict the young man was going through. His mind had been poisoned by the things he had seen and the fear he must be feeling.

"Shoot him, you fucking idiot. If you betray me, you moron, I will get to you. Wherever they hide you, I will find you, and then, and then, I will carve you up into so many pieces, and I'll put each piece through the mincer. They'll have to bury you in a bucket. They'll never know who you were. Now shoot this bastard, you fucking imbecile."

"Bill, most of the Baker gang are dead. The rest will hang, including these two. They have no power over you now. We know that you haven't done anything wrong; you were forced to work for them, and there's no evidence against you. I will make sure that you are fairly dealt with. They will probably offer you a new name, a new identity, they'll let you join the army. Get you a nice job, you can learn a trade, you can box again. With that right hook of yours, I'll give it 6 months, and you'll be Army champion. Think how proud your Gran would have been to see you marching home, smart as a new pin, boots shining so bright you could shave in 'em, medals dangling off your chest. Make her proud, Bill, make her proud son."

Billy 'the brick' Mason lowered his head and his gun. He knew that Joe was right. Whatever happened to him now was better than working for that filth.

"You fucking stupid….." Eddie's invective was cut short as Joe smashed his right fist into his temple.

Sue Cartwright took the gun from Billy's hand and collected the others from the dead body of the guard and the one that had fallen to the floor. With both Bakers unconscious and the guard

462

dead, she was satisfied that all was safe in the room; she went to check on the Frenchman.

Baptiste was coming too; he moved gingerly; he had lost blood, but he would be fine if they could get him to the hospital quickly.

"Go to the window and shout, as loud as you can, 'prozrachnyy', three times. It means clear in Russian. It is the code we set." Baptiste instructed.

After checking the word, Sue went to the window, and the gunfire stopped; after she shouted out the code word three times, silence fell upon the farm.

121

Where is the Money - Wales

"I say. The profits must be huge. I wonder where all the money is?"

All the participants had been searched, and only a moderate amount of money had been found—no more than you would expect a person to carry. Marshall had a little more on him, but not a significant amount. Pritchard-Smythe's men had searched Mynydd farm, but again, only small amounts of money had been found.

Rosie was thinking aloud. "Both the Irish and the London gang must have paid Myfanwy for the livestock. You can't imagine that someone as savvy as her would allow the goods to be taken without payment upfront. Surely not."

"One would normally expect such transactions to be cash on delivery, wouldn't one?" Simon joined in her musings.

"Ooooh, you do talk lovely." Rosie teased her aristocratic partner. "Didn't you say that Marshall had been involved in banking in Switzerland?"

"Yes, he was, or so he claimed." Simon sat up as he caught on to Rosie's idea.

"So, he arranges payments to be made into bank accounts in Switzerland?" Rosie asked doubtfully.

"I don't know how that would work exactly but what was it Marshall said?" Simon referred to his notes. "Marshall said that he had 'Made business contacts with people from across the continent; people you understand who had need of discreet banking services.' So, who is it that needs discreet banking services? Criminals, terrorists, people who can't just open an account at Lloyds and write cheques out like you and me."

"So, his business had been what? Moving money?" asked Rosie.

"I don't know, but I think you might be right."

"He's an interesting Chappy this Marshall, isn't he? Do you think that Robinson and the Major would like a word with him?"

"Yes, I think they would. Shall we have another chat with him?"

Marshall was fetched from the Village Hall by one of the marines.

"Marshall, you said that you would cooperate with us?" demanded Simon.

"Well, one would like to do what one could for the war effort, of course. But given the cloud that I seem to have found myself under and the enemies I might potentially make, I would have certain conditions."

"You want immunity from prosecution?" enquired Rosie.

"Such a clever young lady for a farm girl. Yes, that, and I would prefer it if people didn't think that I had informed on them. Also, as my scheme seems to have failed to come up with the goods, so to speak, certain people would quite reasonably expect a refund. A refund that I am not really able to give; funds have already been apportioned elsewhere as it happens. Since they are not reasonable people, it would be better if they thought that I was not able to, rather than not willing, to pay. Do you see my point of view?"

Simon and Rosie looked at each other. "What do you have in mind, Marshall?" asked Simon.

"Send me back to the Hall. Then call for me again a little later. When I am out of sight of the others, concoct a kerfuffle, some shouts, and then fire off two shots into the air. Tell the others that I tried to make a run for it, and an over-enthusiastic soldier shot me. Better still, wait a few minutes before the shots. Then the story can be that I ran up the path onto the cliffs. There was an altercation; I was shot, and my body fell over the cliff. That way, if the lovely Myfanwy, heartbroken as I am sure she will be, wants to see my body to say her goodbyes, there is an acceptable reason why she can't."

"So, they will all think you are dead, especially your creditors. Not to mention, you will be released from any promises you have made to the widow Thomas."

465

"Yes, the poor woman has lost a husband and a fiancée in a matter of months. She really needs to be more careful; don't you think?"

Marshall's death went down as planned. A marine collected him from the hall as suggested. Shouts rang out, and running was heard. A few minutes later, a marine fired two shots into the air from the cliff tops. In the hall, Myfanwy Thomas sobbed as she feared for her lover.

Henry Marshall had no such feelings for the lady as he sat back in the passenger seat of Pritchard-Smythe's car. The driver was a lunatic, he thought as the vehicle sped through the countryside, its destination unknown to him. But he had few trepidations. He knew that he could be useful to the English; he had already persuaded the two spies of that. They had seen the potential of his working for them. Once he was able to gain their trust, he would be able to slip their bonds. The money would help. There was plenty of it. No doubt the English would demand that he pay it over to them. But they would not know the amount he had received. How could they know? He wondered if he should give over half of it or if he would get away with a quarter. It was still a substantial sum. He was thankful for his own forethought in that he had sent the money in several different directions. He could give them the details of one of the accounts, and they would empty it and, with any luck, accept that as the total amount. Yes, a quarter should do nicely.

The Indian driver and the guard who sat in the back holding his gun to the man wondered why the crazy English man was laughing.

Simon and Rosie were on the phone with Robinson and the Major again. They had given them the details of the interrogations. Robinson was especially pleased with the Marshall situation. He and Major Calderdale were looking forward to having a little tête-à-tête with him.

"Bach, what time is the local high tide? Do you think the unloading will be finished by then?" asked Robinson.

"It's in half an hour, and yes, we have all but finished the unloading. The first of the trucks have left for Slough as instructed."

"Rosie, have you taken care of the little matter we discussed?" enquired Robinson.

"All taken care of Sir." Answered Rosie. Simon looked at her enquiringly, he wondered exactly what she had been doing in the engine room and hold of the ship. The powers that be clearly had their reasons. A job that she was suited for more than Simon. He wondered what. It occurred to him that he knew only a little of Rosie's skills and specialities. However, what was it she had said about Sunflower, his motorbike? She had said that she could 'fix her up in no time at all.' Also, when they had been walking together looking for the cavalry, Rosie had talked about motorbikes and how she could tune the Vincent to run even faster. So, Rosie, the Land Girl, was some sort of mechanical expert, and she had been given a job to do in the engine room of the ship. But what? An explosion? It didn't make sense as Simon was an explosives whiz, top of his class, in fact. Whatever it was, Robinson was clearly keeping it on a need-to-know basis; with that in mind, he resolved not to ask Rosie about it. Sometimes, it was an advantage to be in the dark; ignorance is bliss, after all.

Simon snapped his concentration back to the matter at hand; Robinson was giving out further instructions. "Good, now listen carefully. Here's what you need to do. You will remember our first chat, Bach; you understand how momentous the matters that are involved here are. Political considerations that the likes of us can only guess at. Bach, Percival, I want you to let the prisoners go."

Simon looked at Rosie; he could see that she was as shocked as he was. "All of them, sir?" It was all that he could think of to say.

"Yes, you will need to talk to them first; this is what I want you to say."

122

Alone – Slough Farm, near London

Three hours after the last shot had been fired, Joe Turner was alone at Slough farm, well apart from Father and Son, Ted and Eddie Baker, but they were not much company for him.

Sue Cartwright had taken Baptiste and the young girl from Wales to a nearby Military hospital. From there she had telephoned her report to Major Calderdale, along with Joe's wish list, as he had called it.

Mischa's team had disappeared as silently into the night as they had arrived, but not before they had helped herd the animals into the fields furthest away from the buildings and carry all the bodies of the battle into the house, where they had been laid out in the rooms on straw bales. There were no survivors from amongst the Baker gang, a fact that had surprised even Joe. The mobsters were hard men, cruel and determined, but they lacked the skills and discipline to compete with the Russians in such a fight. They had all used guns before, but not in a military scenario; they fired indiscriminately at their enemy, without thought for what their objective was and without conserving their ammunition. The last 4 men had surrendered, but Mischa had been very specific: there could be no survivors; he had no intention of leaving any of the gang to talk of what happened that night, especially for them to let it be common knowledge that Russians had been involved. Even if the Baker gang had been terminally weakened, he didn't want any of the other gangs in London to know it was his men who had been responsible. He didn't want those gangs to believe that he was making a play to be the top dog in the City; if they did, they would come gunning for him and his men. It was not his way to make trouble for the British authorities, he believed there would come a time when they would fight together. The only people who knew of his involvement were Joe Turner, whom he trusted; the lady Joe had called Miss Hereford, who Joe vouched for and hinted was

British Secret Service; the young girl, who was in shock and appeared to know nothing of what was happening; the boy Billy who again Joe vouched for; Baptiste Barbeau who had the same desire that no one knows about the events of the evening and was also Joe's friend; lastly Doreen who he trusted and loved.

Mischa had wanted to deal with Eddie Baker himself; there was a score to settle, Raspy to think of, but when Joe explained the plans he had for the gangster and his father, he deferred his claim. After all, the man had killed Joe's girl, Amber; he had the right to kill him.

Ted and Eddie Baker had been tied to chairs, blindfolded, and gagged. They were arranged opposite each other across the large kitchen table. As they had regained consciousness, they had struggled a little against their restraints but had soon realised the futility; there was no chance of escape.

An hour or so after everyone had left, a truck had driven into the yard. The lone driver and Joe had unloaded the cargo in silence. The driver had been warned not to take any sort of interest in the manifest, the delivery address, anything he saw, or anyone he met. His orders had been conveyed to him by telephone in his base commander's office; he was to tell nobody, ever, including his commander, of his delivery. Joe had nodded his thanks to the driver and the empty lorry had driven away.

Joe had spent the next two hours hard at work. He had carried the petrol one jerry can at a time into each room, carefully soaking the straw that had been laid under each body. Then he had made the bombs; there were 8 in all, each with a fuse connected to a standard alarm clock, each synchronised to explode at the same time. Three of the larger devices were in the upstairs rooms, carefully placed against the chimney breasts so that the force of the blasts would be directed inwards and destroy as much as possible. Two bombs were placed in the hall and the lounge. The last large bomb, the biggest of all, was placed on the kitchen table. That left two smaller devices, which Joe strapped between the knees of the captives; the men had struggled, not knowing what was happening, but Joe used rope to bind their knees together, the explosives trapped securely in place. The clocks for the two personal bombs were placed on the table in front of the men, the clock dials facing them.

When all was ready, Joe removed the gags and blindfolds, first from Ted and then from his son. Ted said nothing, and Eddie erupted into a predictable tirade of threats, expletives, and anger. Joe said nothing, waiting until eventually the gangster tired and his rant faded.

"Sooner or later, in your business," Joe said calmly. "you're gonna piss off the wrong person. You might think you are the biggest fish in the pond. You were. And in normal times, you would get away with it. The law being the law, and we British, with our sense of fair play, would always give you a fair trial. Then you would get to the witnesses, and low and behold, you are found not guilty. But then, these are not normal times; there's a fucking war on. But you carry on as normal, business as usual; in fact, business has never been better. Lots of horny servicemen for your girls to satisfy; easy pickings to rob people in the blackout. You kill, and you steal, and you rape as though nothing has changed. But it has. The law has changed, just for the duration, but it has changed. Trials behind closed doors, No juries, just a judge. Special laws, special sentences. And, like I say, you pissed off the wrong people. Me."

"And who the fuck are you, just a jumped-up tea leaf. You kill us, and someone will get you; if it's not one of our boys, it will be the law. You'll swing for it; murder is still murder whoever you kill." Eddie took up his bluster.

"No, Eddie, I am not just a thief; I am a thief that works for His Majesty. And HRH is a little pissed off with your dad because he's been dabbling in stuff, he shouldn't have his dirty little fingers in."

"I knew he was dodgy, and you let him into our business; you're a senile, stupid old git." Eddie turned his anger onto his father.

"Shut up." Ted's voice was deep, angry, and threatening, even in his weakened circumstances. Eddie fell silent. "So, you're a snake in the nest. I'd have never had you down as grass. I trusted you, Joe Turner. I treated you well. I was gonna groom you to take over one day."

"I'm flattered, but I always said I didn't want to work for you. I was quite clear about that the first time you asked. But you don't like to take no for an answer, do you, Ted? The thing is, when

470

you asked again, I had a new boss, the big guy in the palace, and his chaps had taken a disliking to your activities in the black market."

"What, this is all about a few cows and sheep you're avin' a laugh."

"If you'd have left it at that, Ted, we would probably have just shut it down. Warned off the farmers, raided the farm here and confiscated the livestock. We might even have thought it wasn't worth the bother and not prosecuted you. But you got greedy, didn't you, Ted? You took it to a level that could cause some serious embarrassment to the government. There are acute food shortages on the horizon, poor bastards drowning in the Atlantic trying to bring in vital supplies, honest farmers breaking their backs to grow more crops, working people diggin' up their backyards to grow a few spuds because their kids are starving, and you Ted Baker, taking the fuckin' piss out of the lot of them. Then, to top it all, you throw your hand in with the Irish boys."

For the briefest of moments, Ted looked at Joe, shocked.

"You think I wouldn't find out about the jobs your lads did up north. Robbing the army, Ted, and not just a bit of fencing, weapons, Ted, weapons to sell to the IRA, what were you thinking?"

"The authorities had no idea who did those jobs; we were not in the frame. You think I am a fool. We did the jobs miles off our patch. Nobody was looking to us for them." Desperation was creeping into the old criminal's voice.

"Who told you that Ted? Probably the same person that told me you done them."

"Backhander? Nah, he wouldn't dare." Doubt now in his voice.

"Listen, Ted, I would love to put you right on a few things, but I think you can work them out for yourself. You see, we are on the clock here, quite literally, actually." Joe turned to Eddie, his face dark with anger and hatred. "I said that you had pissed off the wrong people, well, 2 people. Mischa Agafonov was one. You see, you killed his friend, Mikhail Mihajlovic Medvedev, who people called Raspy, killed him for no real reason; you could have sent him on his way that night with a slap. But no, you beat him to death."

"What's he talking about, Eddie," Ted asked urgently of his son. "You didn't tell me about this. I fucking told you to stay away from the Russians. You imbecile."

Eddie said nothing; Joe continued. "Then you pissed me off."

"What the fuck did you do, Eddie?" Ted was furious.

"Anyway, enough of this. The thing is, time is ticking, and I need to get out of here. Mischa Agafonov wanted to kill you. I think that would have been very unpleasant for you both. I persuaded him that my way would be better. Technically my job would be to take you into my bosses. They would arrange a secret trail, and you would both swing. The thing is, and they are a little embarrassed to admit it, they are a bit nervous because things like that never stay completely secret, tongues wag, paperwork, there's always paperwork and then rumours start. They would much rather that everything just went away. So that is what I have arranged. I am overstepping the mark a little, I must admit. It's not the sort of thing they would normally condone, but what are they going to do? They are hardly likely to rake up the mud by court marshalling me. Besides, if they did, after tonight, there will be very little evidence for anyone to work with. No, I am quite sure that they will let bygones be bygones, and it will all be forgotten about in no time at all."

Neither man spoke.

"In front of each of you is a clock. When the hour hand reaches the alarm marker, it will trigger a detonator, and the explosives between your legs will, well, you have imaginations. That will be in approximately 20 minutes time. I am going to leave you now; I thought you might like the time to settle your differences, kiss and make up. You know family is family, after all. Oh, by the way, one of your clocks is set to explode a minute earlier than the other. So, one of you will watch the other die. You could compare notes and you will find out who it is going to be. But then again, will you know if the other is telling the truth."

Joe Turner walked from the room certain of several things: both men were going to die. Both clocks were synchronised precisely so they would die at the same time. Even if the timers were slightly off, the size of the first explosion would set off the others in a chain reaction. His bosses, although they had not ordered him to kill them, knew his state of mind; they knew what he would do, and they would be happy with his night work. Joe knew that Father and Son would not make up in the time they had left; they would spend it in the mutual torture of recrimination and blame. All evidence of the Baker gang would be atomised in the explosion, and none of the people at the farm that night would ever breathe a word.

The next weekly edition of the Slough, Windsor & Eton Observer carried the following story:

"People should be reminded of the dangers of showing any light at night, warns the Slough constabulary. This follows the tragic bombing of Slough Hill Farm. It is thought that a lone German bomber dropped its deadly load on the farmhouse after seeing a light from the building on what was a clear night. Spotted by several locals in the area, the aeroplane was probably lost and separated from its comrades. The explosion was heard for miles around. The Farmhouse was completely destroyed. Having recently been sold, the new owner of the farm was not known in the vicinity, and it is unclear how many people were at home at the time. It is a tragic reminder that, even in the countryside, the utmost care should be taken with the blackout."

123

The Voyage Home - Wales

Simon and Rosie walked over to the Village Hall together. When they entered the room, Rosie signalled to the guards to leave. The prisoners sat on the floor, silent except for the occasional sob from Myfanwy. When she saw Simon and Rosie, she burst out.

"Where is Henry? What have you done to him?"

"I am afraid that he was killed trying to escape. He overpowered his guard and ran up towards the cliffs. He was challenged by a guard there; he attacked the man and tried to take his weapon. In the scuffle, he was shot and fell from the cliffs. We haven't found the body yet, but rest assured he will get a decent burial. We just need to work out what name to put on the headstone." Rosie's voice was dispassionate and hard.

Myfanwy's sobs had stopped, and she stared harshly at the English spies.

"However, we have some good news for you all. We are letting you go." Simon gave out the surprising tidings. The astounded prisoners were speechless. "You will sail in 30 minutes' time. It seems that our government have no wish to waste time and effort on costly trials. They prefer to let sleeping dogs lie."

"I bet they do", Fergus McDowell interjected. "Be a bit embarrassing if the Great British public heard about the IRA liberating English food and giving it to poor, starving Irish people."

"You seem to forget that your plan failed McDowell. Miserably." Rosie taunted the Republican.

"You're the Bitch that murdered Sean, we don't forget our brave martyrs. There'll be people coming after you, girl. Keep looking over your shoulder, English tart."

"He doesn't seem very pleased with our generosity, does he?" Rosie calmly addressed herself to Simon.

"That's because he knows when he gets to Ireland, he's a marked man. It will be a close-run thing as to who gets their hands on him first, the Irish Government or his bosses in the Republican Army. It seems he acted against orders, and the government is annoyed that he put a potential trade deal with the Americans at risk by operating on British soil."

McDowell couldn't hide his worried looks. The bravado knocked out of him, and he hissed incoherent threats towards his captors. Simon carried on. "The rest of you will be on the ship too, as will the rest of your men, McDowell. Together with the body of your man who unfortunately died earlier and that of Marshall's body if found in time. You will sail to Ireland, where you can either settle or arrangements can be made for you to travel on; Mrs Thomas, I believe you have plans to emigrate to Canada; the British Embassy will issue a passport. You will be allowed to write to your son and him to send you money when he can. However, there are conditions on your release. Firstly, you will never set foot on British soil again. Secondly, you will not discuss any of these events with anybody. You will be allowed to write to your son but no other people in the UK. In particular, you will not have any contact with the press. In short you will not discuss what has happened here or any aspect of it, with anyone, ever. If you break these conditions, then your son will be arrested for the murder of David Morgan and will hang."

Myfanwy was still staring at Rosie. "You know he is innocent. Innocent."

Rosie replied, "Myfanwy, there is no need for you to worry. Your son, with his new wife and baby, will live a happy and prosperous life, I am sure." Rosie let her words hang over the shocked mother. "Oh, didn't you know? Yes, Dot is pregnant. I don't think your Alwyn knows yet, but I am sure he will do the gentlemanly thing. All you have to do is keep quiet. Start a new life in Canada."

Myfanwy Thomas made to object again, but Rosie pressed home the situation. "Mrs Thomas, go to Canada, maintain your silence. Think of the alternative: your son at the end of an English rope. Your grandson born a bastard. What's more, Dot will probably go back to her parents to have the baby. Your own kin will be brought up in England as an English Bastard."

Myfanwy, perhaps for the first time in her life, was lost for words. Rosie had used her worst fears and hatred against her, and her hatred and fury knew no bounds. Yet she had no option but to go along with the demands of these English swine.

Simon addressed himself to the Ship's Captain. "We are leaving what is to be done with you to the Irish authorities. I imagine that they need your vessel and your skills, so you will probably be forgiven for your sins on condition of your silence. The same goes for you, Jones, as a harbour master, you have broken so many laws. Probably the most serious of which is providing details of mine fields and safe shipping lanes to unauthorised persons. I think you can guess the penalty for that. You will be taken to your home to collect a few things, then you will leave on the boat, never to return. On condition that you never discuss your actions with any person, especially the press."

Simon and Rosie gave the orders to Captains Brown and Pritchard-Smythe, whose men efficiently set about their business. One by one, the lorries were reloaded and set off to London. At the last minute, the prisoners were released and allowed to prepare the ship for departure, watched closely by the Marines.

As planned, at high tide, the Irish ship drifted away from her moorings. Piloted by the Harbour Master, she slipped out to sea without any noise or fuss.

The SS Magnolia left the harbour silently and unseen, like a disinterested student leaving a monotonous lecture. The mood of her crew, humiliated and dejected, seemed to touch her own temperament. She coasted languidly on her course for the Emerald Isle.

Douglas McKay, worried for his old friend. He had been chief engineer to the Magnolia for as long as she had plied her trade in these waters. He knew every inch of her engine room. Every valve, every dial, every pipe of hers was known to him. No man had ever understood his lover, as well as Douglas McKay, understood the Magnolia. He could feel in his soul when there was something not right, if even the slightest mechanism was amiss.

Checking every dial, every pressure, Doug McKay was not a happy man. His subordinates raised their eyes to his constant worrying. They knew that in times of peace, he would have stopped the ship already. Only the constant threats of wartime sailing prevented him from giving that order. McKay knew as well as anyone the ever-present dangers to a drifting ship from the silent enemies of U-boats and mines.

124

The loneliness of command - The Irish Sea off the West Wales Coast

As HMS Unicorn, an Undine class submarine of the Royal Navy, serenely made her way through the icy waters of the Irish Sea, Her Master, Cdr Jonathon Ronay, didn't feel the same tranquillity as his boat. He turned his back so that the men could not see his hands were trembling as he silently reread the orders.

Fundamentally Ronay was a man of peace, a servant of Christ. A teacher, a student of the word of the Lord. How had his path led him to this? Why had God chosen him for such acts?

He read the orders again, hoping for a mistake. To his despair, there was none.

Ronay had been an English teacher in peacetime. A lay preacher on the Sabbath. As a Royal Navy reserve, he had dreaded his call-up, but it had been swift. The excellence of his Great War service to the King and Country had singled him out. He was back in the Navy before the war had even begun. His first command was confirmed as France fell to the Germans. His first voyage as commander of the Unicorn, patrolling the Eastern Atlantic approaches, began as the Luftwaffe was first locking horns with the RAF in the skies above southeast England.

It was not that Ronay had doubts about his duty. He felt incontrovertibly that his obligation was to stand up to the evil that Nazi Germany represented. The conflict in his soul came from that unbreakable commandment from God that 'Thou shalt not kill'.

During his service in the first war, his contact with death had been remote. He was under the command of his Captain. He followed orders. He did not pull the trigger. He performed his duties, but he didn't take life. Now, he was the man who gave the order. That pulled the trigger. That took lives. What worried him most was that he was good at it, he excelled at it, he even enjoyed it.

In his hands were more orders to defy God, yet more instructions to murder; he knew that he didn't have the will to disobey them. He longed for the end of the war. When he would join the church and preach Christ's word. He would serve God and hope and pray for redemption. But he felt that whatever he would do, however much good he could bring back into the world, it would be too late for him. He was doomed; he would be eternally damned.

The Unicorn had been patrolling the waters just off the coast where the river Mersey emptied into the sea near the port of Liverpool. The orders to base his operations here had surprised Ronay. He and his crew had become adept at protecting the great convoys of allied merchant shipping as it steamed easterly towards the British Isles. To be here seemed a waste of their talents. When the signal had come in to seek and destroy a cargo vessel off the Welsh coast, it seemed to be too much of a coincidence that they were already in the area. The orders had included the details of the planned route of the ship. The time it would be in position and the last lines of the order, words that would haunt his soul forever, 'no rescue, no survivors.'

As he came across the ship, it was stationary in the water. A sitting duck. Ronay moved the Unicorn until the ship showed on the horizon silhouetted by the moon. Commander Jonathan Ronay felt sick to the stomach as he edged as close as was safe to the fated craft. His mind wandered to ponder on the number of souls who would perish that night before he regained his concentration and focused on the words of his orders, 'suspected illegal armaments shipment must be destroyed, no rescue, no survivors.'

On his instruction, twin tubes were loaded, a complicated process that involved equalising the pressure in the tubes with the outside water. When all was ready, his order despatched the lethal torpedoes.

125

Overheating – Aboard the SS Magnolia – Irish Sea - 1941

On SS Magnolia, McKay was now fixated on one dial. The pressure gauge of the cooling system. The needle was pointing slightly, very slightly, to a lower value than normal. Acceptable tolerance for an engine of this type, perhaps, but not on McKay's engine, not on the Magnolia. He grabbed hold of a young assistant and charged him to stand and watch the dial. The slightest movement of the needle and he should shout out.

McKay busied himself, checking every inch of the cooling system. Every pipe was examined for leaks, and every joint was scrutinised. When the boy shouted testament to a slight lowering of the pressure, McKay ran to a different gauge. As he had feared, the internal temperature of the engine had increased. The cooling system was failing, and the engine would overheat. If left unchecked, it would seize, causing untold damage.

McKay shouted to all his men to look for the problem. Surrounding the engine, the men wiped dry rags over the pipes and looked for the tell-tale signs of coolant leaks. The temperature continued to rise at an increasing rate.

"Over 'ere Chief." A gruff and worried-sounding voice made itself heard over the roar of the engine.

McKay ran to the voice and looked at the joint in a pipe that was being pointed out by an oily finger.

"Stop engine." The chief's instruction was shouted without waiting to check with the ship's captain. It was his call, and he knew that delay could be fatal. Liquid, the lifeblood of the cooling system, was leaking out from a joint by a filter. McKay examined the joint carefully. He wouldn't know for sure until he undid the nut, but it looked like the threads had been crossed. The coupling had been tampered with; of that, he was sure. No way one of his men would have made such a ham-fisted mess of a job like that. To his certain knowledge, there had been no maintenance on this section of the engine for weeks. Nothing he could do immediately as the system would have to cool first.

He walked quickly up to the bridge to give his report.

"Are you saying that this is sabotage?" asked the captain after he had heard the outraged engineer's reason for stopping the engine.

"I am Captain, but it doesn't make any sense. It has been done by an expert. Oh yes, they knew what they were doing all right. And yet, why this? If they wanted to disable the ship, they could have done several things that would permanently damage the engine just as easily. They must have known that we would notice the overheating and stop the engine."

"How long to fix it? How long until we are back up and running?"

"Well, I will have to repair the coupling; I have the parts......."

"Your man didn't ask how complicated it was or how clever you are. How fecking long?" Fergus McDowell shouted, interrupting the engineers' deliberations.

"An hour, an hour and a half."

"Well, hadn't you be getting the fuck back down there and getting on with it then?" McDowell was beginning to fear he knew the reason for the sabotage.

"Well, if you want to borrow my tools and cover yourself in scolding steam, be my bloody guest, you fecking idiot." McKay squared up to McDowell, staring chillingly into his eyes. He knew who the man was, but he had no time for his sort. He feared no man and wasn't about to bow down before a hooligan such as him, whoever he represented.

"This is not helping Gentlemen." The captain mustered all the calm he could. "Doug, cool the pipes as quickly as you can. There's no man I know who could do it quicker or better."

The engineer stared intensely for a moment longer before spinning on his heel and marching off towards the engine room.

McDowell needed a cigarette, but as he headed out the door of the bridge, the captain shouted out a reminder not to smoke on deck. Leaning against the rails, he stared out across the tranquil sea. The moon made a mockery of the no-smoking rule; its light would make it easy for them to be seen from miles away.

As he pondered his fate, Terry O'Hare joined him at the rail.

"The boys are saying that you didn't have the go-ahead for this mission, boss. Are we in trouble?"

"I think I am. But right now, you're on a stricken boat, in a sea full of U-boats, so I wouldn't be worried about what is going to happen in Dublin just yet."

"Well, at least we've got the petrol and the ammo." O'Hare cheerfully suggested, gingerly touching his broken nose.

"What did you say?"

"The bosses, they'll be pleased that we brought back the petrol and the boxes of ammunition. Although I wonder why the Brits let us keep it?"

"What are you talking about?" O'Hare had grabbed the man by his coat lapels and was shaking him violently. "What ammunition?"

"In the hold, the English idiots forgot to unload half of the petrol and most of the ammo. Some of the petrol cans are damaged though. Petrol leaking all over the floor, but don't worry, I told the lads no smoking down there."

McDowell turned back to the sea and stared. As if vainly looking for the source of his destruction that he knew was out there. "You English bas……"

Technically, there were 4 explosions, each one of them capable of killing Fergus McDowell and stopping him from completing his expletives. The first and second were the warheads of the torpedoes as they impacted the sides of the ship, the third was the petrol as it ignited, and the fourth was the explosives of the armaments as their detonation completed the chain reaction. Anyone witnessing would swear that there had been just one massive explosion. But there was only one witness, Cdr Jonathon Ronay, only he who saw what happened that night; alone he observed, through the periscope of His Majesty's Submarine Unicorn, the demonic fireball that leapt towards the heavens, the infernal flames rising high into the night, a penitent man whose thoughts, were thoughts of the fires of hell.

126

Analysis – SOE Headquarters - 1941

"Thank you for allowing us to meet here. I wanted to make sure that walls don't have ears, and I know your security is top-notch." Robinson sat down in one of the old comfortable armchairs that Major James Calderdale had in his office as the officer poured two glasses of whiskey and pushed one towards his boss.

"Not a problem at all, delighted to have you here." Answered the Major.

Robinson caught sight of the label on the bottle and was shocked by the expensive and almost impossible-to-find brand. "Where on earth did you get hold of that?"

"I was hoping you wouldn't ask. It was a present from Joe Turner; he seems to have liberated it from the personal stores of the late Mr Baker Snr."

"That lad has got a nerve; what else has he liberated? I would like to know."

"I think it is a question best left unasked, if you don't mind me saying so. He did have the good sense to send a crate of the stuff to Winnie. I take it you read my report." The Major looked to change the subject.

"Yes, thank you. Good work, James, very good work. You realise that it is a little too detailed. How many copies do you have?"

"No copies, just the original you have. You will notice that I have failed to number the pages. So, if you wish to omit some of the contents, we can always file such sections separately. I lit the fire for such a purpose." The Major smiled.

"As I said, good work."

"Sir, overall, how do you think the operation went? I mean, did we make a difference?" James Calderdale asked, his voice serious and concerned.

"I would say we had our share of luck. Without the death of that Butcher chap, we would have no clue as to where to look for the source of the livestock. But they do say you make your own luck, and I would say we did a very good job, especially with regard to the Irish involvement. If those arms and even the livestock had made it to the Republic, it would have stirred up a hornet nest, I can tell you. Just the other day I was asked by a contact I have in the IRA, unofficially of course, if we had come across Fergus McDowell. I told him that he was someone who we had been keeping an eye on but that he had disappeared. It seems that they, too, have lost track of him; he seems to be a bit of a fly in their soup, a loose cannon. I don't think that they would be mourning him too deeply if they were to find out about his demise; best that they don't know the circumstances, though. On which subject do any of your people have any idea about the sinking?"

The Major shook his head. "The only one apart from us who would have any idea would be Amy Percival, aka Rosie. She was the one who sabotaged the ship's engine and arranged for some of the ammo to be left in the hold. She's a bright one, she'll be able to put two and two together all right. That said, she's prudent, and she knows how to keep her mouth shut."

"Yes, I have to say that her work was exceptional on this mission." Opined Robinson.

"You sound surprised."

"No, no, not at all." There was a slight hesitation in Robinson's voice, which the soldier picked up on and looked at him questioningly. "Well, all right, call me an old stick in the mud, but one does by nature doubt if the women we put into the situations will have what it takes. I know that I am wrong to think that but one can't get away from what one has been taught all one's life. I guess that Amy, Rosie, or whatever she is called, proves that women can be as ruthless as men. It is certainly the case with this young lady. Her work was exceptional. She saved young Bach's life, that's without any doubt, and without her, we would never have stopped the shipment leaving for Ireland."

"If the truth be told one never really knows how any of these young people will do when we put them into the field. They can be the best in their class in training, but it's one thing to cut the throat of a dummy and another to take a life. I have no doubts about Percival; she is as coldblooded an operative as I have ever

484

seen. Smart with it. She is far from flighty either; no danger of her work being compromised by any romantic entanglements would be my guess."

"What are you going to do about Bach?"

"I am going to use him in the next mission suited to his talents." Major Calderdale knew what Robinson was getting at, and there was a defiant note in his answer.

"He disobeyed an order. He was told to get out of there when we knew he was blown, but he blatantly disregarded our instruction."

"He did what he felt was right, and in the end, he was right. Look, if you look at these things like a military operation, then yes, orders must be obeyed. But we teach these boys and girls to think on their feet. Bach knew from the start that his mission stood little chance of success and so did we. His cover was feeble; he looked like a spy. Which we didn't mind because it kept all eyes on him and their gaze away from the land Girl. He knew that if he left when we told him to, they would be suspicious about his sudden departure. They would likely conclude that he had been tipped off, and that would have left them to look for the informant. He, very bravely, in my opinion, stayed to protect that source. He knew that, sooner or later, they would come after him. He put the mission ahead of his own safety. People have got medals for less."

"We don't give out medals, and you know it. There was some talk of him becoming attached to this girl, the niece of the hotel landlady. Any issues there?

"No, I don't think so. She seems to be smitten, but he appears to have remained detached, almost coldly so. As you know, we usually investigate the background of our people, you know, find out about their love affairs, etc., but we drew a blank on Bach. Cartwright seems to think that he had someone whom he lost early in the war, but there was nothing in his background check. He would appear to be popular with the ladies, but he's a bit of a cold fish."

"All right, if you are happy with his conduct, he's your man; you must do as you think fit. Off the record, I think you are absolutely right; he is a good operative. Now, what about Turner?

485

Do you feel he went a little beyond his brief?" Robison switched the subject.

"Once again, we teach these people to be resourceful. We wanted the operation shut down without any public scandal; he got the job done."

"By using his own private army, it would seem, will this be a regular aspect of his missions. By the way, there was no mention in your report of who it was that was shooting up the English countryside."

"Respectfully, Sir, I thought that you would want to keep that information out of any official report. I think that you know who it was that helped Joe out, don't you, Sir."

"Actually, I had lunch with Mischa Agafonov yesterday. Our paths crossed back in the day, during the last war, and then again when he came to England. He was an excellent choice as the leader of Turner's little militia. He will not be advertising his part in the demise of Ted Baker. He feels that the fall of that empire will lead to a vacuum, and competing gangs will look to fill the void, and he has no desire to be a player in that game. He thinks that if it became known that Russians were involved, that would put a target on his back. He is adamant that he wants to cause no trouble for the British Authorities. Indeed, he has offered his services in any clandestine operations we might wish to stage in Eastern Europe at a future date. He said very little on how he knows Turner though."

"Yes, Turner has been evasive on that matter too. Should we push the issue?"

"I think sleeping dogs need their kip, as Mr Turner would be likely to term it. He is an exceptional operative. The information he and Cartwright got about the Baker set-up was outstanding. We have pretty much got our hands on all their assets. As yet, we don't have a total, but it's a substantial fortune that the Bakers unwittingly donated to the war effort. What's more, we avoided any potentially embarrassing court cases, even if it was at the expense of a bloodbath."

"I don't think that we need to be squeamish about that. All the participants were over 21. One thing did surprise me, though." Major Calderdale paused, collecting his thoughts and perhaps wondering if he should hold back his concerns from Robinson.

"The one surviving member of the gang, Billy Mason, said that both the Bakers were alive when he left the farm. Cartwright says she can't remember, a very unusual and uncharacteristic failing on her part. Baptiste Barbeau claims he wasn't sure; to be fair, he had been shot, after all; Mischa Agafonov ignored the question when I asked him. If this Billy is right, then either Joe Turner killed them himself, or he blew them up alive."

"Have you asked Turner?"

"Yes, and all he would say is that both Bakers are definitely dead."

Robinson thought deeply for a few moments before asking. "Are you thinking that Joe Turner tortured them before killing them for some personal reason? Because that is a serious matter. We can't have operatives that behave that way. If they let personal concerns get in the way of their job, that could compromise their missions."

"I have no positive reason to think that; Joe Turner does not strike me as the sort to enjoy violence. I don't see him killing unless he thought it necessary. The fact is, he shut down the black-market operation and the largest criminal gang in London. As you said, he is an exceptional operative, and he completed the mission as instructed."

"We didn't instruct him to kill everyone." Countered Robinson.

"We didn't instruct him not to. Besides, he didn't kill everyone; apparently, he was handcuffed to a chair whilst a battle took place between the Bakers and some unknown rival gang." Calderdale responded defiantly.

"You are very loyal to your people; that's admirable, James."

"I am just like any good shepherd looking out for his flock of sheep, Sir."

"That may be, but what worries me, James, is that your charges are not sheep; they are more like a flock of lone wolves."

Calderdale stared distractedly into his drink; he didn't answer his boss.

After a long pause, Robinson asked. "So, let me be clear, you have complete confidence in Bach, Percival and Turner, your flock?"

"Yes." Replied The Major without hesitation. "Yes, I have."

487

"Good, because I have a little job coming up that I think will be right up their street."

127

Nightmare.

The ship is tilting more than ever now. Instinctively, he is holding tightly onto a rail to stop himself sliding down the deck and into the water that has already swallowed the bow. Laughing, he wonders why he is doing so. No point, he decides, as he lets go and begins the plunge. It's like the slide at the seawater Lido in Lymington. Every possible day during the summer holidays, he would visit with his sisters. He would ride that slide time after time. Screaming his joy with each heavenly plummet until the welcoming water enfolded him in its sybaritic arms and snuffed out his exuberant squeals.

His nanny would call out to him that time was up and they had to head home. "One last go." He would beseech her as he clambered up the iron steps to the dizzy height of the top. "One last go."

He is defiantly screaming the words now. "One last go! My time is up." The deathly North Atlantic waters snuff out his exuberant squeals.

Simon Bach wakes alone. Shaking as always, but this time, strangely euphoric.

Milton Keynes UK
Ingram Content Group UK Ltd.
UKHW020822300924
449047UK00013B/843